Niglíču

She Comes Out Alive
A Story of Wounded Knee

Florence D'Angelo
Paul Oscar Wybrant

Independent Thinking Press—Port Jervis, NY
ISBN: 979-8-9856582-3-1
Library of Congress Control Number: 2023914298
Title: *Niglíču*
Author: Florence D'Angelo and Paul Oscar Wybrant
Digital distribution | 2023
Paperback | 2023

This is a work of fiction. All characters, organizations, and events portrayed in this novel are either products of the author's imagination or are used fictitiously.

Dedication

*The authors dedicate this work
to each other
and
to their spouses,
Sal D'Angelo and Jing Wybrant*

Part One
1890

Chapter 1

Čhaŋkpé Ópi Wakpála ektá ípi.
They arrive at Wounded Knee Creek.

His McClellan saddle always squeaked, and especially so in cold weather. It irritated Major Samuel Whitside. He stood up in the oiled wooden stirrups and waved a gauntlet gloved hand to call a temporary halt to the caravan. The wind flipped up the cape of his royal blue greatcoat and the exposed gold caught the attention of his officers and men. They had just crossed the narrow bridge, passing Louis Mosseau's store and the post office. He knew his troops, weary of field rations, would have enjoyed going inside, but he would not let them. Methodically fingering the fob of his open watch, he noted it was getting late. Obsessive about time and discipline, he knew there was a lot to be done before sunset.

Thirty-two years of sterling service had earned him the respect of his men. His piercing eyes and dashingly bushy moustache enhanced his stern expression and embodied him with undeniable dignity. He was not a man to be crossed.

Whitside scanned the ranks of his officers and nodded towards Lt. Harry Hawthorne. Expecting yet another interrogation from his superior so obsessed with duty, the lieutenant rolled his eyes towards his companion, Captain Wallace. "Here we go again," Hawthorne sighed, urging his dark bay warhorse forward into a quick trot.

Never taking his eyes off the terrain that would become the Indian encampment, Whitside directed question after question at the lieutenant.

"You've instructed Capt. Moylan to station his Troop A and Capt. Nowlan's Troop I as sentinels around the Indian camp?"

"Yes, sir."

"Hmmm. Moylan will establish twenty posts around the Indian camp and his patrols will roam from post to post. But what about the

3

Indian camp itself? Its location?"

Always making sure, Hawthorne thought. *He leaves nothing to chance.* His response was quick. He wanted to please his superior officer. "You, sir, will direct Big Foot and his people to encamp west of the Agency Road here. That'll lock them in between the dry ravine there in the south and that prominent hill on the north."

"That's fine, Harry. And what about your boys?"

"Well, yes. We'll be ready. I will post my battery of two Hotchkiss cannons on yonder hill above the camp with muzzles pointed in enfilade at the Indians. And later today, when Colonel Forsyth arrives from Pine Ridge with reinforcements, he'll bring in another battery. That'll give us a total of four cannons, enough to kill half the Indians in the territory."

Did I see a shadow flicker over the Major's features, Hawthorne wondered? *Was it a wince?*

"Hmph. Tell me about the cannon," the Major demanded.

"Major, Sir, these weapons terrify the hostiles. And being the projectiles will explode on contact even at 4,200 yards, every hostile in this valley will be within easy potshot range."

Whitside nodded somberly. "How long will it take to place the cannon?"

"Once we get started? Thirty minutes. Forty-five minutes, at most. Major, with those big guns looking down on them, the hostiles won't think twice about following orders."

"Hm ... what time is it, Harry?"

"About 2:30, Sir."

"And the date?"

Wanting to shake his head in exasperation, but controlling himself, he replied, "December 28, 1890."

Whitside again scanned the hills. "Those of us who have been in this business as long as I have, have developed a keen sense of smell for situations like this. Yes, our situation here *looks* good, but I don't like the smell of it." Twisting in his saddle again to look back at his troops, he continued. "I want you and your men to be careful with those big guns. Capron will probably take command of all four pieces when he comes in with Forsyth. As you know, Capron's got a real hothead, that German Weiner, in his battery. That makes it doubly important that you keep your wits about you, Harry." And now he looked with truly stern eyes. "We don't want Wiener blowing the gates of Hell wide open. This is not the time to avenge Custer."

"Yes, Sir," Hawthorne replied, and dropped back to ride again with Capt. Wallace.

"What did he have to say?" the captain asked.

With a nervous smile, the Lieutenant teased, "He wanted to know what we had for breakfast. Asked if I was still picking my nose." He drew in a deep breath and then exhaled, puffing a fog of smoke into the cold air. "He also said the situation here stinks."

"Yeah," Wallace agreed, spitting tobacco juice on the dusty ground. "Welcome to Wounded Knee."

****

Pȟehíŋ šašá na akhíšoke.
His hair was red and thick.

Brings Fire sat in the wagon bed chipping off slivers of dry wood from the sides. There was nothing else to do on this long journey to be with relatives. It wasn't the usual way they had traveled. They were not bringing gifts. And never before had the Long Knife soldiers traveled beside them.

One sliver embedded under her fingernail. She pulled it loose and sucked the tiny drop of blood from the wound. With her finger still in her mouth, she tested the stability of a loose tooth. Her first loose tooth. She wiggled it. It still seemed firmly attached, but not for long she had been told. She would lose this tooth but another would come back. That's what her mother had said. But her grandfather's tooth hadn't grown back the second time it came out. *Maybe because it was kicked out? Maybe it was because he was an adult.* When adults lose things they don't always get them back. That's part of growing up, her grandfather had said. He was right. Her father never came back after he went to fight the white soldiers.

Grasshopper, her grandfather driving one of the first wagons, braked, stood up, and stretched. Riding in a wagon, sitting stationary like that, was hard on his arthritic knees. Smiling wryly to himself, he remembered his knees had not bothered him when he had sat astride his war pony. No, then he had moved with the fluid motion of his mount, his thighs aware of the horse's bellowing lungs, his calves pressing in, allowing his knees to flex as he moved up and down to the rhythm. *Where are my horses now?* As a warrior and respected elder, he once could count many that were his, grazing near camp, waiting for his call. Gone now.

Relative to Tȟašúŋke Witkó *His Horse Is Crazy*, Grasshopper was born in the Year of the Whirling Stars, 1833. Many people of the time, Lakȟóta and white, thought the stars were falling. Grasshopper felt that way now; that the stars were indeed falling. He had an uneasy feeling looking out over the terrain. His right hand reached for his medicine pouch, hanging on a thong around his neck. It, and the photo it contained, were still there. He was reassured.

Wind Woman, her mother, sat erect across from her. Brings Fire thought her beautiful although her father would never had allowed his wife to have her hair as unkempt as it was now, with a tangled nest of shorter hairs at the top of her long braids. Brings Fire closed her eyes, remembering the morning routine of her parents. She pictured her father's strong fingers holding the long black strands of her mother's hair and braiding them with soft fur strip. She remembered the dreamy smile on her mother's face. *Where is my mother's smile now?*

Looking ahead, Grasshopper saw the caravan had stopped. Several cavalry soldiers guarded the ambulance carrying the gravely ill chief, Sitȟáŋka *Big Foot*. Following behind the beloved leader were 350 of his Lakȟóta Mnikȟówožu, tired and hungry, and sandwiched between mounted cavalrymen. The halt made him uncomfortable. He looked around. With seasoned warrior's eyes, he saw the terrain was favorable for the hunter, but a trap for the hunted.

"Why have we stopped, Até?" Wind Woman asked from the flatbed.

"The Long Knives probably want us to camp here. They remember what happened two days ago, and don't want us to escape again." He tried not to look, but his eyes returned again and again to the southern side of the valley where the ravine opened to the creek. *Just an arrow shot away,* he thought as his mouth became suddenly dry. He had been here some twenty summers before. Again, he touched the pouch.

"Let me look too, Lalá," Brings Fire requested. Her grandfather stood her up on the seat beside him. She followed his eyes, steady and focused on the distance.

6

"We are not yet there, my grandchild. Almost, though. Pine Ridge is not too far now, but they will have us stay here tonight. Look over there," he said, pointing, "by that line of cottonwoods. That's Čhaŋkpé Ópi Wakpála *Wounded Knee Creek.*"

"You have been here before?"

"Our band made winter camp here two or three times when I was a boy. I've hunted here. Do you see that high hill? We played up there. We could see a long way from that spot." His eyes softened as he continued, "The hills roll on and on and fool your eyes. They are there and then they are not. Mysterious." And then, as another thought intruded, his eyes became cold. "From that hill, you can see everything that moves in this valley." And he remembered how true that had been twenty years ago. He sighed, switched thoughts and remembered the way he had played as a boy, pretending to swoop down the hill and ambush the enemy.

"We called it Wígmuŋke Pahá *Rainbow Hill.*"

"Why?"

"Because from up there the rainbows were bigger and brighter."

The wagons started to roll again. *There are no rainbows here today,* she thought, coughing out the dust that clouded the air.

She climbed back into the bed with the lodge poles hanging out the back and rested on the hides. Warily she watched the soldiers. They looked tired, with drooping heads and sagging shoulders, and some looked sick. But she felt no sympathy for them. They should not have been chasing the Mnikȟówožu away from home and through the hills. She should not be in this wagon traveling to be with relatives.

They are so different from each other, these Long Knives, she thought. *Different faces. Different hair colors; blonde, black, brown, gray and that one over there, red.* As if sensing her eyes on him, the red-haired soldier rode up closer to the wagon and smirked.

Suddenly, Grasshopper pulled in the reins. Attuned to animals all his life, he had been watching the mule pulling the wagon. His gait had changed. There was now a limp. He must have picked up a stone. Grasshopper put down the reins and jumped down from the wagon.

"What are you doing? Get back on there and get moving!" a soldier yelled to him, motioning with his rifle. Grasshopper pointed to the mule whose hoof was now raised. The soldier reluctantly understood and waved him clearance to continue.

While Grasshopper worked with the animal, the red-bearded soldier sidled up to within inches of Wind Woman. She turned to look at him. He raised one hand and spread two fingers while his other hand went to his crotch. Seething, she looked away. She raised her chin. He parted his lips and snaked out his tongue, moving it suggestively.

I'll bite it off, she thought, turning her head.

The soldier leaned over the wagon and cupped Wind Woman's chin, twisting her head, forcing her to see his lecherous gaze.

"You know you want it," he whispered.

But Wind Woman was neither weak nor timid. She grabbed his arm and pulled, shying his horse who sidestepped away from the wagon and whinnied.

When Grasshopper stood up to intervene, the butt of a rifle against his back knocked him to the ground.

The disturbance caught the attention of a junior officer. He struck the red-headed man's shoulder with his riding crop and growled, "I had enough of you, Dawes! Get your sorry ass back in line!"

Dawes, his vulgar and undisciplined ways tolerated by the Army only because he was a valued sniper, turned to Brings Fire and spat a stream of foul tobacco saliva at her. She rose, burning with anger. *"Čhikté kte!"* I will kill you!" she screamed again and again.

Her mother grabbed her skirt and pulled her down. "Stop! You cannot fight them! Stop!" she commanded. Seething and frustrated, Brings Fire leaned back into her mother's embrace and cried.

*****

Líla eháŋni k'uŋ héhaŋ.
It was very long ago.

The caravan came to a halt, and Grasshopper looked over the intended encampment as though he were planning a battle. He could not help but think he was prey to something much bigger than himself. Both seasoned warrior and effective hunter, he could analyze from both angles. He focused on the terrain, thinking he would put his warriors here if they were to be the aggressors, and there, if they would need to flee. He put both his wagon and the one following at the intersection of the Agency Road and the dry ravine.

It was a risky decision, he knew. In the event of a fight, a high concentration of bullets would fly through the area. But the intersection offered the shortest route to the relative safety of the ravine, where they would find brush and shallow caves. Grasshopper shuddered. His band was far outnumbered in men, weapons, and ammunition. And he suspected that the feared Hotchkiss cannon would soon menace his people from that high hill.

Yes, he thought, *this would be the best place. Not a good place, as the chance of surviving was poor, but surely it is better than running through open fields.*

My family must be first. Swallowing hard, he maneuvered his wagon to be clearly in front. Should they need to escape this way, they'd pass the spot of the secret only he and the wanáǧi *spirits* knew. Lost in a long-ago moment, he placed one hand over the pouch on his chest and absentmindedly stroked it with his other. *Long ago, but like yesterday,* he thought, feeling the jump of his heart at the same time.

*****

Wíŋyaŋ kiŋ thípi kiŋ pawóslal iyéyapi.
The women erected the thípi.

Their fingers nearly froze while erecting their thípi. Wind Woman, together with her relatives, struggled in the wind to construct the tripod frame before fastening the lesser poles to create an almost conical dwelling, tilted with its steep face windward, while the gradual slope of the front opened into the entrance. Despite the harsh conditions, they worked swiftly and, within an hour they had established the shelter. Brings Fire longed for the protection and warmth of the soon-to-be fire within. Assisting, as the adults expected, she carried in the blankets and robes and established her own sleeping area. In other times and other places, the women would have erected their thípi to form a camp circle which would have offered some shelter from the wind and a place in the center where the children could play under watchful eyes. But now? The bullying by the Americans left them little time for planning and cooperation.

Brings Fire had few things she could call her own, but she had packed within her folded robe a valued possession: a gift from a

9

grandmother on the night her baby brother died during birth! The braided sweetgrass doll was all she had left from that expectant night. The white man had killed her brother as surely as they had killed her father, for what grieving woman could properly nourish a son whose father had just died? This, she knew with certainty. With her little girl's tears, the doll had become her "brother." On the day she found the copper American coin with the Lakȟóta head stamped on it, she thought, perhaps the white man's magic would bring her brother to life again. In her despair, the wašíču *white men* seemed so powerful and her people so powerless, and so she had inserted the coin inside the doll to be his heart. On this night, however, when she knew the days of such fantasy were over, she withdrew the coin.

Fear of war and a general uncertainty hovered over the camp. The Wanáǧi Wačhípi *Ghost Dancing* had frightened the white population. Ever since Wovoka, the Paiute, began promoting the new religious idea that heaven would punish the whites for their mistreatment of the natives and cause them to disappear by the year 1891 if the dancing continued, the settlers suspected an uprising was in the making. With the recent assassination of Sitting Bull whom the authorities at Standing Rock Reservation believed was inciting a rebellion, Big Foot had struggled to protect his people. He could have taken his band to the Makȟóšiča *Badlands* stronghold or perhaps to join Mahpíya Lúta *Red Cloud* at Pine Ridge, as Red Cloud had encouraged. He chose the latter, but the Seventh Cavalry had intercepted the band on the way. And now here they were on the banks of the Wounded Knee Creek, awaiting an uncertain future.

As the sun set, the cooking pots held a weak stew of dried beef and tímpsula, a powdered wild turnip which added thickness to the water. Using the buffalo horn ladle, Brings Fire dipped into the pot and offered it to Grasshopper. Saying he was not hungry while refusing it meant he was giving his portion to her, and she gratefully nodded her understanding. The People must care for the young first.

"Iná, may I go out to scout round the camp?"

"You may, but, I want you nearby."

"I want to go outside as well," Grasshopper announced. He would see that she was safe.

Brings Fire did not want to go anywhere near where the wašíču, the white men, were congregating. She had been taught they were evil. Stay away! But the coin in her pocket and her desire to surprise her grandfather overrode the fear. Once outside, she sprinted off. Her grandfather followed her with his eyes as she overtook two Húŋkpapȟa boys heading for Mosseau's store. They walked side by side for a short distance, but then the boys broke off into a run. Grasshopper's heart swelled with pride as he saw her race in pursuit and then quickly take the lead, until finally she stumbled up the steps, approaching the front door before the others.

Brings Fire had never opened a wooden door before! She placed her two palms on it and pushed. It did not move. She heard a snicker from a white man sitting off to the side smoking a pipe and became embarrassed. Her fingers went to the crack where the door met the frame as she would have opened her thípi, but before she could try to pry it open, a dark brown hand appeared from behind her and settled on the black latch, lifting and then pulling it. With that motion, she leaned back into the body behind her and, turning, saw a wondrous color, the amber of dark honey from the wild buckwheat flowers the bees so love on the plains. And it was on a boy's face, spread so smooth she almost reached up to touch it! She blushed and lowered her head.

"This is the way to do it," he said as he pulled the door open further and let her pass inside. So mesmerized was she by his color that she barely stammered a grateful response before he disappeared. *This must be Há Sápa, Black Skin, the Húŋkpapȟa boy.* She had heard about him. The older girls found him quite handsome.

*****

Pȟéta Akú wakȟályapi etáŋ opȟéthuŋ čhíŋ.
Brings Fire wanted to buy some coffee.

So much to see inside this strange, four-sided building! She walked down one side and across to the other, examining cooking and eating utensils. So much she did not understand, and she almost dizzied herself with the many colors of the bolts of cloth. She skimmed her fingers over them, and closed her eyes, thinking perhaps she could feel the colors. A red feathered headdress sat on a wooden head with painted blue eyes and such red cheeks to match! *What type of woman is this?* She giggled as she imagined her mother wearing the hat. And then, turning, she saw her own full face in a mirror hanging on

11

the wall. Startled, she jerked back a step. Her face streaked with dust from the road. But the others in the store were as dirty as she.

A blue pillow with yellow flowers brought to mind the prairie in summer. The shiny silver pots brought her thoughts to the thin skim of ice on an early winter pond. *What kind of people create such beauty and yet be so cruel?* She heard others in the store make similar remarks. "Such magic these wasícu possess!" she heard, and yet the magic of the copper coin had not brought back her brother.

The coin! She had almost forgotten why she had come here! She walked to the counter where a white man and his Lakȟóta wife stood. She did not know what to say.

"Háu, Young Lady. "Do you want to buy something?"

She stretched out her hand to Mousseau and presented the copper coin. "Coffee," she said. But the shopkeeper shook his head. *Did this mean no? Why no?*

"Too little. Too little," Mousseau explained, but again she stretched out one hand with the coin and the other for the coffee in return.

"You need this!" he smiled indulgently as he held out a larger coin.

"Wait," Mrs. Mousseau said, taking Brings Fire's hand and placing into it a small bag.

How kind she is, Brings Fire thought. She was not aware that the dark-skinned boy had been watching her, attracted to this girl who ran so fast. She did not see the boy go over to Mrs. Mousseau during the initial attempted transaction. She did not know that he, seeing the coin she held, would never be enough to buy coffee, handed Mrs. Mousseau the only coin he had, a bigger one, and walked out of the store.

*****

Pȟéta Akú haŋblóglake.
Brings Fire talks about her vision.

Long shadows stretched before her when she ran back to her thípi. Her grandfather stood out front, watching for her. She handed him the bag and smiled.

So tired was she that after entering the thípi, she went straight to

12

her robes. The familiar dancing sparks of the fire relaxed her, but sleep eluded her. Squeezing her eyes shut, tears flowed, but she bravely wiped them away. She couldn't cry. *Warriors don't cry!* Isn't that what she had learned from her dream?

Weeks ago she had awakened, shaking. A dream unlike any other filled her...had stayed with her.

"Iná, do little girls have visions?"

"Čhuŋkší, what a strange question to ask, but yes, they do. I, myself, dreamed of Double Woman. Do you know who she is?"

Brings Fire shook her head, and so her mother continued. "If you dream of Double Woman, you can go one of two ways. Either you will be industrious and virtuous and excel in crafting and join the Quilling Society as I have, or," and here she lowered her voice, "or you can create havoc by stealing the men of other women." Brings Fire blushed. Her mother smiled.

But Brings Fire's dream was nothing like that. She wasn't even sure it was an actual dream either. She didn't feel like she had fallen asleep. She felt she had just drifted into another place. *Was that what happened in a vision?* She went to her grandfather. Maybe he would understand.

"Lalá, it is possible that I have had a vision?"

It was hard for Grasshopper to hide his smile. "I do not remember when you went to the mountaintop and fasted."

But motioning to a space on the frost covered log beside him, he invited her to tell the story.

"I was in a different world, Lalá. The colors were so sharp they almost hurt my eyes. I walked out of a forest and onto a grassy plain. No buffalo were there. I walked to a mountain and when I stood beneath it, it towered high into the sky."

"Like Devil's Tower?" he suggested.

"Taller." Her eyes took on a faraway look. "Beneath it, a small river flowed. I followed along its banks and came upon a she-wolf. I was afraid, and yet the wolf's eyes beckoned me closer. The wolf then spoke in a language I somehow understood. 'What do you seek, little girl?' I walked up to her and said, 'I want to help my people."

Brings Fire took her grandfather's hand. "I want to be a warrior. Like you. Like my father was! I tried to tell this to the wolf, but she just shook her head. 'The sun has set on the days of the warrior,' she said. Is this true, Lalá? Will there be no more fighting?"

13

"There will be a fight, Ťhakóža."

"The wolf told me something else. She said I will fight a different battle. Will you help me be ready for it?"

"What you ask is difficult. How can I help prepare you for a kind of fight I do not know?

"Well, then can you teach me to be a warrior like yourself…just in case?"

A warrior like myself? Do I want that for her? Scarred. Now defeated. No, I want her safe. I want her to care for her children. I want her, a woman, to pass on all that is good about our ways so that we, the People, will never die. To humor her, though, he pretended he would do as she wished. It would serve her well if she learned to be conscious of her surroundings and how to react to them, regardless of what her future held.

*****

Wítaya mníčiyapi.
They came together for a meeting.

A rush of cold air flowed over the hair of the buffalo robe pulled part way over her head. The long outer hairs tickled her nose. Brings Fire awoke, smiling out of a dream in which her father had entered the thípi carrying meat for the cooking pot. But, she realized, the cold air was not coming from the raised flap of someone entering. Someone had left the thípi, and she was alone in the dark. *Have I slept long?* She did not think so because the fire looked as it had when she had closed her eyes; soft, welcoming. Even after she pulled her robe up even higher and nestled down under it, she still heard the voices of people outside. They were close, and indeed so close that she could teasingly stretch her foot up against the slanted hide side and touch someone's leg. *No, I won't do that. Those are not playful voices outside,* she thought.

When she became fully awake, she realized where she was, and then, feeling the anxiety of her people, another chill passed through her body that the robe could not warm.

"Come in, come in. It is too cold to stay outside. Sit by our fire, Mitákuyepi *My Relatives*, and let us talk about this." It was the voice of her grandfather, and she sat up as he entered. Several people

14

followed him, but the draft had diffused the smoke and a gray haze made it difficult for her to recognize them all. That they were relatives, as her grandfather's greeting had suggested, was certain. *But were all people our relatives? That cannot be. Or why would we be captives?* As the smoke cleared, she saw that there were aunts, uncles, cousins, among those entering. And she saw Grasshopper sitting in his honored place with the women on his left and the men on his right.

Wind Woman approached her with outstretched hand. "Come, I will take you to my cousin while everyone here talks." But Grasshopper held up his hand. "Hiyá, she should stay. This is her future, too. Let her listen and learn." Though this was an informal council, one of many held in the camp that night, she felt honored to be allowed to stay. She would be respectful and not disappoint her grandfather.

The pipe was passed to Grasshopper, and he smoked; the smoke rising to the ancestors who would witness this gathering and these conversations. The meeting began in silence, as all such meetings did. Brings Fire looked around the circle.

Her two older cousins were there. Both had attended the mission day schools on the reservation and Brings Fire found it fascinating that these two brothers could be so different. Inseparable as children, they had grown apart over the years and now were clearly at odds with each other. As a student, Wašíčuŋ Pȟehíŋ *American Hair,* despite being able to return to his home at night, readily accepted and thrived on wašíču *white* culture. Wearing his hair short and parted in the middle, coupled with his habit of using knives, forks and spoons when available, set him apart from most of his relatives. A Christian now, or so he said, like many new converts, he was enthusiastic about spreading the Word and so he carried about him an air of superiority that irked his brother Matȟó Hótȟaŋka *Loud Bear*, so much that they would not even speak to each other. Teachers considered Loud Bear to be a mission school failure, for as soon as school let out for the day, he would immediately revert to traditional ways. Loud Bear would only speak in Lakȟóta, while American Hair avoid communicating with it whenever possible.

American Hair was therefore the success story of educators who advocated, "Kill the Indian, Save the Child". Many of his peers recognized him as such with the chant, "Dead Indian! Dead Indian!"

15

Although he tried not to show favoritism, Grasshopper clearly favored Loud Bear, the traditional grandson, and was proud when he joined the militant Wanáǧi Wačhípi *Ghost Dance* faction. Brings Fire, so far, had escaped wašíču schooling, and she promised herself she would never stray from traditional ways.

Her eyes focused on the wanáǧi ógle *ghost shirt* worn by Many Crows. The black raven feathers stood out among those of owl and eagle that adorned the neck of this plain cotton shirt. Surely, he had come under the influence of Kicking Bear, son-in-law of Chief Big Foot, and clearly he was ready to defy bullets with the Ghost Shirt. *Would it protect him?* A dutiful son, Many Crows was supporting his aged father, Strong Legs, now toothless and feeble in his eighties. The man, quite old for that time, leaned against his son for balance. Strong Legs' mind was sharp yet, and he drew inner strength from his memories of fighting side by side with Grasshopper. It had been fourteen years since the decisive Lakȟóta defeat at Slim Buttes. His philosophy now was more in keeping with American Horse, a key figure in that battle, and a man who promoted the path of friendly associations with white people and wašíču education for the children.

The silence is good. The smoking is good. Brings Fire could feel it settle the high emotions of those present. Eyes no longer flashed anger across the fire. Wind Woman looked toward her father and communicated with him in spirit as only two people so close can. Her eyes said that he was wise to invite people with different points of view. These were dangerous times, and all opinions were important.

This thípi seems very crowded, Brings Fire thought as she counted the people. Bloody Mouth, Knife, Big Belly, Chases Twice, Hail Hawk, Rabbit, Many Wounds, Grey Wing, wives of some of them whose names she was not sure of, and the unmarried twins, Black Bone and Stitch. She sent her prayers with the smoke, intending to invite the spirits of her ancestors to join this gathering. *Perhaps they are already here.* The people around the fire were visible, but it seemed that among them were others who had lived before, a crowd of people from past and present.

A sudden voice then startled them all. "Wakȟáŋ Tȟáŋka has blessed us all winter without a storm. I ask you, did you notice how high and blue the sky was above the hills today? And tonight, Mitákuyepi, you surely could count all the stars of Tȟayámni *The*

16

Pleiades. All this will change. Tomorrow night a blizzard will come out of the north and we will suffer great agonies. Prepare as best you can."

Waŋblí Hohú *Eagle Bone* had spoken and then sunk, slouched, into silence. A demented man, the People indulged him with much affection. Tonight, though, Big Belly was in no mood for his dire predictions. "This good man often predicts evil, and he does it more as he ages," he said, dismissing the prophecy. Rabbit wasn't so sure. "This winter has been easy on us, but we have suffered other sorrows lately. Maybe his prediction will come true."

Brings Fire saw her cousin American Hair get agitated. It was clear he wanted to command attention and was obviously struggling to control himself. Finally, he blurted out, "The old man is a foolish heathen who talks to spirit creatures who are not there. There will be no storm."

Loud Bear slowly turned to his brother and in a low, threatening voice said, "It would be good if my brother remembered he is in his aunt's thípi and is speaking of an elder present."

Oh, no. Now they will go at each other.

Brings Fire was right.

"My brother is quick to remind me of my manners, but what he is not saying is that he disapproves of my way of living and my beliefs," American Hair said. "The old ways have passed away. It is time to put away our foolish ideas of living free on the plains. There are no buffalo anymore. They have perished, and so have our old ways."

Loud Bear retaliated. "Our ways are who we are, and I ask you, who are you?"

There was a pause of quiet and then came the unexpected reply, "From what pot do you eat? Is it not made of iron? Whose weapon do you use? Is it not the gun of the wašíču? What old ways are *you* following?"

It was time for Grasshopper to intervene. "I have news from Big Foot. A while ago, I came from his Army tent. It is warm in there, and his wife and children care for him. The Army doctor is kind and gives him medicine."

There were murmurs. Only some were of approval.

"Big Foot wants us to meet with Red Cloud, but he is bleeding and coughing. He will not make it to Pine Ridge tomorrow."

Women cried out and wept openly. The men remained grim.

17

"We who are here have many differing ideas," Grasshopper continued. "Let us speak of them face to face instead of hiding these in the corners of our minds." He turned to Loud Bear, "Tell us what you think."

"All here know of Chief Big Foot's attempts to get along with the wašíču. The soldiers know it." Loud Bear glared at his brother and said, "And remember, he even went to Washington to ask for a school. We have chosen to go to Pine Ridge. We were on our way. There was no need for a military escort. Do they think we have lost our way in the wilderness? And yet, look around. Hundreds of soldiers surround us. The Oglála scouts say that more are coming from Pine Ridge. You have seen the cannons. Why are they here? We were already going to where they say they are taking us. They are not fools. Maybe they do not want us at Pine Ridge. Maybe what I hear is right. Maybe they will put us on their train and send us off to captivity far away. To Fort Meade, maybe. Or maybe they will ship us away to a place called Alabama to rot with Geronimo's people. Or maybe they will just kill us all."

American Hair could not let that stand. "These people are Christians. They gave us their word."

"Do you trust their word? Have our people ever been able to trust their word? Look at you. You can read. You can write their words. You dress as they do. Why are you not with them now? I will tell you. They do not see you as their equal ... and they never will."

Loud Bear's supporters nodded their assent.

"My brother," American Hair said, motioning to all around him, "My relatives. Listen to me. We have but few warriors here. Maybe 150. Our women and children are here. We cannot win a battle. We will never win a battle against those cannons. Let us listen to Big Foot. We will peaceably go to Pine Ridge and talk with Red Cloud. We will learn the white man's ways and we will live. We will learn to farm. Any other way and we will die. There will be no need to preserve old ways. No one will be here to observe them."

Fury was building up in Loud Bear, and there was fire in his tone. "Remember when they promised us land for 'The Great Sioux Nation.' Where is this nation? They said it would be ours till the buffalo are no more. They were right about some of it. The buffalo *are* no more, but where is The Great Sioux Nation? Gone." Here, his frustration brought him angry tears and he could no longer speak. He stared into the fire, breathing heavily. When he raised his head, his eyes were wet with passion. "I am not a crippled animal. I will not surrender. Tomorrow is a good day to die."

A child's voice cried out suddenly, "I will die with you!" All eyes turned to Brings Fire, who clearly adored her cousin. All eyes turned to see her as she stood up, defiant upon her robes.

The silence turned to a nervous titter and then, when she repeated, "Yes, I will," gentle laughter erupted. Blood rushed to her face. She could not meet their eyes and looked down. She had spoken impulsively, it was true, but it had come from her heart.

"My little cousin speaks like the warriors of old," Loud Bear boomed. "Perhaps we should listen to her."

Wind Woman walked over and motioned for her to sit down and be quiet. "My daughter speaks of that which she does not know. Men die in battle. Women live on."

American Hair seized this opening to pursue his argument. "Their priests speak of a God who loves us all."

With flaming eyes, Wind Woman shot back, "Their priests teach us to thank God for our destruction. Despite the risks, I say we should hide our guns and use them if we must. I will keep mine."

Black Bone sat up straight. "Mitákuyepi, understand this. There are women, children, and the old ones in this camp. They are weak. They will die. Keep this thought before your eyes tomorrow. If you start a fight, are you willing to live with their spirits who will haunt you?"

Rabbit, a recognized leader, spoke with a strength that betrayed his weakened lungs. "This is wisdom. They are many. We are few. Many of them fought at Greasy Grass, and they know we did too. They want to avenge Pȟehíŋ Háŋska *Long Hair (General Custer)*. They want us all dead. We should not give them an excuse to kill us tomorrow."

"I see it this way," Grasshopper said, finally ready to voice his own opinion. "All have spoken. All have been correct, and all have been wrong. Some soldiers watching us have faced us before in battle. Some soldiers, by their actions, seem new to this type of duty. I hear many of their loud voices. They are drinking that bad water and their minds will be clouded. And they are nervous. This makes me anxious. I say we should expect the worst and be happy if wrong."

As Brings Fire searched the faces in the circle, she saw there was

19

much agreement. Could her cousin American Hair agree to this compromise? She could not read his thoughts. His face was hard as stone.

Grasshopper continued. "Bury your guns so that the Americans cannot confiscate them but do so in a way that you can easily retrieve them without being seen when we are ready to leave. Sing your death songs, but do not provoke a fight. We have never started a fight with our women and children present. I will not do so now. And yet, I do not want to die peacefully in my thípi if my people need to be defended. In case of a fight, grab your gun and keep firing at the Americans until our women and children can escape. The Long Knives are not likely to fire on women and children. Run behind them to the ravine. It is our best escape route. Head east towards Wounded Knee Creek and then south from there. There are pockets in the walls of the ravine near the creek. Hide in them to escape the bullets." He paused. "I have spoken. That is all."

One by one, the guests silently left the thípi to go their own way for a night of fitful sleep. Brings Fire did not sleep at all.

*****

Mílahaŋska akíčhita kiŋ wayátkaŋpi na itómnipi.
The American soldiers drank and got drunk.

The smoke from the Sibley tents on the hill was indistinguishable from that emanating from the ventilation openings of the thípi in the encampment below. Like prayer smoke from the pipe, the swirls of white rose to the heavens and mingled with all smoke and yet it came from people who could find no common ground this night. Grasshopper stood outside the thípi, wondering how it could be that smoke from different fires mingled in the sky without conflict, while those who made the smoke could not find peace with each other. Grasshopper pulled the blanket around him closer as a chill ran through his body. *Something bad will happen tomorrow.* He wasn't so much concerned for his own well-being, he had fought many times before, but he worried for the women and children. He lifted the flap, bent down, and walked inside.

Not far from where the Lakȟóta thípi were, a rowdy group of men gathered around a lantern lit wagon. From the hill, Sgt. Murphy

20

could see the oaken kegs in the back of it. "I guess ole Jim got tired of entertaining the reporters in the back room of his store at Pine Ridge, and figured the business would be better here," Murphy mumbled to no one in particular. He leaned back, looked to the starry sky and held his concertina in two tense hands, gently pumping out a lonesome ballad from back home in Ireland and trying not to think about those drinking whiskey on a night like this. *What an incredibly stupid idea! It isn't like those Indians really want to be here.* He was a little surprised that rebellion had not yet occurred. *But that would be a dumb move.* Though the Indians were outnumbered and outgunned, Murphy knew desperate people could do unpredictable things.

Col. Forsyth also saw this wagon while he walked down the hill. "What's that all about, Sam?" he said, turning to the officer next to him.

"That trader Asay hauled a keg of whiskey over here. Figured there was more money to be made here than back at his store. He's selling whiskey to the reporters and some officers. I'll go down there directly and shut down his--"

Forsyth cut him mid-sentence. "Let it be. The men deserve some conviviality. Just make sure Asay and his partner down there understand that the only enlisted men he is to sell to are the noncoms." Whitside was uneasy about this. The air was already thick with tension, and he started to protest, but Forsyth lifted his hand. "Come to think of it," Forsyth said, "round up the officers and bring them to my tent. The drinks will be on me."

The Sibley tent can comfortably accommodate twelve men, but, with whisky flowing, no one cared it was so crowded that elbows bumped into each other, and tin cups tipped their contents onto soldiers' boots. The raucous laughter emanating from the colonel's tent drifted into thípi, and Lakȟóta children, hearing it in their sleep, cuddled closer to their mothers, who stared into the darkness dreading the dawn.

Col. James W. Forsyth, in high spirits as the center of attention, entertained reporters from back east, accepting congratulations in advance for subduing the mighty Sioux nation. While not vocally boasting of his accomplishments, his actions pointed to his realization that he would achieve a page in history books tomorrow. Children would know and would study his name! He had subdued the mighty Sioux nation and brought the Indian wars to a conclusion, finally! Such a thrill! *"Celebrate,"* his spirit said. *"Celebrate mightily!"*

"I propose a toast," a young officer shouted, barely heard above the din. "To our colonel! Raise your cups and drink." All willingly obliged. "To Thomas Jefferson's Empire of Liberty." All cups were filled and raised again. "Our Empire of Liberty progresses apace from the Atlantic to the Pacific." Fueled by the alcohol consumption, the applause became louder.

Forsyth toasted, "To all of you gentlemen! Your names will grace the illustrious history of our young nation."

He then shouted, "Music! We need music! We need to sing our song. Tell me, men, what is our song? What is the song of our regiment?"

The chorus cheered, "Garry Owen!"

Forsyth continued, "Get that son-of-a-bitch squeezebox player in here. I'm tired of listening to that crap he's been playing ... so sweeeeeet and gentle! Let's give those Indians some real battle cries!" He swung his arm around to point to the entrance but, dizzied with the alcohol, he almost toppled and was steadied by a now whiskey splashed Whitside.

Soon after, an orderly returned with the reluctant Murphy. "Play for us, my good man!" Forsyth commanded.

Now Murphy had a certain affinity for the Indians. He knew what it felt like to lose one's homeland, but he was a soldier and now considered himself an American, and so he played what he knew they wanted. His fingers cramped though when he heard the verse:

"We are the boys that take delight, smashing the Limerick light when lighting, through all the streets like sporters fighting, and tearing all before us."

I can feel it in my bones that something bad is going to happen! They are enjoying these words a little too much!

A worried Captain Wallace barely sipped his whiskey. Turning closer to Major Whitside, he said, "If I may say so, major, tomorrow's going to be a real powder keg with all this drinking. We have tensions in both camps, bucks on both sides are just itching for a fight and we are not far from reveille. Besides that, I'll bet my bottom dollar that bastard Asay has been selling booze to the enlisted men as well. Is there some way we can get the Colonel out

22

of here and into bed?"

Before he could respond, Forsyth left the tent, unsteady on his feet. *Great! An opportunity!* they thought as they followed after him.

"Whew, that felt good!" Forsyth said aloud when he finished painting the frozen ground with his urine and, with difficulty, rearranged his uniform. When Whitside appeared, Forsyth was surprised, but this quickly turned into annoyance when the major laid a hand on his shoulder and guided him away from the tent. Wallace gently held his other arm.

"Where are you taking me? Can't a man go out to piss in peace?" Forsyth's annoyance had now turned into anger.

"To your quarters, sir!"

In jerking his arm away from Wallace, Forsyth fell into Whitside's arms, slurring, "No, I am not going!"

"With all due respect, sir, yes, you are," Wallace said, and they both strong-armed the colonel into his tent.

"I swear to God I will have your heads! I swear to God I will!"

But Whitside was firm as he lowered his commanding officer onto his cot, "So be it, sir. But you have an army to command and the nation will be watching tomorrow. The nation will judge all of us tomorrow." No sooner had the words been said than the colonel dropped off into oblivion. They covered him, rekindled the fire, and left.

With the colonel safely asleep, Whitside took control.

"Wallace, I am going to go back and shut down that party," he said. "You find Asay and turn off that whiskey. God only knows we should have done this earlier, and may God have mercy on us if this damned place blows up tomorrow."

"Attention!" Whitside called to the soldiers in the tent, but he had to give this command twice before the soldiers took notice. "Colonel Forsyth has instructed me to ask all of you to call it a night and go sober up before reveille. Spill your drinks now. Drunkenness tomorrow will be cause for court martial and I won't shirk from filing a report."

The officers shuffled out of the tent grumbling and Whitside looked with disgust at the mess they left.

Meanwhile, Asay was filling an enlisted man's cup when Wallace approached him undetected. Wallace slapped the cup away and drew his revolver, intending to shoot a hole in the keg. Instead, in anger, he used the butt of it to hammer the spigot off the barrel. He then shoved Asay up against the barrel while the stream of whisky drained out against his legs.

Wallace fumed. "You, sir, can go to hell if the situation explodes tomorrow!" He turned to the other man who seemed intent on slinking away. "I know you, Dawes. You've been in the regiment a long time. You damn well know the rules about drinking on duty. Report to me when we get back to the agency! Understand?"

Defiant, Dawes turned and looked Wallace in the eye, "Yes, Sir! You know I will," he sneered.

Dawes stumbled through the trampled buffalo grass, his head pounding. Whenever he got drunk like this, the visions would come: His father ... his brother ... the screaming and then the silence. Quiet. His brother was too quiet! *Why didn't I do something? Why didn't she?* As always happened when he became that drunk, traumatic memories came back to haunt him. He wove through the shrubbery in the darkness until he tripped. As he fell, he grabbed the nearest bush, a buffalo berry bush. When he sought to right himself, one of the inch long thorns pierced his hand. "Damn!" he cried as he sucked off the blood and continued his search for his tent. "Baxter! Baxter!" he called to a companion. "Where the hell are you?"

Baxter woke up to the sound of his name, but he did not answer, did not want to be around Dawes any more than was necessary. The others in the tent felt the same. "Don't answer the bastard. He's twisted! I'm sick of him." They nodded in agreement and rolled over to go back to sleep.

As he staggered around in the dark, Dawes became nauseous. Bending over, he retched, but still he craved more whiskey. *Asay has to have more.* Finding his way back to the wagon proved to be easier than finding which of the many tents was his. He found Asay in the wagon bed mumbling in his sleep, oblivious to the cold.

"Wake up! Wake up, goddammit, I'm freezing my ass off. I need a drink!"

"You sorry bastard!" Asay hissed from beneath his blanket. "Leave me alone! Get the hell outta here! The keg's dry and you know it. Git back to your tent. If the major finds you here, he will bust your ass back to wherever you came from and send me with you!"

"I'm a bastard? Maybe those kids of yours are bastards. Ever think of that?" Dawes threw back his head and laughed. Waddling off, he threw back more taunts over his shoulder. "Asay, I been meaning to ask you. They say your wife likes sweet buggy rides down to the Niobara with the menfolk. Since we be such good friends and all, mind if I buggy the missus down to the river myself?"

Asay, infuriated, half sat up in the wagon. Had he been sober, he would have crushed Dawes with pleasure, but the alcohol dizzied him, and Dawes was able to ramble aimlessly away. No longer laughing, Dawes moaned, "Damn, my head hurts!"

But Dawes was not the only soldier wandering the encampment that night. A group of officers had met and huddled together, passing around a private stash of whiskey. Dawes approached them, but the menacing glare from the one raising the bottle to his lips caused him to keep his distance. *Maybe if I stand here and watch them long enough, they'll let me join their little party.*

However, they moved on through the makeshift village, singing and leaving Dawes behind. Finally, they stopped before an Army tent and yanked open the flap. Inside, Chief Big Foot lay dying.

"Hey, Big Foot, heap big Injun chief, you were at the Little Big Horn. Ain't that right? We're here to pay you back!" Two of the men jostled to enter the tent at the same time. As they struggled, Big Foot's wife armed herself with a kettle of boiling water. Seeing this, the men backed out but, unfortunately, into Captain Myles Moylan, the captain of the guard.

"Back to your quarters, all of you!" he boomed. "Now, or I will place you under arrest. Move!"

Glad now he hadn't joined the men, Dawes slunk into the deeper shadows afforded by the multiple thípi. The cold was clearing his head, and, as it often happened to him, other urges arose. *A woman would be nice right about now,* he thought, biting his lower lip.

Before he could think how he would achieve that, he saw an Indian woman holding the hand of a child walk past the outer edge of the encampment. He followed. He watched as she assisted her young daughter with relieving herself and then scrunched up her own dress to do the same. Her legs, dark in the moonlight but visible, excited him. He walked over, surprising her. "Squaw woman, you should not be out here in the dark all by yourself. How about I take you someplace safe?"

Frightened, she put her child behind her and backed away. When

Dawes lunged for her, she screamed.

"Leave her alone!" A newly recruited soldier on guard duty that night aimed his rifle at Dawes. "I don't know who you are, but you'd better get the hell outta here!' he boomed.

The recruit offered to take her back but she just ran off.

*****

Kȟoškálaka núŋpa átakičhiyapi.
Two young men meet each other.

American Hair did not go to his thípi that night. Instead, he walked as far as he could away from the native encampment and headed towards Čhaŋkpé Ópi Wakpála *Wounded Knee Creek*. He was not escaping, and yet he escaped notice. Alone at the creek, he raised his arms to the sky, threw back his head with eyes closed, and prayed.

Peace enveloped him until it slipped into his consciousness that this was not the position in which to pray. He sank to his knees, made the Sign of the Cross, and prostrated himself on the ground. He was new to the idea of sin, new to the idea of the American God who demanded submission and, in return, offered love and everlasting life. Thomas Didymus American Hair asked his Father in heaven for forgiveness, although for what he was unsure. His joy in his newfound faith pushed him to chant memorized Latin words of praise to this new God. He knew the meaning of the words, and yet his mouth had trouble negotiating the sounds. Sure that Jesus Christ, the Son, at least, would understand his attempt, he began the Divine Praises as his teachers in his mission day school had instructed.

Benedictus Deus. Benedictum Nomen Sanctus e-jus.
Benedictus Jesus Christus, verus Deus et verus homo.
Blessed be God. Blessed be His Holy Name.
Blessed be Jesus Christ, true God and true man.

Blessings to God, yes, but am I blessed this night? He thought back to when he was seven years old. He had gone to school and had his braids cut off. "See how nice you look now?" his teacher had said. "Such an excellent student you will be now!" In the way of the Lakȟóta, hair was cut off when there was a need to embarrass, or as a sign of mourning. In broken English, his little boy voice asked his teacher what he had done wrong. "You are Indian," he was told. "That is enough." Rather than rebel at the admonishment, he determined to win the respect of his teacher. He'd be the best student! He'd become "white." His family could not understand this, but he knew this was the way it had to be. Submission led to acceptance and although, at first, it tore at his insides to submit, he soon learned that in doing so, he earned favor with his white teachers and the priests.

Every morning, he studied English. He learned the history of his country through white eyes. He learned about Jesus. In the afternoon, he learned how to farm. And these lessons excited him! He brought this newfound knowledge back home to his parents, but they, sadly for him, were not interested at all. Instead, they spent their time teaching his younger brother the old ways. Not getting recognition for his successes from his parents, he, instead, strove to become a superior student and, with his natural intelligence, he almost succeeded.

A voice broke into his reflections. Respectful of the prayer posture, the soldier on night watch touched American Hair's shoulder saying, with voice and hand motion, "C'mon, you have to go back to camp." American Hair stood, looked the soldier in the eye, nodded compliance and walked back.

Private Flood continued his rounds for the short remainder of his four-hour watch and then found comfort warming himself within a circle of new recruits sitting close to a fire. They stretched their hands over it, trying to keep warm.

"You ever shot a man?" one soldier said to another.

"Never," came the reply.

"Have you ever shot *at* a man?"

Again, the answer was in the negative.

"Do you even know how to work this pistol?" said another as he drew out his Colt Single Action Army revolver. "They showed me. But I ain't never hit nuthin' with it." That produced some nervous laughter.

John Henry joined in as a questioner. "Since we all are in this together, I wonder if any of you even fought at all?"

A young man with only a hint of a beard responded, "I used to wrestle with my brother." After that there was quiet. These men had no experience in warfare. Only a few months before, they'd been

27

farmers.

And it was only a few months ago John Henry had been a farmer too, if you could call plowing up dry powdered dirt that blew away in the hot 110-degree wind, some sort of farming. If you planted kernels of corn that you could dig up after a month's time and have them look the same, then a farmer he was. If you expected rain that rainless summer of 1890 in Fall River County, west of the Pine Ridge reservation, you would be mightily disappointed. John Henry learned not to expect rain. He learned not to expect to grow crops in the drought. But he did not expect his father to pack up and leave unexpectedly one morning, never to return. The man took their half-starved horse and rode into Rapid City to catch a train going anywhere but there, and that left John Henry in a bit of a predicament. Because he had his mother to take care of and no money to do it, he did what needed to be done. He sent his mother back east to her family where water actually flowed, promising to come for her after he earned some money in the Army. John Henry's heart was heavy sitting around the fire and he was scared.

One of the young men got up and stretched, and his too-short pants wrinkled above his knees, leaving a bare space between the boot tops and the bottom hem. His dress was not atypical, as the Army had not fitted the uniforms for these men; instead, they accepted what the recruiter handed them and later traded amongst themselves for better fits.

"I'm going to get some sleep," John Henry finally said. He placed his hand over his belly and stroked it. Army rations did not agree with him and awakened the acid in his stomach. His tent mate followed, and John Henry knew that soon after lying down under the thin blankets, they would spoon into each other for the heat their bodies would share. The temperatures had been in the 60s during the day but had dropped quickly to 30 and the wind made it seem much colder. But it was not only the wind that made him cold. The tension also did. John Henry felt it in the air, a now silent night awaiting the dawn.

*****

Óta Íŋyaŋke ečíyapi.
Her name was She Runs A Lot.

28

Who-who-who-who-who-who. Over and over Wind Woman heard the short eared owl call for a mate. The sound made her lonely and the night dragged on. In the dim light of dying coals, all sounds seemed sharper. All shadows danced eerily and evoked memories. She thought of her husband in the spirit world now. *Can he hear the owl? Does he call for me?* Wind Woman pulled Brings Fire closer to her and both hearts seemed to beat too fast. *There would be no peaceful journey into Pine Ridge tomorrow. One did not have to be a warrior to sense that.* Her daughter's head rested against the side of her breast. She remembered suckling her years ago, hoping her milk would be enough to sustain her little one's life. *Tomorrow*, she wondered, *will I be able to protect this beloved daughter if there is trouble?*

It seemed to Wind Woman that Brings Fire had known only winters of hardship. She sighed as she gently ran her fingers through her daughter's long hair, separating the tangles at the ends. The world had offered brutal winters in those years since her child was born. There was a time before, though. She remembered those other times when winters were not so cold and food, if not plentiful, was enough to keep everyone fed until spring. *Would they ever come back?*

*****

It was during the winter of what white people called the Children's Blizzard that her own child had received her name.

That day offered no hint of what was to come, although the people had prepared to stay as warm as they could, huddled into shared thípi to conserve what little firewood they had. The snow had made food scarce and all the four-leggeds had suffered. The ribs on all who still lived looked much like the ribs of those who hadn't. Many had died; starved, frozen, and it seemed likely that this band might suffer the same fate. The winter stories that elders could tell were long ago exhausted, and what few games the children could devise in the cramped thípi no longer held any attraction. The warriors had repaired their weapons and had put them aside. The urge to create beaded artwork was no longer alive. Starvation had set in; adults rationed the food for children while they themselves chewed leather

29

to ease the pain of hunger. Though it was still day, the people languished and fell into stupefying sleep.

Óta Íŋyaŋke *Runs A Lot* was not satisfied with sleep, though. At four winters old, she crawled around through the piles of robes, pretending to come out onto the plains to hunt buffalo. She would flatten herself to the thípi floor, wherever she could find space, and raise her head just a little above the "people boulders" to see the herds of imagined buffalo. She would choose the one closest to her, his hot breath shooting smoke from his wet nostrils, snorting and suspicious of her presence. Now she would act, she thought, and she nocked the arrow into the bowstring and, with mighty strength, pulled back and then released. The arrow found the lung as its target. The beast went down, and she prayed over it and offered thanks while she carved out the liver and bit into its life giving nourishment. As she feasted on her pretend kill, she too nodded off to sleep in the valley between her parents' legs, her moccasin clad feet close to the dying fire.

When the sun began its descent into the west, a strong wind whooshed down the smoke hole and sent a shiver through her body. Not under a blanket, she awoke to find the thípi had grown cold. The fire had gone out. She nudged her mother, who just moaned in her sleep. She tapped the shoulder of her father, who, lost in his own dream, shrugged her away. She sat and waited, but it grew colder. She knew the way of the animals as taught by her grandfather, and also knew it was at this time when creatures were too cold to respond, that death would follow to take their spirits away. She loved her family and her little warrior's heart knew it was up to her to do the only thing that would help. She must get fire.

It was not far to another thípi that had pale white plumes coming through the smoke hole, although it was on the opposite side of the circle. The walk was simple. She had gone there many times before. She set out into the blizzard that suddenly happened, and the stinging ice pellets and blinding snow prevented her from finding this oh-so-close thípi with the welcoming fire and extra wood for her family. She walked in circles, lost, and the thípi she found were empty, all empty, and she did not know that she had touched the same thípi repeatedly as by now the bitter cold had frozen her eyelashes together and her unseeing eyes had brought her close, but never to, her destination. Her frozen feet would someday bear the scars of flesh that fell off as it thawed, but she continued until she at last reached a door flap where her fists hammering on it brought welcome entrance into a warmth that shocked her into a faint.

She awakened to the rubbing of her limbs by the women and sat up to drink warm water. She stood up, weaving to get her balance, dizzy with the new flow of blood, and insisted that she should bring the fire to her family. This she did, returning in the arms of Kȟaŋǧí Óta *Many Crows*, holding in one hand a small iron pot containing a smoldering coal and in the other, small sticks to ignite the fire. On that night, she earned her adult name, Pȟéta Akú, *Brings Fire*.

Because a ceremony often accompanied the giving of a new name, Bring's Fire's mother had much preparation to do. Gifts for the people had to be made and so Wind Woman found renewed pleasure in her beadwork. In time, the winter snows melted and soon after, the soft pastel petals of the pasque flower matched the blue of the Spring skies. Finally, it was time for the ceremony. On the chosen day, Wind Woman gently put the new ceremonial moccasins on Brings Fire and presented her, the Hokšíčhaŋtkiyapi, *Child Beloved*, to the camp.

Chapter 2

Oyáte kiŋ líla iníhaŋpi.
The people were expecting something bad.

Wind Woman stretched in the morning freshness of Dec. 29, 1890, and noticed a different excitement in the encampment. She may have heard a woman's song, or perhaps, was it whistling she heard? The heavy buffalo hide that covered the thípi muffled the sound, and when she finally got up to go outside, she thrilled to the morning calls of a chickadee. *Maybe the day will go well after all,* she thought. *No blizzard has come. Perhaps there is no threat.*

Grasshopper walked over to greet her. She noticed he walked with a younger step. She noticed more fire in his eyes. "Até, you look well this morning."

"I am well," he said, pulling himself straighter, squaring his shoulders.

"You think there will be trouble, don't you?"

"It would not be as I would wish, Čhuŋkší *Daughter.* I would never choose to fight with women and children present, but if I must act to protect them, I am prepared to die fighting." He looked towards the cannons and his eyes swept over the troops surrounding the encampment. "We would never win, but we can save some."

Looking deeply into his daughter's eyes, he continued, "I will save you, you and the child, if it is in my power to do so."

She met his eyes and smiled tightly. "I may save you!" She paused. "And I have hidden my gun."

Resting her hand on the fringed leather sheath at her waist, she indicated she also had her knife, a gift from him. The black glass-like blade fashioned from a fractured piece of quick cooling magma obsidian had come from a place the Crow called the "land of burning ground." Grasshopper had slain the Crow warrior and refitted the

32

blade in a buffalo bone handle and given this treasure to his young daughter many years ago. The sinew binding was still strong and the knife effective. Wind Woman would use it today if necessary.

With pride, Grasshopper placed his hand affectionately on her shoulder and nodded.

Brings Fire came to stand beside her mother. "Iná, will we have to fight today? I am ready!"

"What you need to be ready for is to help me pack."

As she turned to begin this task, Napé Ópi *Wounded Hand*, the village crier, approached Grasshopper and the warriors he was conferring with, announcing that they, and indeed, all Lakȟóta men and older boys, were to assemble for council in front of Big Foot's tent. Women and children were told to stay within the camp.

Mother and child stood at the entrance flap and strained to hear the men's responses. Most of the voices were riotous and impossible to fathom, but some powerful voices rose above the tumult and these they could understand.

"Why can't we just pack up and go to the agency?"

"More talk is bad news!"

"What is there to talk about?"

And then there was a sarcastic, "Are they lost? Do they need us to show them the way to Pine Ridge?"

A short time later, Grasshopper returned to Wind Woman. "Hide the weapons, the guns, the knives. Hide the bows. Hide the arrows too. And the awls, hide them as well. Go, quickly, tell the other women."

Finally, there was something for Brings Fire to do. "I will run that way to tell the others." Wind Woman ran off the other way and immediately upon hearing the news, the women started concealing the weapons as best they could as they dismantled the thípi and loaded the wagons.

They could not help but hear Loud Bear's voice, and his angry tone frightened them. Wind Woman knew hot-headed young men often provoke incidents.

"They threatened us all night and would not let us sleep," he called out. "They promised revenge for our defeat of Custer. Now they want to meet? So they can take our guns? Are we to die without defense?"

Grasshopper tried to quell the rising fear with reason. He walked through the encampment urging calm. "They are trying to intimidate us. It is the way of the Long Knives to bully us before doing anything. They like showing off their strength. And besides," he added conspiratorially, "Look at the way they arrange themselves around the council area. They will be shooting at each other if trouble breaks!" Everywhere he did his best to calm the warriors. There were women and children here, he reminded them. That was foremost on his mind. "No, they intend to show off, but they do not intend to harm us. Calm yourselves. Do not become agitated! Do not start a fight!"

This was difficult to do as by now a rumor was also circulating around the encampment that they were not to be taken to Pine Ridge. They were to be taken to prison in Fort Meade, South Dakota instead.

Chief Horn Cloud, a lifetime friend of Grasshopper, called together his sons and all who would listen and gave advice. "Do not start trouble," he counseled. "And stay away from troublemakers." However, if a confrontation was provoked by the soldiers, as he suspected it would, he knew they would act as men and protect the women and children. "To die for the sake of relatives is noble and would satisfy me," he told them. "A good way to die!"

Messages continued to fly back to the women. "Hide the weapons. Keep the children close. Ensure the elderly are in the wagons. Make sure the teams are ready to run. Make the horses ready for escape in case of trouble. And if trouble breaks out, do not fight the Long Knives. Run! Run as fast as you can!"

Wind Woman could no longer conceal her concern. With heart pounding, she tucked Brings Fire into the wagon bed between two bags and ordered her to stay there. Sensing her mother's fear, the child did as she was told.

*****

Mílahaŋska kiŋ mázawakȟáŋ kiŋ wičhákhipi.
The Americans took the guns away from them.

As Brings Fire peeked over the bags, she saw women nervously hurrying to pack the wagons. Back and forth they went, stirring up the dust on the ground as they did so. The dust rose and fell in a swirling motion as the breeze picked it up and swept it high around the women's legs before it fell to the ground only to be pushed around again. *The dust is like the peoples' spirits in this camp. Rising up and then drifting down. One moment, the people are happy. The next, something is scaring them ...rising and falling, just like the dust.*

In another part of the encampment, the feet of Ziŋtkála Zí *Yellow Bird,* the ghost dancer, kicked up even more dust as he stepped and gyrated. The slight breeze of that morning lifting the dirt formed a cloudy, electric atmosphere around the dancer that matched the tension spreading through the camp. Yellow Bird danced and danced. And all people felt uneasy.

He was an imposing figure and his sweat-soaked Ghost Shirt accentuating his virility did little to induce calmness among the Lakȟóta or the Army present. The dance itself was about peace and expectations of a better life, but the Americans instead saw threats and war. The belief that the continuous dancing would ultimately return the Plains People to former glory, implied the elimination of the white population there, and so each step was a taunt that the Army commanders could no longer ignore.

Anxious warriors milled around, their looks threatening. Heated arguments broke out. The officers tried to keep them under control but Yellow Hawk's antics kept tensions high.

"Tell him to shut up. He's getting on my nerves," one said.

Throwing more dust into the air, Yellow Bird exhorted the young warriors. "Bullets won't hurt you! They'll float in the air like this dust!" The eagle feathers in his hair bounced with his stomped rhythm and his green painted face and yellow nose pointed to the sky to which he flung his prayers.

Fearing an escalation, the army interpreter, a mixed blood Lakȟóta, Philip Wells, a man with a working knowledge of the Lakȟóta language, took the medicine man by the arm and told him to sit down and be calm. He assured Yellow Bird that all would work out fine for the Lakȟóta. Yellow Bird stopped, waved his arms one more time, and finally sat down.

While the Lakȟóta men gathered in the council area, the soldiers were ordered to position themselves between the Lakȟóta men and the women of the camp. This wise military decision would strategically make it difficult for the warriors to respond to the cries they would soon hear from the women.

Another decision was not as wise. A circle of American soldiers surrounded the Lakȟóta men and boys assembled before Big Foot's tent. Seasoned soldiers were aghast at this positioning. They found themselves facing each other across the council area! One grisly sergeant called out across the space, "Stu, you old Injun fighter, if trouble breaks, turn around and shoot at the hills. Not at me, for God's sake!" It seemed likely to the experienced men they would face friendly fire if violence erupted. A murmur of nervous laughter rippled around the ranks.

Though dying with blood coming from his nose, Chief Big Foot did not relinquish his role. Coughing, he cleared the blood from his throat, and with strangled voice urged his people not to provoke a fight. If guns had to be surrendered, he instructed the warriors in his tent, give up the old guns, but hide the new. "Convince the American soldiers that we are a peaceful people," he insisted.

Outside, twenty warriors stood up, announcing they had no guns on their person but would go to the camp and get what they could. The Americans allowed these to pass through. Soon after, they returned with mostly irreparable muzzleloaders and other such relics, dumping them in a pile near Big Foot's tent.

Whitside scoffed, "Yesterday they had plenty of very good Winchesters. They're trying to deceive us, Colonel." And so Forsyth had Big Foot brought out into the council area.

"Big Foot, I want 25 guns. Yesterday, when we captured you, everybody had a gun and a good gun too. I want those guns, 25 of them."

The chief protested. "My men have no guns except as you have found. I collected all my guns at the Cheyenne River Agency. What the soldiers did with them, I can only guess."

"Big Foot," Forsyth hotly implored, barely able to control his anger. "You are lying to me in return for my kindness? Am I not treating you well? You have a warm tent and your people have provisions. My doctors are treating you."

And yet we are prisoners, Yellow Bird thought. He jumped back to his feet and once again began his dancing and singing incantations. An elder attempted to stop him. "You provoke the Long Knives. See! The old ones, women, and the little ones are not protected. Do you want to start a slaughter?"

The dancer shot back, "The Great Mystery will protect us. This is what the Messiah in the West has promised. I speak with authority and I tell you, the bullets of the enemy will not harm us." But minutes later, again, he sat down.

Some young men, bitter with the proceedings, went back to the camp and returned with just five more guns. More infuriated than before, Forsyth ordered, "Give me *all* of your guns, or, I swear to God, those four guns on the hill will destroy your camp."

Barely able to speak now, Big Foot whispered his command, "Bring all the guns."

But a warrior protested. "There are no more guns!" Murmurs of agreement rose and the soldiers steadied themselves for confrontation.

Forsyth needed to take action. He ordered his men to search the camp.

How the warriors protested! "Long Knives near our families?" But Big Foot reassured them. "Let them do it. We are not on this journey to fight. They have promised to take us to Pine Ridge. We will join Red Cloud's council and see our relatives!"

Some older warriors were appeased, but many seethed, clenching their fists and yelling their disapproval.

With the warriors contained, soldiers were ordered to check the wagons for hidden weapons. The women were led away while the soldiers went from wagon to wagon, ripping open sacks, rifling through blankets and robes, emptying parfleches which held food for the winter. Any woman or child who interfered was pushed aside.

Brings Fire remained in the wagon as she was told, fearfully hiding under a blanket. She peeked out and saw her mother try to push through the soldiers. One knocked her down. On the ground, she reached for the obsidian knife at her side, but her hand found only the cloth of her dress. Then she remembered. The knife was in the wagon. Her widened eyes shot to her daughter lying on top of its hidden place.

Her wagon was soon to be searched. Thinking she was immobilized for the moment, the unsuspecting soldiers opened a space in their line and Wind Woman burst through, reaching the wagon before they did. She pulled Brings Fire from the wagon, held her close, and withdrew to the relative safety of the other women. The women wailed and screamed their hatred at the soldiers as they watched their possessions strewn about and trampled on the crushed dry grass.

One young pregnant woman could bear it no longer. The beaded cradleboard she had lovingly created was torn apart, and beads flew in a rainbow spray through the crisp morning air. She charged at the men.

"Subdue that woman!" Two soldiers grabbed her arms. Leering, one said, "I think we should search her. She is a mite too eager to get to her wagon." The other agreed.

Wind Woman recognized the red-headed soldier and shuddered. The woman struggled, locked in between the two soldiers, while one reached up under her sack-like dress. When this soldier realized her pregnancy, he, ashamed, withdrew his hand. "You won't do it?" hissed the red-headed one. "Then I will!" and he lifted her dress and exposed her round belly.

I know that man, Brings Fire said to herself.

A commanding voice rang out, "Subdue her, search her, but by God, man, control yourself. Look at her!" Dawes, grinning, released her when his superior drew near. Sobbing, she ran back to her family.

Wind Woman tightened her grip on her daughter's hand while the men reached into her wagon and began throwing things out. *The knife is there! They will take my knife!* Brings Fire, knowing how important this knife was to her mother, imagined what she was thinking and wanted to reassure her mother that the knife was safe. She tugged hard at her mother's hand. When Wind Woman looked at her, Brings Fire smiled and smoothed the fabric of her dress tight against her leg. The shape of the pouch that held the knife became visible. The child had it safely hanging from her own waist.

*****

Ok'ó hiŋglé.
A great excitement erupted.

The women's screams reached the men at the council area and chaos erupted. American Hair surprised his grandfather by wrestling his way through the first line of hardened soldiers to get to the women, but he was subdued by the second line. They knocked him to the ground. Grasshopper rushed to his aid, but he, too, was immediately blocked.

38

"Get back, old man!" a soldier said, pushing a rifle hard into his midsection.

Grasshopper grabbed the rifle barrel, stopping one soldier's threat, but received another as the butt of a rifle caught him in the small of his back. He fell to his knees, a scene repeated with variations around the council area, with much jostling until the Americans restored order.

The warriors heaped a jumble of weaponry within the council area. There were a few Winchesters and old muzzleloaders and even cooking utensils that might serve as weapons. The sight frightened Charles H. Cressey, a war journalist from Nebraska's Omaha Bee, and he prepared in his mind the story he would write. To him, the Lakȟóta appeared as the aggressors. The guns were placed in clear sight of the "savages," and were within easy reach if a fight should erupt.

The surrender of weapons was too slow and too meager for Forsyth. He ignored Wallace's suggestion that he should tone down the situation. Tension was straining the faces of Americans and Lakȟóta alike. The assembly was nearing a breaking point. Instead, Forsyth barked, "Whitside, officers, search the bucks." and then he said to the Lakȟóta, through an interpreter, "Stand up like men, remove your blankets, and surrender your weapons!"

Many young Lakȟóta warriors ignored the order. Around twenty older men complied. Yellow Bird became agitated again and stood up, but two soldiers forced him down.

Forsyth ordered again, "By God, if you won't volunteer like men, then we will force you. Whitside! Varnum! Search them!"

The first three warriors who submitted to the search, gave up two rifles, one a Winchester, along with ammunition belts hidden under their blanket robes. Other cavalry men tried herding the rest of the Lakȟóta into obedience using the force of their rifle barrels. Loud Bear angrily resisted, but Lieutenant Mann interrupted this intended search when he noticed a young warrior drifting to the east edge of the assembly and shouted, "Be ready, men! I think there is going to be trouble."

Meanwhile, most women were busily repacking the wagons, but some were standing on tiptoe to get a better view of the proceedings. Wind Woman did not like what she saw.

From where she stood and from what she could hear, there was chaos, and she feared for the safety of her daughter. "Go, wedge yourself between those sacks. Keep your head down!" she ordered.

As Brings Fire sat on the bottom of the wagon bed, she raised her dress and untied the pouch at her waist. "Iná, first you must take this!" Wind Woman tied this around her, feeling stronger because of the knife.

"Good! Stay down now." With her eyes just above the wagon sides, Brings Fire watched her mother go the short distance to a bush and kick up the dirt and scratch into it with her toe. She couldn't draw attention to herself by using her arms to dig up her Winchester so she squatted behind the bush, looking like she was relieving herself, while she slipped the gun up under her blanket robe.

Now, with her gun close against her side, she climbed back into the wagon. Unseen by the soldiers, but obvious to the woman in the wagon near her, she nodded and asked for secrecy with hand motions. Her cousin cautioned, "Firing that gun will draw attention to us and we shall all die." But Wind Woman replied, "If I need to use this gun, we will all die anyway, but I will die fighting!" Frightened, Brings Fire searched her mother's face. She was serious.

Wind Woman was intent on evaluating the situation. Americans surrounded her people. The mountain guns and troops were to the north. The cavalry camp was to the northeast. To the south, there were more mounted troops, infantry soldiers, and scouts. She spoke to the women who were near, pointing to the escape positions with her chin.

"Hurry! Finish packing. See, we are close to the road! If there is shooting, race your wagon to the south. There are fewer soldiers there, and they won't shoot a woman. The Oglála scouts there won't bother you if there is shooting. And look, you can run to the ravine over there if you need to!"

In and among their wagons, the women strained to see and understand what was going on in the council area, but the men were excitedly shifting places, and voices shouted at each other were unintelligible. The figure of one man became more pronounced. He stalked among the warriors with arms upraised, waving his valued Winchester above his head. Wind Woman could not be sure, but thought this was Šuŋgmánitu Sápa *Black Coyote*, a close relative of Sitting Bull. *What is he doing?*

His voice became clearer when others quieted to hear it. "This is my gun!" he ranted. "I paid good money for this gun! I will not give it to anyone unless I am paid!" Other voices echoed his protest.

Forsyth pointed to the man and demanded that someone shut him up and take his gun.

"He does not know what he is doing!" a warrior yelled to Wells, the interpreter. "He is crazy and deaf. He can't hear you!" Nonetheless, two soldiers came up behind to seize Black Coyote and a struggle ensued.

Wells stumbled in his translation and the only thing that all understood was that they were to remain calm. This, however, did nothing to ease the tension.

And then Black Coyote's rifle went off.

*****

Kȟoškálaka kiŋ henáyos wanáǧi oómani káǧapi.
Those two young men set out on their spirit journey.

Bang.

Brings Fire jolted to attention at the sound of the first shot. It split time into before and after, she would later think. It did not even matter from where it had come, be it from a Lakȟóta warrior or an American soldier, as the effect would have been the same that morning at Wounded Knee. The firing of that single rifle had a deadly energy that triggered an explosion of gunshots and death everywhere.

After Black Coyote's rifle fired, six young warriors threw off their blankets and pointed their rifles at the troops. A mounted Lieutenant Robinson, finding himself in their line of expected fire, wheeled his horse around to get out of the way and shouted to the K troops, "Look out, men, they're going to fire!"

He charged off at top speed up the hill towards the Hotchkiss batteries. K troop opened fire. All the warriors cast off their blankets, and those with guns immediately joined the firefight. Those without guns scrambled into the pile of weapons that had concerned reporter Cressey and seized what they could find.

Most of the women by the wagons had never witnessed a battle scene. In the past, their grief only began when the warriors returned with the bodies of their loved ones. Now, as the first warrior fell, his

41

wife saw it happen and every woman there thought she saw her future. Shocked into an eerie, primitive self-defense mode, the sounds coming from their souls were more animal-like, and their voices rang out loud without words, some in screams, some in high-pitched monosyllables, some in groans, and some in shocked voiceless gasps. They scrambled into wagons and urged the horses into a panicked race towards the Agency Road. Some ran on foot with their children gripping their hands. They tripped over the rocks and the uneven terrain, trying to reach the nearby ravine and its potential safety. Wind Woman was strangely calm though, as she took deadly aim at the soldiers. She left her wagon off to the side, hoping to protect, as any warrior would, the fleeing women and children before she too, with her daughter, ran for the ravine.

There was chaos near Big Foot's tent. Bullets flew in all directions. Warriors fought soldiers hand-to-hand. Smoke and dust rose, making it difficult for Wind Woman to get a clear shot from her position.

On the hill, the artillery was eager to use the big guns. With lanyards in hand, the men poised for the bombardment, ready to use the weapons that would end this conflict once and for all. Captain Capron, fearing premature firing, yelled, "Dammit, calm your nerves! You can't fire until our boys separate from the savages." Not trusting this command to be obeyed, he ordered the friction primers removed from the two guns in his battery. Lieutenant Hawthorne did the same for his.

The Lakȟóta men, trapped within the circle, fought to get free. Gouging, slashing, and firing, they struggled to penetrate the soldier barrier to get to the women and children. Gouged, slashed, and fired upon, many died.

Grasshopper made it through, although not unscathed. With pumped up adrenaline, he and Waníyetu Kté *Kills In Winter*, his kȟolá, *brother-friend*, struggled through the smoke and the hand-to-hand fighting, and broke through the line. Grasshopper did not even notice that a bullet had ripped into his flesh until the loss of blood made him falter. In what seemed like dizzying slow motion, he saw Kills In Winter rip off his shirt and wrap it around his arm. "I cannot stay here. You...hide!" He pointed to a clump of bushes.

Loud Bear fought his way past the soldiers, stabbing with his knife and smashing with the hammer he had found in the confusion.

He was intent on putting an end to the life of Philip Wells; the interpreter was holding the tip of his nose in his hand, perplexed whether he should rip it all the way off or try to save it. A bullet whizzed into the hammerhead Loud Bear wielded and deflected off, sparking, and, with fury, he turned to defeat the soldier who had thus dared to assault him. Running hard, he collided with the runaway mules pulling the whiskey wagon, now carrying a very surprised and terrified Dr. Ewing, who had come to the scene with a picnic lunch. Shoving the mules aside earned Loud Bear one kick to his leg, grazing it, while he headed towards the screaming women.

Terrified, Pvt. John Henry Flood had pulled his revolver when the shots first rang out, but he himself did not fire. The turmoil of smoke and dust swirling gave only glimpses of shadowy figures massed together. He sensed shots were being fired in his direction and he could see Army guns pointed at him from the other edge of the council circle. *Oh my God,* his brain screamed, *Our own soldiers will kill us!* Forcing himself to move, although his knees were buckling under him, he heard someone calling for his mother, "Ma! Ma!" He realized it was his own voice, and he sent an urgent prayer for God to keep his mother safe because he knew he would never be able to keep his promise to return. Seeing neither friend nor foe, he shot blindly into the smoke. He fired again. And again.

A gust of wind billowed a path into the smoke, and he found himself face to face with American Hair. There was a recognition from the night before. There was a moment of "Don't I know you?" but American Hair's arm was already above his head, ready to drive his makeshift knife down through the private's chest cavity. John Henry pulled the trigger.

American Hair stared at him in the disbelieving second before he realized this would be the end of his life. John Henry lowered his gun and reached for American Hair, falling towards him. Friendly fire tore through the private's neck.

Powerless to stop this madness, Father Kraft stumbled through it. He stepped over the two as they lay dying on the bloodied ground and searched for survivors he could comfort.

*****

Aŋpétu waŋží él wičháša kiŋ ká wakté kte.

43

Someday I will kill that man.

So great was the carnage in the council area, that Father Kraft, shocked, was unaware that he, too, suffered a stab wound in his lung. Stepping around those already dead, including Chief Bigfoot, he administered to the dying and tried to assist those wounded. Because the battle had shifted to the surrounding area, he was relatively safe there.

The surviving warriors fought their way to the women in the wagons leaving an adequate separation of forces for Col. Forsyth to orchestrate his next maneuver. He made his way up the hill and ordered the cannon bombardment.

The effect was devastating! Round after round poured out of the cannons and shredded each thípi into tattered strips that were left flapping against the few lodge poles that still stood. The people screamed while the shells blasted their flesh and bones apart, their bodies lifting with the impact before falling in crumbled heaps upon the frozen ground. Those that escaped the initial onslaught stamped a bloody trail as they headed for the creek. The massacre shifted again to follow them.

*****

It strangely took a lot of effort to open his eyes and, as he did so, grains of dirt fell into them. Blinking, he still could not see past a brown wall. *Am I buried?* Grasshopper thought, but then he raised his head and his thoughts became clearer. He was just seeing the grass before him. He was lying on his belly with head turned to the side, his left ear pressed to the ground.

Uŋčí Makȟá Grandmother Earth *She shudders and I hear her moan*, he thought to himself, but then, he realized the vibrations originated with the cannon projectiles that slammed into the earth, and the moans, maybe his. His wounded arm, encrusted with dirt, stretched out before him and he saw the shirt was not completely blood soaked.

Good, he thought. *I haven't lost much blood.* He wiggled his fingers. *Good again,* he thought. *My arm will be fine.* Realizing he was too weak to move much, too weak to run from bullets, he inched his way deeper within the bushes, cocked the pistol he had taken from a soldier he had wounded and maybe killed, and feigned death.

In the distance, a Hotchkiss shell exploded under the horse that was dragging his wagon to safety. His mass swallowed up most of the shrapnel, but some found its way into a little boy running alongside the wagon. The horse dropped, twisting, and the wagon overturned, spilling Wind Woman and Brings Fire onto the ground. Wind Woman grabbed her Winchester from the rubble. Freeing herself from the thípi cover that had landed on top of her, Brings Fire grabbed her mother's outstretched hand and they raced towards the ravine. Hoping the sentinels would not notice the two of them, Wind Woman thought she had a chance of escaping a bullet in the back, and, if her daughter ran before her as she now instructed, her own body would provide a shield.

The sentinel troops under the command of captains Moylan and Nowlan were in a frenzy. Women, children, elders were running in all directions, scattering, hoping to avoid the bullets, hoping to avoid death. Some ran towards Wounded Knee Creek. Most did not make it there. Some ran towards the store, hoping to find safety. Some did. Many ran to the ravine. Moylan screamed, "Don't shoot, men. They're squaws!" The command passed up and down the line. Some obeyed. Some did not.

Kills In Winter, along with some other warriors, made it to the ravine. Seeing Wind Woman and Brings Fire scrambling into it, he ran there. Pushing her daughter down, Wind Woman immediately returned rifle fire. Kills In Winter directed some warriors to go down the ravine to the creek where they might find safety, and then he felt a tug on his leg.

"Will you find my grandfather?" Brings Fire pleaded.

An old woman handed Kills a belt of ammunition she had found on the field. Taking his knife and rifle, the old warrior headed straight back towards the fighting. Most of the assault was now concentrated on the field beyond the ravine and so it was relatively safe to go back among the many bodies in the smoking council area. So many wounded! So many dead! Sickened, Kills went from body to body. "I'll be back," he said to those still alive. "I'll bring help," he promised, not knowing if he would live to make that possible.

He later wondered how he could hear the faint call of his best friend through the booming artillery fire. "Kȟolá!" He would wonder how Grasshopper could see him through the smoke, and yet when

45

Kills saw the upraised arm, he knew his brother/friend was still alive.

Yellow Bird was also still in the council area. Believing his Ghost Shirt would protect him from bullets, he hid himself in the Sibley tent used by the Oglála scouts and was firing sniper shots from there. In an ill-conceived move to stop that fire, a private sliced open the tent but received a fatal hit to his abdomen in return. Lieutenant Hawthorne, upon seeing this, ordered a shell lobbed into the tent, and so Grasshopper and Kills In Winter saw the brutal end of their Ghost dancer, who, indeed, did not die from bullets, but from a Hotchkiss bombardment.

*****

How excited Dawes was using his newly acquired Winchester 1886! The sensuous heat of the rifle barrel warmed his gloved hands and each recoil of shot fired sent orgasmic-like thrills through his body. *This is better than fucking,* he thought as he dropped one Indian after another. Bang. Bang. Bang.

"Dawes, stop shooting the kids!" a soldier yelled trying to grab the rifle away from him. But ramming the butt end of it into the private's gut, Dawes growled, "Touch this again and I'll use it on you!"

*****

"You are not safe here, Khólá." Kills In Winter struggled, half carrying and half dragging Grasshopper to Wounded Knee Creek. There was a hollow under the bank from once rushing waters and he placed Grasshopper there. Bullet ridden blankets were strewn on the ground. Kills heaped some on his friend and camouflaged him with deadwood brush that had washed into a curve. "Do you have bullets?" Nodding that he did, two, Grasshopper pulled himself into the fetal position under the blankets and hoped he would stay warm enough to survive.

Kills raced to the ravine, heart beating in his ears, breath coming fast and heavy. So many screams! So many gunshots! He faltered when he beheld the scene.

There was a woman feverishly clawing into the south bank, shoving her son into the shallow hole. He rushed to shield her and fired to the north at the soldiers. Twisting left and right, no time for careful aiming, he dodged one bullet that whizzed by his head. He watched another burst through a cradleboard and knock the child's mother down.

Again and again he fired until he heard the click in the empty chamber. Weaponless, he raced after the women, his death song steadying him against the carnage, preparing him to die.

"Take him! Take him," a bloodied woman screamed, stumbling into him before collapsing. He reached out his hands for the limp child. Shot through the neck, the child was dead, but he took the body with him out of sight of his dying mother and laid him behind a rock. There was no time now to honor the dead.

"Run! Run! There! Follow the ravine!" he yelled to the women running in all directions, but his commands did little to control the chaos.

Joining the others in flight and looking back over her shoulder, shooting, Wind Woman soon ran out of bullets. Breathless, heart pounding against their chests, mother and daughter ran and ran, tripping and rising, legs torn by bushes they barreled through. Finally, heaving with exhaustion, they found a deep cleft in the ravine's side that offered protection on three sides. "We will rest here. Catch our breaths. Stay. Let me look at what's ahead." Still hearing gunshots, although more distant and infrequent now, Wind Woman scanned the terrain. Smoke was rising from the battleground. A renewed boom of cannons reverberated from there. Seeing the bombardment wasn't over, she yelled to her daughter, "Come! There are hills over there!"

Running out of targets, hands shaking from anticipation, eyes glowing with blood lust, Dawes tried to mount his wide-eyed skittish horse, but she so shied off when he placed his left leg in the stirrup, that he almost fell backwards. Dawes punched the panicked horse in the neck and the horse regained its senses, standing still enough for Dawes to mount and head off towards the same hill that Wind Woman and Brings Fire sought.

With a quick twist backward, Wind Woman saw him, and so she shoved her child beneath twiggy bushes along the base of the hill. but the keen sharpshooter eyes of Dawes noticed the movement. Smiling, he directed his horse there. Wind Woman pushed her daughter hard against the ground and covered her. She was trapped

47

and she knew it.

As did he. He stopped his horse a few yards away. He dismounted, betting she had no gun. *I can take my time here. Savor each moment.* He ran one hand up and down the still warm shaft of his rifle, stroking it.

"Iná, I can't breathe."

"Sssssh. Don't move."

"Iná, the branches…you are pushing my face into the branches…it hurts."

"Quiet!"

Bang! And a bullet whined, deflected off a rock on the far left.

He is playing with us. He could have shot into the bush. She tried to drape herself to cover more of her daughter. *Maybe it will be enough if he just kills me.*

Bang. This time to the right, but the bullet ricocheted into the bush, skimming her leg. "Aiii!" She couldn't help herself, the pain surprising in its intensity.

"Iná, are you alright?"

"Yes. Yes. Quiet! Don't move!"

Bang! He shot into the hill behind them.

Bang! This shot buried itself in the frozen dirt before the bushes, spraying dried leaf matter into her eyes. She blinked and blinked but could not clear her vision, would not move her arm so she could wipe her eyes.

"Iná, are we going to die?"

There was only one thing Wind Woman could do…play into his cruel game. He wouldn't shoot her outright if she stood up. That would be too easy….too quick. *I'll come out…challenge him to a fight…distract him so my daughter can run…can escape.* Decision made, calm settled over her. She remembered how she had wanted to be a warrior. *Today I will die as one.*

"Čhuŋkší, when I stand, get ready to run. Go to the ravine. The fighting has stopped there now. Hide. Your grandfather will find you."

"Iná?

"Do as you are told."

Wind Woman crawled out of the bush and stood, boldly facing him. Now with a clear view, she recognized him. The red-headed soldier. She pulled out her knife threateningly.

48

Such an ugly laugh! First low and quiet…a snicker… and then, when he recognized her, her flashing black eyes, then, loud and vicious!

"It's you! How wonderful!" He stepped back a few paces. If she hurled the knife, the distance would allow him to dodge it. He raised his rifle. There was no need to take proper aim. She was so close.

She crouched and flashed the obsidian blade, daring him to come to her.

"Bitch!" He pulled his own knife and charged.

Outweighing her by 75 pounds, she was no match for him. This was not the playful wrestling she did as a very little girl, sitting astride her laughing father. This was not the coy fighting, the joyous struggles with her husband when he caught up to her running through the tall grasses.

And this time, Brings Fire did not do as she was told. She watched, eyes frozen on the two people. *How can this be my mother?*

Dawes flipped Wind Woman over onto her back and made a mistake that would mark him for life. When his one hand went to his waist to loosen his pants, he freed her left hand. Grabbing the knife from her pinned right hand during his momentary distraction, she slashed the razor sharp blade across his face, a neat incision from his ear to his mouth. Stunned, he released his own knife jammed into the ground by her right hand, stared at her, then backhanded the obsidian from her hand. With blood streaming down his face, and her nails raking his cheeks, he wrapped his hands around her throat, gagging her into unconsciousness.

Then he sat back on his knees and looked to the bush, the bush Brings Fire was standing before, frozen.

The pain had yet to set in, and so he stared at Brings Fire and screamed. "Watch this! Watch this!"

He pulled down his pants, pulled up her mother's dress and pumped his hate into her. Drained within seconds, he struggled to his feet. "Wanna see something else?"

He bent over, grabbed his knife and the neck of Wind Woman's dress and hauled her into a limp sitting position. "Remember this!"

Brings Fire saw the blood spurt from her mother's neck, pulsing little red geysers, while he laughed.

The scream would not rise from her little girl's throat. No sound came at all from her wide open mouth. When Dawes stumbled towards her, she ran and ran and ran, swearing someday she'd kill him.

*****

Winúȟčala yámni awáŋyaŋkapi.
Three old women protected her.

When Brings Fire opened her eyes, she found herself next to her mother lying still on the ground, and thought, *Why are we lying out here in the open? Why is she sleeping out here?* She had no recollection of her frantic run from Dawes. She did not remember her return. She stood up, perplexed. She shuddered. She cried.

What had happened to Iná? Where did everyone go? A sudden flash of the fight whipped across her mind. She shook her head. *I don't want to see this!* Again it came...now pulsing bursts of red. *Red! Something about red? Iná? Iná?* The world suddenly felt enormous and she, suddenly, tiny; small... vulnerable.

A crow cawed in the distance and then another echoed a response. She heard more noises; muted and far away. *Moans?*

Iná, wake up! Though she knew what death looked like, her mother couldn't be dead. Those blank staring eyes? *Those cannot be on Iná's face! She is asleep. Yes. Asleep. And in a dream that makes her eyes look that way.*

But Iná should not be lying there like that with her dress pulled up! She'll be cold!

She pulled down her mother's dress, and covered her with her own blanket, covered the blood on her chest, hiding it. A gust of wind raised the blanket edges, moved the blanket up and over Wind Woman's face. *Yes, that's better.* But she tented the blanket over her mother's nose so she could breathe and laid small rocks around the perimeter of the blanket to hold it down.

The sun was lower in the sky and clouds had formed. The temperature had dropped. *I'll go for help, Iná. Wait here. I'll be right back.*

Her feet did not feel the stones along the creek bed. They were numb and she stumbled. *Oh, my knees!* She looked at her hands, stinging now, scraped from before, and was surprised. *How did this happen?* Still, she walked on and on...so far.

50

Relief warmed her when she turned the bend and saw three grandmothers. Using sticks they scratched into the loose dirt on the bank. One looked at the sky, worried. Too tired, too traumatized to walk further...*and walk where? Where was safety?*... they thought to burrow in a shelter, but even as they dug they knew they would never have the strength to complete it before the storm came.

Brings Fire stepped towards them, and the one who had searched the sky saw her. "I'll help," the little girl offered, not knowing what else to say. "Then will you go to my mother?"

"Where is she?"

"There," Brings Fire pointed in the direction of the hills. "She's asleep there and won't wake up."

The old woman looked to the others. They would be able to offer no help to the woman most probably dead. They, weak, could not walk that far, and a storm was coming. The best they could do is care for the girl so she wouldn't perish.

"We will go," she said to pacify the child. "Later. In the morning."

There was no food to share, nor any fire, but one of the three sisters, one who in her youth had been vain about her beauty, even now carried grease in a small sack on her belt to smooth out the wrinkles the harsh sun created in her face. She reached her fingers into that pouch and drew out some grease to apply to the face, hands and feet of the child. "This will help against frostbite." She ripped a strip off her fraying dress and applied the cotton to cover the child's wounds.

Soon the digging stopped. It was pointless. The sky had darkened and the cold had deepened, numbing the old women. The three sisters doubted they would live until dawn. The oldest opened her dress and pulled Brings Fire's head between her sagging breasts, breasts that had nursed babies who later became warriors fighting alongside Crazy Horse and others who had refused reservation life. Wrapping her blanket around the two of them, the old woman hoped her body would protect the child through the night. The other women huddled around her, as close as they could get, wedging themselves into the small nook they had made in the bank. Tenting themselves with their torn blankets, their warmth lasted a few hours until each grandmother, one by one, entered the spirit world.

The blizzard hit as the dawn sought to give light to the day. Starting as rain, it froze the blankets, and then the sisters, together, sealing off the space within that held Brings Fire, unconscious, but yet somehow alive. The wind heaped drifts around the huddled bodies, and they almost went unnoticed when the searchers came that afternoon, scooping up frozen bodies and heaving them into wagons.

*****

Hardened, he thought, by the day before, a newly recruited soldier was on burial detail when he came upon the mound in the snow jutting out from the bank. There had been other mounds that he pried from the frozen earth and tilted over revealing stiff bodies. This one was bigger though. He asked for help. When they soon determined this to be a trio of women, they tried, for necessity, to separate the sisters so the bodies could be tossed onto the wagon, but they could not. They new recruit kicked at their stiff corpses, over and over, jamming a shovel in spaces between their bodies until they finally disengaged. A child was hatched within their circle. Fighting tears and nausea, he had to break the arm of the oldest sister to release Brings Fire. When he felt the child's unexpected breath on his hand, blood left his face and he almost fainted. Images of his baby sister back home flashed through his mind.

"Throw it up on the wagon. Just don't stand there!" he heard the corporal yell. "There are plenty more to clean up!"

Ignoring this and subsequent orders, the soldier lifted the cold, limp child and held her tight against his chest, breathing warm air into her face. He mounted his horse and galloped with her pressed against him all the way to the rescue center in the church at Pine Ridge.

*****

Kills In Winter did not later remember much of the night. He could not later imagine from where he got the strength to usher woman after woman to shelter at Holy Cross Episcopal Church in Pine Ridge. How he even found the church was mystery to him. But exhausted though he was, he left the warmth of the shelter before dawn, before the storm hit, to look for Grasshopper.

He was not hard to find, struggling to get up as he was from beneath the heavy blankets and tangled brush. The movement had reopened his wound and droplets of his blood smeared easily over the thin crust of new ice. Kills called to him.

"Khólá! I'm coming!"

Snow was beginning to fall. Small hexagonal flakes of white graced the corpses with purity.

"Here. Let me help you up."

"We must find my daughter ... my granddaughter...my grandsons."

"Loud Bear is at the shelter...a church."

"This church...a white man's shelter?"

"Yes. I'm taking you there."

"No. I must find my daughter!" He jerked away from his brother/friend. "My grandchildren...they are out there."

"You will be no good to them dead. There is enough death here."

Oglála scouts on horseback spotted the two survivors and approached to offer help. Mounted behind one, Grasshopper hung on with his good arm and was taken to the church at Pine Ridge, and placed on the straw bedding beneath the Christmas garlands.

Wood was constantly fed into the potbellied stove, glowing near red as its heat radiated throughout the room. As Grasshopper's body warmed, his frozen hands and feet thawed and painfully tingled to life. Coupled with the loss of blood, exhaustion overcame him and he lost consciousness.

Kills went to the door.

Loud Bear held it shut.

"You will go nowhere, Uncle. It is too late."

Scowling, Kills pulled against the door opening it a crack. Wind whooshed in with whirling snow.

"The storm is here. It is too late...but come. I'll show you someone."

The bundle of a motionless child lay on straw in the corner. A dark-skinned boy knelt before her, trying to drop warm broth between her parted lips. He turned to Loud Bear. "She won't take it. She won't swallow." There were tears in his eyes.

"Who is he?" Kills asked.

"He says he knows her. Doesn't want her to be alone."

"She will recover?"

"The doctor does not know. She has no real wounds, but she was very cold. She does not move."

53

"Where is this doctor?"

"There."

Loud Bear pointed to a young man with short and straight black hair, who was examining a patient across the room. *White man* Kills thought derisively. But when the man turned to administer to the next patient, Kills was surprised. *No. Not a white man...maybe Lakȟóta? How can this be?*

Dr. Eastman, 1890 graduate of Boston University and the first Native American medical doctor certified in western medicine, had arrived at Pine Ridge in November. Never did he expect to be thrust into this triage situation.

"Is her mother here? Your brother?"

"They have not been found."

"I will go to her grandfather and tell him."

With heart hammering against his ribs, Kills weaved a path through the moaning injured, and swore revenge. "Wíŋyaŋ! Wakȟáŋyeža!" he kept muttering to himself. "Women and children?" he repeated in a loud voice. "Why?" Caregivers looked at him and tearfully nodded. A wounded young man called out, "Grandfather, I will live to fight alongside you!" Kills leaned down and touched the man's shoulder, "Someday. Someday soon ..."

He found his way back to Grasshopper and crouched beside him. "Kȟolá, wake up! Your granddaughter is here. She needs you!" When there was no response, he tried again. "Kȟolá! Your granddaughter!"

The words broke through the fog of a dream. He had been on the battlefield. Smoke. So much smoke. Gunfire and smoke. He tried to push his way through it but could not move. He tried to yell for her, but the sound would not come. Finally, from deep in his dream he heard, "Até! *Father!*" He woke up, heart pounding, eyes blinking.

"She is here, Kȟolá! Come. Let me take you to her!"

"My daughter?"

Kills In Winter turned away and lowered his head. "Your granddaughter."

Grasshopper sat up quickly and the world spun before his eyes.

"I will help you."

Standing, Grasshopper was astounded by what he saw, sickened by what he heard. There on the left, a woman keening. There on the right, a young man sobbing. A child cries. Another wails. Whispers.

54

Angry voices. And there in the far corner, quiet. There, where his granddaughter lay.

Respectfully, Há Sápa rose when the two old warriors approached. He stepped out of their way.

Grasshopper knelt before his too still granddaughter and stroked her face, smoothed back her hair, the ends matted with blood. He looked up at Kills. "Hers?"

"No. Not her blood."

Then, my daughter's! By rolling hair over hair, the dried blood crumbled off into his palm. "My daughter," he sobbed. Swallowing hard, he turned his attention to the living.

"Kȟolá, lie next to her. Hold her. She will know you are here."

Shooting pains ran through his arm from lying on his side. The pressure reopened the wound, but he was not aware of it. "Tȟakóža! Tȟakóža! …wake up," he whispered to her. "Wake up."

Working feverishly to ease the moans and mourning of the survivors, Dr. Eastman couldn't help but notice Brings Fire in the arms of her crying grandfather. He went to them. "Let me see to your wound," he said to Grasshopper. Though his Lakȟóta words were clearly spoken, Grasshopper did not respond. The doctor repeated them.

"My granddaughter needs a doctor, not me!" Grasshopper shot back vehemently. "If you can do anything, make her well first!"

Eastman spoke gently to the old warrior. "She is warm now. That is all I can do. I cannot heal her spirit. I cannot take away all she might have seen. But if she wakes up, she will need her grandfather." The doctor touched Grasshopper's bloodied bandage. "Let me remove the bullet."

A crude operating table had been set up in an enjoining room. Designed to be more of a closet, the area was cramped but afforded some privacy. Eastman beckoned to it but Grasshopper would not leave Brings Fire's side. "I will stay here. Take out the bullet here."

"Lie flat."

Scalpel and probe were brought to the doctor. Bandages. Carbolic acid. Needle. Thread. Luckily the bullet was lodged in the fleshy part of his upper arm and its removal, quick, and far less painful than the sundance the old warrior had once endured.

Lamps burned dully throughout the night. Some people slept. Most did not. Eyes drifted to the door, hoping it would open and a loved one appear. The door did not open, although the wind had died down a bit, and, with it, the expectation that a miracle would occur.

Loud Bear became the center of attention. He was one of the few there who had witnessed what had gone on in the council area, and he was eager to tell of it.

"Did you kill any of the soldiers?" someone asked.

"I hit many," he boasted, and then laughed, "But I did not wait around to see if they were dead. But I will tell you the best story. A Long Knife from across the circle aimed his rifle at me, and I thought I would soon die. Luckily, I ducked when the rifle fired. Another Long Knife was behind me, wanting to shoot me, too. He also fired. With one duck, I killed two Long Knives!"

Murmurs of approval rippled around the room. No one believed such an outlandish story. No one believed that anyone would have noticed such a coincidence in the heat of battle, but the story was a good one and it raised their spirits.

As the day dawned, attendants snuffed out the lamps, and the people began moving about. Dr. Eastman and his American wife circulated among the patients, evaluating conditions, medicating with what little they had at their disposal, and feeding warm oatmeal to those who could eat it.

Grasshopper sat up when they approached. The doctor offered to check Grasshopper's wound. He refused but allowed him to look at Brings Fire. She remained unconscious and the little gruel they smeared on her lips and pushed between them to encourage eating did not awaken her. Gentle pressure on her throat provoked a swallow response and thus drops of clear broth entered her. But Grasshopper could see that the doctor still did not think she would survive.

Turning to Eastman's wife, Elaine, who also spoke the Lakȟóta language, Grasshopper asked, "Why? Her wounds seem slight. No bullets are inside her. No bones are broken. She does not have frostbite. Why is she like this?"

She answered kindly, "Some wounds are invisible to the eye. Besides, it is not just her body that has been hurt."

Kills In Winter laid a hand on Grasshopper's shoulder. "Your grandson and I will go now to find your daughter and his brother."

*****

56

Soldiers were still out with their wagons and the dead were being hauled to the mass grave that had been dug on the hill where the cannon once stood. American Hair must have been among those buried there. His body never was found. Finding the bodies of those who had hid in the ravine was more difficult than expected with the wind still whipping the snow around.

Loud Bear pointed to the silly antics of a crow tossing a small pouch into the air, trying to detach the bright beads sewn onto it. The bird flapped his wings and a gust of wind lifted him up with the pouch dangling. Then he would descend and stand on the pouch pecking it. Over and over.

Too many times, Loud Bear thought. "Are spirits at work here?" he wondered out loud. He often attributed the unknown to spirit interference and was especially attentive to the actions of animals who might embody such entities.

Kills In Winter thought about that, not dismissing the possibility, but he also had a particular affinity for crows and marveled at their intelligence. *Maybe this bird is telling us something. We should at least look.* He walked towards the bird, but the crow stood its ground, cawing loudly. "Kȟaŋǧí *Crow*, what do you have there?"

That the crow had found anything at all was hard to believe. Americans had already stripped the bodies of curios to sell. Walking closer, Kills' foot hit what he, at first, thought was a long rock. He bent, brushed aside some snow and found the body of Wind Woman. Reverently, he tumbled away the stones that held the blanket so neatly in place and revealed her face. His first thought: *She is at peace.* His second: *The child must have covered her.*

Even the grey-black complexion and staring eyes did not erase the beauty of this woman Loud Bear had called aunt. He fell to his knees, withdrew a knife and slashed his arm in grief, vowing he would kill the man who had done this to her.

Her dress had frozen to the ground. Ripping it loose revealed other horrors. Not only had her throat been slashed but her pubic mound had been scalped, a macabre souvenir some fashioned into a purse. They would not tell Grasshopper this. Nor would they carry her to the mass grave. Until such time they could make a proper burial scaffold, they placed her body in a niche within an outcropping of rocks and heaped stones on it to protect her from hungry animals.

They returned with the beaded čhekpá ognáke *navel pouch*, that the crow had seemed to direct them to. Within it was the dried coil of Brings Fire's umbilical cord, connecting her, as they believed, to the stars.

*****

Mniyáta napéwičhayúze.
Mniyáta greeted them and shook their hands.

How could he not cry when they handed him the beaded pouch? Shaped as a turtle to ensure long life, striped blue and white with multicolored beads on the feather-tasseled legs, the pouch's beadwork was unique. Grasshopper remembered seeing the love on his pregnant daughter's face as she crafted it the winter Brings Fire was born.

He wiped his eyes. "And your brother? Where is he?"

Loud Bear choked out, "He, we did not find."

Grasshopper knelt beside Brings Fire, his fingertip topped with the now cold and congealed gruel. He placed it to her lips. *Daughter. Grandson. Gone. Will she be taken from me too?"*

"Eat!" he pleaded. Time and time again he tried, turning her lips a pasty white, but there was no response. An hour passed. Two. Finally, the tip of her tongue greeted his gruel laden finger. Did he imagine this? He tried another and then was sure there was a response. Another, and her lips closed on his finger. He felt a gentle sucking and his spirits rose.

"She needs water! She is thirsty," he said, hopeful at last. Her eyelids fluttered. Snapped open.

"I'm here, Thakóža."

But she didn't see him. Her mouth opened in a silent O. She was not at the church on a bed of straw. She was not anywhere she knew, and then she was not anywhere at all. Her muscles quivered, her limbs shook, her eyes closed again.

"Thakóža, Thakóža! I am here. You are safe! You are safe now!"

Doctor Eastman had been watching. There was nothing he could do to rescue her from this trauma. With wet eyes, he turned away.

The day turned into night once again. Again she opened her eyes.

58

Again he was able to coax her to swallow. She even sat up. But she didn't speak. Grasshopper held her in his arms, rocking her in the darkness, whispering the songs she had loved to hear, telling the stories he had told before. But all she did was stare.

"Grandfather."

It was the young dark-skinned boy. "This doctor cannot make her well, but I know someone who can."

Exhausted, Grasshopper did not acknowledge the boy.

"Grandfather? I *do* know such a healer. He is not far from here."

Disbelieving, Grasshopper said, "Do you? And who are you that you care so much for my granddaughter?"

Há Sápa did not know why this girl felt so special. He had only encountered her days before when the two of them had run to the store. Instead, he avoided the question and offered, "The lodge of Mniyáta *At The Water* is not far. Do you know of this Oglála healer? Let me go to see him. Perhaps he will help your granddaughter." And without waiting for consent, he left.

Grasshopper did not expect his return. He was just a boy, after all.

However, hours later, Há Sápa stood before him, shivering, hugging himself from the cold. "My father's wagon is outside. Come with me. We will take you to the healer. If we leave now, we will reach there before dark.

Although many had left the church, taken in by relatives within the reservation, the more seriously injured stayed with their caregivers.

"I know this boy," one said. "I know his father. He is not Lakȟóta, but his wife is. You can trust him."

Why should I trust these people I do not know? Grasshopper thought. *They say the father is a black man who speaks our language badly. Black, but maybe more wašíču than one of us.* He thought more, considering the actions of the boy. *And yet the son seems truly Lakȟóta, despite his skin and hair. See how he cares for her?* And knowing in his heart that his granddaughter would not survive here in this place, he finally decided that there was no choice but to trust the boy to take them to this healer, Mniyáta.

Wincing, Grasshopper stood up with Kills In Winter's support. Loud Bear carried Bring's Fire to the wagon, wrapping his own blanket around her. As the wagon bounced along the rutted paths, Há Sápa spoke excitedly. "I did not find Mniyáta at his lodge. His

59

relatives said he was near Pahá Wakȟáŋ, a sacred place. When I found him there, smoke was coming from the top of the thípi. It seemed to welcome me and yet I was afraid to go forward to this place so wakȟáŋ *holy*. But then, the healer stepped out and just said, 'Bring her here.' I waited, expecting more words, but he lifted the entrance flap and was soon out of my sight. How did he know, Grandfather?"

Grasshopper could not answer that. With a grandfather's love, he knew she was a special human, as all humans are, but perhaps now, she is being confirmed as something more. He quietly sang victory songs to her. She must live. She must get well. For him. For all of them.

*****

The sun setting behind Mniyáta cast a long shadow towards their wagon. They stopped before the medicine man facing the soon to be dying rays. Wearing a leather buffalo horned cap, as he turned to greet them, the buffalo tail hanging from the tanned hide swished over the healer's back. An old man, he was imposing still. His eyes sparkled, and yet his smile was sad. As the men climbed from the wagon, he walked to greet them, extending his powerful hands in welcome.

"Napéčhiyúzape lo!" he greeted each formally, welcoming them with a good heart to his lodge. After he listened to their story, Loud Bear carried Bring's Fire into the warmth and laid her as instructed on a plush robe. Mniyáta looked upon her in wonder. "In a vision I saw her coming, but she was a young woman astride a pinto pony of all colors. The pony stood with front legs on one side of the riverbank and hind legs on the other. She appeared as a bridge between the two sides. That she is a child surprises me."

He looked into her staring eyes and turned to a pouch hung from the lodge pole. Withdrawing a gummy substance, he applied it to her eyelid, and held it closed, effectively gluing it shut. He repeated the process with the other eye. "I want her to see only what I want her to see," he said. With scarred, gnarled hands, he gently examined her body, checking for broken bones, flexibility and wounds. Mniyáta agreed the American doctor had treated her well. "Her body will heal soon," he said. "And with time, her heart will also recover."

Mniyáta took his pipe and smoked in silence. Bending over her, he blew smoke into her nostrils. Singing incantations, he prepared the first of her medicines and pressing his index finger and little finger of his free hand to her forehead he said, "Open your mouth, child, to receive this medicine from our Grandfather." He smeared the buffalo potion on the tip of her tongue. Repeating this twelve times accompanied by twelve songs of healing, twelve times she swallowed it until finally, Mniyáta put down his drums and rattles and faced Grasshopper.

"I will go away from here for now to a certain place to pray. You will stay here. The child is out of danger. Her skin will heal rapidly, but the path to heal her spirit will be difficult. Much will depend on you. Be attentive to this. If, with your help, her spirit fully survives, she will be a leader of her people." Wrapping himself in a big buffalo robe, Mniyáta stepped into the approaching darkness. "I will return when she is well."

Within a few days, the crust on her eyelids crinkled, and then crumbled off. She still barely moved, although she now was eager to accept soup and the medicinal teas Mniyáta had prepared and left behind.

One morning when Grasshopper lifted the flap of the thípi, and the sun shone in, she opened her eyes and saw. The warm thípi felt womb-like, and she met the smile of her grandfather with one of her own. "I was away, Lalá. I was with Iná. She is happy now. She told me to take care of you. I promised I would."

Tearfully he nodded. "Tȟakóža, we will take care of each other."

*****

How brightly the sun shone! How warm it felt to sit outside wrapped in the softness of a well-tanned buffalo robe. Brings Fire leaned back against the thípi, directly facing the sun with her eyes closed. Her eyelids' interior glowed an unsettling orange, reminding her of something she could not name. Within it were waves of red and her heart beat faster. She stared deep into her eyelids, transfixed. Shadows swayed there suddenly, dulling the colors. And then the colors disappeared into darkness and she opened her eyes.

Standing before her was Mniyáta, the man who had cured her, but she did not recognize him until he spoke. "I remember your songs," she said. "They called me back, but I did not want to come."

He chuckled. "And yet you are here now."

"I need to be," she responded.

Mniyáta sat down outside the thípi next to her, and resting his back against the sun warmed hide, he too closed his eyes and they sat for a while in silence. Finally Brings Fire spoke to this older man who, out of respect, she addressed as Grandfather.

"Grandfather, Lalá says you gave me back my life. I am grateful."

"I cannot give life. Only Wakȟáŋ Tȟáŋka can do that." He sighed looking to the sky. "Your spirit is not yet healed, little one. Still, there is something missing. Something that you must do."

"Do?"

"I did not see this clearly in my dream about you. What I saw is that you were on a horse who straddled a stream of water. What this means, I can only guess. You yourself will find out someday."

"I don't understand."

"Now you do not have to."

Knowing it was proper to gift a healer, she said contritely, "I have nothing to give you."

He laughed and shook his head. "There is no need."

She held up the beaded bag for him to see. "My mother kept this for me." She took the beaded turtle bag from around her neck. "I know it is wakȟáŋ, but I think am too little to have this now and I have no mother or grandmother to keep it for me."

"It connects you to them. It connects you to the earth. You can wear it or we can bury it."

"Or you can hold it for me until…until…I am better."

"This is unusual…but I will do it."

Conversations were slow with the healer. He chose his words carefully. He left empty spaces between them. Understanding poured into the quiet.

"You have a new life now."

It was true. Her life there in the holy place, away from the People, was quiet. Alone with her grandfather, she felt peace. Each day was the same. The only visitor was her grandfather's brother/friend. He brought them food. Flour. Beans. Her grandfather hunted but there were but few animals to nourish them. The two men talked, but she had nothing to say.

"You need a new name. You are no longer Brings Fire."

"Why, Grandfather? It was a name I earned. My parents told me the story ..."

"Your name must reflect your new life. Not your old. You must give up your name for a time and take on a new one. I call you Niglíču *Comes Out Alive*. When your spirit heals, you may, if you choose, take back your old name. Then Brings Fire might mean something different."

"How will I know when this is to be?"

"You will have counted your coup. Then you will know."

"My coup? I am to be a warrior then?"

"There are different kinds of warriors."

He withdrew a pouch tucked into his shirt and handed it to her. It was still warm from his body, pliable when it folded into her hands. "Take this now in return. This medicine is wakȟáŋ, powerful." After she took the tanned fawn bag, he abruptly stood up. He looked sad.

"You are leaving?" she asked.

"Yes," he said without further explanation. "Stay in this lodge as long as it pleases you."

He walked away, mounted his horse and, holding her bag, headed west.

Chapter 3

Tȟáȟča pȟá kiŋ yustósto.
She stroked the deer's head.

T he medicine man's lodge was further upstream than those of the village. Its buffalo hide outer cover was warmer than American canvas, and the insulated lining kept the cold at bay. Nestled within a cottonwood grove whose trees stretched to the bank of a now pitifully thin trickle of a stream, their thípi was canopied by branches. Shallow rooted, one tree had blown over nearby, and so brittle-branched firewood was readily available.

Kills In Winter brought them their food allotment and the monotonous routine of limited beef, beans, corn, flour, and salt kept them barely nourished. Their wagon had held dried food for that winter of 1890 and 91, but that wagon, and their stock of winter supplies, were among the "spoils of war" that the wašíču had distributed among themselves. Niglíču dreamed of the rich. dried chokecherries beaten with fat and meat, which they called wasná *pemmican.*

"Lalá, wake up! You are sleeping too long. I want to go outside. I am tired of getting better. I am better now!"

Grasshopper was suspicious of her cheerfulness. *Why doesn't she cry? Why does she never speak of that day?* Whenever Wind Woman was mentioned, the girl spoke of her as though she were just away somewhere and would return. *Does she just pretend her mother is still alive? Does she really believe it?*

Although his wound had healed, his muscle-stiff arm pained him when he pushed himself up from under the old buffalo robe. Niglíču grabbed the robe playfully, uncovering him, and he shooed her away with his good arm. Laughing, she walked backwards, tripped over a thick fold in the hide, and tumbled into the softness of her own sleeping place.

Suddenly serious, she said, "I do not think I have ever seen a buffalo."

He realized she probably was right. There were yet a few buffalo when she was born, but none had been in this area for years. Pulling the robe up over her head, covering her, she shook her body as she had seen cattle do, and asked, "Did they do this?"

With dreamy eyed expression he replied, "Tȟakóža, they were wondrous animals. Let me tell you about them." Together they would spend hours like this with him speaking of the old ways when buffalo herds thundered in a black mass covering the plains, raising dust as high as the clouds.

He told her stories of Lakȟóta heroes like Crazy Horse, Red Cloud and Sitting Bull.

"You were like them. I know you were!"

He smiled, and then told her stories of how the People had once lived without horses.

"Like now? They lived like we do now?"

He wanted to say no, not like now, because now we are prisoners and then we were free, but he didn't want to hurt her. "Yes, in some ways like now."

"The medicine man said there were different kind of warriors, but what does this mean?"

"I will not use my words but those of one greater than I. Sitting Bull said a warrior is not one who fights. It is one who sacrifices. Someone who takes care of the People who need him."

"But I had a ceremony. Am I a warrior? I am to care for the People. I am hokšíčhaŋtkiyapi, *child beloved.* Iná says..." She stopped. *My mother says? Iná alive?* Suddenly she felt dizzy.

Now. Now I have to say this. "Your mother, when she was alive, knew you would become a special kind of warrior. She is gone now," and he said that with emphasis because his granddaughter needed to hear the words spoken..."but you will grow to be a strong woman like her."

She shook the words from her ears. *No! No!* She stood up. "I will go outside now."

Grasshopper sat in silence, thinking. *What will it mean to be a warrior now? What kind of sacrifices will warriors make against this overwhelmingly powerful enemy intent on destroying us? What can I prepare her for?* He shifted position, warmed his hands over

65

the fire. *Whatever comes, she will need to know our ways so she can teach them to her children.*

Shrugging off his robe, he stood. *I will teach her.* Even as he thought these words he knew it would not be enough. She would still have to know the ways of the enemy to survive.

*****

Grasshopper ran his hand down the straight path of aligned growth rings on the bow stave, admiring his workmanship. The applied sinew had hardened and needed to be buffed smooth. Within a few days' work, he'd be able bend the arch of the stave backwards to string the short bow and make the needed adjustments for flexibility and strength. The bow was for his granddaughter and he wanted it to be perfect for her.

He could not teach her woman's ways. He had never learned more than rudimentary skills. Watching the women of his family fascinated but did not motivate him to learn their craftmanship. But his granddaughter needed something to do and had showed interest, in the past, in shooting arrows. Her father had made her a mock bow. He will make her a formidable weapon. Someday she might live where there will be game and she will be ready. Someday she may need to defend herself.

Knowing nothing of correct bow lengths, she assumed the short bow was for her grandfather. *Maybe we will be leaving this place? Maybe there is a place of buffalo somewhere? Maybe we will find bigger game than the puny rabbits my grandfather sometimes snares for our cooking pot.*

Grasshopper sat on a log and planed off tiny slivers of wood in places still too rigid for his liking.

"Thakóža, come sit by me."

Niglíču, always drawn to the stream, always digging into the bank and surprising him with smooth stones, and once an arrowhead, obediently went to him and sat.

"I am making this for you."

Her eyes brightened. "For me? You will teach me to be a warrior?"

Not answering, he put the unfinished bow aside and stood up. "We will walk."

Expecting adventure, she was disappointed that they did just that.

66

Walk. And walk slowly. Through the trees and back. Grasshopper sat back down the log, picked up the bow and continued his work.

She stood there perplexed.

"Thakóža, what did you learn?"

"Learn? We walked among the trees."

"What could your enemy learn from your walk?"

She thought a little and then realized the walk indeed had been a lesson.

"The enemy could guess whether I was young or old? Strong? Weak maybe?"

"Go on."

"Maybe that I was a girl? Maybe how tall I was? Whether I was rushing. Limping. Alone." She paused. "I understand now."

"Go now. Pretend you are the enemy. Follow your tracks and see your story. Tomorrow we will follow the tracks of something else and learn that story, too."

Grasshopper had decided he would teach her independence. She would learn how to protect herself and be self-sufficient. He was getting older, he acknowledged, and knew someday life might require her, even at a young age, to fend for herself.

A fresh snow fell that night. When dawn came, Grasshopper watched Niglíču sleep snug and warm under her robe. He stood before her and stared. The staring did not awaken her. He continued. Without a sound. Finally, she became aware.

"Better," he said. "But a little too slow."

After a breakfast of a tasteless flour biscuit and watered-down coffee, they followed rabbit tracks. The next day and on repeated days after, they did the same. They noted the same pattern, and the same trail to the creek. One morning, Grasshopper woke Niglíču before dawn.

"Go. Meet the rabbit when it gets to the creek."

*****

Winter was a time for dreaming. Winter was a time for storytelling. Some nights Kills stayed there and the two old warriors told tales of their youth which later morphed into her dreams. There in her sleep, Niglíču was neither young nor old, nor male nor female, nor even an odd combination of them. She just existed and flowed without

67

assigned roles or particular cultural barriers, being and doing everything with seamless transition.

One such dream was memorable. It was a dream of earth tone coloration and floating shadowy images. She was approaching womanhood and sat cross-legged before the fire wearing breechclout only. She dipped her fingers into pouches of powdered clay and rubbed the clay together with the grease she held in her other hand. Her palm formed a bowl for the mixture of ochre paint. Her long black hair hung behind her shoulders. She closed her eyes and applied the paint sensuously to the outer portion of her eyelids and then zig zagged it down her cheeks like a path of tears. Dipping her fingers into the reddish-brown clay, she then drew a line passing from her ear to the corner of her mouth. She had seen such a face before, but she could not remember where. Ugly scars decorated her body and these she covered over in black and white, and then traced long black lines from her collarbone slipping down to encircle and accentuate the areola of her budding breasts.

In her dream, she stood up, ready to hunt, and felt powerful. She entered the central circle of the village, drawing considerable attention from the men and looks of disdain from the younger women. An old woman with a featureless face handed her a bladder of water from which to drink. She raised it high above her head, leaned back and let it splash down into and out of the corners of her mouth, trickling down to spill in and out of her navel. A breeze blew, and she stretched her arms to embrace it, pulled herself into unity with it, and then she strode from the village to hunt, bearing only bow, arrows and her mother's black obsidian knife.

Swirls of many hued browns and greens stood before her. She entered the visual whirlpool, floated through it, and came upon a buck grazing on grasses pushed up through reddened snow. She nocked an arrow and pulled back effortlessly. The deer turned, presenting a perfect target and yet she did not release the arrow.

Instead, with weapon in readiness, she approached the big buck, and he turned his head away as though he did not want to see the arrow that would kill him. She inched closer and was so close now that an arrow would be unnecessary, and so she dropped the weapon and withdrew her knife. The deer turned to her, and yet did not move. Face to face now, her left hand lifted his chin exposing his neck. She placed the tip of her knife at his jugular and pushed gently. He shuddered, and warmth flushed through her body as she realized she now had the power to end his life. How strange was that moment of decision! A gentle energy lifted her and the buck out of that landscape, out of that reality, and held them above it, waiting.

Was it their spirits in another realm that would determine the earthly decision? she wondered. The dream blinked, and she was there again on the blood tinted snow, but now with the decision made. The buck breathed out a plume of warm tobacco scented smoke and she inhaled it, tasted it, and lowered the knife. She exhaled, and the moist nose of the buck touched her nostrils as he breathed in her scent. She stroked the animal's head, and, for that moment, they were one.

The dream ended.

*****

Gnugnúška: "Até lená tȟawíčhoȟ'aŋpi čha yuhá iyótiyewakiye."
Grasshopper: "I struggle to carry on the customs of my father."

Their seclusion had lasted long enough. It was time they rejoin the people. That his granddaughter would sometimes sit by herself and stare emotionless disturbed him.

"What are you thinking about?"

She couldn't really answer because she wasn't thinking about anything at all. She didn't think he believed her though. He just shook his head.

She needs the company of the People. She needs little girls and boys around her, laughing and playing.

Loud Bear had prepared a place for them. The thípi was small, the hides patched and thin, but the People had been generous, his grandson said. There were cooking utensils and blankets.

Niglíču didn't want to go.

This little gathering of twenty thípi is not really a village, Niglíču thought as they approached the band of relatives. A village held happy people, smiles and laughter, children running, meat drying on racks, rich stew smells coming from open thípi flaps, hunters returning with meat slung over the pack horses, warriors boasting of deeds, dogs growling over meat scraps, and horses tied outside of the thípi of a young woman. There was none of that there. But as desolate as it appeared, Niglíču knew she would have to accept it as home.

People came out to greet them, and she knew by the tightness of her grandfather's hand on hers that this was not easy for him either. Back there, they could pretend nothing bad had happened.

It didn't matter that Kills entered the thípi with them. It did not matter that the booming voice of Loud Bear filled the inside with his boasts. That there were blankets and a pot, food in bags and a backrest for her grandfather made little difference.

What did matter was that there were no ashes. There were stones arranged in a circle for a fire but they surrounded cold, dry earth. Flames had never risen from that empty space. Food was never cooked by a fire there, hands were never warmed over it. *Where is my mother that there is no fire here? Where is my mother? Not here. Never here!*

Dead. My mother is dead.

Finally she began to cry.

"Ťhakóža, what's wrong?"

She couldn't stop crying. No comfort from her family nor from the hug of an old woman who claimed to know her, could stop her sobs. She cried until she had no strength to cry anymore.

When she quieted, they heard a scratch on the thípi covering, and Grasshopper welcomed a boy inside. Twiggy sticks were tucked under his arm and he carried a fiery coal precariously balanced in a tin pan. Há Sápa said, "My aunt sent me to give you this."

*****

They leaned forward into the dim firelight. Grasshopper poked at the flames. Niglíču studied the shadowed creases in her grandfather's face and wondered if he was feeling what she felt. Alone. Though now there were others nearby, their conversations heard through the thin hide of the thípi had ceased, one by one, as night deepened. Perhaps only she and her grandfather were yet awake.

"Ťhakóža, you should sleep."

"Will we always live here now? Can we ever leave this place?"

"For now we will live here. Who can say what will happen later?" He paused. Added another stick to the fire. "Your blankets are there," he said, pointing.

She knew what he meant. There would be no more talking that night.

Grasshopper watched his granddaughter while she slept and thought about all who had been a part of his life when she was born. Maštíŋsapela *Cottontail Rabbit*, his wife, was there. How beautiful she had been despite, and maybe because of, the smallpox scars that had patterned her cheeks. He smiled thinking of how she had said, giggling, that the scars were from ardent rabbit kisses. Cuddled, standing beneath the buffalo robe before her father's thípi, he had kissed each scar, laughing at her silliness. How he had loved her! But then the white man's coughing sickness came. Gone was his wife, her sister and brother-in-law. All within weeks. And then a few years later, gone was his son-in-law, Niglíču's father, dying from a bullet wound to his belly.

He fingered the old medicine pouch that hung from his neck but did not feel comforted. For not only did this contain the four medicines, tobacco, sweet grass, sage and cedar to promote harmony between the physical and spiritual worlds, but it also contained a photograph, a reminder of what he had done, and regretted doing, that long ago day near Wounded Knee Creek.

*****

Her grandfather was there at the fire when she opened her eyes. *Still?* No, he had not yet rolled his blankets. The sticks he was adding to the fire were those he had gathered after his morning song. The thípi flap was flipped open and crisp morning air flooded the small enclosure, bringing with it the now familiar yeasty smell of wígli uŋ káğapi *fry bread*. This bread made from the weevil filled flour the reservation provided was not something her mother had prepared but Niglíču enjoyed the sweetness of it and the sugar it was dipped into.

"Wake up! I have food!"

Kills in Winter entered, sat by the fire and unwrapped the small cloth bundle he was carrying. "Eat!" he offered.

"You cook now?" Grasshopper smiled, not believing it.

A slow smile spread across Kills In Winter's face, deepening his dark creases, and exposing chipped teeth. "I did not make this." He averted his eyes, still smiling.

Turning serious, he said, "There are many widows here now." He

71

looked pointedly at Grasshopper, and then nodded towards Niglíču, whispering, "She needs a woman to teach her how to be a woman."

*****

Tȟuŋkáŋ Wašté Wiŋ *Pretty Stone* and Čhaŋhásaŋ *White Birch* were cousins, and what with battles and diseases, they had found themselves to be widows with no close family ties. In times past, this would have been unusual, as everyone seemed to be related to each other in some way and they would have found a home among their other relatives. Now, though, these two independent women, who no longer required a male hunter for food, shared a thípi in this small village, and were content in their relationship. Both were mature women past childbearing age, and not particularly attractive. They were, however, hardly indifferent to the fact that a few bachelors were still around.

When Kills In Winter first entered the camp, Pretty Stone had taken notice. He appeared to be a vigorous man and healthy, older than she, but he smiled at children and petted the camp dogs as he walked past, although, sadly, without looking at her. She casually asked about him, and learned that true to his name, he had been a good provider at one time for a larger family. The people gave him a small temporary thípi not too far from hers, expecting he would ultimately join the families of his relatives in another equally small, impoverished village. That he chose this camp appeared odd until she realized he wanted to be near others of Big Foot's decimated band that had settled there. He most especially wanted to be near his friend, Grasshopper, and the little girl they called Niglíču. Pretty Stone now paid a little more attention to the way she looked, took a little more time to brush and plait her hair, and observing his patterns, tried to be in his path at least once a day.

One day when she walked past him all bundled up in wašíču clothing that could not keep her warm enough, a gust of wind flipped up the ragged and dirty hem of her long cotton skirt, and flapped it against his leg, causing a hesitation in his stride. He looked at her and smiled before walking on. Emboldened by the smile, she met him that next morning with a fresh breakfast of fry bread, the bread that he now shared with Grasshopper and Niglíču.

"So, Kȟolá, who gets up this early to give you fry bread?"

Grasshopper's eyes twinkled teasing his friend. He knew how much Kills in Winter enjoyed the company of women.

"There are two widows, cousins, with a thípi near you. You could call to them right now and they would hear you."

Laughing, Grasshopper shot back, "Would they come if you called?"

"Maybe one would," Kills In Winter smirked. It felt good to be at ease with his friend again.

"Maybe they can teach my granddaughter. They are good?"

"I do not know how good they are, but this one makes excellent bread. Maybe together we can find out how good they are in other ways."

"Maybe you will have to find out alone," Grasshopper replied, as the mood turned back to solemnity. It was hard for Grasshopper to feel happy. It was hard to feel like a man when all that defined his manhood was fading away.

Did Kills In Winter not see this? he wondered. *We have no weapons. We have no ponies worth talking about. We have no need to be warriors. We cannot hunt. We cannot roam. We cannot even make decisions.*

He thought of Niglíču. He thought of the women he saw here. *They are sad, yes. They too lament the passing of the old ways, but,* he thought with a twinge of jealousy, *their basic role has not changed much, although the method of fulfilling it is different. They still will bear and care for children. They still prepare food. Clothing, although different, will always needs tending.*

Intuitively, Niglíču knew that the conversation between the two men was going to be about her, and so she slipped out of the thípi, excusing herself from any discussion she might not want to hear. She wanted her family back, she wanted what used to be, she wanted a mother, and she wanted to sleep at night without the feeling of terror that might slip into dreams. She did not want to hear the frantic soundless screams that no one else could hear, the screams that woke her with a palpitating heart.

She ran, her feet kicking up clumps of snow behind as she made her way to the partially frozen river where she squatted on the bank and watched the water flow beneath the clear ice. She wanted to be a little girl again.

White Birch Woman came upon this girl at the river's edge and saw her slamming rocks into it, shattering the icy surface into shards that became prisms in the slanting rays of sunlight. She surprised Niglíču by quietly kneeling down next to her and swooping her bladder water carrier into the newly created ice hole, filling it with morning water. Looking to the sun, she greeted Niglíču.

"This day will be beautiful. Can you feel it?" Rising and holding the bladder stretched and dripping in her right hand, she offered her left to the child and said, "Come with me. I want to show you something." They retraced Niglíču's footprints. "While you were running away, you missed something. I am fortunate to have seen it!" She pointed to a patch of čhaŋtȟéča *baby's navel or anemone.* "Do you see how it is pushing the seeds away through the snow?" She laughed. "Anemone flowers away from its mother. So will you too. That is the way it is."

Still hand in hand, they walked back to the village.

*****

Wičháša núŋpa kiŋ Wakȟáŋ Tȟáŋka čhékiyapi.
The two men prayed to the Creator.

As the weeks passed, an unusual alliance formed between Grasshopper, Kills In Winter, the two cousins and Niglíču, one that did not conform to the traditions of past times and yet was not quite a foreshadowing of the future either. With the concern for Niglíču drawing them together, they helped each other much as a traditional family would, uniting to teach Niglíču the worlds of both women and men in Lakȟóta society. Under their attention, she began her recovery.

"I see my cousin has become a little woman!"

Loud Bear saw Niglíču kneeling before the fire, modestly, in the way of women, under the watchful eye of Pretty Stone. He startled her, and she pricked herself on the wašíču needle as she tried to push it through the heavy leather of the moccasins she was learning to make. When Pretty Stone turned to her own sewing, Niglíču waved the drop of blood on her fingertip at Loud Bear in a gesture of *See what you did?* He looked at her and motioned for her to go outside with him. Pretty Stone, along with the other adults in Niglíču's life, was lenient with Niglíču because of her trauma. If she wanted to speak privately with this cousin, the older woman was glad that the girl desired to talk to anyone at all other than her grandfather. Seeing the affirmative nod from Pretty Stone, Niglíču put down her sewing and went out.

"How have you been, Little Cousin?"

He had been away for what seemed like weeks, and he was not comfortable with the change he now saw in Niglíču. There was a smile on her face, but not in her heart.

"I am fine."

"Have you used your snare yet? I have seen a few rabbits by the creek."

"Not yet." Both were quiet, and then she spoke in a hurried but hushed voice. "They have forgotten I am to be a warrior. Grandfather no longer teaches me. He sends me here to these women. They are good to me, and I am learning, but I do not want to learn these things. I want to be like you." This type of praise flattered him and even this, from a young girl, his cousin, thrilled his heart.

"I came here to tell you a secret. You must promise to tell no one." Niglíču was familiar with his secrets. This grown cousin had often confided in her, but mostly about plans he never achieved.

"We have been dancing."

"Oh, no! You know the soldiers forbid this! The camp police will catch you!"

"We go into Makȟóšiča *The Badlands*. We climb down deep into the crevices there. The rock walls hide the light from our fire and there we dance. We have been collecting guns as well. We will be ready."

"Ready? Ready for what?"

"Wovoka teaches that The White Robe (*Jesus*) of the wašíču says the Kingdom will come soon. Buffalo will fill the land again, and our old ways will return. It will be as before. We must dance and pray, and this will happen. No one can stop us!"

"Do you really believe this?"

"Yes, and I will train to be one of the most courageous warriors. Maybe I will be the one to lead our people in this new time."

"Then I want to dance too! Take me there. With you."

"Cousin, that I cannot do."

Her eyes clouded with tears she wiped away. Rather than go back and continue her sewing, she headed towards the creek, kicking at the dusting of snow, dirtying it with the muddied soil beneath. With head down, she did not notice the man who approached from an intersecting path. He, so absorbed in the prayers he mumbled under his breath, did not notice the child at the intersection and so they collided. She stumbled. He caught her.

"Whoa, young lady!" Father Bastiat exclaimed smiling. He held her before him, steadied. Startled, Niglíču saw only pale white hands against her dark skin when a shadowy memory of another time and other white hands flashed before her. She jerked herself out of his grip and ran away.

He stood there and saw her disappear into the bushes, much as a spotted fawn fades into the woods back home in New York.

Crouched low and hidden, she watched this black robed man. She knew him to be a white man's priest: she had seen such men before but never had she been touched by one.

This, Fr. Bastiat's first close encounter with the Lakȟóta he had come to save, unnerved him. He picked up his heavy bag and continued his walk through the village, heading for the modest cabin he would call his own. His two-week train journey across the United States from New York City had left him tired. The curtain across the top bunk of the open accommodation Pullman car had not afforded him the solitude he felt he needed to pray, and yet here in this desolate landscape, he felt a little too naked to talk to his God. He had just begun to thoroughly enjoy the newly opened Bronx parks with winding paths and towering trees and had felt, and felt foolish for thinking it, that the shield of their protective canopy afforded him a bit of security from the constant surveillance of a loving but all-knowing God. He had gasped as he disembarked from the train; the openness of the land stunned him. He was here and God was very much here too ... so close and scarily so. *In this place you cannot hide from God.*

He was sure the people were aware of his presence, though no one came to call on him that first day. But the cabin his Order had commissioned for him appeared sturdy. Wood had been stacked outside. A few sacks of government issued food sat on a table with two chairs beside it. There was a lantern. There were two buckets. One he supposed was for scooping water. The other? He looked through the window. There was no outhouse. On a shelf above the stove he saw a pan, a pot, a coffee pot, two dishes, two cups and a few utensils. A narrow bed hugged the wall. Two blankets covered it. He breathed in deeply to calm his nerves. He had taken a vow of poverty. He had volunteered as a missionary here. God would provide and he would adapt.

When darkness closed in, he could see the village fires in the distance. He could smell their bacon scented smoke. But there was no noise from there save for a few barking dogs. Grateful for the bolt on his door and the latch on his shuttered window, Fr. Bastiat knelt before the crucifix he had affixed to the wall, made the Sign of the Cross and prayed. *God, come to my assistance. Lord, make haste to help me.*

He was not blessed with sleep that first night and so he did what he often did in such cases. He made up stories to comfort himself, and this one was to be autobiographical. How did he come to be here in the wilds of South Dakota? He, a man born and raised in New York? With eyes closed, he imagined others reading the story of his life long after he had left this world. He would start with how he came to be a priest. He would start on the day he met Father Xavier. He fell asleep, however, exhausted, after the first composed word, and later relived it in a dream.

*****

The road that ran between Boston and Fordham University was well traveled, and Father Xavier, a Jesuit priest, used it a few times each year to assure that the newer university, Fordham, maintained the standards that were expected of a Catholic institution. One afternoon while trotting down Boston Post Road and nearing his destination, the clopping of his horse's hooves had a decided clink to it and, looking down, he saw a shoe had come loose and conveniently so, he thought, and maybe providentially so, near a blacksmith. Dismounting, he walked his mare the short distance, and observed the smith hammering away with a sort of controlled fury, bending the glowing iron into the shape he desired.

Being an astute priest, and one for many years, he guessed it was not really the iron the blacksmith was trying to bend to his wishes, but perhaps something else. Being an outspoken man and one willing to take chances and ruffle a few feathers, he approached and said, casually, as though this was a most normal thing to say, "What are you hitting there, sir?"

Barely looking up, John Bastiat responded, "Why, a shoe, of course."

"Are you sure?"

Now this irked Bastiat. For one thing, he was not in the mood for games. For another, the unspoken answer hit too close to home. He turned to see a pleasant smile and asked how he might help. While he hammered in the nails, the two struck up a conversation and, little by little, the priest was able to coax Bastiat to tell a bit of his life. On the surface, it did not seem all that unusual. Bastiat had begun life as a poor New York young man who had left farming to apprentice himself to a blacksmith. Of course, the blacksmith had a daughter, and of course, young Bastiat fell in love with this beautiful girl and later married her. Time went by and now he had his father-in-law's business.

"Have you children?" the priest asked and watched a cloud cross over Bastiat's eyes.

"No," came the short answer.

Probing now, and not because of curiosity, but because he felt Bastiat wanted to confide something but was hesitant to do so, the priest asked, "Your wife is well?"

The cloud darkened, and Bastiat gave no answer. Fr. Xavier waited. "I see," he responded.

With flashing eyes, wet with sudden tears, Bastiat shot back, "No, you do not see!"

Ah, thought the priest. *This is where the hurt lies.* He probed no more.

Bastiat went back to his hammering, and Fr. Xavier stood to leave.

"How much do I owe you, sir?" he said.

"Nothing," was the reply. "I just hammered in a few nails."

Feeling dismissed, the priest led the horse towards the door of the stable.

"Wait," Bastiat called. "Please."

So many questions! So many questions poured from the soul of this man. So many "whys"?

How could God allow his wife and unborn child to die? Why had he offered to hold that sick boy while the mother descended from a carriage before his shop? Why had he kissed this fevered child? Why hadn't he noticed the pocks? Why had he gone home and then kissed his pregnant wife? Kill both wife and child with a kiss? Why? Smallpox had run rampant that year in New York City. He had survived it, but his wife died days after contracting it from him. He had prayed. How he prayed and yet God hadn't heard him! Bastiat's whole body shook, sobs bursting forth with the questions that had no answers. Fr. Xavier just held him until Bastiat, exhausted, slumped forward, holding his head in his hands.

"Pray with me now, son," and he did, and somehow a peace descended on him and he knew now that God had heard and answered, although what the answer was, he was not sure.

"Thank you, Father," he said.

"I did nothing," Xavier replied, "but allow a few nails to be withdrawn."

Later, Fr. Bastiat would look upon this encounter as a turning point in his life. He felt God drawing him back to the Church, even hearing the call to minister to others as Fr. Xavier had ministered to him. Becoming a full member of the Jesuit community took many years, and after several, but before taking the ultimate step, Bastiat needed to fulfill the required missionary work. He chose the conversion of the native people of Pine Ridge as his mission.

Chapter 4

Pȟaŋkéska hokšíčala kiŋ pȟóskiskil oyúspe.
She again and again cuddled the foreign doll.

oud Bear sat with his grandfather, together grieving the loss
of American Hair. That he was apparently buried in the mass
grave on the hill was appalling. They customarily laid their
dead on a scaffold or in a tree, far from the reach of animals, far
from the mud a corpse might lie in, too high for a person to walk
upon. And relatives near the scaffold could talk to the deceased,
assure them they were not forgotten. All this was denied those buried
together on the hill. Loud Bear forgave the grievances he had held
against American Hair, remembering only that they were brothers.
What gave the young man hope was the dancing. Surely the old
ways would return. Surely this Jesus his brother so believed in would
make the world right again. Wovoka had promised this, and many
believed him. But Grasshopper did not and sank deeper into despair.

One evening, in early summer, Loud Bear brought encouraging
news. A relative had been found, a relative who had been inquiring
about the survivors of the massacre. Neither man had met this
woman before. This daughter of Grasshopper's cousin had married a
white man, an agency clerk by the name of Bordeaux, and lived near
the Pine Ridge Agency. It was this relative, Wáčhiŋhiŋ *Soft Feather*,
herself an iyéska čhiŋčá *half-breed*, who was seeking this
information.

"She is our blood relative. Do you want to meet her?" Loud Bear
asked.

Grasshopper fondly remembered his cousin, Soft Feather's mother.
When they were but young children, they had played together at the
large summer encampment and she became like a sister to him.
When she matured, she married a trapper and he did not see her
again. He had heard years later that she had died from the white

80

man's many-scab disease called wičháȟaŋȟaŋ *smallpox*. He was curious now about her daughter and so he agreed to go. All three would go, he decided, and meet this new cousin of theirs!

Procuring a wagon for the trip was not nearly as difficult as obtaining a horse to pull it. The Americans had confiscated or destroyed all horses fit for either hunting or battle. However, they eventually located a kind man who could spare his mule for the duration, and so the three set out the following morning. From his schooling, Loud Bear knew enough English to ask directions to the house, which was reported to be large, and certainly too spacious for this childless couple. An old Lakȟóta man, sneering, directed them to the white and tan two-story building. That this was a structure for two people to live in was incomprehensible to Niglíču.

Climbing down from the wagon first, Loud Bear tied the mule to the hitching post. Niglíču cautiously descended, holding onto the wagon a little longer than necessary as she eased her right foot to the ground. Her left was still on the wagon board when she felt her grandfather's hand on her shoulder, reassuring her. When she approached the three-foot-high white picket fence that encircled the house, she wondered what type of creature this fence would deter.

Surely this would not stop a deer who would leap over. Surely not a small animal who could dig under it or wiggle through the spaces! Perplexed, she ran her fingers over the painted wood, and wondered if it was from this kind that their new friend, White Birch, had earned her name.

"Lalá, this is to keep things out? It is very short."

Loud Bear laughed, happy to explain. He too felt the fence was ridiculous. He thought his response would be better than Grasshopper's and so answered, "This fence says that the land in here belongs just to them."

"Just to them? Who gave it to them?" Niglíču asked.

"The white man took it from us."

Grasshopper did not correct him although what his grandson said was only partially true. *Was any land theirs?* A group of people may claim land but they never possessed it. It passed to whomever was the more powerful. *And how could any one person say a piece of land was theirs?*

Niglíču ran her hand over the rounded tops of the pickets, up one side and down the other. *Little hills. Up and down.*

81

The people at the gate made Soft Feather uneasy. She stepped back from the window so she could not be seen but could still watch these strangers. Her husband was not a popular man. Ambitious and brusque, he wielded his minor authority over the workings of the reservation with an eye to becoming powerful. And she, of mixed heritage married to white man, was not trusted by either the Lakȟóta or the white population there. *Why had he married me at all? To prove how "fair-minded" he was? Or was it that my husband had received favored treatment in land allotment because his wife had Lakȟóta blood?* She shook her head to clear her thoughts. *How odd that I think these things so often!*

The younger man opened the gate. She didn't expect that and she tensed. *But there is a little girl here. These strangers would never harm me with a child present.* She passed by the oval hall mirror, looked at herself, and went towards the door.

Although her father was white, he was a dark Frenchman with straight black hair, and so she had not lost all her Lakȟóta features in the mix. They were just tempered in a way that made her exotically attractive, although her figure owed much of its curvaceousness to a diet rich in sweets. In fact, at the moment, a pie was in the oven and she smelled the burned sugar of the berries as it bubbled out from under the crust onto the stove bottom, smoking. She turned and hurried into the kitchen. Her husband would scold her for a burned pie!

There was a rap on the door.

She lifted the pie to the top of the cast-iron stove and removed some water from the heater at the side to wash away the juices that had dripped onto her new linoleum floor. Wiping her hands on her apron, she walked to the door, opened it a crack, and asked in perfect, although slightly accented, Lakȟóta, who they were.

Loud Bear began the introductions.

"My relatives!" she exclaimed and opened the door wider. But when invited in, Niglíču hung back in her grandfather's shadow.

The deep booming of the grandfather clock in the hallway marked the girl's first step into a wašíču house. It was noon and the twelve bongs coming from that tall giant with a swinging arm frightened her. Seeing this, Soft Feather crouched before her and reassured her that this only told the time of day and that she need not to be afraid, but of course, this meaning was beyond her comprehension. There were no Lakȟóta words for time as defined by white society. Niglíču understood only that this wooden monster with brass decoration helped white people tell if the sun was up or down. *Odd.*

Odd, yes, but not nearly as odd as the hard flowers on the floor she was walking on. She was not sure where to place her feet. She had discovered linoleum, and it was a genuine wonder to her and made her forget the clock. Such colors! Such a pattern! In fact, she was paying more attention to the house interior than to her new cousin. Her cousin, however, was paying quite a lot of attention to her.

A beautiful child, Soft Feather said to herself. *See how straight she stands. See those big eyes watching, taking everything in. She has intelligence, this one does. Bathe her and dress her up, educate her, and she would be a daughter anyone would be proud of.* Soft Feather thought quickly while Grasshopper and Loud Bear told the story of Wounded Knee. She heard their words, "no parents left," but her heart was saying, *Maybe she can be mine!* She had been married several years but there had been no pregnancies. She yearned for a child. And this one would be a relative.

She served them pie. Poured them coffee. They spoke in their native Lakȟóta, something that had been denied her since she married. Mr. Bordeaux forbade that language in their home. To please him she had to become "white", as though in transforming her, he was fulfilling a mission that would promote him to a higher position. *See what I can do?* She had recognized this early on in their marriage, but now she had no choice but to stay with him.

Despite her sincere hospitality, Grasshopper was uncomfortable in her home. To a man used to being on the move, settling in different areas with the seasons, pursuing the once massive buffalo herds, the house bespoke permanence. There was too much of everything, too much to ever pack up and move to another location. Foreign smells he recognized as white man's soap tightened his lungs. The sweet-sticky fruit filling that had at first slid so smoothly down his throat with the first piece of pie, now made his stomach queasy with the second wedge.

Loud Bear looked comfortable, however. Squared rooms, table and chairs were not unfamiliar to him who had received schooling. He leaned back on his spindly chair and belched loudly. Soft Feather giggled. She would never dare such a breach of etiquette with her

83

husband around.

And Niglíču was mesmerized by all she saw. After her initial shyness, she bubbled over with questions. Grasshopper had not seen her smile so much since the tragedy.

When once again the grandfather clock startled him with its bong, Grasshopper decided the visit was over. It was good that he had come. It was good to see another relative, but now he wanted to be away from this foreign way of life. The destitution of the small village suited him better than this.

He rose to leave but then Soft Feather stopped him. "Wait, please," she insisted. "I have something to give the child."

They listened to the stairs creak as she ascended to the second floor. Niglíču ducked and anxiously looked up when she heard the wide floorboards overhead groan. Never had someone walked directly above her!

"This is for you, my little cousin," Soft Feather said when she came down the stairs. She held out the curly yellow-haired, pinked cheeked porcelain doll to Niglíču. "It was mine, but I think she would want to be yours."

Niglíču did not know if she should touch this realistic looking baby, but when she felt the soft body beneath the lacy dress and looked into its blue eyes, she was spellbound, and cuddled it.

"There now," Soft Feather said, "You and your new baby should come to visit me again."

On the ride home, Niglíču explored every inch of her new baby, dressing it and undressing it, holding the lace up to the sun and peering through it, running her fingers through the baby's hair to separate the tangles. She wondered whose hair it had been before the baby received it.

*****

It was late afternoon when they returned to the village. Loud Bear stopped the wagon before Grasshopper's thípi. "Will you come with me to the river when the sun rises tomorrow?" Grasshopper asked his grandson. Though an unusual request, Loud Bear did not question it. Saying he would be there, he then drove off to return both wagon and mule.

When the sky glowed red and orange, but just before the sun

84

added its white-yellow brilliance, Loud Bear stood outside the thípi waiting. The curious request had bothered him during the night. He knew his grandfather stood alone at the edge of the river each dawn singing his morning song. Once his grandfather had confided that the river's flow over his bare feet connected him to all that was.

Grasshopper emerged from the thípi soundlessly, and because Niglíču was still asleep, he gestured for his grandson to follow him. When they had walked several yards away, the older man finally spoke. "I used to be alone there, but now, further down the stream, I see the new Šinásapa *Black Robe (priest)* and he sings, too. I want to know what he is saying." Though Grasshopper could understand and speak some English, he was not nearly as proficient as his grandson.

Fr. Bastiat was growing to enjoy the intimacy of open-air prayer and had found the dim, stuffy cabin too confining for the outpouring of his soul. He would walk to the riverbank and stand on its highest point and pray Lauds, the Morning Office. He did not feel comfortable praying in Latin. He thought in English, and he reasoned he should pray his personal prayers in the same language. Facing the rising sun, he would kneel on the damp grass and begin his prayer with, of course, the Sign of the Cross, rosary in hand, followed by

"Come to my assistance, Lord!

Make haste to help me!"

Grasshopper and Loud Bear, camouflaged by morning shadows amid the shrubs and tall grasses that took advantage of the water source, watched and listened.

"Creator of the earth and skies

To whom the words of life belong,

Grant us truth to make us wise,

Grant us the power to make us strong..."

"What does he say? What is he singing?"

"This is his morning song." Loud Bear whispered. His translation was in spirit similar to that of Grasshopper's morning prayer song. Grasshopper had felt it was so, and for a moment felt kinship to this priest. "You can go now," he whispered to his grandson.

Grasshopper could not later understand his compulsion to join the prayer. No longer hiding, and surely observed by the priest, Grasshopper walked several yards downstream to his usual spot, removed his moccasins and stepped into the icy water that braced

85

him. Raising both arms in offering towards the sky, he began his morning song.

*****

Bastiat walked the long way back to his cabin, a path that led him through the outermost perimeter of the village. It was there that people relieved themselves. It was from there that foul fumes assaulted his nostrils.

Prior to coming, he had studied the Lakȟóta culture enough to know that these were not the "filthy savages" they were so often in newspapers portrayed to be. Left to their traditional ways of moving from place to place, their camps were most often clean. When their camp area was fouled with human and animal waste, the camp moved. The wastes were soon naturally absorbed and ultimately nourished the lush buffalo grasses.

Such movement was not possible now. Circumstances dictated the camp had to be close to both flowing water, a limited resource, and a food distribution center. And the government wanted the people to settle into cabins. Bastiat knew disease would flourish in this current situation. He would teach them how to adapt. As he made his way to his cabin, he decided his task for the day would be to dig a deep hole. Over this, he would build an outhouse.

Years of smithing had made his muscles powerful, but years of preaching had not kept them strong, and so after a few hours, Bastiat, sweating, decided this was enough for one day. He sat down on a log and hiked up his robe to cool down. Bending forward, he flicked away the dried mud that clung to his hairy legs.

Há Sápa did not live in the village. His father, a freed slave who had joined, and then deserted, the US Army to marry a Lakȟóta woman, had built a cabin nearby months before the massacre. And so by slightly altering his path to the village, the curious boy was able to spy on the priest. He surmised the priest was digging a hole for an outhouse. He had helped his father do the same thing not that long ago. But because he was a bit of a rascal, Há Sápa feigned ignorance.

"Someone died? You are digging a grave?"

The boy's English startled the priest. He looked up to see a dark-skinned boy staring at him.

86

"Why, no. I'm digging a hole for an…"

"Outhouse?"

"Why yes."

The boy walked over to the hole, inspecting it. "It is deep enough now." He looked around. "You have no wood?"

Feeling strange that he needed to explain himself to a boy, Bastiat confided that he had yet to order wood, or indeed any tools needed for its construction. He'd go into town tomorrow to take care of that. That apparently satisfied the boy who began to walk away.

"Stay…please. It would be nice to speak to someone who can understand me."

Há Sápa smiled. Sat beside the priest. Because of the boy's willingness to supply answers, the priest plied him with questions and learned more practical information about the people he intended to save for Jesus than from all his previous studies.

*****

The trip to town was productive. Wood was ordered. Nails, hammer, and saw were purchased. He'd need hinges. Maybe he could make some? A crate with supplies he had sent from New York had arrived too and all would be delivered to him the next day. He certainly looked forward to it. He hadn't expected such Spartan living!

The walk back to his cabin…he couldn't yet call it home…was invigorating and he was in high spirits. His meeting with the boy convinced him that he might be more successful with the village children. If he could befriend them, then maybe he could reach their parents and begin his mission. With that in mind, when he walked beside the river, he was happy to see the little girl who had run from him before.

From a distance, she appeared to be bathing a doll…a porcelain doll too, and how she came to get such a doll was unfathomable. He walked closer but stopped when he realized she was not bathing the doll at all! *She was making it dirty?* He stepped behind some bushes to watch.

No, it was not mud that she was grinding into the white porcelain face, but dried berries made into a mush. When the doll's complexion darkened, she smiled thinking she had succeeded in making the doll's skin like her own. But then she splashed water on it for a test. Her hand brushed over the stain and it immediately faded. Again and again she ground her mixture into the doll's face. Again and again it washed off, only dirtying the doll's hair. The priest watched with tears in his eyes, understanding.

And then he had a thought. Ink! Ink would darken that porcelain if she was careful not to scrub it off.

Finally I can help! He quickly rushed back to his cabin and opened his box of inks. He was a calligrapher at heart and appreciated the old art of handwritten Bibles. The magnificent swirls of the ink on the first words of a chapter mesmerized him. There were only a few material things that held great value to him, and one was his wife's mahogany brass edged and sloped writing box. Now, when he opened it, and as always happened, it felt as though her spirit rose from it and entered his body along with the smell of the colored inks in their squat little jars. "Such an artist she was with her pen!" he sighed.

He did not linger, though, as he did not want the little girl to leave before he got there. Quickly he mixed a little brown and a little red into another jar and, after screwing the cap on tightly, rushed back to the riverbank. She was still there! He approached slowly and, as she caught sight of him, she hid her doll. He beckoned to her, but she retreated deeper into a clay alcove. Opening the jar, he dipped in his finger and painted a round patch of the skin on the back of his left hand with the ink, almost perfectly matching her skin coloration. She watched warily as he extended his stained left hand and motioned for her to give him the doll. Hesitantly, she offered it, and he applied the stain to the doll's left hand in the same manner. He bent to the stream and tried to wash the stain off, but it continued to hide the white porcelain behind it. Niglíču met his eyes, questioning. He held out the jar as an offering to her and she accepted it. Pleased, and understanding this was a small but important step that he did not want to push into something greater yet, he returned to his cabin.

The following morning, the empty jar stood outside his door.

*****

Gnugnúška owáčhekiye thípi kiŋ ektá yé.
Grasshopper went to the church.

88

Mathó Nážiŋ *Standing Bear*, who managed the post office near the Pine Ridge Agency, greeted Bastiat. "Good afternoon, Father. You are new here."

"Indeed, I am," Bastiat said cheerfully. "I am Father Bastiat. Has any mail come for me?"

Two letters were there; one from his Jesuit superior, and this he put aside, knowing it to be an inquiry about how things were going, and the second was a thick envelope from his brother in New York. It was this brother, George, who had approved and championed his decision to go out west, to make a difference in the world beyond saving the souls of the people in his small affluent parish. George and his wife were active in The National American Women's Suffrage Society. Bastiat was hesitant, though, to help that group for he was unsure of his position on women's rights. While the Catholics spoke of the equality of all people, the bias of the Church was towards a separation of roles for men and women. He thought of his wife. As the years passed since her death, she had grown increasingly saintly in his eyes. She would have been content with the way things were.

Bastiat tucked the first letter into the leather pouch he had slung over one shoulder and eagerly opened the second. Tucked within folded newspaper clippings from the New York Herald and the New York Times, Bastiat found the long letter and felt a pang of homesickness. New York seemed so far away! Engrossed in family news, he did not notice the tall man who stood before him, waiting. The man cleared his throat.

"Excuse me, Father, I would like to welcome you here."

Startled, Bastiat looked up.

"My name is Pierre Bordeaux. I am one of the Agency clerks. How are you settling in?"

After answering truthfully that he was doing well enough, but that he had a lot to learn about the Lakhóta people, Bordeaux offered his help.

"I live very near here. Come to my home, have coffee with me and we can talk."

Bordeaux, a Catholic himself, was happy to have Jesuit help in civilizing these Indians. His wife was transforming, he was proud to say, although she still insisted on using her Lakhóta name, Wáčhiŋhiŋ *Soft Feather*, when introducing herself to other Indians.

He would never say the Lakȟóta, but had compromised with its English translation, for now. Mostly, he called her Mrs. Bordeaux in the company of others, and especially with white people.

The priest consented and they walked to the clerk's home together. Bordeaux opened the door to their spacious home and called his wife. "Mrs. Bordeaux, I have brought company!"

Soft Feather appeared from the kitchen, wiping her floured hands on the apron that encircled her wide waistline, and welcomed the priest. They sat together at the table and Bastiat observed that the husband did all of the talking. The priest directed questions to Soft Feather and she glanced at her husband before answering them. Her measured responses appeared to be reflections of her husband's thinking and not necessarily her own. Fleetingly, he thought of his brother's arguments in favor of the female vote.

"Father, are you thinking of building a church there? Those Indians from Big Foot's band have a hard time settling down. They talk incessantly about moving to another area. Their location is too dirty, they say. They are always moving! How can a man prosper if he is always moving around? A church might encourage them to build cabins. Why they insist on those teepees is beyond my comprehension!"

Bastiat agreed, in theory at least, but he did harbor a sort of romanticized fantasy of life in a thípi. He wondered what it would be like living in a space without corners. Would it be more natural? More like a womb? Softer? He had never been in a real, lived-in thípi. Surely the ones set up at exhibits could not tell their true story. His mind flew off as it often did and this time it went to imagining a round church. What would that feel like, and where would the altar be?

"Father?"

"Oh, excuse me. I am so used to being alone and letting my thoughts fly at will. Yes, I will build a small chapel there, and soon too, before winter, and maybe someday, a bigger church."

He then surprised himself by telling them his plans. The people are hesitant around him, he said, but he was hoping to develop trust with the children. Maybe he would tell them stories. Make them feel welcome. Maybe this would reassure the parents. He told them the story of the little boy and the girl with the doll.

"A girl? With a doll? Why, that is my cousin!" It seemed to

Bastiat that this was the first time he really heard Soft Feather speak. "She was just here a few days ago. I was the one who gave her the doll!"

"But look what she tried to do with it," Bordeaux interjected. "And you, Father, did not help matters any by letting her get away with it. Indeed, you fostered it! To save them, we must kill the Indian! Don't you see that?"

He wanted to say he agreed because, after all, that was his intention in coming here. Make them good Christians! Show them the way! But there was something overbearing in the man's tone that held him back from speaking aloud and so he just nodded agreement, and this seemed to satisfy Bordeaux.

"Well, I must be getting back soon. Thank-you for your hospitality." Bastiat excused himself and rose from the table, but perhaps he rose too hastily. He shook the table and coffee spilled onto the lace tablecloth. Soft Feather hurriedly sopped it up, blotting it with the white satin napkin, which caused an unsettling thought to pass through Bastiat's mind. Her dark skin against the white satin seemed wrong. *Why? Am I truly without prejudice?*

Bordeaux offered a horse to carry Bastiat back to his cabin, but he declined, preferring to walk the dusty trails. Along the way, his feet kicked up the dry earth, purposefully. He paused and watched it settle to the ground and wondered how this parched land could support the farming life the agents were asking of these Lakȟóta people. The priest bent down and scooped a handful of soil into his hand and let the dust trickle between his fingers leaving behind several small stones. One caught his eye. Bands of orange and brown rounded the small stone and on one side twisted and twirled with a black stripe. Prairie agate. He had seen it before, although not quite in this natural state. Rubbing it clean, he remembered a time in the past.

Newly married, he had brought his bride to Manhattan to experience the American Museum of Natural History. What a crisp and glorious fall day it had been! They had left at dawn and their horse had been strong, swift, and steady, easily traversing the fifteen miles with little direction from himself. He smiled remembering how he and his wife teased each other under the heavy lap blanket that both concealed and warmed them in her father's hooded buggy.

How she had marveled at the specimens in the hall of rocks and minerals! How he had wished he was rich enough to buy jewelry studded with the swirling rainbow agate that she so loved! "Buy one for me someday..." she had insisted, "when you have your own business. Make it into a pendant! I don't need gems," she had said. "These are beautiful enough!"

And now I have one...but have no wife to give it to.

Overcome with sudden loneliness, he raised his tear-filled eyes to the sky and sent a prayer for his wife to heaven. A bird appeared, a hawk he supposed from the shape of its silhouette against the blue, circling once before diving towards the ground behind the trees. *The stone. The hawk.* He shook his head, thinking of the story of Crazy Horse that he had read. *The world is filled with coincidences!*

He put the stone into his pouch and walked on.

*****

Grasshopper surprised Niglíču one day, calling her away from a sewing lesson with the women. "Come with me!"

Eagerly she left the thípi and followed him to a clearing by the creek. "What? What do you have for me?" she asked. She anticipated a surprise because her grandfather's eyes twinkled like they used to. Smiling eyes, she thought, belied the solemn set of his jaw.

He stretched into a bush, more dramatically than was needed, and she laughed when he feigned pain from the thorns. *What's in there?*

"Can I help?" she asked.

"I cannot seem to reach it. I found it there this morning," he lied.

"What? What?"

"Come and see!"

Never did she suspect that among the thorny canes would be her new bow! Never would she have anticipated the quiver full of arrows!

"For me? You finished it?"

He smiled, neither affirming nor denying. Once before he had made such a gift, a bow for his daughter, and he had given it to her with the promise that now she could protect herself and her family. But what was a bow against a soldier's rifle? How could he have known that there was no weapon they could have made that would have beat a repeating rifle? And yet Grasshopper made this bow for

92

his granddaughter because she had wanted one. *It will give her confidence! Practice will sharpen her senses and occupy her mind! And maybe she will find meat!*

Niglíču eased the bow from amid the thorns and admired the simplicity of it. It was not decorated. Nor was the leather quiver. He had made her a weapon. Should she choose to decorate was her decision.

With one hand on the leather-banded grip, she tried to draw back the string. There was little give. Her arrow would not go far.

"You must practice. You must grow strong to be the master of this bow."

*****

Grasshopper wondered about this strange Black Robe who had yet to come walking through the village, had yet to ask people to come to his little morning ceremony ... the ceremony where he raised the piece of bread and the cup, appearing to give thanks before consuming them all alone. His granddaughter had seen the priest do this. She spied on him, lying close to the ground behind bushes. He, foolishly she thought, was not aware of what was going on around him, especially later in the day when he began rubbing the stone. First, he would dip the stone into a bucket of water and then he would take what appeared to be sand and rub it over and over the edges of the stone, sliding the sand with the pressure of his thumb deep into crevices. He'd dip the stone into the water, admire his work and begin again. Watching the priest was far more interesting than staying in the camp and she could report to her grandfather all that she had seen.

"Be careful. Stay at a distance!" he warned, although he did not really believe the priest to be a physical threat to the child. The man appeared harmless, but caution should always be taken with the white men.

But the more he heard about this priest, the more curious he became. It was after their morning songs, sung at such a distance from each other that they barely heard the others, that Grasshopper watched the priest wade upstream to deeper water and greater privacy and followed him. There Fr. Bastiat removed his black robe and undergarments and fully immersed himself, splashing and

93

washing with abandon. He appraised the priest as a man and guessed his age and physical condition to be comparable to his own.

I will go watch this man's ceremony. I will see for myself what he does.

Niglíču had reported that the priest had dragged logs from near the stream and arranged them before a makeshift table with spread-eagled legs that he had constructed. The logs were old and rotted, but still their circumference was too big for campfires. The priest had chipped off the bark on top and so created a smooth surface for seating. While the priest was in his cabin, Grasshopper sat in the shadows on a log farthest from the altar.

Inside the cabin, Bastiat was preparing for Mass. The linen, embroidered and now neatly folded, would serve as the altar cloth. The purificator veiled the chalice, and the paten held the unconsecrated host. Two tiny cruets, one for water and the other for wine, waited. He would bring the heavy Lectionary outside first. Bastiat felt ridiculous doing this, knowing full well that no one would be in attendance. This had been the way it was since he had arrived and set up his "church." It made him feel very lonely. He walked outside to place the book on the altar and did not notice Grasshopper at all. He walked back in and got the other necessities and then, facing away from the congregation to the east, for he arranged his outdoor chapel so it faced the sunrise, Bastiat, together with his imagined congregation, turned to God in adoration and supplication.

Grasshopper sat and watched quietly until he saw the priest maneuvering items on the altar table. Unable to see clearly what was going on, he walked up closer and, in fact, so close that his face reflected off the chalice when Bastiat raised it during the Consecration. Startled out of his prayerful state at the sight of the Indian face, Bastiat almost spilled the now Precious Blood and returned the chalice quickly to the safety of the altar.

Someone is here? Bastiat turned to see Grasshopper motioning with his hands to continue. Flustered, Bastiat continued the Mass, but now it was more of a shared communion. But not completely shared. Fr. Bastiat did not, could not with clear conscience, offer the Host to Grasshopper. With eyes reverently closed, he consumed The Body of Christ alone.

When the Mass was over, neither man knew what to say.

Grasshopper stared at the crucifix and asked, "Wiwáŋyaŋg Wačhípi?" He then pointed to the wood of the Cross and said, "Čhaŋwákȟaŋ." Bastiat did not know Grasshopper meant the Sundance and the Sundance Tree, and realizing this, Grasshopper pulled down and over to the side his loose shirt at the neck revealing the scars on his chest, while repeating, "Wiwáŋyaŋg Wačhípi." Suddenly appalled in realizing that this Indian was comparing himself to the Lord Jesus Christ, Bastiat immediately shook his head vehemently and said "No!"

Grasshopper met his eyes with a hard stare. He withdrew his hand from his shirt covering the scars he was proud of and turned to leave.

"No. No, wait!" With a sudden insight that this man might understand more than his former parishioners did about the meaning of self- sacrifice, Bastiat touched the man's shoulder and said, "I was wrong ... Yes ... like that."

Chapter 5

Šinásapa kiŋ ȟtayétu háŋ athílehaŋyaŋ wičháhi.
In the evening, the Black Robe came to visit them.

Niglíču took her bow practice seriously. She escaped the village area early in the morning and so avoided the two cousins and their lessons. There were a few other little girls in the camp, but these children did not interest her with their hoop games. And now even her porcelain doll bored her. Disappointed that her arrows were not propelled with enough force to hit her target, she stopped using the arrows and concentrated on her draw. Scrunching her face and tightening her jaw, she pulled back the string and released. Over and over.

It was at such practice that Loud Bear watched her, smiling. He approached from behind. "It is hard to bring down the enemy without an arrow." Though his face was solemn, his eyes danced.

"Cousin, I need to learn more of the wašíču language. Grandfather says it is good to understand the enemy. Can you teach me?"

"What do you want to learn, little cousin?"

"How do you say, 'Čhikté kte'?"

How he laughed! This little cousin was so amusing! "And why do you need to know this?"

"I want the white men to know that I will kill them. When I am a warrior, I will need to know how to say this."

Seeing how sincere she was troubled him. "If a time comes when women will need to be such warriors, it will not be wise to forewarn the enemy."

"But I want them to know the arrow comes from me!"

Knowing it was time to stop the foolishness of this conversation, he told her to mimic this: "I am a little girl. Please do not hurt me."

"I am a little…" She stopped, realizing she was being mocked. "You will see. Someday you will see." She had vowed one day she would avenge her mother's death and it was this that was compelling her obsessive practice with the bow.

*****

"Who is there?" Loud Bear asked. He sat nearest to the closed flap of his grandfather's thípi when he heard the unusual tapping. A normal request for entrance was a scratch and so he was suspicious.

"Father Bastiat."

Deciding it was time to take some initiative of his own and be a more forceful presence in this small village, Bastiat decided to visit Grasshopper. The man had, after all, come to Mass.

Loud Bear frowned, but Grasshopper motioned for his grandson to open the flap.

Bastiat entered, bowed over and was immediately overcome with intense emotion. Perhaps because he had expected something else and found the interior so unlike the hovel he had envisioned, he stood there speechless. The primitive nature of the place prompted a flashing vision of the Nativity, and he instinctively made the Sign of the Cross.

Loud Bear muttered in Lakȟóta, "He comes in and immediately claims the place."

Bastiat, without thinking, began a house blessing.

"Lord, Father, almighty everlasting God, in your goodness send your holy angel from heaven to watch over and protect all who live in this home..."

Loud Bear stood up, glaring. Grasshopper narrowed his eyes but remained otherwise motionless.

"... to be with them and comfort them, through Christ our Lord."

Angered, Loud Bear stormed out leaving the priest to realize the precarious situation he was in. He had not meant to offend, but clearly he had done the wrong thing.

A moment of tense silence followed. Grasshopper motioned for the priest to sit on the side opposite the cooking fire. Thinking the Black Robe had not invited him to share the ceremonial meal at Mass but not letting that deter his hospitality, Grasshopper instructed Niglíču to fill a bowl from the pot of starch-thickened stew suspended over the fire. But upon receiving it, Bastiat knew the girl had not offered it willingly.

97

The stew was a pasty blend of flour and potatoes, but the bacon flavor and wild onion he detected saved it from being tasteless. No one spoke as he ate it, and he nodded his appreciation when finished. Declining more, the priest tried to make himself understood. "I want to help you," he said slowly with carefully enunciated syllables. "I want to be a friend."

Grasshopper gave no indication that he understood, although he knew the English words "friend" and "help." Spoken by a white man, those words were not to be trusted.

Not knowing what else to say, the priest laid his bowl down, and reached into the sack he carried slung over his shoulder. Grasshopper wary, tensed. Bastiat noticed but smiled reassuringly. He withdrew a small, paper-wrapped object.

"This is for your granddaughter. She has been watching me, but she does not think I saw her. May I give this to her?"

Grasshopper, half understanding, nodded. Bastiat extended the package to Niglíču. She took it and opened it when her grandfather indicated she should. When she saw the polished stone with its brown and amber swirls within red and white bands, her eyes lit up. Bastiat looked at her, smiled warmly and said, "Now you can be like Crazy Horse." Thanking them for their hospitality, he got up to leave.

Kills In Winter passed by the priest while walking towards Grasshopper's thípi but thought little of it. The priest had become more visible lately, but so far had not been interfering. But as he grew closer, he encountered Loud Bear walking in the opposite direction. The young man appeared in a foul mood.

"What angers you?" Kills asked.

"My grandfather met with the Black Robe."

"This bothers you?"

"Yes, it does!"

"Walk with me."

Loud Bear spat out the words. "Priests make promises. Life will be better. Jesus will save us. Where is this Jesus? Wovoka said dance. Jesus will come. He has not come. The buffalo have not come back."

"You have given up hope? You no longer dance?"

"The only hope we have is to fight."

"Fight them and you will die."

"You talk like an old man. You used to be a warrior. What are you now?"

Kills did not answer. He did not know the answer and Loud Bear walked away.

The thípi flap was open now and sun shone through the triangular entrance and brightened the interior. Kills In Winter invited himself in. Turning the stone over and over, Niglíču held it up to him. "See?"

"What do you have there?"

"A stone."

"You found such a colorful stone?"

"It was a gift from the Black Robe," Grasshopper answered for her, already suspecting that this visit had a purpose other than socializing.

"You are such friends with this man now that you are letting your granddaughter accept his gifts?"

"No, not at all. I am studying him," Grasshopper said.

"Studying him?"

"Yes."

"Why?"

"It is always best to know the enemy's ways."

"And what have you learned?"

"I am not sure. He seems like he is good, but ...."

"He claimed our thípi!" Niglíču heatedly interjected.

"He did what?"

"Loud Bear said so!"

Grasshopper looked at Niglíču, "If you hate him so much, return the stone."

"But ..."

"Listen well, Ťhakóža, I have every reason to hate the wašíču too, but I am no fool. Right now, they have beaten us. If I want to beat them, I need to understand them. *You* need to understand them. And you do not do this from far away. The stone is not just a stone. It is your opportunity to learn about the enemy. See it as such."

"In this he is right, child. But be wary. He will want to make us as they are," Kills In Winter cautioned.

"He can want many things. That does not mean they will happen," countered Grasshopper.

It was dark when Loud Bear returned. He breathed out the white man's alcohol and slurred his speech. Niglíču was asleep. He sat with Grasshopper and talked long into the night.

"She is almost 7 winters now. She has no parents. The agency police will take her away from you so she can go to the white man's school."

"No one can take her from me."

"You will see. They have taken others. The school is far away. Carlisle they call it. When she comes back, she will be different. She will speak their language. Some do not come back."

"Where do they go?"

"They die."

*****

Wagnáye!
I have failed her!

The morning was cool and the sky clear, and as Grasshopper stretched his sleep-stiffened muscles outside his thípi, he thought it would be a good day to travel if only to get the humiliating food handouts. He hated ration distribution day. He lived now, not as a warrior-hunter, but as a diminished man.

He hated standing in the long line outside the distribution building. If he had a wife, she would be the one standing in line, sparing him the humiliation. She would hold the ration ticket.

Grasshopper sat with Loud Bear on the wagon's bench. And because Loud Bear was too heavy with the whip on the overworked mule's back, Grasshopper held the leather strap and used it sparingly. There was no need to hurry, no need to be impatient.

Niglíču sat behind him in the wagon bed shared with Pretty Stone and White Birch. Though the distance was short to the center, the day was windy and Niglíču was cold. "Can I sit up there with you?"

She climbed up and squeezed in between the two men. Grasshopper stretched his blanket around her shoulders and she immediately felt his warmth. His right hand held the ration ticket, crushed and wrinkled. Why he did not put this into the pouch he always wore hanging from his neck and fingered so often disturbed her. Surely this card would last longer there. Her mother had stored it in her beaded pouch. *Why didn't he?*

When they arrived, the long line had already formed and the hungry Lakhóta stood uneasily before the scrutinizing stare of the reservation police and officials. The atmosphere was tense as the

100

agent and his assistants walked along the line speaking the English they assumed few others knew, pointing to various families or individuals and recording notes into long ledger books. Grasshopper took his place on the line and listened to the discouraging message passed down through it. The flour was mealy, and the beef was tainted! A hard knot formed in his stomach, and the thought erupted that if he should find any excuse, any excuse at all, to fight and die right there, he would do it. But Niglíču stood by his side, and he controlled himself for her sake.

The wait was long, and the children grew restless. Many left their parents and went to play, running this way and that in tag-like games. Niglíču spotted Há Sápa among them just as he accidentally bumped into an official, knocking the ledger from his hands.

"Watch where y'all goin' you ... nigga? Well, lookee what we have heah! A niggah Injun!"

The official grabbed Há Sápa by the shoulders and looked him straight in the eyes before his hand flew out and smacked him hard across the face.

"Learn yo place, *boy*!"

How could Niglíču understand that to some, the War Between the States had not ended, the Emancipation invalid? How could she know that even the now deceased, but still revered Lincoln had held to his belief that white men were superior to those with dark skin. What she saw only was that the older boy who had been kind to her, the boy who had smiled at her while he had stood beside his mother on the line, was now sprawled on the ground, holding his face before laughing white men. She broke from the line and ran to his defense. Standing between the officials and Há Sápa, she clenched her fists and yelled at them, "Ayústaŋ pe! *Stop it!*"

"Ah see we have a little spitfire heah," one official laughed, lunging for her too.

Suddenly a strong weathered hand latched onto this arm and spun the official around. Grasshopper crouched there, ready to fight, and armed only with his knife. *A good day to die!*

The long line quickly evolved into an angry crowd surrounding the incident. Warriors squeezed through the women to get to the front. Officials, panicked and outnumbered, drew their guns. Suddenly, barreling through the crowd, Bordeaux appeared in the center. "Put the guns down! You will not turn this into a riot! Stop!

Now!" he commanded. "There will be peace here while I am in charge!" He saw the boy on the ground. He saw a little girl ready to defend him. "Cowards! All of you!" he yelled to his subordinates. "A little girl scares you? For this you will besmirch my record?" He turned to the crowd and waved them away. "Go back to the line. Get your food!"

Heaving deep breaths, Grasshopper held tightly to Niglíču's hand and walked back with the crowd, now forming a still angry and very irregular line before the distribution building. Impassioned voices filled the air. The people no longer stood patiently. They paced. They rocked back and forth on their feet. They made the guards nervous. Loud Bear, away at the time of the incident, now milled among the people, his excited voice adding to the tension.

When Grasshopper reached the front of the line, it was Bordeaux who asked to see his ticket. He noted that the man received food for just himself and granddaughter. No parents were mentioned. No siblings for the girl.

"Note this man. He is new here. And he is responsible for *her*," he ordered the clerk with the ledger.

He looked Niglíču up and down, but she faced him squarely. "Might do well to civilize her some. Maybe Carlisle," the clerk suggested.

Later, when they stood before the distributors and an *X* was placed next to their names to show they had received their rations, they did not notice the other citation next to Niglíču's name, but Loud Bear, who stood next to them as a self-appointed bodyguard, did.

That night, the late August air chilled the small village, and Niglíču slept warm under the tattered robes. Loud Bear sat with his grandfather and Kills voicing his concerns over his small cousin's future.

"The wašíču have marked her. They have noticed her," he said.

"What does this mean, 'marked'?"

"When they come to take away children to send to Carlisle, they will come for her. I know how this works. An orphan is easier to take away. They will not ask your permission and you cannot stand in their way. You will die first. They will find an excuse."

Turning to Kills In Winter, Grasshopper asked, "Can this be true?"

"I cannot say for sure, but they have taken children and, if they live to return from that school, they are not the same."

They sat in silence, the smoke from their pipes looping through that which came from the slow burning embers of their firepit. Finally, Loud Bear spoke.

"There is another way. Send her to Soft Feather. Her husband is an official and has influence. She can go to that school run by Wičháȟpi Yámni *Clarence Three Stars*. It is close to where your cousin lives. You can still see her."

"But before you were against this," Grasshopper protested.

"Things are different now."

"I will think about this."

Long after the other men left, Grasshopper weighed his options. He could try to leave this place and head for Canada as had Tȟatȟáŋka Íyotake *Sitting Bull* a while ago. But without horses, guns and supplies, he would be putting his granddaughter in even more harm. And Sitting Bull had returned, unhappy with the situation there anyway. Soft Feather's home was not even a day's ride away. Maybe his granddaughter should learn to read the white man's words, speak the white man's tongue. She would learn quickly. She would not have to stay there long… just long enough so that she would not be taken with the others. Soft Feather was a relative. She would take good care of her until it was safe for her to return.

He watched his granddaughter turn in her sleep exposing her shoulder and back to the cold. He crawled over to her and pulled up the blanket to cover her properly. *How I will miss her!*

*****

The scratch at the thípi entrance came earlier than he expected, and Grasshopper jolted awake with heart pounding, not even realizing he had just nodded off. The three soon set off on what Niglíču thought was a high adventure; a visit to that house of wonders where that generous relative had given her sweet foods and a gift. She cradled her ink-stained doll and sang songs learned from her mother.

When they approached the house, Niglíču's excitement sent shivers of guilt down her grandfather's back. Niglíču was unaware that if Soft Feather accepted the proposal, she would not be returning home with him, and her new life would begin.

A surprised Soft Feather, home alone while her husband worked, opened the door to them. "I'm so happy you came again! Come in!

103

Come in!" She ushered them into the kitchen and offered them breakfast. She encouraged Niglíču to help prepare the batter and soon all were laughing while Niglíču vigorously whisked the ingredients together and then looked ashamed of the splattered mess on the table. "Here. You clean it up!" Soft Feather smiled, and Nigliču swirled the soapy checkered washcloth across the smooth oiled wood of the tabletop and traced the sudsy paths with her fingertips.

See how happy she is! She likes it here!

When the hearty breakfast of fried cakes and maple syrup was finished and fingers licked clean, Nigliču was sent outdoors to see the Halladay Self Regulating Wind Engine spin its swirling sun rays round and round. After several minutes, Loud Bear came to stand beside her. He looked sad.

"It is nice here," he said softly. "Do you think so?"

"Yes," she answered. But he rarely spoke in this gentle way. *Is something wrong?* she wondered.

"Soft Feather is a good woman. She cooks well."

"I cook better," she replied.

"Maybe. But I think she could teach you different ways to make food. Like today. You had a good time in there before."

"It was good. But I miss practicing with my bow. I think we should leave now."

"No. You need to come inside now with me," he said, his voice hardened.

Soft Feather and Grasshopper sat at the table. "Your relative and I have been talking. Sit, Ťhakóža. I need to tell you something…something you must try to understand."

She sat next to him, suddenly afraid. He, too, was sad. *Why is everyone sad?*

"I am an old man and having a little girl like you to take care of is hard for me."

I don't understand this. When had this happened? Have I been bad?

"You are to stay here with Soft Feather. You need a woman to care for you. It is nice here. There is food. Here you will go to school."

"I don't want to stay here! I want to be with you! I promise. I will be good. I will take care of you! I will cook! I will learn to sew your moccasins!"

He ignored her protests. How it hurt him to do that! How his heart was breaking! "I will visit when I can."

"No! No! I won't stay!"

"Tȟakóža, you will do as I say. You will stay here. You will learn the white man's way to speak. You will learn to read the white man's words."

Soft Feather joined in, her words earnest and gentle. "Little cousin, I will be like a mother to you."

Grasshopper stood up. "Learn quickly. Then I will come."

Desperate, Niglíču looked at Loud Bear. "You will take me?" But he averted his eyes and walked outside. Grasshopper followed.

She stood there, hardly able to breathe when the door closed behind them. Tears clouded her eyes and she felt suddenly dizzy. Swallowing hard to push back the food that had risen into her throat, she fell to her knees hugging her stomach. A cough turned into the gag which brought up her breakfast, an ugly brown splotch on the hard pretty flowers of the hallway floor. Still bent over, a chill seized her. Shivering, she began to cry.

Soft Feather didn't know what to do. The happy child she had agreed to mother...keep forever if only that would happen!...had turned into a...she couldn't even describe it but to think...trapped wild animal.

What have I agreed to? She ran to the door, flung it open, and yelled, "Wait!" But the wagon had turned the corner, and no one heard her call. Flustered, with two hands on her cheeks, she went back inside, closed, and locked the door behind her. *What if she tries to run away?*

But Niglíču was not going to be running anywhere. She had rolled onto her side and drew up her knees, clamping her hands between them and stared blankly at the grandfather clock, ticking away a life of its own.

Soft Feather stood over Niglíču and took a deep breath. *I'd be upset too, being deserted by my family.* She knelt beside her and lifted her unyielding body into her arms and rocked her. She had forgotten the words to the song her mother had sung to her when she was a child, but she remembered the melody. Humming it, she smoothed back Niglíču's hair and prayed she was doing the right thing by keeping her.

Soon her new daughter's body relaxed. Though Niglíču's eyes remained closed, Soft Feather wasn't sure her breathing matched sleep. *Was she pretending?* She lifted her up and put her on the couch, there gently removing her vomit soiled skirt. There, covering her goose-fleshed skin with a woolen blanket.

She cleaned the mess on the floor, rinsed out the skirt and hung it above the stove to dry. Biting her lip and rubbing her hands up and down her arms, Soft Feather shook with fear. Her husband would be home in a few hours. *How am I going to explain this to him?* Anticipating the beating she was sure to get, she thought of ways to please him and possibly avoid it. Her fingers traced the still sore bruise beneath her skirt. She forgot which of her many transgressions had earned it.

Cleanliness was important to Bordeaux. Neatness. Order. Everything had a place and was in it. More as self-preservation rather than her own need for these, the house was immaculate. Maybe if she made the girl so...clean, not smelling of wood smoke and bacon, hair shiny and carefully braided...French braided!...just maybe she could escape his wrath. How stupid she had been to accept the child without his permission! But how could she have passed up the opportunity for a child she so badly wanted?

She set the large washtub in the center of the kitchen floor. When enough water was heated, she filled the tub.

"Come, little cousin, wake up now. I will give you a bath."

Niglíču opened her eyes. She hadn't been sleeping, nor had she really been awake. Hazy thoughts of denial, dreams of her mother and father had overshadowed her reality but now these vanished instantly with Soft Feather's words. Now, instead, a heaviness so weighed her down that she did not want to move.

Soft Feather sat her up. Undressed her there on the sofa. Naked, she was carried to the kitchen. Naked, she was immersed in the warm water. Never had she sat in such deep warm water. Never had her hair been covered with white suds that smelled like flowers. Never had a soft sponge slid over her skin and between her legs. The warmth melted her into submission and encouraged Soft Feather.

Throughout the bathing, Niglíču never said a word, never acknowledged that she even heard the gentle praises Soft Feather heaped on her. But when she was helped out of the tub and stood chilled on the cold kitchen floor, she did react. Urine spilled down

106

her legs.

"Oh my!" Soft Feather exclaimed, putting the towel on top of the puddle. "On my!" she said over and over as she hastily covered Niglíču with a billowy white blouse she would later belt at the waist to form a long dress.

She sat Niglíču on a kitchen chair and ran her comb through the child's long black hair, untangling strands that had been long neglected. She parted the hair three ways and began creating the then fashionable hair style that had originated in North Africa.

"How beautiful you look now!" Soft Feather observed, but Niglíču continued to look at her with blank eyes.

*****

Neither man spoke on the way back to the village. What words could fill the emptiness of the space on the seat between them?

Grasshopper saw smoke rising from his thípi. He had left only smoldering coals; nothing that would cause the quick bursts of grey that faded into the white sky. The two men approached cautiously. Lifting the flap, they saw Kills in Winter there. Behind this friend were his belongings piled off to the side.

"I will stay here with you awhile, Khólá."

Grasshopper nodded, grateful.

"We are two old men, but we are not dead yet. Your granddaughter will come back to us."

*****

Wičhíŋčala kiŋ líla wíkhophe.
The girl was afraid of things to happen.

Niglíču didn't eat nor did she move from the couch while Soft Feather hurriedly prepared her husband's favorite dinner, while she coiffed her hair and changed her clothing, and patted powder on her face to whiten her complexion. She then sat on the porch swing, creaking it with back and forth motion. From afar she appeared the picture of complacency. From afar no one could notice her skipping heartbeats and the tightness in her throat as she waited on the porch for her husband's return.

And then she saw him.

How handsome he looked with his broad shoulders and dark hair neatly parted and flattened still, even in this late afternoon! How his long strides seemed purposeful! How his erect posture exuded confidence! It was easy to see how she had been captivated by him, so different from the men that had hung around her father's trading post. Here was a man who could protect her, she had thought. Here was a man whose promises of a life apart from reservation poverty had tempted her. But if she had ever loved him, she surely did not now. He did not raise her up. Forcing her to submit to his demands, he made her life miserable.

Once she had been pure and honest. Now, with him, she mostly lied.

"Welcome home!" she said sweetly, patting the space beside her. "Dinner is almost ready. Sit here with me awhile first" She raised her face, offering him a kiss. She took his hand and stroked his fingers the way he liked it. "I have something to tell you. Please don't be angry with me."

These were words she had used before. Normally they preceded a confession of a trivial action, and he expected the same. "Yes?"

"A relative came to visit today. A cousin of my mother. He is an old man and sickly," she lied. "I do not think he has long to live. His granddaughter has been placed in his care since her parent's death. He brought her to meet me." She stopped when his face darkened.

"I have told you time and time again, there will be no Indians in my home." His words were slow and measured, menacing.

"I know. I know. But I did not invite him, and the girl looked so sweet and helpless. A beautiful child. Intelligent." She bowed her head and lowered her eyes making harder for him to detect that her next words were lies. "He came because he heard how good you are to the people here. He came because he knows you want the children to learn new ways...to learn to read and write so they can live good lives...so they can forget the old ways. He now believes he wants this for his granddaughter."

So vain as to believe this, Bordeaux responded, "He is a wise man, then."

"Yes. I thought you would think so." She paused, a picture of meekness. "Mr. Bordeaux, you know I have always wanted children, but God has not given us any." She turned her tactics to use the

108

religion he had once embraced. "Maybe He has a special mission for you. Maybe He knew that you could change one child, one child to prove to others that they can do the same. The people would look up to you. The government would recognize how good you are."

"Perhaps," he said, thinking of the promotion he might get.

"The girl is here, Mr. Bordeaux."

"Here? Now? Without my permission you have a girl here?" He stood up, angry. "Where is she?"

"Please. Please. Don't be angry. She is inside. She is upset!"

"SHE is upset? I AM UPSET!" he roared. He pulled his arm back to slap her and was deterred only by the people who had walked by, turning their heads towards the commotion on the porch. "God damn you!" he hissed under his breath.

He stormed into the house looking left and right and saw Niglíču sitting stiffly on the couch. Three long strides had him standing before her. "Look at me!" he demanded. She raised her eyes and looked through him.

Forcibly, he cupped her chin and lifted her face. Narrowing her eyes, she tried to wrench her face away, but he held fast and lowered himself to her level. *I know this girl.*

Grandfather. Old. Orphan. Suddenly things seemed to fit. *We were going to send her to Carlisle.* A quick thinker, he saw the opportunity. *Fix her myself. Everyone knows how wild she was that day…dirty little animal facing the police! What a feather in my cap to subdue her!*

He released her, rose and turned around smiling. "She is beautiful," he said to Soft Feather. "You are right. I can fix her. I can kill the Indian in her. Just like I did in you. Wait and see!"

Soft Feather had escaped the beating but not the guilt she would carry watching her husband break the spirit in this little girl.

Again, Niglíču would not eat.

"When she is hungry enough, she will," Bordeaux calmly observed. If there was to be a battle of wills, he would win. He held all the cards.

Hours passed and still she did not respond, but she kept her eyes fixed on Bordeaux, a dull focused stare that seemed to him to have fire behind it. When night descended, Soft Feather dressed Niglíču in a long white cotton flouncy edged gown, far too big for her, and tucked her shiny hair into a nightcap.

"She needs proper clothing," Bordeaux observed. "Buy some tomorrow."

Soft Feather led Niglíču to the stairs and, after stumbling a few times trying to ascend them, Niglíču learned to hike up the front of the gown to free her feet. Mr. Bordeaux, amused, watched them just as he had watched the dressing of Niglíču too, which Soft Feather thought odd. When Niglíču lifted the front of her skirt too high, exposing her thighs, he smirked and thought with some satisfaction, that his work was going to be challenging. Even more interesting than the transformation of his wife!

Soft Feather opened the door to the small room with one window covered by a curtain of lace panels. The bed commanded the center of the room and was flanked by a nightstand on one side which held a single glass of water. Soft Feather provided an ornately lidded bowl for relief during the night, if needed. She spoke in a halting mix of Lakȟóta and English. She could not think of a Lakȟóta word for such a thing as a chamber pot. Nor could she find a word for the footstool next to it. "Oáli," she blurted out, but then laughed nervously to herself. "No, that means 'ladder'," she remembered. But Niglíču understood and climbed into the tall feather bed and lay down in its deep softness. She was exhausted and so gave in to the warmth of it. She submitted to the heavy covering, the tucking in and became still. *The woman is kind to me. Would Grandfather leave me with someone he did not trust?* She thought not, but now she wasn't sure of anything. Wasn't it just this morning that she had felt safe?

She did not sleep long. Lying still under the covers, Niglíču let her eyes travel across the harsh corners of the room. Lit by the moon, the flowered wallpaper did not make her feel like she was on her back in a meadow. *Was it supposed to? Was there a story behind the flowers that all looked the same?* The thípi covers in her village before had paintings that told stories. *Do these people have stories they are proud of?* Unreal wallpaper flowers: they were without a scent. Stiff wallpaper leaves: they were without a sway in the wind. All dead but trying to look alive. She turned her head to the left and to the right and felt the emptiness of space. The room was so big! She looked straight up, hoping to see moonlight peep through the smoke vents, but there was just the blackness of the solid ceiling. She listened for the heartbeat thump of the wind on a flexible buffalo hide but instead heard the wind slap the solid frame of the house, rattling the shutters.

The silence was not broken by the crisp crackle of a flaring ember or the soft snore of her grandfather, but by the hard echoing of voices raised in argument below her. How odd that voices should rise from beneath where she was to sleep. The sound seemed to come from within the complaining earth itself, and it frightened her.

She crawled up from beneath the covers and sat cross-legged on top. The gown twisted around her waist, constraining her, and she removed it and sat naked in the scant stream of moonlight that had found its way through the glass pane of the small, closed window. She walked over and spread her hand on the cold glass and felt a disconnection between the sky and herself. *What am I breathing if not the sky?* she thought. She had seen a window lifted before and marveled at its versatility and so she tried to raise this one, but she did not notice the nail hammered into the frame track that would make opening impossible. Suddenly feeling claustrophobic, she tiptoed over to the door and tried to gently turn the enameled handle. It would not turn. She remembered the kitchen door and the twig-like metal that made it impossible to open when it was inserted into a hole there. *I am a prisoner.* The events of the day plowed through her thoughts. Wasn't it just this morning that her grandfather woke her to the prospect of an adventure and a visit? What had gone wrong? What had she done that her grandfather no longer wanted her? If she escaped from here, where would she go? Who wanted her? Who needed her? Even more exhausted now, she pulled the blankets from the bed and made herself a twisted nest under the window and crawled into it, seeking womb-like comfort as moon shadows played over her sleeping form.

*****

"Mrs. Bordeaux, do *not* think I am pleased by what you did today. You had no *right* to do this!" When his voice was that stern, the veins on his neck throbbed. Soft Feather knew better than to comment. She stood with head bowed and accepted the tongue lashing. "Now that it is done, however, I will make some rules, and you had better follow them. Do you understand?" She nodded, with eyes toward the floor. "Number one: She will not leave this house *at all* until I say so. Is this understood?" Again, a nod. "Number two: We speak only English in this household. Only English!"

111

"But, Mr. Bordeaux, she knows no English."

"Then she will have to learn pretty quickly, don't you think? Well?"

"Yes."

"Good. That's enough for tonight, then. I will kill that Indian in her. Just wait and see! Didn't I fix you?"

"Yes."

"Now prepare for bed. I will be there shortly."

And soon after, if Niglíču had been awake, she would have heard the rhythmic groan of their bedframe.

*****

Čhuŋkšíuŋyaŋpi kiŋ mniákaštaŋ-wičhuŋkhiyapi kte.
We're going to have our daughter baptized.

Niglíču supposed she had been asleep because she, all at once, realized the brightness of the room. Such did not happen in a thípi. She did not move from her nest of blankets, though, even when she heard the click of the lock. When Soft Feather walked in, Niglíču remained under the covers. She had no intention of leaving them now unless she could get a clear path out of the room and out of the house.

"Good morning! How are you? Did you sleep well?" Soft Feather greeted, although it was clear to her that Niglíču had not slept well. The little girl tightly shawled herself with the blankets and did not answer. "Are you hungry?" Soft Feather asked. Then, with a look over her shoulder to see that Mr. Bordeaux was not around, she repeated in Lakȟóta, "Loyáčhiŋ he? *Are you hungry*?"

"Hiyá! *No!*"

"I heard that!" Mr. Bordeaux yelled from the hallway. "Teach her to say 'no' or, better yet, 'yes,' to whatever we say." Soft Feather could release her breath now. She thought her husband had heard her speak, too. "I will!" she responded cheerfully.

Soft Feather lifted away the blankets and noted with both understanding and dismay that the child was naked. "Stand up so I can dress you!" The room was cold and Niglíču shivered, her skin puckering even more when she realized Bordeaux stood in the doorway appraising her.

112

"Give her the clothes. She can dress herself."

He smiled, taking sadistic pleasure in watching the girl try to cover her nakedness with his wife's blouse.

Breakfast was a tense affair. Niglíču sulked before the plate of uneaten food, while Mr. Bordeaux rattled on about how appreciative she should be with this bounty before her. Soft Feather tried coaxing her to take at least a bite, but the girl rebuffed these efforts, and finally clamped a hand over her mouth, defiant.

"Let her starve then!" Mr. Bordeaux stormed. "Take her to her room and leave her there. She'll come around soon." He left the house without further word, and Soft Feather knew better than to disobey him.

"Wait here!" she told Niglíču. "I must go to the store to buy you clothing."

With no choice but to wait, Niglíču stared out the window. She saw Soft Feather leave and walk towards the store. She watched her return an hour later. That evening at dinner, Niglíču was led into the dining room and sat in the tall chair. Her stiff new clothing rubbed against her. Her socks and improperly sized shoes squeezed her wide feet used to walking barefoot. She had no choice but to wear them, but no one could make her eat. And so, she didn't.

The next few days brought little change. Niglíču drank enough water to survive but ate so little she became thinner, dark circles hanging beneath her eyes. Bordeaux's rule was that Niglíču should stay confined to her room until she behaved gratefully, but since the rule did not specifically state that she was to have no company there, Soft Feather brought up her rocking chair and spent most of the day sewing little girl dresses and speaking, in English, of various news and events while her husband was at work. She knew Niglíču did not understand most of what she said but she hoped her presence alone might be of comfort. How she wanted to speak to the girl in Lakȟóta! But she didn't dare. If ever her husband found out, this seeming truce between them might be shattered.

Nights were the loneliest times for Niglíču. Never before had she slept alone. Always some family member had been there. When she couldn't sleep, she stood in front of her window with both hands pressed flat against the cold glass.

Loud Bear could see her, although the glass played mirror for her, and she could not see him. Each night he checked on her and each night he reported back to Grasshopper that she was well, something he could not prove but hoped was true.

When four days passed with little progress, Bordeaux started to doubt himself. Neighbors noticed the little girl in the window and inquired when they could meet her. Husband and wife made excuses. *She does not feel well today. She still is shy.* But both Mr. and Mrs. Bordeaux knew these would be acceptable for only so long, and then it would indeed look like they were imprisoning the child. This would not sit well with Bordeaux's superiors.

What if I'm not successful? Enough people knew by now what he was attempting to do and so a failure would be disastrous, he thought, to his career. He needed a way to divert the potential failure from himself. The next morning he awoke with an ingenuous plan. If he failed, he would say it was God's fault...or God's plan...whatever worked best. And for this to be credible he would need the help of a priest. The new Jesuit? Bastiat?

Yes! He would find him and bring him home. Saddling his horse in the early dawn, he mounted the frisky mare and rode hard to the village where Fr. Bastiat was trying to establish his base parish. He found him at Mass, nearing the point of consecration, and so Bordeaux knelt as the lone parishioner to partake of the Eucharist.

"I need your help, Father," Bordeaux began. Bastiat's eyes brightened.

"A little Indian girl lives in our home and my wife and I would like you to baptize her so that she can become more completely a part of our small family...and a part of the Church, of course."

His first baptized Indian! How exciting! He was making no progress at all with his parish of zero attendants. "When would you like me to do this?" he asked.

"Today. This evening. Come for dinner to celebrate a new Catholic."

"I will. Gladly!"

Upon returning home, Bordeaux called to his wife, who was still upstairs with Niglíču. "Mrs. Bordeaux, we are having company for dinner! This house needs cleaning! Dinner needs to be planned. Come down here! Now!"

Soft Feather hurried down the stairs, but not before locking the door to Niglíču's room. "Who is coming? What is happening?" Her face was flushed in exasperation and that excited him. His hands

114

took hold of her shoulders and a wide smile spread across his face. "The new priest is coming for dinner! He will baptize the girl. His first baptism, he said! Won't that look good? All because of me!"

"Tonight?" She glanced around the room. There was much to do. She had been neglecting her usual duties and was surprised her husband had not noticed before. He saw her look. He noticed now.

"Don't worry! You have plenty of time! Leave her up there until you are ready to bathe and dress her and then you can bring her down when he comes!"

She frantically rushed around, dusting furniture and washing floors. She took a small ham out of the smokehouse and roasted it coated with honey, dug up and washed some potatoes and carrots stored in barrels in the root cellar and prepared to boil them til they were soft. Once done, she was finally ready to tackle the job of making Niglíču look ready to become a baptized Catholic. She went upstairs.

Although Soft Feather opened the door cautiously, a whirlwind of a child charged her, determined to rush past into whatever freedom she could find outside of that room. But Soft Feather was faster. Grabbing at the blur of motion, she latched onto the child's long hair and jerked Niglíču back into the soft, wide expanse of her bosom.

"Oh no, you don't, little cousin of mine. If you are to become my daughter, you will stay right here and do as I say, and what I say is that you are getting a bath and cleaned up because tonight a priest will baptize you and Jesus will make you happy again." How hollow those words sounded to her! How likely will a forced baptism make everything better?

Fr. Bastiat arrived right after the clock bonged for the sixth time. Hardly able to conceal his excitement, he had been waiting for the sound, standing off a bit behind some bushes. Bordeaux greeted him graciously at the front door and ushered him into the living room where he saw a little copper colored girl with hair piled on top of her head in contrived waves. With her head down, ringlets of curls shielded her face. She sat on an overstuffed chair as if she were glued in place, as well she might have been by the way Bordeaux glared at her when he thought he was not being watched. Bastiat had been a priest for a long time and so had observed many domestic situations. He was not comfortable with this one. *I think I know this girl. Why won't she look up so I can see her face?* It was only when

115

the girl was called for dinner that she raised her head in defiance. Her eyes flashed when she looked at him. *Niglíču! How did she end up here?*

Bastiat lost both appetite and enthusiasm watching Niglíču pick at her food. Encouraged to eat more, the priest declined, claiming the food delicious but filling. After Soft Feather had cleared all dishes, the talk turned to the baptism. But the questioning that came next surprised Bordeaux.

"Mrs. Bordeaux, are you Catholic?"

"Yes, I am."

"Do you believe in the basic tenets of the Holy Roman Catholic Church?"

"Excuse me, Father, the what?"

"When you recite the Apostles Creed you are saying them, the basic tenets. So, do you believe them?"

Looking at her husband, who nodded, she said, "Yes, of course!"

"You certainly do *not* believe that Jesus Christ is really present in that bread and wine at Mass, though, do you?"

She giggled involuntarily. "No, of course not." At that, Mr. Bordeaux got very red. Damn her! Of course she was supposed to believe Jesus was present!

"Mr. Bordeaux, when did you last attend Mass?"

"Why just this morning, remember?"

"And the last time you went to Confession?"

"I don't remember that, Father."

"Does this child know who Jesus is?"

"We both have spoken to her many times about the Holy Family. She knows how to make the Sign of the Cross. Show him, Niglíču." And he motioned with his hands for her to follow. She mimicked these actions without feeling. *It is better than being hit again*, Niglíču thought.

"When the person I baptize is beyond being an infant, it is my custom to interview her first. Would there be a place here where we can talk alone?"

Mr. Bordeaux looked annoyed.

"You may use her room, Father," Soft Feather offered.

They all walked up the stairs together. Bastiat noted that there was a key still in the keyhole of the bedroom door. "Thank you," Bastiat said, placing a hand on Niglíču's back to guide her inside. He looked

116

pointedly at Mr. Bordeaux while he pocketed the key, daring the Bordeauxs to object or say something, and then he gently closed the door in their faces.

Niglíču walked over to the window as she always did and placed two hands on the glass. Bastiat put his hand on her shoulder, ignoring the shrug that suggested he remove it.

"Niglíču, look at me." Maybe she did not understand, he thought. Surely she recognized him, but her eyes said nothing. "Listen to me," and he began repeating names; Grasshopper, Loud Bear, Kills In Winter, White Birch, Pretty Stone, but he said all this in English. And then finally he remembered the title of the person he had never met. "Iná," he said. "Your mother."

Niglíču whipped her head around. *There you are,* he said to himself and then said aloud to her, "Let me try to help you." Her eyes glazed over once again, and Bastiat knew she had retreated from the world. He stood beside her for a moment and then went to the door. The Bordeauxs were waiting in the hallway, looking anxious.

"I cannot baptize this child," he said. "She does not know what the sacrament is."

Infuriated, Bordeaux walked the priest to the door, never saying goodbye. It was not prudent to have such a man as Bordeaux as an enemy. Still, the priest wanted to help the child, but without her cooperation, and that of her new parents, there was nothing he could do. He returned to the small village depressed, but eager to find out how this child had ended up in a home he knew would destroy her.

Bastiat slept a troubled sleep that night, haunted by vivid dreams of being lost and alone in a strange land with no way to either communicate or escape. The dreams made him moan. His mouth was dry when he awoke and the taste in it was of an uncomfortable version of the former night's feast. There was yet some coffee in the pot brewed yesterday, so he poured the stale liquid into a cup, drank it all, but was unsuccessful in removing the bitterness in his mouth and in his heart.

Later, during Mass, as he raised the Host before the brass crucifix, the face on the corpus shimmered and Bastiat had to steady himself as dizziness overwhelmed him. For that split second, the face of Christ had become the face of Niglíču. *I am going crazy,* he thought, shaking his head.

117

He could not keep Niglíču out of his thoughts. Believing God had called him to help her, he was determined to meet Grasshopper that day and discover how she had ended up there.

*****

Grasshopper paced back and forth throughout the night. How could he sleep while he awaited the return of his grandson? Loud Bear had not returned with his report on Niglíču. Something must be wrong.

Kills stepped out into the dark night. "Come in. Go to sleep. Your grandson is not a boy. He will be back."

"Yes. Not a boy," but still Grasshopper was anxious. Loud Bear had changed. His anger had turned into bitterness and his bitterness into despair. Often, he smelled of mnišíča *bad water.*

*****

The sun had fully risen when Loud Bear stumbled through the dry buffalo grass on his way to the village. Bastiat heard the reed-rattling swoosh before he saw the young man weaving through it. *Loud Bear! What luck! Now I have an interpreter!*

"Loud Bear, may I speak with you for a moment?"

The excess of alcohol that had made Loud Bear giddy earlier in the night, now made him dizzy and foul tempered. Aching from the fight he should have avoided, outnumbered and doomed to defeat, he was in no mood to speak to a priest. Ignoring the greeting, he ambled on. Obligated to report to his grandfather, he dreaded the beratement he was sure to receive. Grasshopper had warned him about mnišíča and he, as usual lately, chose to ignore it.

Bastiat caught up to him. "Excuse me, but I need your help translating. I saw Niglíču yesterday and I'm concerned for her."

Scowling, Loud Bear turned to confront the priest, but the motion upset his balance and he swayed, about to fall. Bastiat reached out to steady him. Caught him.

Overreacting, Loud Bear whipped out his knife intending to threaten, but in trying to pull away from the priest, his knife tore through the black robe and nicked the priest's forearm.

"Aaaah! Bastard!" the priest yelled, clamping his hand over his arm to stop the bleeding. Seething, he turned back to his cabin.

118

Loud Bear's mistake sobered him, but his pride prohibited an apology. Realizing, though, that this hostile action towards a priest could land him in jail, Loud Bear trailed behind Bastiat and waited outside. Soon after, the priest appeared, the makeshift bandage on his arm mostly hidden by the torn sleeve.

Without apology, Loud Bear offered, "I will help you."

With implications that a refusal would have caused more trouble, the priest narrowed his eyes threatening and affirmed, "Yes. You will."

Grasshopper was, soon after, relieved seeing Loud Bear emerge from the clump of trees. But he was taken aback when he saw the priest following him.

"Tȟakóža, where have you been? Why is he with you?"

"I was where you told me to go. I watched the house. She is still there."

Walking up next to his grandson, Grasshopper became more aware of how inebriated the young man was. With obvious disgust and sarcasm, he said, "You have done more than I asked you to do."

"I am a warrior. You cannot tell me what to do."

"A warrior would not need to be told."

Answering the second question, Loud Bear said, "This priest wants to talk to you. I said I would help with the words."

The priest then told Grasshopper how sad and ill Niglíču looked. He said she was not the same girl he had seen a few weeks ago. He spoke of her blank look, her thinness, her apathy. That place is not good for her, he concluded.

Grasshopper nodded, clearly disturbed with this news.

"You said she was well?" he scolded Loud Bear. "You told me this every day!"

"How could I know without speaking to her? I saw her in the window. That's all."

The conversation became heated and Bastiat thought it best he leave. When he rose, the rip in his sleeve parted, exposing the fresh blood that had seeped through the bandaging.

Grasshopper rose too and put his hand on the priest's arm. "You are hurt?" He saw the look exchanged between the two other men. Something had happened between them.

"It is nothing," the priest said. "An accident." He left them, knowing he would return at another time.

When Bastiat was beyond the range of hearing, Grasshopper angrily confronted his grandson, and demanded an explanation. "You did that to him?"

"He grabbed me."

"You are a fool! Their holy man? He will remember this."

"It is but a scratch!"

"He will report you. You endanger us all by your stupidity. Do you remember how you told the People how much you despised the ways of the wašíču? Do you remember? And now you have taken their bottle and behave like the worst of them!"

Loud Bear knew the insult was justified and he was embarrassed. But he could not bring himself to admit it to his grandfather and so he hardened his face. "I will check on my cousin tonight," he asserted and then, without further talk, he left.

While acknowledging the priest's bravery, Grasshopper wondered if he should trust the man's words about Niglíču. *But what reason could he have to lie?*

*****

Wičhíŋčala kiŋ owáyawa-ta gloí.
She took her girl to school.

"What did she say to him? I'm going up there and knock some sense into that ..." Bordeaux was livid. Soft Feather placed herself between him and the stairs.

"Don't stand in my way! Move!"

"You will *not* touch that girl!"

"I won't? Try and stop me!" He moved to push her aside, but her bulk served her well now.

"Move or I'll ...."

"Do what?" she said in a low, steady voice. "Hit me? Again? Do it then and see what kind of promotion that will get you."

"Bitch!" he spat, walking away. Soft Feather went up the stairs and locked herself in the room with Niglíču. She smiled to herself. It was a good thing she had the only other key.

"Tonight, we will sleep together, little one. And tomorrow I will take you to a new school."

Soft Feather felt better than she had in years. Confident. Proud of herself for standing up to him. *I'm not alone now. I have relatives. I have choices now. Maybe my mother's cousins...MY cousins...will take me under their protection. Maybe I do not have to stay here in this ugly house, cooking and cleaning and satisfying this evil man. I can take care of the girl there. I can raise her as my own there.*

Soft Feather removed the pins from her hair, and the black veil of it fell well below her shoulders. Niglíču watched. Something about the action made her think of her mother. Soft Feather shook her head, freeing herself of the curls, and there was a look of animal satisfaction on her face. The woman raised her chin in confidence, and Niglíču found she wanted to be near her. Soft Feather lifted her dress over her head and then began loosening the whalebone corset. She slipped it down to the floor and stepped out of it easily and then stood up and raised her arms high in a stretch that cared not that outlines of her voluptuous rolls of flesh could be seen under the cotton shift she wore. She walked over to Niglíču and undressed her too, and then she brushed the girl's hair into the straightness she was born with. Soft Feather jiggled the nail in the window track until she could pull it out and then she opened the window wide. Cold air rushed in. Taking Niglíču's hand, she walked over to the bed and thus out of sight of Bordeaux, who stood below the window, watching. He started walking towards town.

Niglíču did not feel that the softness of the feather bed was so suffocating when her body rested against that of Soft Feather. She had rolled into the pit made by the woman's heavy body and felt peace wash through her. For the first night in several, she slept peacefully.

In fact, they slept well past the dawn and well past the time Bordeaux left for his duties as agent. For the first time in years, Soft Feather felt free to speak Lakhóta, and the two spoke almost as relatives would of people they knew and customs they once had shared. Niglíču even smiled. Soft Feather convinced her that attending the local school taught by former Carlisle students would be on a trial basis. "Try it," Soft Feather had told her. "If you do not feel comfortable there, we can try something else."

Niglíču felt a nervous happiness while walking hand in hand with Soft Feather to the one room school. *It's like an adventure,* Niglíču thought, but then she thought of the last "adventure" she had looked forward to ... the one that landed her there with Soft Feather ....

Maybe this will be alright. Maybe ....

Once outside the schoolhouse, they walked through a noisy group of children playing near the teacher supervising them from the schoolhouse steps. After a gentle push, Niglíču shyly left Soft Feather's side to go to him. As the teacher led her inside the building, she turned once to look back at Soft Feather, who was wiping tears from her eyes.

"Come with me," the kind teacher said.

Soft Feather slowly walked home, her thoughts filled with plans for her new daughter and herself. She did not, however, return in the afternoon to pick Niglíču up from school. By then she had died. Mr. Bordeaux said he found her body at the bottom of the staircase when he returned home that afternoon. He said it appeared as though she had accidentally fallen.

*****

Waná išnála okáptapi.
She was the only one left.

When Niglíču first saw her tall and handsome Lakȟóta school teacher, she wondered what he had done that made him so ashamed that he cut his hair short. It was not as short as the wašíču, but still, it did not even reach his shoulders. She could not have understood that he had just recently graduated from Carlisle and his hair had not yet grown back. Sympathetic to the confusion a child new to any sort of formal education would experience, he crouched before her, smiling during the introductions, and extended his hand. She took it reluctantly and entered the schoolroom. The eyes of fifteen children followed her as the teacher guided her to the front row bench on which sat other children of her age.

"Class, this is Niglíču. She visits us today to see how she likes our school. Niglíču lives with Mr. and Mrs. Bordeaux. You may know Mr. Bordeaux is an agency clerk."

She was told, in English, to sit and that command she remembered from the Bordeauxs. She held the gray slate slab and white chalk on her lap the way the other children were doing. She watched the teacher guide the chalk into making pointy shaped figures on the big slate attached to the wall. These looked nothing like the figures she saw on painted thípi. These looked nothing like the drawings children scratched into the mud by the creek. And yet they must have told a story because when the teacher stuck each figure with an arrow like stick, the children, all together, made a sound.

Perhaps this was a game, Niglíču thought. Perhaps the figures were a sort of poor animal drawing and once struck, the children would cry out the pain the animal felt. "Ahh, Buh, Cuh, Duh, Eh." Strangely, the teacher found this game important and so began emitting the cries while the children drew those and other odd shapes on their boards. *How strange the wašíču ways were!*

When this game was through, the teacher passed out books to each child. Such a mysterious thing was this book. When Niglíču opened hers, she jerked back in surprise. The ink drawings of the trees, animals, and people were all upside down! The little girl next to her took the book away and handed it back, right side up. Niglíču felt foolish.

The little school was lucky to have these old McCuffey Primers, and the teacher watched that the children handled them carefully.

The children all pointed at the words as they recited together from the first lesson.

"A rat ... a cat ... a cat ... a rat ... a cat and a rat ... a rat and a cat ...."

Later, an assigned pupil collected the books and then distributed Ray's Arithmetic. The first lesson had pictures of balls labeled one to ten. The first row of children counted while pointing to the balls.

"One ...one, two...one, two, three ..."

They continued up to ten. Niglíču realized what they were doing and tried to memorize the sounds of counting. Seeing his new student taking part, the teacher helped her along.

"Yes! Good! One, waŋzí ... two, núŋpa ... three, yámni ...."

Finally, Niglíču understood something! She relaxed. It seemed, though, that they were sitting still for a very long time and it was growing uncomfortable. Niglíču stood up to stretch and walk around. There was immediate silence.

"What are you doing?" the firm voice of the teacher said. Niglíču did not know what the words were, but she knew she was being reprimanded. *Why?* The teacher pointed to her seat and then used words she had learned at the Bordeaux household: "Sit down!" She sat, unhappily. School was not so nice anymore, and she was getting hungry. Her stomach growled. The room got warm and Niglíču realized from the short shadows near the windows that it was midday already. The morning had gone quickly.

The situation improved dramatically once the teacher announced lunchtime and recess. All the children became excited and ran to get their lunch bundles or pails. They took them outside and sat on the grass, but Soft Feather had neglected to give Niglíču any lunch in the morning's excitement. Niglíču sat apart watching the others eat until the teacher's wife, noticing, gave her some warm bread. An older boy sat next to her and asked, in Lakȟóta, where her family was and why was she living with the Bordeauxs. She replied nicely that her family was away for a while and so she was staying with her cousin. An image of her mother doing beadwork floated up from her memory and then this turned into Soft Feather sewing clothing. The two images vacillated. Soft Feather was doing beadwork. Wind Woman was sewing dresses. Then the images became smoky until it seemed they were of the same person. Niglíču started to sweat.

The distraction of a game of tag erased the images and Niglíču raced with the others round and round the schoolhouse on well-worn paths until the children all collapsed in a heap, one on top of the other with Niglíču underneath a lighter skinned boy. The sun glinted red in the highlights of his hair, and Niglíču's mind flashed back to the day a wašíču had killed her mother. She became her mother in her heart and the boy became that man who had killed her and she cried in terror and beat her fists against the unsuspecting boy who stood up as fast as he could and prepared to face her. The teacher was there in a second to intervene, standing between them, but the fire had left Niglíču, and she knelt with head nearly touching the ground as she rocked forward and back. The teacher turned to the children gathered in a circle around her and whispered, "She was at the massacre." They stepped back.

The subdued children returned to the classroom with the teacher while the schoolteacher's wife tried to console Niglíču. Only one thought swirled in Niglíču's head. *Iná, my mother, is dead. Dead. Dead. Dead!*

Niglíču was not aware of much else that went on in the classroom that day until a large map was unrolled and tacked to the exposed inner wood of the log cabin schoolhouse.

"This is a map of the United States of America. We often write it in abbreviated form. U. S. A. This is the country in which we live.

This is the country you are a part of now."

"Mílaháŋska Tȟamákȟočhe. Long Knife Country," an older boy known for some belligerence, blurted out.

"*Your* country, now," the teacher corrected. "Yours as much as theirs! And here," he said, tapping with that smooth stick again, "is South Dakota. South Dakota has been a state for almost two years."

Niglíču had a limited understanding of maps. Her grandfather had traced map-like images on the ground when he went hunting. It piqued her interest.

"Now," the teacher exclaimed as he unrolled another map to tack on top. "This is a map just of South Dakota. We are here," he said, pointing to Pine Ridge. "And these are the Badlands," he stated, pointing towards a lower portion of the western side.

"Makȟóšiča, the bad land they gave to us for farming," the belligerent one said. Niglíču could see the teacher getting annoyed. Niglíču did not understand the word "farming."

"And here," the teacher pointed further northwest and tapped harder on the map, "are the Black Hills--."

The same student interjected again. "The good land—Ȟesápa— they took away from us." The look that flitted over the teacher's eyes suggested he might agree with the boy's sentiment.

The lesson continued with cities and towns and resources, and the words flew over Niglíču's head as she studied the map, trying hard to understand what the symbols meant. That blue line was water, she could see. If she headed anywhere northwest, she would have to run into it. Her thoughts surprised her. *Headed? Am I going anywhere?*

As the school day neared closing and the children were working independently, practicing their numbers and letters, Niglíču walked up to the map. She placed her right hand on Pine Ridge and, with her left, she traced her way to the Black Hills. The teacher watched her. He knew she had most probably been told of the sacred importance of the Black Hills. He did not know that the Wasúŋ Wóniya Wakȟáŋ, or Wind Cave in those sacred hills, had always fascinated her. He could not know that in the course of his teaching, she had decided she would find this entrance to the spirit world and journey there to be with her mother. The teacher walked up to her. He pointed to both places and said the English words, wanting her to repeat them. She did, and he was pleased that finally she was participating. Her bright eyes that he mistook for curiosity in learning were not for that reason

125

at all. She was afraid. What she had decided to do would take courage. She wasn't sure when she would leave though. And she wasn't sure how long it would take to get there. The map only showed she was here and it was there. The space in between those two places didn't look long. She could find berries to eat along the way. It didn't matter if she arrived hungry. The spirit world would provide food. Her mother would feed her.

A bell rang and the other students stood up immediately, smiling. "What? What?" she asked the girl beside her.

"We're going home now. School is finished for today."

Niglíču watched a group of siblings walk from the play area. She watched a mother hug her child. A grandmother came and took the hands of two boys, leading them away.

"Your new mother will come soon. She must not have known the time we end," the teacher's wife said.

Soon, every child was gone. Both teacher and wife were cleaning the school room. Niglíču sat on the bottom step and waited. Waited more. *I am all alone. No one comes for me.* She walked away from the school, down the path. All alone was a scary feeling. She started to shiver. She started to remember that day. Flashes. *There was the knife. I gave it to Iná. There was a man who was hurting her. Cutting her. With the knife. The knife I gave her.*

"Iná, I'm sorry…"

She started to run…northwest.

*****

Šinásapa wičháša wakháŋ kiŋ Niglíču olé.
The priest went looking for Niglíču.

As Bastiat was walking into town, he saw a small funeral procession coming towards him, heading to the cemetery. A solitary figure, dressed in black, walked directly behind the wagon carrying the coffin and a handful of mourners processed after. As it caught up to him, he stopped in respect and stood to the side of the road to let it pass. His hand, raised in a Sign of the Cross blessing, caught the eye of the black suited mourner and Bastiat recognized Bordeaux, who quickly looked away.

I wonder who died? thought the priest. A sick feeling knotted his

126

stomach. *Not the girl. Please, not the girl!* That the coffin was too big for a child reassured him this could not be the girl who was being mourned. He walked on, passing by the few curious people who watched the procession pass. One old man called to him.

"Father, I am surprised they did not ask you to say something over the grave. After all, you were just there a few nights ago."

"Do I know you?" Bastiat responded warily.

"I don't think so, Father, but my name is Peters and I pride myself in knowing what goes on around here. It's a small town. Hard to hide anything."

"Hide?"

"Why, that there was Mrs. Bordeaux, gone to meet her Maker all of a sudden-like."

"Soft Feather Bordeaux?"

"That's the one. Bordeaux says he found her all twisted and dead at the bottom of the stairs. Maybe that Injun kid they had pushed her."

"Surely they don't suggest she did!"

"I don't know about that, but I do know the girl went missing."

"Missing? They don't know where she is?"

"Well, the Injuns might, but I can tell you, Bordeaux doesn't. It's a wonder they aren't out searching for the kid now."

Bastiat reversed course and hurried towards the Lakȟóta village. *She wouldn't have killed Soft Feather. Maybe Bordeaux,* he smirked, *but not her. Maybe...and probably...the woman just fell...an accident...but where is the girl?*

He was out of breath when he reached Grasshopper's thípi.

"Where's Niglíču?"

Grasshopper and Kills were standing outside, and neither could understand the priest's fast speech, a frantic rambling of words and hand motions that attracted the attention of others.

White Birch knew more English than the others. She stepped forward and told the priest to slow his words so she could understand.

Grasshopper fired questions at her. "What does this Black Robe mean? Who is dead? Where is my granddaughter? What happened?"

Bastiat tried to piece the scenario together, but he was guessing, his heart pounding with concern. *It was only assumed that Niglíču ran away. And if she did, wouldn't she be there now? She had already followed the road. She wouldn't have gotten lost! Maybe she's.....* He couldn't bring himself to say..."dead too."

127

Search parties were formed. Groups were sent out to traverse the land between the town and their village. They would cover the entire area. They would not let up until she was found. Word of her disappearance reached the school and then other pieces of the puzzle slid into place. Yes, she was there. Yes, all day. She could not have pushed Soft Feather. Yes, she left alone.

The priest wanted to join in the search, but he could not ignore the crushing need for prayer. He felt God pushing him to his knees. *Pray! Ask and you shall receive!*

When else have I prayed like this? Yes! For my wife! But what good did it do? Where were you then, Lord?

In response, he heard Isaiah's verse: *for my thoughts are not your thoughts and your ways are not my ways, declares Yahweh. For the heavens are as high above earth as my ways are above your ways, my thoughts above your thoughts.*

"Tell me then, Lord! I don't know your thoughts! I don't know your ways now! Tell me!" the priest cried out loud, kneeling before the crucifix.

"Seek and you shall find."

There was a new moon that night. Some men continued to search in the blackness, but Niglíču still wasn't found.

Father Bastiat slept, bent over in prayer. When he awoke, stiff and painful, his mind was suddenly clear. *They are looking in the wrong places. Niglíču would never run away back to this village. She felt unwanted. She would run from it.*

Thank-you Lord!

But he'd need a horse if he was searching. There were a few in the village. Maybe he could borrow one? He ran to the village, surprised he could still run at all after all the years walking. There, next to a thípi was an old swayback. There next to the thípi was an old man taking burrs from the horse's mane.

"I need your horse! Can I use your horse?" The priest motioned with his hands, hoping to convey the message. "The horse! The horse! I will look for Niglíču!" The old Indian understood then and nodded yes. "Go!" he said. "Look" he said.

The horse was without an American bridle but the old man fitted a leather thong in his mouth and handed the end of the reins to the priest. Bastiat mounted quickly. Riding bareback was not new to him. With his robe draping over the horse's hindquarters, Bastiat urged the horse into a trot. He rode well, being familiar with horses, and the old gelding responded with more enthusiasm than the priest expected. Alternating trot and fast pacing, the priest reached the schoolhouse as the teacher was preparing for the day. After a brief introduction and explanation for the visit, Bastiat grilled him.

"Think!" Bastiat said, "Was there anything to suggest where she might go? Think! Anything!"

The teacher relived the day. Reading lessons. Math. Then the map. *What is it about the map?* "I do remember something now."

"What?"

"She was tracing this map with her hands. One hand was resting on Pine Ridge. See, come here and I will show you!" They walked over to the map and the teacher imitated Niglíču's hand motions. Bastiat's mind worked quickly. He could not imagine where she was heading, but if she went northwest, she would have to hit the river. There was no way around it. And if she had no food or means of obtaining it, she just might stay by the river. Thanking the teacher, he hurried off towards the northwest, intending to ride up and down that river until he found her. It was a longshot he knew, but the only lead he had.

*****

Niglíču started her escape walking. She skirted the town but saw a lot of activity near the Bordeaux house and figured they were about to search for her. She felt sorry she was hurting Soft Feather. She vowed if she could leave the spirit land, she would go back and explain. Someday. Then she ran. There were no landmarks that she recognized. At first that did not frighten her. She would just run into the wind. Isn't that what the teacher said? The cold wind came from there? Isn't that where she wanted to go? And the wind that evening was cold. It penetrated her cotton dress. When it started to get dark, she found hills in the distance that she could head for in the morning. Maybe she would run into a stream. She was thirsty.

Exhausted, she decided lying in a niche between some rocks would protect her for the night. They did block the wind, but they did not keep her warm. She covered her legs in the sandy earth, burying them.

Her lips were dry and cracking when she woke up, and when she stretched them in a yawn, they bled. She dabbed at them with the back of her hand, smearing the blood, and then sucked her lips into her mouth, swallowing the bloody drops that oozed out. She was so thirsty! She was so hungry! Had she traveled a straight path to the northwest, she would have been near the White River by now, but as it was, she had zigzagged around rock formations and still had about five more miles to go. Motivated by thirst, she brushed off the dirt and got up to leave.

The day turned hot. Finally, she stumbled upon a tributary leading to the river and she stood in the barely wet bed of it and scooped out handfuls of mud until a puddle formed. From this she drank, and of this she vomited. The wet mud attracted insects, and they flew around her, biting when they could. She stamped at them, leaving angry little girl footprints in the mud. Slipping, she struggled up the small embankment and followed alongside the tributary, hoping it would lead to fresh water. By the end of the day, she reached White River, and she threw herself into its cloudiness and drank freely of it. Her wet dress clung to her as she propped herself up against a steeper bank, falling into a deep sleep.

She was more than reluctant to leave the river. She was terrified of leaving it. There was water and never had she felt such thirst. She drank. She bathed. She drank some more and even was brave enough to eat some crayfish raw and so partially satisfied her hunger. She feasted on late blackberries growing along the bank. She looked to the northwest and saw endless miles of walking. *What if I never find the Wind Cave? Maybe I should stay here? Maybe I can find my way back to Grandfather?*

Hungry and so chilled, Niglíču looked for a place to sleep that night. The limestone and volcanic ash sediments that gave the river its name had been carved away from the riverbank at a curve leaving an alcove protected on three sides. Niglíču gathered dried grasses and made herself a nest there. Protected from the wind, Niglíču huddled into it and slept.

*****

Bastiat was no fool. He knew he would travel into territory that was unknown to him and realized he should go prepared. He rode through town and stopped at Kooken's store. The owner looked at

130

the disheveled priest and gave him his immediate attention, now ignoring the women fingering the bolts of cloth while asking him questions about its quality.

"What can I get for you today, Father?"

"I need some supplies. A canteen, jerky, matches, a knife, and yes, do you have a used rifle that is in good working condition? You do? Yes, then that too ... and some bullets. Oh, and a compass."

These seemed unusual items for a priest to buy all at once. The owner gathered the products and totaled the bill.

"Add this to my account, please," Bastiat said as he hurried out the door with the owner looking incredulously after him. Kooken turned once again to the women. "I wonder what he is up to," he said. "Is he going to shoot those that don't convert?"

Stuffing what he could into the pouch he wore slung across his chest, crowding the small New Testament of the Bible within, Bastiat mounted the horse and felt prepared for the journey. He had not used a compass in years but managed to find northwest and headed in that general direction. It did not take long before he noticed the old chestnut he was riding was not sound. His gait suggested his left hind leg was lame, for the tip of the hoof sometimes dragged over the ground. He knew then he could not push this horse too hard, or he might do a lot of solitary walking.

The terrain soon became studded with rocks and the horse stumbled frequently but righted himself. He looked almost embarrassed about the faltering, but he did not need to be coaxed forward. "You are a tough old gentleman, aren't you?" Bastiat observed out loud, and the horse twitched back his ears to listen. When the terrain became harder to maneuver, Bastiat dismounted, sparing the horse his weight, and they walked together, with Bastiat cradling the big horse's head in the crook of his arm. "You need a name," he said as he affectionately pinched and jiggled the sagging lower lip of the horse, who shook his head, clearly disliking the action. They walked a little further until the terrain became flat and smoother, and Bastiat let the horse graze a little before remounting. "I shall call you Ned. And Ned, we have places to go and now we must hurry."

Hurrying would have been easier if Bastiat knew where he was hurrying to. The land opened flat around him and his chest seemed to expand with it. He zigzagged through the plains that lay between

Pine Ridge and White River, looking for a trace of a young girl passing through. Ned appeared quite bored with this adventure and hung his head, tired now from doing more on this day than he had in recent years. When darkness came, Bastiat hobbled the horse and let him graze while he stretched out on a bed of gathered buffalo grass, tucked his hands into the sleeves of his robe and gazed at the stars. They felt so close to him he reached out one arm and pretended to touch the North Star, the only one he knew, and then stretched out his other as though to embrace all of them. Instead of feeling them within his hug, he felt they swallowed him up whole and that he was now a part of that magnificence, swimming in the sea of it, losing himself in the process and finding he was actually all of it. His breathing stopped and all motion around him followed suit and the individual sounds of the night harmonized into a single voice and he knew he was hearing God. "This is prayer," he thought. "Dear God, help me find the girl!"

*****

The cool night had left him stiff, and standing up was difficult. No longer could he just sit up and then rise as he had as a young man. He rolled over and onto his knees and then boosted himself up from there and, as he raised his head upon standing, he saw before him the rich orange of Ned's chestnut coat illuminated by the rising sun. Ned tossed his head and walked over, apparently refreshed. Bastiat appraised him. Ribs were exposed but Bastiat was confident he *he?* could fix that with some grain. He ran his fingers down the barrel of the horse's chest and indulged in a secret pleasure he had enjoyed as a blacksmith. By tucking his hands into the armpits of the horse, his cold stiff fingers were warmed. Bastiat laughed at himself, and the horse whinnied. He next slid his hands over the old muscles of the horse, and tracing them, found them firm still, and was surprised he had not noticed before the brand on his left thigh. He had seen the US brand on Ned's left shoulder, but this newly discovered brand of 7C made Bastiat wonder if this horse of the 7th Cavalry was one of a few that had survived Custer's last battle. Some quick calculations would make this horse at least twenty years old, but upon peering into Ned's mouth, it seemed the horse was younger.

"What sights have you seen, Ned?" Bastiat wondered as his

affection for the horse grew.

Putting aside thoughts of a hearty farm breakfast, as he was feeling very alive that morning, and hungry, he satisfied himself with some jerky and set off again on the search. He knew Ned had to be thirsty and so he let the heightened senses of the animal lead him to water. It was not too far away; although, from a distance, the tributary was unnoticeable beyond the tall grasses. Luckily, a distant thunderstorm had soaked enough water onto the soil for this little stream to flow. Both man and horse, side by side, drank from it. Bastiat stood up, stretched, and looked around. Further upstream, he saw what appeared to be indentations in the mud on the bank. He walked towards them eagerly.

Upon closer inspection, Bastiat's heart was thrilled to recognize the footprints of a child. Perhaps he had been right! Again, man and horse zig zagged over and back across the tributary to pick up the trail even as the day grew hot and Bastiat's black robe became suffocating under the intense sun. A sweaty foam bubbled at Ned's mouth. Bastiat dismounted. He would walk the horse.

Bastiat unbuttoned the top of the robe and stretched the opening, feeling the heat of his body rise out of it. He unbuttoned more and then finally, with a look to heaven for forgiveness, lifted the robe over his head and stood in his short-sleeved, white union suit. *Why not?* he thought to himself. And having gone this far, he bent down and pulled up his pant legs. Looking down on himself with his manhood clearly outlined and his feet enclosed in bulky boots, he laughed again. He was feeling so free! *What is it about this land that makes me feel so?* He unbuttoned the top of his underwear and felt a breeze tickle his hairy chest. "How good it feels to be alive and here in this place!" he said in thanksgiving to his God as he rode off towards the White River.

With the use of the compass, he arrived at the White River further north than had Niglíču. He wasn't a good tracker, but he searched, going northeast against the river flow, and when the first few miles yielded nothing, he changed directions and headed downstream. He knew she was somewhere along the river; she had to be, his heart said.

And then he saw her; her crumbled body lying by the river's edge.

*****

133

Hačhóla Šuŋk'ákaŋyaŋke glí.
He Who Rides Without Clothes has returned.

He desperately hoped she was just sleeping. Ned splashed noisily downstream and yet she did not move. His heart raced as he dismounted and walked towards her. With his shadow covering her, he observed her breathing; slow and shallow, but steady. His impulse was to take her in his arms, but he decided she would startle and try to run and then, when he caught her, she would be frantic. He wondered if he should just sit there and wait for her to wake up, which seemed strangely logical, but this, too, would spook her when she opened her eyes. Sitting beside her little shelter, he forgot what he wasn't wearing, but closed his eyes and remembered his mother sitting next to him when he had pneumonia as a child. Fevered and almost delirious with it, he had drifted in and out of consciousness to the sound of her singing. He remembered the peace it gave him, and so he sang softly. He looked at her intently, willing her to hear his whispered hymns, but as he sang, she became more like a daughter and he less like a priest. His songs changed to those of his mother's.

Au clair de la lune
Mon ami Pierrot
Prete-moi ta plume
Pour écrire un mot.

He placed his hand on her arm ever so gently, and she murmured. He stroked it gently, and she grumbled. He lifted a lock of her hair from over her eyes and her eyes twitched and then opened. She saw him as though still in a dream. He saw her muscles tighten. He sang softly again and did not meet her wide eyes with his own. Knowing she was preparing to bolt, he rested his hand around her wrist, and she knew from the firmness of it that he had captured her.

"Niglíču. OK," he said, pointing to himself. Looking at her, he continued, "I am good." *Surely she knew the word good.* You are good." He knew that sounded ridiculous, but how else could he tell her she was safe with him? She shivered as she sat up. Bastiat watched but still held her hand, not trusting that she would stay with him. *And why should she?* He thought of the way he was dressed. *Does she even recognize me?* He then reached into his pouch and

134

withdrew a long piece of jerky and handed it to her. She grabbed it greedily, hunger taking precedence over all else.

He motioned for her to stand and pulled gently. She rose hesitantly and then collapsed. He caught her as she fell and her body against his felt hot. She was more than just exhausted. She was sick and shivering harder now.

His priesthood preparation had not included training to care for the physically ill. The only other experience with the sick he had had was caring for his wife before she died. He got down on his knees, holding her limp body to his chest, and prayed. "Help me, Father! Please God, help me!" She moaned awake and fought him. Certain she did not know who he was, he called her name again and again. In her near delirium, there was no recognition, and she clawed at him and kicked him until it appeared the only way to subdue her was to wrap her in something. *But what?* He had brought no blanket, which he now regretted. His robe, draped over Ned's neck, was several feet away. *But he was a military horse, after all,* Bastiat thought. *Would he come when called?* Bastiat whistled.

Standing at attention at once, Ned raised his head and ambled over. While struggling with a tiring Niglíču under one arm, Bastiat grabbed his robe, and pinning the girl's arms to her body, wrapped the robe twice around her tightly. With difficulty, and surprised that he could even do this at all, Bastiat mounted Ned with the girl tucked under his arm. She struggled when he sat her before him, but Bastiat saw that the fever was again taking hold and she was weakening. Wrapping his arms around her, he urged Ned into his fastest walk in what he hoped was a direct line to Grasshopper's thípi, several miles away.

It was nightfall when Bastiat rode into the village with Niglíču sleeping against his chest. The people cheered when they saw Niglíču, and for that moment, Bastiat felt a warrior's pride. There were tears in Grasshopper's eyes when he saw his granddaughter and he held out his arms to her. Bastiat unwrapped her and lowered her into them. Her fever was raging now, and she unaware of her surroundings. All attention focused on the girl and her grandfather.

Slinging his robe over his shoulder, Bastiat regretfully led Ned back to the old man who owned him. But this grateful old warrior refused the reins handed to him and shouted a stream of Lakȟóta words into the gathered crowd, who cheered once again. The priest did not know, at first, that he was being gifted this horse for the rescue of the girl, and he did not know for quite a while that the gleeful old man had also given him his Lakȟóta name, Hačhóla Šuŋk'ákaŋyaŋke *He Who Rides Without Clothes*.

Part Two

137

Chapter 1
1892

Šínasapa kiŋ owáčhekiye thípi waŋ káǧe.
The Black Robe builds a church.

He had to agree with the men who had hauled the lumber to the site. His new church was unusual.

"But Father," they said looking at the stone foundation footprint, "your church would be wider than long if you put the door there."

"That's true," he had replied, "but you have to imagine that this will someday just be the vestibule for the big church I will build here someday."

"Do many people come here for worship?"

"Not yet. But they will."

That optimistic outlook faded as the weeks went by. If he was lucky, a handful of people came to his outside Mass and these, mostly women who were friends with Pretty Stone and White Birch. The two cousins came to Mass faithfully every day and might someday become his first baptized converts.

It was the day before Palm Sunday, April 9,1892, and now, after a winter spent constructing the building, it was done…or done enough to celebrate Mass inside. The long windows in the shape of a cross that streamed the morning sun onto the altar had no glass, but the waxed paper would have to suffice until he could get more funds. Fr. Bastiat opened the double doors centered opposite the altar and looked in. *Impressive! And I built it myself!*

He would leave the doors open all day he decided. Maybe someone would be curious and go inside. Taking his knife, he walked to the river. There were tall reeds there...cattails he called them… and he would use these instead of palm branches to decorate his church.

The next morning, he chided himself for thinking this first day of Holy Week would be different than the others.

No people had come to Mass that first Palm Sunday of his mission. No one held reeds aloft to be sprinkled with holy water from a shiny aspergillum. No one. How disappointed he was! But he made excuses for them. It had rained in the early morning hours. Maybe they didn't know this Mass would be celebrated inside.

If only I could speak their language. Then I could make them understand! Then they'd come.

Obviously, the people could not comprehend the words used in his Latin Mass. But he wanted them to understand at least the Gospel readings! He had sent away for some translations but he so mangled the pronunciation that he doubted anyone could draw meaning from them.

Deciding he would not let his blessed "palm" branches go to waste, he carried them into the village and distributed one to anyone would take it. "Holy" he said to each recipient, indicating the reed. "Wakȟáŋ."

While he was in the village, Niglíču was in the church. Since her rescue, she had little contact with this priest and, as ill as she was, she barely remembered the experience at all. Mostly she remembered feelings rather than actual events. She remembered her initial panic when his hand gripped her wrist. But she also remembered how safe she later felt with his arms around her. That remembered comfort confused her. He was a wašíču *white man*…but he did not feel like an enemy. He gave her magic to dye her doll's skin. And he had given her the stone. Made it for her. She wanted to trust this man.

Throughout the building process, she had spied on him, curious. When the dark-skinned boy visited the priest, she even felt a little jealous of their friendship.

Now, thinking herself alone in the church, she explored it. She touched the ink drawings tacked along the walls. A man tortured. Women crying. A whip. A thorny headdress. Nails. Death. *Who was this man? Why was he so wakȟáŋ that the priest draws his story?* She stood behind the table, not understanding it was an altar. *At Soft Feather's house, we ate around a table but there are no chairs here. Just planks of wood over there to sit on.* The lectionary lay atop the altar. She lifted the heavy cover and stared at the print, remembering her only day at school. *A-a. Ah*. She found the second sign and traced its mystery with her finger. *B-b. Buh.*

Bastiat had returned and found her there, now his time to spy. He watched her turn the pages identifying the two letters and smiling at the game she was creating. Over and over, she tapped the book, presumably on the two letters she sounded out each time. *A-a Ah. B-b Buh.*

She wants to read!

He closed his wet eyes and prayed. *Dear God...let me teach her...*

*****

The spring boreal chorus frogs were particularly noisy that early April Tuesday night of Holy Week, and their call made him lonely for the spring peepers of New York. One night the world was silent and then the next a far call would be heard and then finally an explosion of spring sound. "Winter is over," the tiny frogs sang in New York and here their South Dakota counterparts echoed the sentiment.

Bastiat sat outside in the dark, planning. *These people will see Holy Week. They might not understand what I do...they probably won't participate... but they will see it!* He hugged the blanket around himself and walked to the church to lock the doors for the night. Inside his dark cabin, he knelt in prayer. *Jesus... Passover Lamb....Jesus, who takes away the sins of the world, have mercy on us..."*

Awakening to bird song, the priest boiled water for his coffee and went outside to feed Ned. The lean-to backed against a cabin wall provided minimal shelter for the horse, but the animal adapted, his thick wooly coat starting to shed now with warmer weather. The extra grain, an expense the priest couldn't easily afford, had fattened the horse. No longer did ribs show.

He walked over to the church and opened the doors wide and then went back inside his cabin to get the necessities for Mass. Four women stood outside the church door. Delighted, Bastiat ushered them in to sit in the front row. He showed them how to make the Sign of the Cross and they imitated him perfectly, pleasing him even more.

Mass was kept short. He didn't want to overwhelm them. After

140

the dismissal, he invited the women to look at his hand drawn Stations of the Cross. They pointed and gestured, and Pretty Stone asked who the bearded man was.

"Jesus, this is Jesus. Very wakȟáŋ. God's son. The Great Spirit's son. He is your friend. He loves you."

Apparently all four understood the words if not the meaning and yet they nodded respectfully.

"You tell stories about this man? This dead man who loves us?" They shook their heads, confused. "This is what Mass is?"

"Yes. Yes!" he nodded enthusiastically.

"Why did they kill this son?" White Birch asked.

What words can I use to explain this? "You come every day and you will learn this."

The four exchanged words the priest did not understand and then Pretty Stone said, "We come."

"Can you bring others? Children?"

"We bring."

Bastiat thought the day could not get any better! Singing "How Great Thou Art!" he walked to the river. Wild roses grew along the bank. He would use the green thorny canes to make a crown...a crown for the Son of God.

Niglíču watched this black robed priest bend the canes and cut his hands twining them into a circle. He used several canes twisting them together. And then she watched him hold his creation over his head and gently lower it, wincing. *Like the man drawn on the paper.* A thorn cut into the priest's forehead, and she watched him look down and make the Sign of the Cross. He then raised his head, closed his eyes and smiled.

*****

On Good Friday morning the priest dug a hole, not particularly wide and about 18 inches deep. He scooped out the last few inches of dirt with his hands keeping the hole narrow enough to wedge in the 8 foot tall 2 by 6 inch plank he intended to plant there. The crossbeam, a shorter scrap leftover from his church construction lay nearby.

At 2 PM, Father Bastiat took down his drawing of the second Station of the Cross and attached it to the tall plank and then dragged this tagged wood into the village. He could have carried it, the people noted. It didn't seem that heavy and yet the priest hoisted one end over his shoulder and dragged the other end making a jagged scar across the ground.

"What is he doing?" the people wondered.

The priest stopped in the center of the village and curious people came forward. He showed them the drawing and the crucifix on the end of his beaded belt. He tried to explain that the plank was the upright beam of the cross. He sprinkled Holy Water on the beam, blessed it and then kissed it. Inviting the people to also kiss the pine plank, only White Birch and Pretty Stone came forward to comply.

Kills watched, annoyed. "They kiss the wood. They should kiss me. I can do more for them than that piece of tree."

Há Sápa stepped forward. Niglíču watched him turn to the people and then, as though in defiance, he, too, kissed the wood. Following his example, little children approached the wood, giggling. *Was this a game?* They planted their closed lip kisses and ran back to the encircling crowd.

Motioning for the people to follow him, the priest led them to the church and reverently laid the wood on the ground and the crossbeam over it. Taking hammer and nails, he skillfully drove in each nail to affix the beam to the plank. Beside the box of nails lay four railroad spikes, each about a half foot long. He picked up one and motioned to a young warrior to come forward as a volunteer.

The man shook his head. The priest motioned to another, pointed to the nails on his large dangling crucifix as explanation but that man also refused.

Grasshopper stepped through the crowd. "If the Black Robe needs help nailing himself to that wood, I will gladly do it," Grasshopper snickered in his native language and the people laughed at his sarcasm. Niglíču cringed. *They are making fun of him... a holy man. Would they have dared this with Mniyáta? Does the Black Robe have power too?*

Grasshopper knew, of course, that no one would be nailed into the wood. That wasn't the way of the Black Robes. Still, he hammered in the spike where Jesus' hands would have been. He hammered in the one that would have pierced His feet. He hammered another to affix the crown the priest had made.

"Will you help me lift the cross?" Bastiat asked.

Together the men raised the cross above the hole and sank it into the ground. While Grasshopper supported it upright, the priest wedged in the supports. Stepping back, the two men shifted it back and forth until it stood perpendicular to the ground. The priest offered his hand in thanks.

At that moment, Kills grunted disparagingly. "My kȟolá is Christian now?

Chastised, Grasshopper refused the handshake. "The Black Robe suffers nothing with his pole. How does this help the people?"

*****

Over and over Fr. Bastiat practiced what Há Sápa taught him…Three sentences:

"Leháŋl *Now.*   Ní úŋ *He is alive!*   Ečhétu. *It has happened."*
Has there ever been a more succinct way to sum up Easter Sunday? Fr. Bastiat thought as he prepared for the most important Mass of the liturgical year. When he stepped out of his cabin, the morning breeze threatened to tear the large paper drawing he had made of the resurrection. Quickly, he hugged it to his chest and faced with back to the wind while walking to the church doors. A baby cried inside. *A baby? In my church?* How surprised he was to see several women sitting on the benches! How surprised he was to see a few children too!

"Christ is Risen! Christ is truly risen! Alleluia!" he greeted them enthusiastically, forgetting about his intention to say the sentences he had practiced. Remembering, he went to each person there and said, mangling the pronunciation, "Leháŋl *Now.* Ní úŋ *He is alive!* Ečhétu. *It has happened."*

He tacked his drawing to the altar and turned to leave to get the other Mass necessities. Only then did he see Niglíču in the shadowy back corner of the church. He clapped his hands together in a prayerful pose and bowed to her, smiling. "Christ is truly risen!" he said to her. "Risen indeed!"

Chapter 2

Tuktél owáštečaka waŋží él phiyá uŋkíthipi kte.
Let us remake our home in some pleasant place.

Horses were not always a part of Lakȟóta culture, but once they were able to be stolen from competing tribes and bred judiciously, they became the means for measuring a man's wealth. Grasshopper had not known life without the horse, nor had his grandparents or the prior few generations. When their war and buffalo ponies were taken away by the soldiers, the Lakȟóta were left with horses beyond their prime, once sleek and proud horses now good only for modest transportation within the reservation. And they were few. And neither Grasshopper nor Kills had one.

Niglíču's bow practice had made her a skilled archer but game had soon been depleted near the village. She was eager to hunt, but she needed a horse.

And the priest had one.

Under Bastiat's skillful care, Ned became quite an attractive animal in comparison to the half starved ponies of the village. A tall American Horse, he towered over the Indian ponies. Carefully groomed, his chestnut coat shone. His gait was lively and Niglíču was very jealous when one day she saw Há Sápa trotting him through the grassy plain.

She waited for his return on the path to the priest's cabin, surprising both boy and horse with her sudden appearance.

"Why are you allowed to use the priest's horse?"

"Why are you annoyed that I am?" he countered. He liked Niglíču, but she unnerved him with her forcefulness, so unlike the other village girls. But in response to her scowl, he offered the explanation. "I trade with him. I teach him our language for a time, and he then gives me equal time with his horse."

"How often do you teach the priest? I have not seen you riding before."

Há Sápa lived a distance away. His father, a black man and former cavalry soldier, did not feel comfortable living close to the village. He supposed he was trusted but perhaps it was his own insecurity as a former slave that made him aloof, wanting a private life. Perhaps he felt it best to shield his massacre traumatized wife from people. Perhaps he felt guilt that he was not there at the massacre to protect his wife from the mental anguish she had experienced. But no matter the reason, the man kept a physical distance from the village, only occasionally allowing his son to visit relatives there.

"I go when I visit my aunt."

Niglíču stood aside to allow horse and rider to pass, but already she was devising a plan.

*****

Grasshopper watched the people evolve. Through both necessity and despondency, they allowed themselves to be drawn into dependency on the white man. What they ate was controlled by the white man. What they wore was also. The people were even turning from their white man's canvas thípi to the construction of small cabins, anchoring their location and strengthening their reliance on the white man for life's necessities. But worse than that, Grasshopper saw once virile young men decay into spineless ghosts of their former selves because of their alcohol addictions. That included his grandson, Loud Bear, and this sickened Grasshopper.

"We will move from this place," Grasshopper confided to Niglíču one night.

How happy she was! Certain her grandfather would be returning…somehow…and she did not know how…to the lifestyle of his own childhood, the one she had so often heard about during winter stories, she did not expect his next words.

"We will move across the creek."

Across the creek? Just across the creek?

"But that is not far."

"It is far enough so we do not have to watch our people become lazy. Far enough so we do not become like them."

"Grandfather, you will never be lazy!"

"It is my grandchildren's welfare that I think of."

145

They scouted the area across the creek, looking for a place close to, but high enough above the creek so flooding would not concern them. They searched for a place where wood for fires could be found, a place where thickets might hide rabbits. A place that might shelter them from winter winds.

There was no such place within range of the hated distribution center they were shackled to. But one spot seemed better than all the others, except that it brought them closer to the church. He weighed his options deciding proximity to the priest preferable to constant exposure to a dying culture.

"We will stay here."

It did not take much effort to move. Pretty Stone and White Birch assisted, though they lamented their departure. He invited Kills to join them not knowing that his kȟolá had already decided he would take the two cousins as wives.

"Bring them too."

"They would not want to come. They want to be near the church."

"You allow this?"

"I do not control them," Kills In Winter replied. "Not yet anyway."

"Kȟolá, I do not remember you controlling any woman!"

Despite coaxing, Loud Bear would not leave the village. He had joined other like-minded men creating mischief where he could. Once ghost dancers, stamping and trembling with passionate expectancy for their savior to come to eradicate the white men and restore the buffalo herds, now they spent their nights in the addictive shadowy oblivion that whiskey hung on them.

"What honor is there in that?"

But each entreaty was met with rebuttal. "What honor can be found here?"

His explanation that there is honor in preserving the traditional ways fell on deaf ears. *The white men force change on us but there are ways to resist that uphold our dignity. These I will teach my granddaughter.*

*****

Niglíču was not forbidden visits to the village. She had become close to Pretty Stone and White Birch and she felt even more welcome in their thípi now that Kills was there. In this thípi there was laughter.

146

In their thípi it felt like the times before *that* time.

She wandered along the creek on her way home, happy, kicking into the banks where the soil was soft just for the pleasure of seeing the small cascade of soil tumble over the edge of the water to wash away with it, a plume of tan fading clear. Once. Twice and then the third hard kick higher on the bank. The soil crumbled as expected but a dark object protruded from the indentation of the bank. Curious, she reached up to pull it free.

But when she touched it, smearing off the dirt, she discovered it was some sort of metal. She dug around it and revealed a blade, rusted but not fragmented. Gently she pulled on it, but it did not give. There was a handle and soil had caked it firmly into the bank. Digging more unearthed a bone...a jawbone, canine in nature, with teeth attached, the blade jammed into the hollow of it.

She recognized its power immediately as a chill swept through her. *Wakȟáŋ!* In trying to disengage the knife from the bank, the metal blade pulled loose.

"I'm free," she heard whispered, but it wasn't the knife speaking but the bone. *A bone cannot speak,* she rationalized and yet the sound was so real. Fragile, the bone disintegrated in her hand, its dust falling through her parted fingers. Only the teeth remained. A strange calm swept through her. She heard not the birds nor the rush of water. She did not hear her grandfather approach. As though in a trance, she saw a spirit wolf and it spoke to her without words. *I will be your guide.* She vaguely was aware she fell to the ground.

"Tȟakóža! Tȟakóža! ...wake up!"

It wasn't difficult to wake up... the passage smooth and warm.

"What happened? Are you sick?"

He won't believe me. No one will. But I had a vision. I have a spirit guide. "I must be tired. Maybe I'm hungry," was all she said. Worried, he took her hand, and they walked home.

*****

It was a sad story, this telling of how Niglíču's father died, and Grasshopper had told it many times before, but it was worth retelling.

"Your father was a brave man. He fought in many battles. He counted many coup. He made one big mistake, and you must learn from it. He came upon a wašíču that a Crow warrior's arrow had

147

taken down. The wašíču was crying out in pain when your father rode by."

At that point, Grasshopper's hand went to the pouch he always wore and Niglíču wondered why her grandfather did this during conversations like these.

"Your father felt sorry for his suffering. He tried to pull the arrow from the man's leg, but it would not pull free. Your father knew he would have to cut the flesh around the arrowhead. He took his knife from the sheath and the white man shot him. Maybe the man was afraid your father was going to kill him. Maybe the man was just full of hatred. Your father struggled back to his horse. He never made it back to camp before he died. You were very little then. You were told he died in battle. In a way, he did."

With wide eyes brimming with tears, Niglíču said, "Why are you telling me this now, Lalá?"

"The people in the village are learning to trust the wašíču. I do not. And I do not want you to make the same mistake as your father. Do not trust the white man. Always think that he wants you dead."

"All the wašíču are like this?"

"Átiyuha? *Absolutely all of them?* That I cannot say. But how can you tell which one is good… which one is bad?"

I can tell, she thought, but didn't dare say out loud, not then. *I can tell the Black Robe is good.*

*****

She did not tell her grandfather that she was going to see the priest the next morning. But worse than that, she lied about it.

"Come with me to check the snares. Maybe we have caught a rabbit. Take your bow. Take arrows. Maybe we will walk far and find game."

How surprised he was, and disappointed too, that she declined. "I want to bead my medicine bag today. The wolf's teeth need a special place."

*****

The direct route to the church would lead her to the creek. She had crossed it before at this point. Some parts were naturally waist deep and other parts the priest had made deeper so he could wash himself better. He had piled rocks making a little bridge, a little waterfall. Stepping gingerly from rock to rock, she could cross without getting her moccasins wet.

Which she did after her grandfather was out of sight.

Fr. Bastiat was grooming Ned when she stepped into the clearing by the makeshift corral.

"He looks good."

The priest's eyes opened wide, and his smile dimpled his cheeks. Nodding, he replied, "Yes. Your English is good too."

She made the hand talk signals for *Question. You trade.*

These he recognized but misinterpreted to imply she wanted to trade for the horse. He replied similarly. *No. No trade.*

Knowing he was not understanding, she tried another tactic. "Há Sápa talk. Teach you." She made the sign for *ride horse* and then pointed to herself, "I teach you. I ride."

Finally, he understood. "You will teach me your language? Yes?"

She nodded.

"And I will let you ride the horse?"

She nodded more vigorously.

"Yes. This is good trade," he agreed.

She smiled. "Yes. Good trade."

He had been getting better with nouns, picking up words here and there from the women who attended Mass. Those were easy, but it was the verbs that he was having trouble with. The language was so full of verbs for everything…specific verbs for very specific actions. And what he felt should be really easy, like saying "I go" turned out to be so complicated. "Am I going there from here? Am I taking someone or something with me? Am I going instead of someone else?" and that was only the beginning of what the women tried to explain to him...each way of going requiring a different verb. He would definitely not start with that verb!

"Tell me," he said, and then pointed to himself and gestured with his fingers running. "I run."

She told him, "Waíŋmnaŋke."

He laughed and garbled the word. *I am never going to run anywhere if I have to say that!*

He pantomimed "I walk."

"Mawáni."

"Wait," he said. He hurried into his cabin and came out with a pad and pencil. "Say it again?" He listened carefully and tried to write the word phonetically. Mawáni wasn't difficult but how was he to write waíŋmnaŋke? There were no such English sounds...no such nasalization that almost sounded French...no symbols to transcribe. He would have to learn these words by listening only and, not being used to studying that way, this scared him.

This first lesson was short. She was eager to ride the horse! She mounted clumsily without a saddle, but Ned was patient. She gestured for the gate to be opened but the priest shook his head.

"No. Not this time. You stay in here until I can see how well you ride. Next time," he said, supplementing words with gestures. He wanted to be sure there would be a next time. She would have to work for this privilege of riding his horse.

*****

Wíŋyaŋ nawíŋȟ yaŋké šni.
She does not sit as tradition expects.

She wasn't gone long, but even so, Grasshopper had returned before she. "You did not take your bow, and your medicine bag has not been beaded." he observed. "Where did you go?"

Wanting to lie, she was unsure what it would be. He might have been in the village. She could not say she was there, and she never went anywhere without her bow. She was trapped into telling at least part of the truth.

"I went to see what the Black Robe was doing."

"Why did you not tell me this before? You have spied on this man many times. Everyone knows this."

Before she could respond he continued. "Ťhakóža, I will tell you how a warrior acts. No man can decide for another and so a warrior acts according to what he feels is best for himself and his family. A chief is just the leader of whomever wants to follow him. Do you understand this?"

"Yes, I do and that is why ..."

"You will listen to me first and then you can talk. A warrior does not hide his decision. He speaks it openly and the others respect him for it, even if they do not agree with it. It is his life, and it is his decision. Do you understand this too?"

"Yes."

"Now you can talk."

"I do not know what to say, Lalá."

"Why did you go to the Black Robe?"

Niglíču told him about her conversation with Há Sápa and her desire to learn horsemanship. He understood his granddaughter and wondered which of his horses of long ago he would have given her if the many years had not fallen between then and now. He once had a beautiful pinto mare who walked with head held high. She would shake her shiny black mane and rear up with excitement, pawing the air with white socked forelegs when he came near. Her rising revealed her freckled underbody, which faded up to the whiteness of her broad chest. She was born for racing and responded to the gentlest pressure of his knees. Such a beautiful animal, he remembered, and heavy with foal when last he saw her. What a delight it would have been to see his granddaughter riding this horse across the plains!

The conversation continued. "Your plan makes sense. Your deceit was unwise."

"I am sorry, Lalá." She had disappointed her grandfather, but he did not say whether he approved or disapproved of her plan.

Later that day, she approached Grasshopper and Kills In Winter, who were smoking together.

I will tell them what I want to do. I will tell both of them after I sit with them for a while.

"Háu," she addressed both of them, sinking to cross-legged position to join the two men.

Grasshopper hid his grin as he saw his friend pull his shoulders back in indignation. *She addressees us as a man. She sits like a man.*

"Tomorrow, I want to go to the Black Robe and help him learn our language," Niglíču said to them, matter-of-factly. "He will let me ride his horse in trade."

*****

Šúŋkawakȟáŋ kiŋ mayánuŋ.
You stole the horse.

151

Bastiat knew how unlikely it was that the cavalry would see the US brand on Ned and demand his return. *Impossible,* he thought, but Ned was looking rather good. With blanket padding as a saddle, his swayback was barely visible, and Ned could be mistaken for a younger horse.

There was, however, that niggling question as to whether Ned was actually stolen, or could he be considered one of the spoils of war. If the Indians had won the war ...or was it just a battle?...they would have had a right to the booty which could include the enemies' horses. Who knew the circumstances for Ned's procurement by the old Indian?

Still, that brand made Bastiat nervous. He had become quite fond of the animal.

I can rebrand him, Bastiat though. He had made branding irons before, although he had never actually branded an animal. He looked at the brand, ran his fingertips over it, imagining what metal piece would turn the brand into some other character. He made exact dimensional sketches superimposing one design over the other to see how the new brand would meld with the former. Finally, he was pleased with his result. Placing a JES brand right before US made JESUS, a very appropriate brand for a priest, Bastiat thought. Jesus would own the horse!

That part was easy, but disguising the 7C was problematic. *Perhaps I can turn the 7 into a cross by adding a top and arm. That curve of the C can become the left half of a heart. I would only need to create its mirror image on the right.*

He pounded the glowing metal into the form he wanted. When cooled, he placed his creation over the existing brands and made adjustments. Finally, it was time for the branding.

It wasn't long before he realized the idea seemed better in its planning than it would be in its execution.

The branding irons were resting in the fire. Bastiat tied Ned to the fence post. Nauseous and so filled with the guilt of hurting his beloved Ned, he tied a cloth over Ned's eyes. Ned was trusting and did not move. Bastiat felt sicker. *I am going to have to do this three times!* he said to himself. *And I have to do it right. Perfectly. Please God, help me!* He wondered how much help God would give him, though. *I am, maybe, after all, stealing a horse.* Worse yet, he was inflicting pain. He put a grain bag on Ned's head. He had even added sugar to make it sweet.

Bastiat carried over the brands while Ned was munching away. With Ned's nose in the feedbag, he was not aware of the smell of hot metal. Bastiat prepared himself for the big brand. SIZZLE. Ned jumped and screamed into his bag. After his forelegs hit the ground and he trustingly settled down, SIZZLE again. Seeing what he believed was an accusation in Ned's eyes, the priest thought, *I betrayed you!* But once again, he applied the iron. *Three times!* He dropped the irons, ripped off the eye cloth and feedbag, and immediately toweled cold water onto the new brands. Ned calmed down. Bastiat looked at his handiwork. The JES sat crookedly before the US and the 7C had turned into a tipping cross with an irregular shaped heart next to it. *Not good...but adequate.*

Mathó Hí *Bear Teeth*, the old man who had gifted Ned to Bastiat, laughed so hard that his necklace jangled, the two bear fangs rattling against the three human teeth in between. The priest was such a joy to watch...so amusing! The old warrior found life around the village boring, so he assigned himself the task of scouting the outskirts of the village, bringing him to the perimeter of the priest's camp every day.

Bastiat heard the laughter but was too embarrassed to seek its source. Surely his squeamishness must have been obvious to the observer, whoever he was. Surely, he must have looked foolish!

The next day, Bear Teeth was waiting outside the priest's cabin before dawn. Betting the Black Robe would get up early to check on his horse, he was not disappointed. Bastiat, however, was surprised to see him. Hopeful that the man was there for Mass, he smiled a welcome.

"Good morning! I am so happy you are here, but it is early for Mass yet."

Bear Teeth surprised him again by speaking a halting but understandable English.

"No Mass. Take this," the man said, handing Bastiat a leaf with mashed vegetation in it. "For horse." The old man then dabbed a bit on his skin and Bastiat understood this was for the brand burn.

"Thank you!" Bastiat said accepting the mashed coneflower root, trusting it would be helpful. A quick look towards Ned, waiting impatiently for more grain, told the priest the horse had suffered no ill effects.

"You steal horse."

Bastiat's tanned face blanched. "No, you gave him to me, remember?"

The man grinned, revealing but one tooth in the front of his lower jaw. "I steal horse."

Bastiat could not help himself. He knew anyone could see the horse's poorly branded hide was a botched attempt to cover the horse's true owner. His face turned red. The old man smiled even wider. *Now we are partners in crime,* Bastiat thought. *Save me, Lord!*

The priest truly could not help it. A laugh burst forth, an uproarious laugh from the depths of his being gushed out and Bastiat, doubled over in laughter, clapped the old man on his back until they both laughed hysterically.

"Come," the priest said as the laughter subsided with both men out of breath. "Have coffee!" and then, "What is your name?"

The old man withdrew the necklace that had been jostled beneath his shirt. "Mathó Hí *Bear Teeth*," he said.

*****

That afternoon Bastiat trimmed Ned's hooves. The horse was cooperative under the former blacksmith's care. He didn't shoe Ned. There was no need for what the horse did now, and besides Ned had good conformation and structurally sound hooves. The drag on his hind leg had improved too with proper attention. The priest took his time, remembering fondly the years he did this for a living.

Of course, this time would have been better spent reading scripture, preparing the homily, or even walking into the village trying to garner favor to increase his parishioner total. But the morning spent with Bear Teeth listening to the old man's boastful stories of bravery had felt so good! And understanding some words in that conversational mix of Lakhóta and English made him just want to be a man for once. Not a priest. Maybe just for one afternoon, he thought.

It was a hot day, and the priest was wearing his shirt open to the waist and half tucked into his trousers. He did not wear clerical garb while working. It seemed foolish, he thought, and no one seemed to care, anyway.

To Grasshopper arriving later, Bastiat now looked like any other white settler, and it triggered an uneasy response. The black robe had made the priest appear neutral, less threatening and thus more approachable.

"I come. See horse." Grasshopper surprised the priest, who dropped the leg and looked up to see Grasshopper and Niglíču opening the corral gate.

Wiping his hands on his pants, Bastiat invited them closer. "Yes. Yes. Come and look."

Grasshopper ran his hands down the horse's legs, patted his chest, paused over the fresh brand and then opened Ned's mouth.

"Old horse."

Bastiat felt he should qualify that with, "But sound. He rides well."

"I ride him." Grasshopper was not asking a question and Bastiat felt it was a test.

"Yes. Sure," he said, looking Grasshopper square in the eyes. "Why don't you take him for the day and ride far?"

Is that surprise I see in the grandfather's eyes? Bastiat thought. *Good. He hadn't expected this.* "And Niglíču can stay here if she wants. She can teach me more."

Holding a clump of mane in his hand, Grasshopper deftly mounted the horse. He did not grunt in painful exclamation, although he wanted to, for his muscles had not stretched into mounting a horse in many months.

"Oȟtáyetu, I come back."

"You mean 'evening'?" He motioned the sun going down.

"Yes."

I trust him with the horse. He trusts me with his granddaughter. Finally, I'm making progress!

There were no exciting Lakȟóta lessons that day. Bastiat simply questioned a solemn Niglíču and scribbled down phonetic spellings of words he wanted to know. He saw how sad she looked and tried to cheer her with food and teasing, but her head would just turn in the direction she expected her grandfather to come. Clearly, she was uncomfortable with him. She wondered whether she needed to stay.

"I see you have your bow. You have arrows. Can you show me how you shoot?" Much of this was pantomimed and Niglíču couldn't help but smile at how silly the priest looked.

"Come! Come!" he said motioning. He went into his cabin and took out his pad and a pen. On it he drew what might have been a deer or a horse or maybe even a dog. *He isn't good at drawing animals,* she observed.

Ripping out the page, he took it to a tree several yards away and affixed it to a branch. "Can you hit this?"

Her arrow pierced the paper where the animal's shoulder was, ripping the impaled paper from the tree. He drew a smaller target and again she hit the mark dead on center. Soon the ground was littered with torn paper. Soon they felt at ease with each other.

Well before sunset, Grasshopper returned. Slung over Ned's shoulders was a small mule deer. "Good horse," the old hunter said, dropping the deer to the ground before dismounting. "Give to people," he said, gesturing towards the deer.

*****

Šiná tȟaŋníla waŋ mahél íyotakapi.
They sat down inside an old blanket.

The children playing tag in the cottonwood grove kicked up yellow leaves that swirled in the brisk air. Exhausted, Niglíču and Há Sápa fell backwards into the wind-swept piles of gold and rolled, laughing as leaves tangled in their long hair.

"That was fun!" Niglíču exclaimed, breathless.

"Can I ask you a question?" Há Sápa looked at her seriously.

"What?"

"Why don't you ever play with the other girls in the village? You go there so often anyway to see the Black Robe."

"I just like to play with you."

"So, you like me more than the others? Boys or girls?" he asked.

"I like you."

"More than the others?"

This sounded silly to Niglíču. *Of course, I like you more than the others. Why do you think I spend so much time with you?*

The sun was setting, and the orange hues of the sky deepened and striped themselves with reds and yellows. The temperature dropped. The children had spent many evenings that past summer watching the sun go down, but today it seemed too cold to just sit. Their sweaty bodies cooled quickly.

"Let me get a robe. We can stay warm for a while before you go,"

156

Niglíču said.

Returning with a large old blanket, she sat down next to him and draped it over their shoulders, half covering their heads. With the blanket cocooning them, an unfamiliar tension heightened their awareness of each other. For a moment they were silent.

Há Sápa spoke first. "Did you ever see two young people stand outside the girl's family thípi wrapped in a buffalo robe?"

"Not lately," she replied. "But I did before."

"They talk in whispers," he said. "I wonder what they talk about?"

"Maybe they tell stories," she said.

"Maybe they tell each other that they like each other."

"Don't they already know that? Why else would they do it?"

"Here," he said, "Let's try it and see how it feels."

"Try what?" she asked.

"Let's try talking that way. Let's pull the blanket over our heads."

She couldn't explain why that made her uncomfortable.

"This is a small tent," she giggled. "And..." she said pushing him a little away... "you smell."

"I think he puts his arm around her like this." Há Sápa said, clumsily stretching his arm around her back. But he did not know where to rest his hand. Deciding on the hair draping over her shoulders, he boldly stroked it.

"What are you doing?" she asked. "We are supposed to be talking. Talk. Say you like me."

"I do like you, Niglíču."

She giggled nervously. "You sound so funny! Your voice sounds so different. You seem so serious! I will never do this with a boy!"

She started to get up, but his arm around her tightened, scaring her.

"Stop it!" She pulled herself up, taking the blanket with her.

Not twenty feet away Loud Bear walked towards her thípi chuckling.

Há Sápa too stood up, embarrassed and angry. He hated being made fun of by anyone, and least of all, Loud Bear. Once he had respected him, but not anymore. He was no warrior. All he did was drink whiskey.

He turned to Niglíču, angry. She, after all, caused all this with the blanket! "Your hero cousin is soft and growing fat."

*****

157

Grasshopper was gathering wood for the fire when Loud Bear approached. The young man walked heavily, weighted to the earth. His shoulders sagged slightly forward, unnoticeable to anyone other than his concerned grandfather. Though Loud Bear was a subdued version of his former prideful self, Grasshopper thought he could affect a reversal and restore the man's self-confidence. He'd find a way, somehow.

"I see my little cousin spends time with the Black Robe. She rides his horse. No one else rides his Jesus horse."

The Jesus horse! The village still found the brand funny and Bastiat, embarrassed, tried unsuccessfully to cover it with a blanket when he rode. Niglíču, though, rode bareback and her bent knee pointed directly to JESUS.

"She has made a trade with him. She teaches him. He lets her ride," Grasshopper explained as they entered the thípi.

"She will learn wašíču ways. That is not good. Look what happened to Soft Feather. Look… look…what happened to my brother."

"Ah, but you, too, seem to be learning the wašíču ways, Ťhakóža. Stay with me here. Let me teach you the old ways. Then you will not need their whiskey."

"I do not *need* their whiskey."

"Prove it. Stay here!"

"I already know all I need to know. What is there to know here anyway? We go to the supply building and get food. We eat."

Just then, Niglíču walked into the thípi carrying the blanket.

Loud Bear sneered at her. "Your blanket is full of leaves. Did you drag it on the ground? Did you lie down on it or, maybe, share it with someone?"

His grandson's bitterness angered Grasshopper. Clearly it upset his granddaughter who narrowed her eyes and left without a word. Perhaps it was best that the young man find his own way. All men must do so.

Chapter 3

Líla osní.
It is cold.

I must be getting old, Fr. Bastiat thought when he felt jealous of the horse for the heavy blanket thrown over his back. He mounted quickly, eager to spend the extra allowance he was given to buy a suitable coat for his new environment. *I'm sooo cold!* He hunched his shoulders and buttoned up his sweater before riding to the store.

One thing he did not like about belonging to an Order was that he had to ask for money. He understood the vow of poverty and accepted it with his mind, but his heart often wanted the freedom to earn and spend as he saw fit. He had once secured a prosperous living as a blacksmith. He had had more than enough money for his family's needs.

Well, he told himself, *not much of a family. Just my wife and I. My wife ...."*

His marriage seemed so long ago, as if in another lifetime, and yet he would often roll over in his sleep expecting to find her there, wanting him as much as he wanted her.

Such daydreaming passed the time on the way to the store. Welcoming smoke rose from its chimney promising a warm interior. Once inside, Bastiat requested to look at the Montgomery Ward mail-order catalog and was handed the small volume. Thumbing through the pages, he found the entries for men's coats and decided on a long woolen one. The decision was straightforward. There were no illustrations and few choices. He thought of the clothing stores in New York, but reasoned there was no need for a store to stock much clothing here. No one could afford it. As had become his custom, he picked out some hard candy for Niglíču, along with the sugar cubes to satisfy his spoiled horse.

Niglíču would come a few times each week to ride Ned and speak Lakȟóta to him. He was a fast learner, but so was she. Her English was improving far faster than his Lakȟóta and the lessons were enjoyable. A prideful gleam flashed her eyes when she corrected his many errors. Puffing herself up like a schoolteacher back East, she fixed his mistakes, not allowing him time to think for himself.

Just as he finished placing his order, he remembered something else he had to buy.

"Rope! Yes, I need some sturdy rope. About 50 feet worth. Do you have any?"

The shopkeeper said, "Why certainly, Father. You fixin' to hang somebody?"

Bastiat laughed. "No. No hanging. I have other plans.

*****

Ómayakiyapi čha philámayayape ló.
Thank you for helping me.

That night, the expected first snow fell. He knew it would. He had thought the cold, gray, and heavy clouds stretched across the wide sky and the bitingly crisp fall air had promised it. The snow had just dusted the ground, but now he felt he should work faster to complete his project.

He was going to build a bridge. He hoped Niglíču would still visit him during the winter, but that little river might rise and prevent it. That she might walk over the ice and break through in a deep spot scared him. The image of her floundering in icy water was unbearable.

Is it a good thing for a priest to become so attached to one child? But how can I help it?

"But I'm to be father to all my children!" he said out loud, but he knew that was not a satisfactory answer. It could be used to both justify and criticize his special feelings for Niglíču. These words ... father, children ... now sounded strangely odd when thinking about his relationship with these people. "Father? Children?" He said them again. They were the right words. The Church had taught him to think that way. He was a priest, and this made him God's representative on earth and his mission was to save everyone and

160

bring them home to Christ. But these people did not look to him as a father and he could not think of these individuals as children. "Grasshopper? I should call him my son?" He had to laugh. But then he stopped and looked sheepishly around to see if anyone was nearby. He talked to himself more often now and, not being so far from the village, he wondered if anyone noticed.

He began cutting down a few trees. There were few to choose from, but he estimated four would be enough if they were straight for about ten feet and had a diameter of eight to twelve inches. A small stand of cottonwood stood not too far upstream, and he was determined to get them.

Soon four trees lay on the dry grasses. Bear Teeth watched him from a distance...but Bastiat expected him to amble closer. The laughter and coffee they had shared created an interesting relationship. If they were completely alone, Bear Teeth might start a conversation. If they were near others, the older man kept his distance.

"You cut wood for winter?"

Bear Teeth could now speak simple English sentences more fluently.

"No!" the priest replied, but since found he could not find the words for bridge, he left it at that. Bear Teeth looked confused. The priest already had a cabin. What need did he have for this wood if not to burn?

Bastiat continued in English but, waving his arms, gestured his intentions. "I am going to make a small bridge to cross this river."

"Why don't you walk on the rocks?" the old man gestured back.

"The river might rise."

How strange that we can actually have this conversation with such a jumble of languages and signs ... and understand each other?

After a few minutes, Bear Teeth continued with words and pantomime, "Why don't you cross the river where the water is shallow?"

"I want to cross the river in a certain place."

Bear Teeth made no response to that and just sat silently while Bastiat chopped away the side branches, throwing them into a pile by the water's edge. The work was hard for him. Exhausted, he went back to his cabin after working the first tree. When he went back the next afternoon, he saw the branches were gone, the swish marks on

161

powdered soil suggesting somebody had dragged them towards the village. Bear Teeth was waiting nearby. Bastiat called to him.

"Did you take the branches?"

"Yes."

"There were a lot of branches."

"Yes."

"You must have made many trips."

The old man shrugged. He did not think of the trips. He thought only of how warm his thípi would feel with the hot fire those small branches would make as they burned.

From then on, when Bastiat placed the branches one on top of the other, he did so with the thought that they would be dragged and so faced them all in the same direction. And after he finished the day's work, he had Ned haul the branches closer to the village.

Ned also was assigned the job of dragging the logs to the location where Bastiat wanted to make his bridge. Kills, one day, was crossing the river on the way to see Grasshopper when he saw Bastiat struggling to get Ned to climb the small bank on the other side of the river. The priest wanted the log that Ned dragged to be positioned so that each end would be resting on an opposite bank. Kills was curious, but he said nothing and walked on.

Grasshopper welcomed Kills warmly. The two friends had not seen each other lately. Kills had traveled to be with his extended family camped elsewhere. They sat inside and Grasshopper offered Kills his pipe. While smoking with his friend, Kills mentioned the priest's behavior.

"Kȟolá, I think he is building a bridge. Maybe he wants to visit you often and does not like to get his black shoes wet."

"Why would he want to see me?"

"He will want you to join his church. He will want your granddaughter to join his church. My women go there every day."

"Your women go every day?"

"Yes."

"You will stay with them in this village?"

"Yes. I will stay."

"It is hard to have two women, Kȟolá. I do not think I could do this. They are jealous of each other?"

"It is not like when we were young men," he winked, "and these are not young women. It is easier now." At this, he paused, both men

162

reflecting on their youth. "I can no longer hunt. I do not bring food. But both women tell the Americans they are the woman of the family and so we get double rations. I will grow fat," Kills said, but he was not smiling.

That evening, Grasshopper suggested to his granddaughter that they should go for a walk to see what the Black Robe had been doing. They walked down to the river and there, at their usual crossing were logs roped together spanning the river.

"Can I try it, Lalá?"

He nodded, as there was no reason not to let her, but he did not like this bridge. It felt like an intrusion. This bridge was more than just the rope and logs. This bridge would allow the Black Robe easy access to his thípi. It was as though the priest had invited himself, without permission, deeper into his life.

The next day, Bear Teeth awaited the return of Bastiat to finish his bridge. The old man was curious ... and bored. At the very least, the priest was interesting to watch.

But he saw Grasshopper first. The two men exchanged greetings.

"You wait for the Black Robe?" Grasshopper asked Bear Teeth. The old man nodded.

"Do you know when he will come?"

"I think soon. After his ceremony."

Grasshopper wanted to question the priest and so he sat by the riverbank and waited, looking towards the path from which he expected the priest to appear. He did not have to wait long.

It was a fine day for a walk, Bastiat thought, and so he left Ned behind to munch contentedly on his daily ration of grain. "I'll be right back," he said to the horse as though Ned cared about anything else while he was eating. "I just have to tie a few more pieces to finish that bridge."

When he got to the water, however, he was taken aback. He was not alone.

Grasshopper called to him. "Why did you put this here?"

"Why? Because your granddaughter can use it to come to see me. The river might be hard to cross in winter."

Grasshopper could not disagree with the logic of the bridge for his granddaughter's safety, but he shouted to Bear Teeth across the river in purposely rapid fire Lakȟóta, "Why does she need to go to him at all?"

"She wants the horse," Bear Teeth yelled back.

"She knows how to ride a horse! She has been riding since she was three years old."

"Maybe she wants *that* horse."

The two men continued their long distance conversation while Bastiat moved the log closest to downstream away from the others so he could get a rope around it. He was struggling with it when the end slipped off the bank and fell into the river and away from the others. The priest stepped into the stream and attempted to lift the log back into place. It was heavy. He kept dropping it.

Grasshopper felt a bit of satisfaction seeing the priest unable to make his bridge. Bear Teeth felt differently. He went to help. Priest and old man together tried to lift the log, but Bear Teeth could be of little help. He slipped on a rock and fell into the water, crying out in pain as his arthritic knees slammed into the riverbed. Bastiat tried to lift him and now both struggled in the cold water.

Seeing this, Grasshopper scrambled over the bank to assist. He steadied Bear Teeth and admonished him to get out of the water. He would help instead. Straining under the weight of the log, Grasshopper and Bastiat bumped into each other as they, too, slipped on the river rocks. At one point, Grasshopper lost his balance and started to fall, but Bastiat grabbed hold of his shirt while the warrior reached for the priest's arm. In their unified effort to maintain balance, Grasshopper forgot they were from different worlds. It surprised him. He stepped away from the priest, confused by this momentary sense of camaraderie.

The moment passed, however, and they hoisted the log into place. Bastiat thanked Grasshopper for his help, but the warrior merely nodded and walked away.

*****

Táku wáta he?
What did I eat?

One day, the women returned from Mass smelling different.

"What is this smell?" Kills asked when they entered the thípi. It was not unpleasant. In fact, he found it aroused his senses.

"The priest smudges us now," White Birch answered.

164

The frankincense and myrrh had arrived along with the censer. How eager Fr. Bastiat had been to swing the smoke exuding pot to and fro before his parishioners, purifying them! This was something they could relate to, so similar to their own practice of smudging. Though the odor differed from their sage, cedar or sweetgrass, the oil and resinous sap of the priest's incense was intoxicating to the women.

"And we like it," Pretty Stone added, smiling.

Kills frowned. His women enjoyed this celebration too much.

"And we also like the stories he tells from his big book. Some are funny. Some are very sad," White Birch added eagerly. "And I like the way he tells them, using his hands to make signs we cannot really understand, but are so amusing to watch!"

Pretty Stone watched their man's eyes grow darker. She should not want to make this man so jealous that he would forbid them their morning pleasure. "We hope the smell pleases you," she said flirtatiously, leaning up against Kills. "We want to make you happy."

This cousin was more attractive than the other, and she often surprised her new husband with sensual experiences that made him forget how old he was.

"I like this smoke," he finally admitted, inhaling deeply of it with his nose buried in her still black and shiny hair.

*****

Later that afternoon while the women mended moccasins, they thought about the priest. "What does he do when the ceremony is over? Play with his horse? Chop wood? Build that silly bridge?" They tossed ideas back and forth, but concluded he had a lonely life.

"Maybe we can make a meal for him?" Pretty Stone suggested, and her cousin agreed.

A few days later, they arrived one evening at his door carrying a cast-iron pot with a steaming stew inside. He was happily surprised and a bit embarrassed to greet them wearing work clothes rather than his traditional robe, but he invited them to step inside out of the cold. They shyly said they would not do that, but they handed him the pot cradled in leather so he would not burn his hands. Muttering something that sounded like "šuŋ ... something," they left in a hurry, like giggling little girls, pleased to bring pleasure to a lonely man.

165

Closing the door behind him, he set the pot on the table and stared into it. It looked quite good. It smelled good too. He was not sure what they said it was, but he was almost positive it had to do with a horse. He had never eaten horse meat before and was tempted to throw it out, as it seemed repulsive to him. Eat Ned? He could never! He would rather starve! But he knew he would feel bad throwing it away, for these women seemed so happy to give it to him.

He now justified eating a horse. Horses ate grain and grass after all, as did cows, and he had no problem eating beef. The horse had to be old. Maybe it had just died? They could not waste this precious meat and neither should he. It looked like beef stew after all, even though the fat did not look quite the same. He remembered something about horse fat differing from that of a cow.

As the aroma filled the room, he became tempted to try just a little and then, after tasting it, that little turned into a lot and before long the pot was empty. *I will sleep well tonight!* he said. *The winds can blow outside all they want, but I am warm and full and grateful for this bounty!*

The next day, he walked into the village to return the pot. The two cousins were outside of their thípi, feeding a chubby white puppy, who nipped playfully at their fingertips.

"Thank-you for the stew," he said bending down to jiggle the puppy's ears.

"Did you like it?" they asked together.

"Yes, very much!"

"We are glad," said White Birch. "Next week we will make you more. We will cook this one and share it with you again."

It took a moment only before he realized what they were saying and what he had eaten.

Not šuŋkawakháŋ! Not horse. Šuŋȟpála. Puppy. I ate a puppy! God forgive me! Bastiat said to himself as he turned away, pale and nauseous.

That white puppy played in his dreams. Nursed in his dreams. Cuddled in a little child's arms in his dreams. Followed him around everywhere in his dreams and shadowed him in his daylight hours. When Bastiat next saw the two cousins at Mass gazing at him and enjoying the holiness of the Bible stories, he pictured them butchering the puppy. He avoided going into the village. He did not want to see that the puppy was missing. But then he remembered.

166

There is still time! he thought. *Well, maybe,* he added. *What does next week mean to a people who do not have weeks?* Still later, he thought, *I will trade for the puppy. What do I have that they might want?*

He rummaged through his belongings. "Nothing," he cried out. "I have nothing they would want!" Then his eyes rested on the blue swirls in his marbled rosary beads given to him as a going away present by his sister-in-law. The beads rested on the shelf above his bed, and these were rarely used. "This they might want!" he shouted, but the echo came back and reminded him these were blessed. *These beads are not jewelry,* his conscience said. *Should they lie nestled between the breasts of a woman who eats puppies?* He pictured the beads there and quickly changed his thoughts.

Yes! Yes! Anything to save that puppy!

Before he could change his mind, he grabbed the rosary and hurried to the village. He found both Pretty Stone and White Birch carrying water to their thípi.

"Hello," he said, trying to appear casual. With his heart in his throat, he swallowed hard and asked, "Where's that cute little puppy?"

"What puppy?"

"The white one I saw the other day."

"Oh, that one," Pretty Stone said, looking down.

"Is he ... gone?"

"Gone?"

"Did he run away? Was he ... eaten?"

"Oh no," she reassured him, "not gone, but our man does not want to share him. He likes puppies. They are not easy to find now. He was lucky to get those two."

"Your man?"

"Yes, Kills In Winter is our man."

"You said, 'our'?"

"Yes. Ours."

Why didn't I realize they were not just living with him, but that they were indeed wives to him? Oh my God!

Kills stepped out of the thípi and eyed the priest with disdain. "What does he want here?" he asked White Birch.

"I only know he asked about the white puppy," she answered.

"Why does he ask about this puppy?" Kills shot back.

167

Looking down and now feeling ashamed, White Birch confessed, "We took him some stew from the other puppy. He probably wants more."

Bastiat could understand a few words of this conversation and so he volunteered, "I would like to trade for this puppy."

Kills grew interested. Trade was something he understood well.

Just then, the puppy rounded the thípi, dragging a chewed rope. He jumped up on everyone and Kills slapped him down. Cowering, the puppy peed in submission.

"Worthless dog. Tomorrow we eat him," Kills said. He could see from the Black Robe's face that this horrified him and so he played it up even more. Kills bent and rubbed the puppy's exposed stomach, round from his last meal. "This will taste very good. Tender," he said as he stroked a thigh.

Bastiat blanched. He took the rosary out from his pouch. "I trade with this," he said, holding up the beads which glistened in the sunlight. Both women said, "Ooooooo." Clearly, they were impressed!

"I have two women," Kills said, hoping to enhance the bidding.

"They can share," Bastiat countered.

Kills turned to Pretty Stone. "Tell this wašíču that my women would rather share their man than their jewelry."

She told him. He looked disappointed. *Maybe my man has gone too far*. She wanted those beads, but so did her cousin.

The bargaining continued. The puppy, sensing a more compassionate person, walked over and nibbled on the hem of the priest's robe. Bastiat looked down and saw that this dog would be huge based on the size of his feet. He was also not pure white. There was a streak of gold running down his back and a certain wolf-like look in his eyes. He was a mix of something, Bastiat observed. Wolf? The puppy looked up at him with trusting eyes. The priest was smitten and Kills knew it.

"Tell the Black Robe he has other beads at his belt. If he trades us both these beads, we will let him have the dog," Kills said to Pretty Stone. He smiled flirtatiously at her. "They will look good around your waist." She translated the deal to Bastiat.

No! was his first thought. He fingered these brown bone beads and their heavy chain a lot. They were always with him. They jangled as he walked. With their heavy cross, they symbolized his priesthood.

These were not jewelry! These were his badge, his pledge of priesthood, his connection to the Blessed Mother! To be worn by this woman? He pictured her dancing before her man with the cross swinging seductively in front. He shook his head. *Where do these thoughts come from?*

"*No!*" he repeated.

Kills called the dog over. He withdrew his knife from his belt and knelt down.

"Stop! Here!" the priest called out, pulling his rosary free from his belt and handing it to Kills. "Take this too," he said, placing the smaller rosary in his hands.

Kills smiled broadly. "Tell him I was only going to cut the rope from the dog's neck. But thank him for the trade. It was a good one for me. Wolf dogs do not taste as good as other puppies, anyway."

Bastiat picked up the squirming puppy and headed for home.

*****

Ipáhiŋ kiŋ yakpúkpa.
He chewed the pillow into pieces.

Clearly, this puppy did not like to be held. Within a few yards of the village, he wriggled out of the priest's grasp and fell in a heap to the ground. He got up quickly and dashed about, circling Bastiat and yipping at him playfully. The puppy thought it was a delightful game when the priest went to grab him! He dodged the hands and circled behind the priest to nip his ankles. Giving up on restraining the puppy and convinced the dog would follow him, Bastiat walked the path home. The puppy circled round and round his new master's legs, nearly tripping him and causing the man to wonder if perhaps he had acted a bit hastily in trading for this dog.

When Bastiat got to his door, he paused. *Now what?* he thought. *Do I take him inside? I can't just leave him out here. I have no barn.* Ned had only a lean to and that would not keep the pup in. And he had already proven that rope would not hold him.

He held the door open, and the pup bounded inside. This new experience of being inside excited the pup, and he ran around dribbling the urine his young bladder could not control.

It had been a long time since Bastiat had lived with a puppy. His childhood pet, Sam, was a mixed breed hound who, when not out running with his nose either in the air or close to the ground, slept peacefully before the hearth and lived on the leftovers from family meals. However, within a few hours, the priest knew this puppy would be nothing like Sam.

For one, the puppy was not interested in just smelling things. He wanted to destroy them! The pup discovered he could use the leather of the priest's shoes as practice for someday tearing apart a rabbit of the same size. The padded pot holder beside the stove was so rich in smells that it easily substituted for a prairie dog. The priest wondered just how many times had he said "No!" that afternoon. Hundreds? Thousands? And each time he corrected the pup, the animal cocked his head in confusion at the priest as though to say *Why?*

But the pup had quiet times too when the priest could hold the animal next to him on the bed and stroke his fur and fondle his toes. Even here, he could see that somehow this pup was not just a dog. Not only were his paws huge, but his toes were noticeably different from those of the dogs the priest had known. The two middle toes of the puppy's front paws were so much longer than the others! Bastiat wondered if those were the toes of a wolf.

Although clearly hungry, the puppy balked at the idea of eating the oatmeal the priest provided. He licked at it and slopped it over the sides of the bowl. He walked all around the bowl as if a different approach would change the bowl's contents and, in the process, made slushy footprints on the floorboards. Finally, as hunger overtook his fussiness, the puppy consumed the meal, but it did not agree with his digestive system. As the hours passed, the priest dealt with the subsequent diarrhea, holding his nose as he tried to scoop up the watery mess.

"OK, this is not going to work. He needs meat. If this animal is indeed part wolf, and if it indeed needs to eat a lot of meat, where am I going to get this?" Bastiat thought out loud, now realizing just how big a commitment this animal would be.

"You had better learn to hunt for yourself, little fellow ... and soon!"

Emotionally attached to this puppy by now, the priest was hesitant

170

to take the puppy out for fear he would lose him, but the puppy soon showed that he had no intention of leaving the priest's side. The dog ran and played, and thankfully now relieved himself outdoors. However, the pup showed no interest in going back inside, the outside being a more powerful lure than his master. The dog followed the priest diligently to the door and then ran off when the priest opened it. Only meat, the priest's supper, lured the dog into the cabin.

After adding more sticks to the stove, the iron-radiated heat made both priest and pup sleepy. Bastiat slid beneath the bed covers and laid a blanket on the floor for the pup. After pawing it into a wrinkled nest, the pup settled into its softness. Content, the priest fell into such a deep sleep, he didn't notice the pup had later clambered onto the bed and chewed on the pillow. Needle-sharp teeth punctured it. Strong jaws had dragged it from beneath the priest's head, feathering the floor.

Chapter 4

Wičháša kiŋ hé tuwé he?
Who is that man?

T he enticement of an open door pulled the pup away from the pillow. There were evening chores to be done and the dog raced to the door, his feet slipping on the wood floor as he scrambled outside. The pup beat the priest to Ned's corral. "Don't bother the horse," Bastiat called out. But the horse would not allow the pup to race around him, barking, nipping at his heels. And so, with an effective kick, the dog fell silent and slunk off with tail between his legs. "I told you so," the priest smiled.

Thankfully, the horse hadn't been as thirsty as on previous warmer days and so the priest did not need that extra tedious trip to the creek to fill up the horse's bucket. He put more hay in the manger, kissed the horse and headed over to lock up the church.

The darkened building looked as empty as the priest expected it to be. The priest walked inside, knowing his way around without light. The pup, however, stiffened as he entered, raising his head to sniff the cold air. Observing the dog's hesitation, Bastiat stepped back outside.

"Who's in there?" he demanded, placing one small emboldened step before the other as he cautiously advanced.

He heard a shuffling movement from behind the benches and the puppy scooted behind him, tail neatly tucked against his abdomen. *Great protector you are going to be,* the priest thought to himself as he removed the candle from the brass candlestick by the doorway and lit it. With the candle in his left hand and his heavy candlestick "weapon" in his right, Bastiat inched towards the intruder. A bottle clinked to the floorboards. The priest smelled whiskey.

"Hi, Padre!" The voice was unfamiliar, slurred.

"What are you doing in here? Who are you?" Bastiat demanded

forcefully. But his nervousness was made evident in the dancing candle flame, the fast melting wax dripping onto the floor.

"Want me to hold that for you, Padre?"

The priest was taken aback at the intruder's boldness. "Stay where you are!"

"In answer to your question, I'm thinkin' of joining your church. Wanted to see how it feels bein' in here."

"You're drunk and you want to keep warm. That's why you're here!" Bastiat blurted out. "Go! Now!"

Bastiat held the candlestick threateningly while the inebriated intruder staggered to his feet. He was a man the priest judged to be in his twenties, a rakishly handsome man, dark skinned like the Lakȟóta, but the waves in his long black hair testified to a European ancestor. His English was fluent with barely an accent. *I wonder where he is from?* the priest thought. *Surely not from around here. I would have noticed him.* Lurching and mumbling to himself, the man left the building, and it was only then that the puppy barked after him. "A little late," the priest said as he locked the church doors behind them.

*****

The black and nickel cooking stove was enough to heat the priest's small cabin and supply him with any hot water he would need. Bastiat had prepared another large pot of oatmeal by boiling the rolled oats first, and now that it had simmered to a less than perfect consistency, the priest ladled it onto two plates, one for himself and one for the puppy. "It's all I have tonight," the priest apologized, and yet they both ate greedily and had leftovers for breakfast pancakes. "I am cooking for a dog now," Bastiat laughed to himself.

There was not much to do once darkness had fallen. Say prayers. Read scripture. Prepare a homily that was understandable. Say more prayers. He checked to see the door was properly latched and that the window shutters were secured. The sudden appearance of the stranger last night made him uncomfortable...and strangely guilty. *Should I have offered him food? Should I have offered him God?*

He sank into his sagging bed and the warm pup nestled into his side, comforting him. He pulled the blankets up around both of them and slept.

173

*****

The church was colder than it should have been when he opened the doors the next morning. While peculiar, it wasn't until a breeze chilled his back while he prepared a fire in the stove that he noticed the side window was open. *He must have come back!*

He walked over to where the stranger had been, expecting to clean up the mess there but surprisingly the floor was clean. Jittery, he finished the fire and went inside to don his vestments and prepare for Mass.

Promptly at 9AM, he rang his bell outside the church door, a signal for those within to quiet down and stand for the procession. Carrying a crucifix and staring focused on the altar as an example to the people, he walked in. He did not notice who sat mid-center of the first row.

Fr. Bastiat turned around, and the stranger, sitting between two young women, smiled broadly and saluted him. Blood rushed to the priest's face. *Why is he here?*

As Mass continued, the priest noticed the stranger made the Sign of the Cross at the proper time and recited the Lord's Prayer without faltering. As he monitored this stranger, he saw him edge, little by little, to the left. There was a young woman there who, at first, did not notice that the distance between the man and herself was growing smaller. She blushed and moved away. Bastiat caught the twinkle in the stranger's eye. Clearly, he was enjoying more than Mass.

After Mass, Fr. Bastiat stood at the door to thank those who had attended, if not actively participated in, the celebration. "God be with you!" he said to each bidding them farewell. Many responded as they had been taught, "And with your spirit."

The stranger exited last.

"I see you have come back," Bastiat said to him.

"I told you I wanted to find out more about your church. And I wanted to see who came here. I see there are a lot of women, but no men today," he said.

Bastiat narrowed his eyes replying, "I noticed you *did* see the women."

"Yes, that's true," he winked. "I always see the women," the

174

stranger said laughing as he walked away.

*****

The puppy growled and the hair stood up on his back. Two people approached. Bastiat had hoped Niglíču would come but he did not expect Grasshopper. Wary, the pup approached them cautiously, swinging his tail low.

"Hello! Yes, the puppy is mine. I got him yesterday."

Niglíču ran ahead to see the pup, and the dog wagged his tail wildly at her touch, an instant bonding. "I like this dog!" she said, wishing she had the words to explain this was more than just liking, that she felt a familiar affection like she had known him before.

The pup shied away from her grandfather, not allowing a touch. "I saw a dog like that in Pahá Sápa, *the Black Hills*," Grasshopper said interspersing English and Lakȟóta. "In a valley between two mountains, he stood. So far away, I thought he was wakȟáŋ."

"Holy?"

"My eyes could not see clearly. I thought maybe I was seeing a white buffalo calf."

"Yes. I remember reading this, but I could not understand why. They are a rarity for sure, but why holy?"

"Why do you want to know?" Grasshopper did not want to explain Ptesáŋwiŋ, White Buffalo Calf Woman, this sacred supernatural woman who first brought the sacred pipe and the teachings. *What are these to the Black Robe?* He smoothed his hand over the yellowed stripe that ran down the pup's spine…a white dog and yet not all white. He had never seen a white buffalo but had heard that, like this dog, the white buffalo calf may not always stay white. *Was there a meaning in this change?*

"I want to understand what the Lakȟóta people believe."

"Why? Because you want to change us?"

What honest answer could the priest give without being offensive? Yes, he wanted to change them. Yes, he wanted to save them! And so he did not answer at all.

Grasshopper took the silence as proof that Bastiat was not different from the other wašíču. Strangely, he felt disappointed.

"Please, let me explain," the priest said, and getting no reply, he continued. "Wakȟáŋ Tȟáŋka, God, loves all people. I want to teach

175

you about Him."

"Do the wašíču believe in this God?"

"Yes, most do."

"Do they listen to his words and do they do as he asks?"

"Yes, many do. They try hard to do His bidding."

"Do the soldiers believe in this God?"

"Yes! They even have a chaplain ... a priest to guide them."

"Then I already know about the teachings of your God."

Bastiat didn't know how to respond to the implications of that. How many Christians acted as Jesus commanded? Love one another? As I have loved you? Is that the way the white man treated the Indians? He was embarrassed.

Niglíču called the puppy to her. "Ȟé! Ȟé!" He ran to her, his tongue lolled out in a smile. "See, Lalá, he likes me!" She held up the puppy's thick legs and wide paws. "And look at him! He will grow as big as the white buffalo calf you thought you saw in the mountains. No, he will grow as big as the mountains themselves."

Bastiat had not yet named the dog but "Ȟé" was a good name for this dog who would grow as big as Niglíču's imagined snow topped Black Hills mountain. *Yes, a good name,* he thought to himself. *But not Ȟé. I will name him Mountain.*

Niglíču stayed after Grasshopper left for the village. The puppy so animated her that her speech came faster than the priest could recognize the words. But he didn't stop her. She seemed so comfortable with the animal and so childlike. When Mountain tired, flattening himself on the cabin floor, she continued to pet him softly. When she once again spoke, it was unclear whether she was addressing the dog or the priest.

"I will tell you about Ptesáŋwiŋ."

It was difficult to find a single way to tell the story to the priest because each storyteller she had heard added his own nuances. When she began, it was immediately clear to the priest that he should take notes that could be useful for another homily.

The spirit woman gave the People the čhaŋnúŋpa, she said, the red bowled medicine pipe with twelve eagle feathers and seven circles representing the seven rites. How could the priest not see the symbolism there! Twelve feathers…twelve apostles! Seven rites…the seven sacraments!

"Wakȟáŋ Tȟáŋka is everywhere," she explained. "and powerful.

But not everyone can see the holiness. And so not everyone has the power."

Fascinating, Bastiat thought, relating these ideas to Catholicism. *How rich my homilies will be!*

Well aware that Catholicism had a rich history of Christianizing heathen activities and holidays, Bastiat set about making connections.

And December 8, the Feast of the Immaculate Conception, would be celebrated soon and the priest prepared. He drew what could pass as a white buffalo calf. Alongside it, he drew the Virgin Mary in a cloud. He dressed her in the traditional blue and white robe and darkened her skin. *Her face probably was tan anyway,* noted the practical side of Bastiat. *She did live in an arid area.* He was getting rather tanned himself, he thought. Weather-beaten.

Dried flowers and rose hips decorated the altar on Mary's feast day. Propped up in the center was his rendering of the Virgin Mary of the White Buffalo. Singing "Immaculate Mary" in a voice best described as cringeworthy, the priest processed in and faced his usual parishioners, all women except for the now identified stranger, Ike.

The Gospel reading was from John, "The Wedding Feast," and the theme was that Mary was like Ptesáŋwiŋ in that she was a pure and holy messenger who said we were to follow certain rules and rituals. She commanded, "Do as He tells you," and Bastiat stressed the "He" was Jesus and suggested that Ptesáŋwiŋ would have wanted them to follow Jesus, too. The priest said that he would show them how some of their rites were similar to the Catholic sacraments. His passion was evident and the women were pleased.

"Fancy footwork there, Padre. Nice job," Ike complimented at the end.

*****

Tȟókayaya he?
Is he your enemy?

Later in the day, Kills overheard his two women talking about that day's Mass.

"What he said made sense," White Birch said to her cousin.

"Couldn't Mary and Ptesáŋwiŋ be the same person? Maybe she

177

appeared to different people with the same message," Pretty Stone added.

"Didn't Ptesáŋwiŋ tell us all people are connected?" White Birch continued persuasively. "Isn't it said if you mixed all colors of people together you would get the color of blood and that means we are all one people?"

Kills had enough of this talk and told his women to be quiet. "Go outside!" he told them. "Speak that foolishness there!"

But he wondered how the priest knew their stories so well now. *What power does this man have to change our stories to suit his?*

He went to Grasshopper with his suspicions. "It is your granddaughter who tells this Black Robe our stories I think."

"I will call her and we can ask."

Niglíču had been practicing with her bow and it was not usual for her grandfather to ask to speak to her then. She approached the two men nervously.

Grasshopper began the questioning immediately. "Did you tell the Black Robe the story of Ptesáŋwiŋ?"

"I did. He wanted to know. He asked you. Do you remember?"

"I remember not telling him."

"I remember you saying you know all you need to know. But I need to know more. Is that wrong? Didn't you say we must know our enemy well?"

"You can look at me and say he is your enemy?"

Realizing he had trapped her, she raised her chin boldly and looked at both of them. "No. He is not my enemy."

Grateful that she did not see the same look of disgust on her grandfather's face as was so clearly displayed on Kill's, she took a deep breath. "And I think he is not your enemy either."

"Tomorrow I will go to see this ceremony. I will see for myself how he twists our stories," Grasshopper asserted.

*****

There! I found it! After flipping through half the book, Fr. Bastiat finally found the illustration he was looking for: St. John the Evangelist, painted as a serious young man with long hair. He held a scroll. An eagle with outspread wings hovered behind him. A shaft of lightning zigzagged across the sky as background. St. John, Son of Thunder!

To the priest, the painting could almost be interpreted as a representation of Crazy Horse, their Lakȟóta hero. Serious. Long hair. The Eagle. Lightning!

He was sure he could make his parishioners see this! While preparing his homily the night before, even he was amazed at how easily the two images linked and he felt rather clever, and even vainly proud of himself, that he had discovered this. When he opened the church that morning, he propped the book upright on the altar, open to the painting. *Let them see as soon as they arrive! Let them guess who the man is!*

Grasshopper did not sit on the makeshift pews. He was not there to participate after all…just to observe. He sat cross-legged against the wall by the door, impossible to miss by the entering priest who faltered in his singing when he saw the old warrior there.

The priest knew suddenly that he would be scrutinized, that his every move would be judged. He did not know Grasshopper's motive but he was certain he wasn't there to worship. Strangely, Bastiat thought his Mass was on trial and that Grasshopper was judge and jury.

Holy Spirit, give me the words…

Given the strength to ignore the judgement, Fr. Bastiat gave an admirable homily directing it mostly in word and tone to Niglíču who sat between the two cousins. He carried his book from the little sanctuary to the pews and invited the parishioners to look closely and see the similarities between the image of St. John and their perception of the never photographed Crazy Horse. They nodded their understanding approvingly…even Niglíču did… but when the priest carried the book to Grasshopper, the old warrior turned his head aside, emphatically declining participation.

Ike, who apparently had formal schooling, raised his hand to get Bastiat's attention.

"Padre, you were saying that the apostles had formal names and that we can change our own name to one of theirs if we want. We could be called Matthew, Mark, Luke, John, Judas…"

"I never said Judas!"

"Well, I already have a white man's name anyway. Did any holy wašíču have the name Ike?"

"I don't know. I don't remember any…maybe Isaac… but you are not supposed to ask me questions during Mass."

"Why not? You are teaching!"

"Later, Ike. Later!"

The Liturgy of the Eucharist commenced with the priest facing the altar, reciting the Latin mysteries leading to the Consecration.

The congregation was supposed to be silent but when the priest raised both the host and the cup, a child called out,

"Ímapuze!" The child was thirsty.

Flustered, the priest continued.

"Líla lowáčhiŋ!"

Now he is hungry! Bastiat interpreted.

The child toddled the few steps to the altar and tugged on Bastiat's robe. The priest looked at him sternly. This had never happened to him before. No one approached the altar itself during this holy time. True, this was a child, he thought, but he said, "No!" He turned towards his parishioners and the look he gave the mother of the child caused her to quickly gather her son, sit, unbutton her loose blouse and offer him her breast.

The priest blushed.

No parishioners were invited to partake of the Eucharistic Meal as none had even been baptized. When Mass was over, all parishioners left, but Grasshopper stood in the back with Niglíču.

"I have a question," Grasshopper said. "Can I ask now?" he continued, with a hint of sarcasm in his voice.

"Yes! Let's sit and talk." The priest was glad for the opportunity, but wary. One of his personal goals was to baptize this man. If he did, many others would follow suit.

"Every morning, the people come to hear you. They sit and you talk. They pray with you, I think. Then you eat. They do not get the food you say is wakȟáŋ. They want it and you say no. Why is this?"

"They are not ready."

"What does this 'ready' mean?"

"They are not pure. Their spirit does not know God."

"That child is not pure? He does not know God? How can you know who knows Wakȟáŋ Tȟáŋka?"

"There are ceremonies. There are rites. You have rites that White Buffalo Calf Woman gave your people. We have seven rites too. I can explain them. Maybe you will find them ...?"

"Hiyá. That is enough of your God for now."

He was unusually quiet as they walked home. There was much to think about, but little he could put into words. He did not find the ceremony offensive. Nor did he think the comparison of Crazy Horse to John was disrespectful. Grudgingly he admitted he could even see why all could not be included in this ceremonial meal. This was so even among his own people and their ceremonies. But he was content in the way he related to Wakȟáŋ Tȟáŋka and saw no reason to change.

*****

A slab of ham. Dried peas. Onion. Bacon. A carrot. Fr. Bastiat looked at the ingredients he had on hand and decided he could surprise Niglíču with a soup. He had no recipe but he figured if he simmered these long enough in water they might resemble something his mother made on cold winter days. *If only I had crackers!*

The mixture came to a rapid boil easily on the hot stove but the priest played with both the fire and the position of the pot and got it to slowly bubble. The cabin was filled with the familiar scent of his childhood home when Niglíču arrived around noon.

She brushed off the snow from her thin blanket cape and stomped the slush off her feet in the doorway. Shivering, she immediately went to the stove to warm her hands over the top.

"Here. Let me make the fire hotter so you can warm up!"

"Your soup smells good," she observed.

The small sticks he added to guarantee flames rather than glowing coals, made the stove sizzling hot, boiling the soup to overflowing. Splashes danced on the stove top, fascinating Niglíču. The priest took her arm and gently pulled her back. "Too close. You'll get burned."

He remembered the same admonition applied to himself and his brother long ago. When their mother wasn't looking, they'd spit on the stove and watch the saliva bubble into evaporation. He smiled wide at the memory.

"What is so funny?"

"Funny? Oh, just remembering something…" Suddenly playful he said, "Watch this!"

He stepped away from the stove, bent down, squished up his

mouth to stimulate saliva flow and then propelled a thimbleful of spit onto the side of the hot stove. Hissing when it hit, the liquid slid down until it all disappeared. Bastiat looked at her expectantly. "Well?"

The spitting was so unexpected, she did not know how to respond. She surmised by his twinkling eyes that this was not an acceptable custom, but rather a playfully defiant action.

"Well? You try it!"

"I spit on your stove?"

"Yes, do it. Watch it 'evaporate.' Watch it disappear. Evaporate. You say the word."

"Evaporate?"

"Wonderful! Now do it!" he laughed.

She, too, worked her mouth to gather saliva. Looking to him for approval, she concentrated and sent a stream of saliva next to where his hit. It hissed. It slid down and bubbled away.

He clapped his hands. "Bravo! Bravo!"

They made a contest of it: whose spit could survive the longest in its path down the iron. How they laughed! How the priest realized how much he loved her!

*****

Tuktél úŋ héči slolyé šni.
He didn't know where she was.

It snowed every day the week before Christmas. There was not much accumulation, but the days were windy and raw. Niglíču did not come to see the priest, although he took his straw broom and swept the snow from his little bridge each day. Mountain would bound before him to and from the river, tasting the snow and burying his head in it only to shake it all off in delighted excitement. He was growing rapidly, looking more wolf-like as he shed the puppy fur in favor of a dense winter undercoat. He would trot alongside Ned as Bastiat rode into town and would follow the priest as he entered buildings there, making the patrons uncomfortable with his wolf-like presence.

A package waited for him at the post office! A Christmas gift from his brother he was sure…the one gift he could expect every

182

Christmas. He cradled it under his arm on the ride back, deciding not to open it until Christmas Day. There was little else to mark the holiday in the village…little else anywhere save for the pine wreath on the post office door.

"Don't you dare touch this!" Bastiat warned the dog when he placed the soft package on the table.

*****

Niglíču worried about her grandfather. There appeared little that interested him since the first snowfall. While he did everything that needed to be done, there was little to do save for gathering wood and adding sticks to the fire he sat before for long hours of the day. She had become responsible for the cooking. It was she who checked the traps and followed trails in the hunt for small game.

One day she spotted turkey prints. The bird's three front facing toes pressed deeply into the snow over and over while the rear toe dragged a linear trail behind, making the bird easy to follow. It was rare to find a turkey so close to the village, their flocks having been decimated by desperate reservation hunters. She found him, thin and old, scratching at dried leaves, pecking for seeds and sent her arrow into him, proud of her skill but sad for the bird, alone when he should have been wintering with a flock.

She expected her grandfather to be jubilant. It had been a long time since they had eaten this meat. Surely he would get excited. Surely now he would smile.

He did smile. Wanly. "Do you know how to prepare this meat?" he asked. She nodded. There were many ways but she thought it would last longer as a stew. "I know where there are onions. The ground is not frozen. I can dig some. We have beans. We will eat well tonight."

Why are there tears in my grandfather's eyes?

"Lalá, why won't you smile anymore?

"Winter is hard on an old man." But it wasn't just winter. It was all that used to be in winter that was not now. *There should be a circle of my relatives here,* he thought. *I should be able to smoke with a cousin. The children should gather and listen to a grandfather tell stories. Maybe I would ask if someone wanted to hunt with me. Maybe I would be busy making arrows. I would see the women making moccasins. There would be joy here even in this cold! And even in the hunger, there would still be hope.*

"I miss them too," she said as though she was privy to his thoughts. There were still nights when she dreamed of her mother, the way she was in the good years. Not that day. She was thankful she did not have many memories of that day anymore. Except for sometimes. Then she'd remember almost everything. Except she could not remember the man who murdered her mother. When she tried to, all she saw was red.

*****

What a temptation that package was! He squeezed it, bent it, determined it was pliable and most probably unbreakable. He sniffed it. Partially untied it and then stopped. *No! I'll wait at least til Christmas Eve!*

The clock struck midnight. He had lain in bed waiting for those twelve chimes. Enlisting the dog in this unwrapping adventure, they walked in the dark to the table. The priest lit the lantern. The dog yawned and whined.

"Ok. I'll let you out first. I have to pee anyway."

Once inside, he carefully untied the strings. Gently unfolded the package ends. Eagerly lifted the folded over flaps and then he saw it.

The blues were exquisite. The crocheted stitches created wavy hills and valleys of alternating light and dark blue rows. Opening it to its full length and width, he saw the blanket would cover his bed. Mountain mouthed the tasseled edges. "Not for you, boy. Not for you!"

Swirling the blanket off the table, he carried it to his bed marveling at its heavy woolen weight. *How warm I will be beneath this!* After flattening the wrinkles and smoothing it evenly, the priest stepped back to admire it. A gift of love for surely his sister-in-law made it for him and he imagined the hours she put into its making. His brother had chosen a good woman indeed!

It took but a moment before Mountain decided to make the blanket his own. He jumped onto   the bed and began a frenzied pawing of it, twisting and bunching it up before he laid down on the heap, satisfied.

"Stop! Stop it right now!" Bastiat shoved the dog off the bed but

Mountain's sharp nails caught on a stitch and so the blanket was dragged off with him. No longer was the blanket perfect. Now there was a pull.

Dammit!

Stretching the yarn on either side of the pull disguised it, but the priest knew now this blanket would only be destroyed should he use it. Sadly he refolded it. Sadly he wrapped the brown paper around it for safekeeping and retied the string. *Merry Christmas! Merry?*

*****

Napé kiŋ hatȟúŋ. Ayábleza he?
His hands are chapped. Did you notice?

"Lalá, tell me another story."

A gust of wind shook the outer covering of the thípi. The whoosh of its force made Grasshopper look up. "Maybe it will snow again."

"We will be warm enough in here," Niglíču observed, sliding closer to the fire. "And your stories will make the day pass quickly."

He smiled. He knew his granddaughter enjoyed the tales of the past but he also was wise to her strategy of trying to cheer him through storytelling.

"Tell me the story about the good white man and the war pony... the one where you would kill the man if he tried to take the pony that was hurt. The story that happened by the new railroad."

"I have told you this many times. Why do you want to hear it again?"

"It is a good story, Lalá. It says that all white men are not bad."

He frowned knowing she wanted the story retold so that she could feel that it was not wrong to like the priest. The story was a short one. He and Kills were young then and riding near a fort built, in part, to protect the railroad. There they saw in the distance a pinto that appeared lame. A white man, maybe a soldier, saw it also and rode up to it before they could. The horse's leg was tangled in the reins, hobbling him. If the white man claimed the pony as his, they would shoot him. It was a Lakȟóta pony, painted and beaded as a war horse. They watched as the white man cut the reins and removed the bridle. They watched him shoo the horse away, and so they spared his life. When the white man left, they caught the pony. It was, in fact, one

185

he had offered his future father-in-law for his wife.

"You said you had thought the horse was wakȟáŋ."

"Maybe it was. Your grandmother rode him for many years." He thought of another story that he had not told…a story of a white man he had not spared. His hand went to his medicine pouch to rub the crinkled photograph through the leather.

"Who will tell this story when we are gone Lalá?"

He had no answer, but she did. One day she would write it all down, like in the priest's big book.

*****

Christmas Day passed like so many other days for the priest. He recounted the story of the Nativity during Mass, and judging by the nods of the women present, they understood his words though not their significance for all of mankind. The story was a good one they thought, but a fantasy. A young woman has a child with no human father? Possible in their stories too, but not in their everyday lives.

"Christ is born in you too! Alive within you right now!" Bastiat proclaimed, but the women cocked their heads in confusion and whispered among themselves during the rest of his homily. Their children gave them immense pleasure but they did not want this white child called Jesus, too.

There was no other celebration after Mass and it started to snow. And because it had been days since he last saw Niglíču, he started to worry about her. Maybe she was sick. Maybe she was cold…He added more wood to the fire. His eyes traveled to the package still on the table.

She would like that.

Inspired, he combed his hair and donned the black robe. He huddled into his new coat, pulled his hat down over his ears, grabbed the package and told Mountain they were going for a walk.

Ned, lonely, neighed his eagerness to leave the small corral. "You can't come this time, old boy. We are crossing the bridge."

The snow was light, falling gently to whiten his path. The wind had died down leaving a serenity befitting the day. Once over the bridge, Mountain bounded ahead, barking his excitement. Niglíču was his playful companion!

Nuzzling his way through the thípi door flap, he entered

186

boisterously, tail wagging furiously as he covered Niglíču's face with sloppy licks. Even Grasshopper had to laugh at this surprise visit.

The scratching by the doorway ended the laughter.

"Hello! May I come in?"

Niglíču looked at her grandfather. He motioned his consent.

"Yes, come inside out of the cold," she invited.

The warmth inside surprised him. He stood there. Grasshopper did not invite him to sit. It wasn't Niglíču's place to do so either.

Awkwardly, the priest extended the package. "It's Christmas Day and I wanted to give Niglíču this gift."

Again Grasshopper nodded his consent and so Niglíču took it, smiling nervously. Clearly her grandfather did not welcome the priest's presence inside his thípi.

"Open it!" the priest invited. His eyes sparkled. This gifting made him happy!

Having never received a wrapped gift before, Niglíču fumbled with the paper but then, with eyes wide, she saw the blue.

"My brother's wife gave it to me, but you will soon see this is not for a man." He glanced at Grasshopper for affirmation, but, in receiving none, continued. "She made it all by herself," he said as she unfolded the blanket, "and I think you will like it. It will keep you warm.

She tossed it over her shoulders, and it draped down in dark blue folds covering her whole body. Her face beamed her happiness.

But the image angered Grasshopper. She looked like one of the "loaf-arounds", people who camped near the forts for handouts. They'd do many things—ugly things—for whatever handouts they could get. Women got gifts, if they were lucky, for the sexual favors they bestowed on the trappers, traders and soldiers. *This life is not for my granddaughter!*

Overreacting, he spoke slow and menacing, "Wašíču, take your blanket and go. She does not need your blanket!"

Wašíču. White Man. It wasn't that he did not know the word, and it wasn't that he found the word so offensive either, but the way Grasshopper had said it made him feel like that was all he was to these people. White. Not a priest. Not an individual. Just a white man.

Tearfully, Niglíču handed him the blanket. He rolled it into a ball

187

and tucked it under his arm.

The two men looked directly at each other and neither dropped his gaze.

"I'm sorry you feel this way," he said as he left. The quiet he left behind was not peaceful.

"I'm sorry," Niglíču said to her grandfather. "I do not want to make you angry with me."

"You did nothing wrong, Ťhakóža."

And yet they did not talk more that day save for what words were necessary.

*****

The next morning Niglíču rose before the day fully brightened and added sticks to the embers of yesterday's fire. She dropped coffee beans into the one metal pot they had and added water to boil. She would surprise her grandfather.

He was tense while he had slept and he awoke stiff. Groaning, he sat up and arched his back in a stretch.

"Here is your coffee, Lalá. And you were right yesterday. I do not need a blanket from a wašíču."

Wašíču. She had never called the Black Robe this. It is wrong to hear this coming from my granddaughter. It does not show respect. The man had saved her life after all.

"Ťhakóža, I have been thinking. Did you notice Bastiat's hands yesterday?"

Bastiat? Since when does he call him 'Bastiat'? she thought.

"His fingertips are cracked. The skin is red and raw. He does not have the right things to wear on his hands this winter."

"I did not notice, Lalá."

"You have a pile of rabbit pelts. Why don't you make him something for his hands? You might persuade him to trade that blanket for them."

A trade. Grasshopper was grateful for this inspiration.

Niglíču's eyes brightened.

"Yes, work all day on these before he trades the blanket to someone else. Tomorrow we will see if he will make this trade."

*****

188

It was too cold to go to the water for a morning song. Too cold to even consider it. Grasshopper stood outside the thípi and sang from there. Softly. His granddaughter still slept. She had worked on the mittens for long hours into the night.

The sky was also too pink for his liking. Cold. Pink sky. He knew snow was coming, and he dreaded it. Ending his prayer song early, he went in search of wood to bring inside to dry. There was little to be found close by anymore.

In his youth, when they had wintered in the forested Black Hills, this wasn't a problem. The towering ponderosa pine covered the hillsides in black. He remembered snapping off the lower dead branches and cracking them across his knee for easy carrying to the thípi. He remembered the taste of the tree's sap which he had chewed to the delight of his senses.

Winter was better then. Their thípi were warm. Parfleches were filled with stored food. When storm winds had whistled through the trees, he remembered the security of buffalo robe blankets; he remembered the warmth of his wife's body under them.

Now he worried. Canvas tents did not retain the heat as well as hides. In cold such as this, in storms such as the one he suspected would arrive later in the day, old people might die.

The first flakes of snow fell before Grasshopper returned. He had managed to find enough wood to last a day if used sparingly. Adding none to the burning embers, he woke up Niglíču and spread the wood out to dry for use when they returned.

"Wake up, Thakóža. If we are to trade today, we should go before the snow falls heavily."

*****

Mountain was outside Bastiat's cabin and the low growl from deep in his throat caught the priest's immediate attention. But the growl soon turned to a whine and then a happy yip as Mountain recognized Niglíču.

"Good morning!" the priest said, nervously walking over to greet them with hand extended. *Why is he here? Is he going to tell me to stay away from Niglíču?*

Grasshopper extended his own hand, surprising the priest who clasped it tightly.

"I'm glad you came. Come in. Come in. We'll have coffee and warm up."

"Your hand is cold. My granddaughter has something you need. She wonders if you will trade for it."

"Trade? Hmmm. Well, we will see. Come inside and we can talk."

When they went inside, Niglíču immediately shrugged off her blanket and went to the stove. Grasshopper noted, with a twinge of uneasiness, just how comfortable she acted in the priest's cabin.

"Thakóža, show the priest what you have."

While she unrolled what looked to be a ball of hide, Grasshopper continued. "She made napíŋkpa otóza. I do not know the way you say this."

Niglíču held out the mismatched mittens, one obviously longer than the other and both larger than was necessary.

"Mittens," Bastiat said. "Those are called mittens."

Both men saw the poor quality of the mitten construction. She had basted together two sets of cut-out outlines of Grasshopper's hands with the fur side out and allowed for extra room. Then she had turned them inside out, leaving the fur inside and the soft leather out. Neither mitten was like the other in any other way. The thumbs were of different lengths, as were the overall dimensions of the mittens. While Bastiat tried them on, Niglíču looked to the floor apprehensively.

She did not, therefore, see the two men exchange a smile when Bastiat held up his hands, modeling the misshapen mittens.

"These are beautiful and so warm!" Bastiat exclaimed. "I do not think I have anything of such value to trade for these."

She saw the twinkle in his eyes and relaxed. He understood. "You have a blue blanket."

"Ah, yes. I think I have it somewhere."

"It is on the chair over there," she pointed out.

"So it is. Then we have a deal? A good trade?"

"Yes."

Grasshopper looked towards the door. The wind had picked up and snow beat against the window. "We should go now."

Just then, a gust blew open the unlatched door and a swoosh of snow swirled into the room.

"Stay. Please. It's warm in here. Wait til the storm dies down at least. Come, have some coffee. I was just about to make pancakes. Eat with me." Bastiat went over to the door and latched it shut. Niglíču looked towards her grandfather. Clearly, she wanted to stay.

"Thank-you. We will stay until the storm is over."

*****

They sat across the table from each other drinking coffee, two older men from different worlds who could not find words to say to each other. Both men directed their attention to Niglíču who served as the intermediary between them, translating their halting attempts at conversation in the other's language.

"What happened to your grandfather's finger that it is missing the top piece?"

Grasshopper held his tin coffee mug with both hands wrapped around it, apparently savoring the warmth. That his left pinkie finger was missing the top knuckle was apparent.

"My grandmother died of the white man's coughing sickness. My grandfather was sad."

Confused at first, Bastiat then remembered that this self-mutilation was a sign of mourning. He shuddered, not wanting to imagine the procedure.

"My wife also died of a white man's disease." His poking finger made dots on his face and arms indicating smallpox.

Niglíču was surprised white men died of these diseases too. After she translated, Grasshopper looked directly at the priest and asked what he did to show he mourned. Bastiat thought a moment and then indicated his black robe. "I became a priest."

Grasshopper nodded his understanding and asked if the priest had children.

Bastiat's eyes filled with tears. "Yes," he said, and held his hands around an imagined pregnancy. "My wife and baby died together."

Needing to change the subject, the priest stood and removed a wood and glass vial from the peg by the door.

"Come here, Niglíču. Look at this."

She went to him, and he pointed to one of the two vials on his thermometer and barometer combination.

"See this silver stripe. It shows how hot or cold it is. It grows tall or gets smaller when it is hot or cold. Watch."

191

Keeping his finger at the level the thermometer first showed, around the 60 degree mark, he walked to the stove. Amazed, Niglíču saw the stripe grow longer. The priest brought the instrument to the window and leaned it against the small glass pane. Immediately the stripe shrank.

He placed it on the table and once again the stripe slowly rose near the original line. "See these numbers. One, two, three,… thirty, forty, fifty,…these measure…these count…the heat. If it is near thirty, then we have cold…ice. If it is near 90, then we are very hot." He fanned himself to indicate this.

Curious now, Grasshopper asked for the explanation. Niglíču replied with her limited understanding, "This line counts the heats. Okȟáta. Many okȟáta. Few okȟáta."

Grasshopper frowned. *This is impossible. There is no such idea…no such word as heats. And if there was, why would anyone want to count them?*

He abruptly got up and walked to the door, opening it to see how the snow was falling. Already there were drifts. Already it obscured his vision. Strong winds buffeted the cabin. The storm had intensified rapidly, but he had traveled through worse conditions. "Come," he directed Niglíču. "We go now."

Bastiat reached out his arm to block her. "No. She cannot go out in this. She is safe here. Can you say she is safe out there?"

Though angered at the interference, Grasshopper thought back to the time his granddaughter had earned her name, Brings Fire. He remembered the frostbite she had endured, her cries as the blood flow returned. He remembered how grateful he was that she survived that cold night of the massacre. *No. I cannot say she will be safe out there in this storm. What if something happens to me?*

"We will stay. Maybe the storm will end soon."

But the snow did not taper off, nor did the wind cease. The temperature rose enough to add freezing rain to the mix, weighing down tree branches and shrubs with ice. Ned whinnied in fear at the sound of cracking limbs. Ice clung to his mane and tail, his shelter not affording sufficient protection.

But inside the snug cabin, the fire crackled warmth. The water boiling on the stove made the air heavy with moisture that froze on the window. Niglíču scratched pictures in the ice. A horse. A dog. A family…parents with children.

"We used to tell stories on days like this," she said, looking towards the shelf of books. "Are there stories in those?" Niglíču walked over to the hastily built bookshelf on the wall. Several books were there and she took down one.

"What book is this? Does it tell a story about your God?"

"That book is called *Adventures of Huckleberry Finn*. It is a story about a little boy who gets into trouble and a Negro who ran away from his master."

"Negro?"

"Yes, a man with black skin."

"Like Há Sápa?"

"A little like that. Yes."

"It is not about your God?"

"No, not this one."

"Can anyone make a book?"

"Yes."

"Will you tell me this story?"

"I'll read it to you someday. But it will take a long time to read. There are many words in this." He paused. "If you let me teach you to read, you can learn the story all by yourself."

Grasshopper scraped the frost off the edges of the window frame where the draft seeped in and looked out. More to himself than to the others, he said, "This storm will invite the old ones to die."

Old ones, Bastiat thought. *Like the old woman who sat in the sun before the thípi of her widowed daughter-in-law. I bring her food. Candy. She loves candy! Her skin is so thin and parchment-like… it seems to pull away from the tendons of her hands when I help her stand. Her clawed hands are always cold, are always a lifeless gray. But when she smiles her toothless smile, I see the beauty she had been in her youth. Will she die today?*

"No!"

To Grasshopper, he said, "Do you know the old woman who sits outside her thípi every day?"

The warrior nodded, and his eyes brightened.

"Come with me. Let's bring her here!"

Grasshopper shawled himself in his blanket while the priest donned coat, hat and his new mittens.

"Stay here, Niglíču! Stay with the dog and keep warm. We'll be back soon."

193

While the two men left together, Grasshopper, the stronger of the two, led the way, breaking the path. His step was determined and sure in the snow while Bastiat stumbled through the drifts, lagging behind.

No smoke rose from the thípi apex. When the men entered, they first noticed the pitifully small fire, mere glowing embers the blanketed women huddled before. A young boy greeted them. "Grandfather, I am cold."

Grasshopper wound a blanket tightly around the old woman while the daughter-in-law and her young son stood by. The old men made a seat of their entwined hands and scooped her up. Seeing the fear in the younger woman's eyes, the priest invited, "You come too."

Together they plowed through the snow and arrived at the cabin breathing heavily. Inside, they tried to stand the old woman up, but the change from extreme cold to the warmth of the cabin disoriented her. She could not support her weight, and her knees buckled. Niglíču pulled back the blankets on the bed and they laid her down.

"What is this? Where am I?" Oyé Wašté *Good Track* sank into the softness of the mattress, but her eyes flashed around nervously at the unfamiliar surroundings.

"You are safe here, grandmother," Niglíču reassured her, pulling up the blankets.

*****

The room darkened when evening came, and the people quieted with the waning light. The priest served them beans and they scraped their plates clean. Fresh coffee warmed them. The boy grew sleepy and his mother tucked him in next to the old woman. Bastiat added more wood to the stove and suggested they all go to sleep. "Tomorrow when the snow has ended, there will be much to do."

But Mountain was restless, pacing before the door. "Go out if you want, but I'm not going with you!" the priest said. He opened the door and the dog darted out, disappearing into the snow.

Several minutes passed and the dog didn't return, unusual behavior for the pup who shadowed the priest all day. Bastiat opened the door, whistling, searching in the darkness, and thus chilling the people inside.

"Uŋčhúwitapi! *We are cold!* Close that!" the young widow

protested. The words were unfamiliar to the priest, but her tone made the meaning clear. He stepped into the storm, closing the door behind him.

Grasshopper wasn't going to sleep anyway. The wood floor was hard and cold in the corner where he lay down wrapped in his blanket. Hugging his blanket tighter, he went to the door. The priest was out there a long time. He called out to him, but there was no answer, only the excited barking of the dog in the distance.

"Lalá? What's wrong?"

"The Black Robe has been outside too long. I will look for him." When she started to get up, he admonished her, "You stay. Sleep."

Several yards from the cabin, Grasshopper, squinting as the icy snow pelted his face, was able to discern a hunched figure slowly coming towards him. The dog appeared to be helping drag something...or someone. He ran to them.

"Bear Teeth," Bastiat gasped between heaving breaths. "I can't get him to stand. He's too heavy to lift!"

Together they hoisted the barely conscious man up. Each man draped an arm over his shoulder and stepped forward. Bear Teeth did not respond with a step of his own, so they half-dragged him to the cabin.

Once inside, they stripped him of his soaked clothing, sat him in front of the stove, covered him in their blankets and offered him hot coffee. As the warmth from the cup allowed circulation in his hands to begin, he grimaced in pain. Grasshopper noted the white of the old man's fingertips did not grow red with the warmth. *Frostbite!*

Slumped forward and shuddering with waves of chills, the old man explained, "I saw you take the women. I had no more wood for my fire, so I tried to follow you."

"He needs to lie down," Bastiat said, looking around for where to put him. There were no extra blankets to cushion him on the floor.

"Bring him to me," Oyé Wašté said. She turned on her side, away from the child, and lifted the blanket. Noting the priest's hesitation, she smiled. "I have done this before."

A flush of blood rose into Bastiat's cheeks. Oyé Wašté pulled aside her blankets and welcomed the naked old man into her embrace, hugged his shivering body to the warmth of her own.

*****

195

Oyé Wašté was the first person to awaken in the morning. The cabin was completely dark, but she felt the dawn. How odd, she thought, to feel dawn. She could not see it as the snow had drifted up over the window and no light was coming through. She decided to just lie still and listen. On her one side, the old man slept peacefully, his breathing slow and even. On the other, the breath of her grandson, sharing her pillow, blew dreamy whispers into her ear. The soft sounds of a blanket sliding over a person changing a sleep position made her think of the many people, old and young, who had slept in her thípi. A steady ticking from a box on the shelf seemed a heartbeat. She expected, in her half sleep, to see glowing embers on the ground, but instead saw a faint red glow from the airspace around the top of the stove door. Someone had tended the fire during the night.

Had someone gone outside during the night? she wondered. *Did he make a path?* Loathe to leave the cozy warmth of the shared bed, she needed to go outside, nonetheless. Her bladder was full.

She turned her head, and instantly the dog awoke. He padded over to the bed. His nails clicking on the hard floor were a new sound to her.

Slowly, the room brightened enough to see the sleeping forms on the floor. The sun must be shining, she thought, as the snow in front of the window looked translucent. The dog walked over to the priest, who was sleeping propped up against the wall near the stove, still half holding a small pile of wood on his lap. Mountain nudged Bastiat awake. He wanted to go out.

Still sore from yesterday, the priest held onto the stove to stand up. Facing the crucifix on the wall, he genuflected before turning towards the door.

She whispered to him as he passed the bed. "I go out, too." Lifting the blankets, she slid herself up to the top of the bed and swung her legs over the child, surprising the priest with her flexibility.

He quietly helped her the rest of the way out of bed and re-covered the two others there. Taking his black robe off the hook by the door, he draped it over her shoulders, and opened the door. Some snow fell off the roof, but snow had not drifted in front of the door. Mountain bounded out and made a path which Oyé Wašté followed. Bastiat made another toward Ned's lean to. The old woman soon

196

followed him.

"I will stay outside for a while. I don't want to wake the others," she said in a mix of Lakȟóta and English. She ran her gnarled fingers through the thick and shaggy winter coat Ned had grown. "My husband gave many horses for me. Six," she said dreamily. "He had many horses." A tear ran down her cheek. Moved, Bastiat wiped it away.

"Come with me. Inside the church. We will make a fire there and it will be warm for Mass."

They walked into the darkened church together. She had been there before, although not each day or even each week. He genuflected before the tabernacle and made the Sign of the Cross and she imitated him, sensing the holiness of the empty building. Incense hug heavily in the air. *Wakȟáŋ,* she thought.

The church soon warmed, but he wasn't sure the people would come today. The storm had passed, but the sun had yet to melt any snow.

Oyé Wašté sat in a front pew with her head down and eyes closed: a picture of prayerful meditation. He knelt before the altar, grateful that he had opened his cabin to the old ones. But rather than being filled with a sense of God's approval, he felt chastised. *Why, Lord?*

He became acutely aware of the crucifix behind the altar. *It feels like He is rebuking me! What is it, Lord? How have I displeased you?* he prayed. And then it was as if Jesus was speaking to him directly. *Why did you not bring all the people into the safety of My house last night? Is not this church that you built their home too?*

*****

Ike called himself a freighter which technically he was, but he did not earn the usual high pay of 70-80 dollars a month an experienced freighter working for Deadwood's Northwestern Express Transportation Corporation did. To be a freighter, a man could either be a driver or a "swamper". Ike was the latter, the man who assisted in the loading and unloading of the 5,000 pounds of cargo a wagon could carry. And though he was hard muscled and experienced, he was not a reliably steady worker and so he was paid considerably less.

He had been at the tail end of a run to Pine Ridge, carrying

197

thousands of pounds of dry goods to the store there, when the storm hit. Four oxen pulled the load and he had walked beside them, preferring this to the bouncing in the wagon. Right before they finally reached their destination, one of the usually surefooted beasts misjudged the depth of a rut and stumbled into it. Ike heard the leg bone crack before the unfortunate beast bellowed its pain. There would be no saving the animal. A bullet to its head ended its misery.

"Lot of meat gonna go to waste here," Ike observed to the driver, his superior in position. "I know some people who could use it."

"Ain't your meat though, is it? You got no right to be giving it away."

"Might be I'd trade for it."

"You ain't got nothin' to trade worth those thousand pounds of meat."

"I'd trade my month's pay if you'd be willing to collect it and explain the circumstances in Deadwood."

The driver thought but a minute before accepting the proposal.

"One more thing," Ike bargained, knowing full well the driver also had no authority to make the deal and would quietly pocket the money for himself. "I'd need help dragging the animal to the village for the people. It'll glide along well enough on the ice."

Snow quickly covered the carcass they secreted behind the church building early that stormy night.

Chapter 5

Ťhaló kiŋ yunáyewičhakhiye.
He shared with them the meat he had received.

"**P**adre!"

Closing the door to the church to retain the heat inside, the priest was surprised by the call.

"I was wondering if you would have morning Mass today. The village seemed a little quiet, so I figured I'd come here to see if you got the whole village converted now. After all, I was away for a while. And you never know the power of the Lord!"

"So good to see you, Ike," Bastiat said with a not-so-subtle hint of sarcasm.

"Where is everybody?"

"Sleeping I suspect." He gestured toward the cabin.

"My, you do work fast indeed, Padre. Not only did you convert them, but you moved them right in with you too!"

"Ike!"

"But there's still more. You didn't get them all, but they'll be coming today for sure. In fact, I invited everyone."

"They're all not coming, Ike. Why would they come because YOU invited them?"

"They're coming for the meat."

"Look, Ike. I don't know anything about you, but I can see you know enough about being Catholic so you know those words are offensive. You can't call the Body of Christ *meat*!'

"Padre. Padre. Not *that* meat. Come let me show you."

A few yards behind the church, a humped mound of snow rose above the sparkling surface. He scooped enough away to reveal the animal, face down, it's long horns spread across the ground.

"Meat for everyone, Padre. You can give a feast. The people will like that...respect you for it too."

"But it's…"

"Yours to do with as you want."

"Why are you doing this, Ike?"

"Let's just say I have a few sins to make up for."

The last time the priest prepared meat from a kill was when he was a boy and had shot a deer. Now he imagined the thick skin of the ox, a hide that someone here might find useful if removed correctly. And the horns? They'll find something to do with those too.

"Ike," the priest said, exasperated, "I don't know what to do with this. How do I cut this up? How will I give this out? How will I cook this?"

"Padre, all you have to do is tell the people it is theirs…the women will know what to do and will welcome doing it too. It's been a long time since they had a whole animal of that size to butcher and cook!"

*****

The snow behind the church was trampled red and muddied around piles of ashes. Crows paced through it all looking for scraps left over from the feasting. There was little for them to find. The people had indeed come. They had feasted and carried back with them meat for their stew pots.

And such a feast it was! Bastiat had to swallow his revulsion and turn away when the ox carcass was gutted and the people began eating organs raw, passing to each other burgundy slivers of shimmering liver and beige-gray strands of intestine.

He looked down, remembering, and saw a small patch of untouched snow, smooth porcelain white with a glimmering puddle of melt in the middle and he flashed back to his boyhood. He sat at the dinner table, next to his younger brother. The empty plate before him was streaked bright with the slanting rays of setting sun coming through the kitchen window, and his tears, one by one, puddled onto it, the second tear bursting into tiny glistening rings upon the first. He focused there, frustrated, listening to his father describe Indians doing exactly what he had just seen that day… eating the raw entrails of a cow they had just slaughtered. "Savages, that's what they are! Savages!"

He didn't have the words then, nor the intellectual development to confront his father, but he knew the man was wrong. He knew his father was not seeing with the eyes of God, but then he couldn't understand that his father's vision was clouded by turbulent waves of western expansion. *I understand now, Father. But you were still wrong.*

His reverie had been broken with a tug on his sleeve. "I told them you wanted the hide, and they will save it for you," Oyé Wašté had whispered to him, smiling and wiping a smear of blood across her cheek. "My daughter-in-law and I will make a robe for you," she stated, still hugging his now stained blanket tight around her. "Wašíču blankets are not heavy enough," she had laughed.

The sun was low in the sky now and the priest was exhausted. Only Ike had remained behind.

"You did well today, Padre," he said. "The people will speak of this day." He looked around. "I think everything is in order. If you're OK, I'll leave now."

"Where will you stay?"

"I'll find a place."

"Stay here."

"That's a fine offer, Padre... I will."

*****

He had not been in his cabin all day and strangely now, when he entered it with Ike, it was less of a cabin and more of a home. *The people have blessed it.* He hung his robe on the peg and noticed the long gray hair that stretched from the neckline to the sleeve. Touching it reverently, he thought of the old woman who had worn the robe that very morning and so he left the hair there, a memorial to the day.

"Padre, I almost forgot. I brought you something." Ike pulled a small package from his chest pocket, a golden contrast to his drab shirt. The bright colored Duke of Durham label added further incongruity. Bastiat recognized it as the new, popular way to use tobacco. Cigarettes. Ike offered him one.

"I don't smoke, Ike."

"You don't have to, but they do. Give one of these out once in a while and make friends." He withdrew one for himself and lit it from the stove. "Here, take a puff. Smoke with me."

One puff was enough. Bastiat coughed. Ike laughed.

The priest went to the shelf and took down a bottle of wine. "I use this for Communion," he said. "But I don't think God would mind if we shared some." The tin cups for the morning's coffee had yet to be washed and he had no others. Taking a rag, he wiped the interior of two and poured in the wine.

Handing one to Ike, he asked, "Why do you call me 'Padre'?"

"My grandfather was Mexican. A good man. I spent some time with him after his wife died. She was Indian. Apache I think. And I was a small boy. Anyway, he was Catholic and saw to it that I was baptized and learned about Jesus. I remember him referring to the priests that way."

"How'd you end up with the Lakȟóta?"

"My mother was Lakȟóta."

"Your father went to live with her people?"

"My mother never said where my father went."

There was a long silence. "Sorry to hear that, Ike. Fathers are important. They make their sons men."

"The Lakȟóta can have many fathers. My uncles are like my father. My mother's brother raised me as his own."

"However did you get your name, Ike?"

"That is a good story, Padre. When I was little, I'd walk around the camp like I was guarding it. The people would tease me, calling me Akíčita Čík'a, Little Scout. That became my name. When I applied to scout for the Army, they asked who I was. I told them. The sergeant said, 'Hell, I cain't say that. You're Ike.' I kinda liked it and so that's what I call myself now."

"I noticed the children today called you something else, though."

Ike laughed. "Iktómi. Spider. The trickster in their stories. I like that one too ... a lot." A sly, one-sided smile slipped across his face.

"You were an Army scout? How did that happen, and how did you ever end up here?

"Padre, that's a long story. Best not told. What about you? How'd you end up on a reservation?"

"Another long story, Ike."

"You ever hear of Wovoka, Padre?" Without waiting for an answer he continued, "He's a Paiute who learned about Jesus. He had a vision that God would come and save the people from the white men and that the buffalo herds would return. I saw him. Heard him. In Nevada. Convincing guy."

"He's the one with the Ghost Dance?"

"He's the one."

"Have you danced?"

"I've done all sorts of dancing, Padre."

"The Ghost Dance, I mean."

"I have. Padre, let me tell you something. The Ghost Dance and Wovoka's teaching were nothing like what they've been saying at Pine Ridge. I never heard Wovoka say anything about shirts that stop bullets. That was dreamed up here. Even after the Wounded Knee massacre, there are still some people who think the old ways will return. Even now that they see the Ghost Shirts did no good at all."

"Ike, I want to teach the people the real things about Jesus. Let them believe in something real."

"Guess that's the problem, Padre. How do you know what things are the real ones?

*****

Niglíču wówapi káǧa čhíŋ.
Niglíču wants to write books.

The day was warm and the cabin was stuffy. Leaving the door open gave Mountain free access to the outside which he took full advantage of to dig through the ashes and roll around on the fat smeared snow, perfuming himself in the scent of meat. No longer was he white. He padded triumphantly into the cabin and shook himself, splattering soiled snow on the floor. Resting his forelegs on the priest's knees, he barked.

"I'm not going outside! Can't you see I'm trying to write the homily for this Sunday!"

The dog cocked his head and lolled his long tongue. Bastiat had to laugh at the dog's rendition of a smile. He laughed that he was now talking to a dog expecting him to understand his words. And finally, he laughed wryly thinking any of his parishioners would care what his homily was about anyway.

"Ok ok! I'll get dressed! I'll go out with you! Wait, ok! Sit! Good boy! Sit!"

Trees dripped their melted ice on them, but when no longer under their canopy, the two walked under a cloudless blue sky. Many branches had fallen under the weight of the precipitation. The people would, at least, have kindling for their fires.

Their wandering led them to the bridge, although Bastiat admitted it wasn't just chance that had brought them there. He wanted to see Grasshopper and Niglíču again. He had an important question to ask.

His reception was warmer than before, but not as inviting as he had hoped. Clearly Grasshopper was suspicious of this visit's intent. The priest initiated small talk, but then running out of things to say and hoping to find common ground, he brought up the subject of Wovoka. He soon found Grasshopper was weary of the promises of this so-called prophet. The buffalo were not returning. The wašíču would not be leaving.

"You did not come here to speak of Wovoka. Why are you here?"

Blushing, the priest explained that he wanted to teach Niglíču how to read and write. It would be like she was in a white man's school, but his school, and because she would be under his protection, this would save her from being sent away.

The reasoning seemed sound, but Grasshopper gave no indication of his feelings. Instead, he called Niglíču. Breathless, she ran to him with the dog at her side leaping up in his attempts to grab her furry mittens.

"Stop that, Mountain! You'll knock her over!" Ignoring him, the dog leapt again, and this time did indeed knock Niglíču to the ground. He straddled the laughing girl and they wrestled for possession of the mittens.

Growing concerned that the playful growls might be turning aggressive, the priest yelled at Mountain again.

"The wolf-dog will never hurt her," Grasshopper assured.

"How do you know?"

"The wolf is her spirit guide."

Leaving no opportunity for explanation, Grasshopper addressed his granddaughter. "Thakóža, the Black Robe wants to know if you want to learn how to make the words in his books. He wants to know if you want to learn how to tell what these signs in his books mean."

She turned to Bastiat. "Padre, I would like that."

The priest blushed. "No, no! You are not to call me this. The word is wrong here. Ike uses it but not you! Call me ..."

A sudden warm inspiration from his past, a picture of his French-Canadian grandfather, rose before his eyes, causing him to say impulsively, "Pepére. Call me Pepére."

Grandfather. He presumed to label himself this using a term he had called his own grandfather. But he would not translate the word unless they asked. Kinship was very important to the Lakȟóta, he knew. Children often called older men by that term, regardless of their actual relationship. But he knew he was implying a more intimate kinship and felt a twinge of guilt at this deception.

They planned she should come to him every other day for her schooling. On one day she would go with her grandfather to further learn the ways of her people. She would learn to track game and sharpen her skills with the bow. Perhaps, but not to her liking, she would also practice the skills Lakȟóta women would need to know. On the other days, she would learn with the priest. To Bastiat, it seemed a fair compromise.

Busy making plans for her education, he grew careless as he walked home. Thinking about books he could send for, *maybe my brother can help?* he slipped on the ice but quickly balanced himself, proud that he did. He envisioned the chalkboard and on what wall he would mount it. He could feel the smooth chalk glide over its surface. The idea of being her teacher so excited him!

The bridge was just somewhat white and so the priest gave the safety of crossing no thought at all. But the snow packed into the crevices between the logs had melted in full sun, only to refreeze into ice later as the skies became cloudy. The ice glistened with a film of water on top and when Bastiat stepped on it, his left leg shot out from under him and, wrenching his right ankle to balance himself, he fell down hard on the logs.

He looked around. Thankfully, no one was there to see his embarrassment. "And," he said out loud, and proudly to Mountain, who was barking excitedly from the bank of the nearly frozen river, "I did not even fall in!"

*****

Huŋká kiŋ otákuye-káǧapi na...
The huŋká establishes kinship, and then...

205

His good fortune did not last, as it took but a moment for the pain to come. When it did, it radiated up from his ankle with a ferocity that surprised him. He managed to get on his knees, but he could not stand without pressure being put on that ankle. And because he did not know if it was broken, he crawled the short way to the end of the bridge to avoid making it worse. However, finding this method to be so slow and difficult, the priest hoped that by leaning down on Mountain's back, he could push himself up to a standing position and hobble home without causing more damage.

"Mountain, come! Good boy!"

The priest grabbed hold of the loose skin on the back of the growing dog's neck. "Stay. Good boy. Stay!"

Afraid of the frantic hold restraining him, the pup squirmed. Desperate, Bastiat tightened his grip scaring the dog even more. Mountain twisted, pulling Bastiat forward until he lay face down on the wet snow. Shivering now, but more from stress than from the actual cold, the priest knew he needed to get to the cabin quickly. It was an easy distance to travel under ordinary circumstances, but now it seemed impossibly far.

Since I can at least crawl, I can do this, he said to himself, but his long black robe made crawling difficult. His knees ground the robe into the snow. Flipping over onto his back, he hiked up the soaked front. Tucking it into his belt made crawling more efficient, although much colder, as he now had only the cotton of his union suit between his skin and the very wet ice.

Gradually the cold dulled his thinking into a willingness to embrace the sleep it offered, but Mountain nipped at him and danced around him, barking. The sound echoed.

*****

Ike was on his way to bring the end of a bolt of floral calico to a woman he wanted to impress. For unloading the shopkeeper's wagon that afternoon, the proprietor paid Ike as usual with extra merchandise. In this case, there was a foot of cloth left over from the bolt, enough for a headpiece…enough even to make ribbons to braid into the woman's hair. He fantasized parting silky hair and weaving ribbon through it.

Until a freighting job materialized, Ike subsisted by trading. Little cash was earned for the odd jobs he performed. Sometimes the payment would be stale loaves of bread or a pie. Other times it might be a defective tool or a meaty bone for stew, but always it was something the reservation Lakȟóta did not have ready access to and thus it served Ike well to get a free meal, a place to sleep or, better still, whiskey. And maybe a woman to spend the night with, as he dreamed about now.

Ike sauntered along, imagining, when suddenly, he heard the barking.

The priest's dog? None of the camp dogs had so deep a bark.

He followed the sound towards the bridge and then spotted the priest, a heap of black against the muddied snow draped with the body of the barking dog.

Ike ran to him. "Padre! Padre!"

Roused, Bastiat lifted his head. "Help me!...I can't walk...my ankle...so cold."

"Don't worry. Stay still! I have you!" Ike bent over the priest, grabbed his arms, and tried to hoist him up. "Damn, you're heavy, Padre!" After a slippery struggle, Bastiat wobbled on one leg, balancing himself with a hand on Ike's shoulder.

"Can you walk like this?"

One painful hop made it clear that Bastiat could not, and so Ike bent over and offered his back. "Climb on and hold tight," he said. Struggling under the weight, Ike was able to carry him to the cabin.

Once there and in dry clothing, Bastiat quickly revived in both body and spirit.

"I don't think it's broken. You were lucky. And the snow has kept the swelling down too. But I'm going to splint it anyway. "

"Thank you, Ike," Bastiat said shyly, embarrassed by his neediness. "How can I ever repay you?"

Because there was no immediate response, the priest became uneasy. It wasn't that he did not trust Ike, but the man was an enigma, living in and between both worlds with curious dysfunction.

"Well, Padre. I was meaning to ask you something, anyway. I travel a lot, and I usually find a welcoming ... er ... thípi to spend the night in while I am here, but sometimes I am not so lucky. On nights like that, I wonder if I could sleep in the church. I won't be disrespectful with Jesus living there and all, and I don't think God would mind me keeping warm in the winter."

207

"You want to sleep in the church?"

"If I could, Padre."

"In the church?" Bastiat repeated. and then he surprised himself by saying, "No ... but I suppose you could stay here…when you're not *lucky*."

"Share this cabin with you? I'd appreciate that. And by the way, given your circumstances, I'm going to stay here a few days. "

"I'm fine. I can hobble along inside here well enough."

"Inside, yes, maybe. But you need wood for that stove. You have that horse that needs exercising. I wouldn't mind doing that. I'd be careful with him."

*****

The priest's ankle healed quickly. With Ike's help he was able to limit his activity, only walking when necessary. Niglíču came daily, with her grandfather's permission, and performed household chores along with her schooling. Within a few weeks, Bastiat regained his independence and church attendance picked up after he instituted free flapjack breakfasts following the Sunday service.

Chapter 6

Waȟtéšni šíčapi kiŋ! Waktáya yo!
Those bad rascals! Warn him!

The river was high after the thaw and the moist earth warming in the sunshine exuded the smell of Spring. Ike was in high spirits. He would soon be back to hauling freight and would welcome some cash.

The new owner of the general store was not happy when Ike asked to be paid in coins that day for unloading the supply wagon. Pointing to a poster tacked on the wall, Ike explained, "I see The Medicine Show is passing through in a few days and to tell you the truth, I could use some of that medicine they sell."

"Hell, I could get you some "medicine" as good as that...or better...from right around here," he said slyly. It was rumored he sold whiskey to the Indians on the reservation, a punishable offense.

But Kickapoo Sagwa tasted different. A mixture of alcohol, beer and laxatives, it was said to cure just about anything. However, Ike did not have medical problems. It was the warm, foggy feeling he got as a side effect that he loved.

He had met the Indian, Dr. Yellowstone, and Texas Charlie a few years before and though they had many offshoots of their Connecticut based company, Ike hoped he would see them again.

*****

Ike found Bastiat, Grasshopper, and Niglíču together close to the cabin. The priest was pacing out a distance. "One, two, three ..." he said as he counted his short strides. Step by step, with one foot directly in front of the other, he estimated the distance. The others watched quietly.

"If you want, you can build the cabin this wide," he said, and then turning the corner, Bastiat stepped forward another eighteen steps, "and maybe this long. You can make it bigger, but for the two of you, that should be enough."

"Hey Padre, what are you doing?"

"Ike, I am glad you are here! I am trying to explain to Grasshopper the dimensions of a cabin we can build for him. Maybe you can help." Ike turned towards Grasshopper, who did not look like he was particularly interested in the excitement the priest was exhibiting for this project.

Ike spoke to Grasshopper in Lakȟóta and then said, "He thinks this is much too big for him. He wonders why he would need so much room.

"I am trying to get him to see that there would need to be a loft or another room for Niglíču and that there would have to be space for the fireplace and table and the door would need to swing in and this requires careful planning."

"Padre, what he wants is more like a wooden thípi. And what he would really like are buffalo hides so he can make himself a true home."

"Well, he will never get that!" Bastiat said in exasperation.

"Maybe I will," Grasshopper replied.

Sensing an argument brewing, Niglíču changed the direction of the conversation.

"We have not seen you lately," she said to Ike. "Where have you been?"

"Well, Little Cousin, your English is certainly getting better. I've been working. And," he said, "I have some money. And ... the Medicine Show is passing through here soon."

"Medicine Show?" she said.

"Ah, that's right. You do not know what this is! Padre, do you know?"

"We have similar things back East, Ike. Nonsense. Foolishness. All of them."

"But fun, Padre. Come with me! Let's all go!" He described what they would see: the actors, singers, trained dogs, and the competitions.

"Lalá, can we?"

"I will not go, Ťhakóža," but seeing her disappointment he added, "But you can go."

210

*****

A few days later, the three of them set out to experience the Kickapoo Indian Medicine Company's performance. While the company's goal was to sell its cure-all medicines, it employed planted testimonials in the crowd and entertainment to entice the buyers to purchase what they normally would not buy. It was a mostly good-natured con job and as the unlikely trio approached, they could hear the shouts and laughter of both the performers and the small crowd.

They arrived in time to see a small white dog prance on hind legs and spin in circles. Niglíču clapped her hands in delight. She had never seen such a small dog like that poodle! A young boy was juggling five balls in the air while Texas Charlie pointed out this was only possible because of a medicine he sold.

A deep hollow sound came from the back of the brightly painted wagon, followed by a jolting melody from the organ. Niglíču's eyes went wide, and her hands rose to her ears, but she walked over to see the painted lady pumping heavily on the foot pedals and flying her fingers across the white keys. The bouncing body movements jiggled the white tops of her bountiful breasts, barely hidden by the low-cut, tight bodice of her red dress. Men watched appreciatively as she sang. A showman yelled over the music that her lung power—and he winked when he said that—was because of the Sagwa she consumed daily.

Bastiat guided Niglíču away from the scene.

"Come see the shooting contest!" Texas Charlie bellowed over the din. "Prove what a good shot you are and win a bottle of the best medicine in the world!" Many men tried to beat the Indian with his rifle for the promise of a free bottle. Most failed but enough won to encourage participation. Finally, a red bearded man came forward with his rifle. "Hey, isn't that the new storekeep?" someone said.

Niglíču had not yet been to the store, but she felt she knew this man and it scared her. She took a step backwards, peeking out from behind Bastiat, and watched the man swagger drunkenly to the scratched mark on the ground, the point from where he would shoot. He turned around to face the crowd and spat.

"I can beat that savage with my eyes closed! If there weren't

211

ladies present," and he looked lustfully at one, "I would tell you how this rifle killed so many injuns you could pile them up ten feet high, easy."

"Put your money where your mouth is, sir," said the showman.

Niglíču watched as the bearded man raised the rifle to his shoulder. A chill ran through her body that she could not explain. Bastiat tightened his arm around her.

"Are you cold, Niglíču? Should I get a shawl for you?" The priest was always prepared. He had tied warm clothing behind Ned's saddle.

She shook her head.

Closing one eye, the red bearded challenger fired off a perfect shot.

"I told you all. Nobody beats me! Nobody! I am the best there is! I am the best there ever was!" He bragged on and on until the crowd sickened of his self-praise and drifted away.

"I will bet you that bottle that my little cousin can throw a knife better than you anytime!"

Was that Ike? Bastiat thought, searching through the departing crowd.

Ike walked over and placed a hand behind Niglíču's back and pushed her forward.

"My cousin ... against you. What do you think?"

"Ike, what are you doing?" the priest asked incredulously. "No! Stop!"

"Quiet, Padre."

Ike then guided Niglíču through the crowd. "Please, no!" she whispered to him. "I don't want to do this!"

"Ssssh! You do have your knife, right?"

Many turned back to see this new entertainment. The red-bearded man recognized Ike.

"Don't you work for me?"

"Sometimes."

"That's your cousin? That little girl?"

"She is."

There was something in the man's eyes that angered her. Something in his tone that was belittling. Something about his hair..."

Not only was Niglíču developing skill with the bow, but she also was taking great pride in throwing her knife. After seeing this practiced in town during a trip to the food distribution building, she became fascinated with the idea. Ike had picked up the skill on his many travels and he showed her the rudimentary aspects of it. Weeks later he had watched her at practice and was impressed. He was confident she could beat the storekeeper, wobbling even more in his drunkenness.

"Well, my lady," said the bearded man, who bowed low before her with an ugly sneer on his face. "Do you want to go first?"

The showman moved the rifle target closer. The bullet hole from the winning dead center shot drew her eye. Focusing on it, she shot her knife forward. The tip pierced that bullet hole and the crowd gasped. So did Bastiat.

Ike faced the storekeeper, "Your turn," he said, but the man just handed him the bottle of Sagwa and walked away through the crowd.

Guess I'm not gonna be working for him anymore, Ike thought. *But it was worth it.*

*****

Drumbeats coming from the far side of the medicine wagon drew everyone's attention away from the knife throw. Because there was no profit to be made there… and because the show's attendees did not appear to be spending their money freely, the showman needed to gather the crowd before it dispersed without buying their products. Dancing Indians usually were a draw.

But maybe a knife throwing Indian girl might be something to consider. She's drawing the crowd here, the showman thought. *Maybe we can get her to join our show!* But once he saw she was with the priest, he quickly abandoned that thought. *Damn!*

"C'mon," Ike said. "Let's go see what that's all about." He led the way past the painted lady selling "medicine", held up his bottle as a salute to her, and walked to the area from which smoke was spiraling into the sky.

A leather-faced old Indian with no discernable tribal affiliation evident in clothing, hairstyle or jewelry was beating a slow rhythm on the drum. A buffalo horned headdress sat heavily on his head, furrowing his brow. Niglíču looked at Ike. This did not look like a Lakȟóta medicine man to her.

A younger man, but past his prime, and naked except for the

213

breechcloth, walked towards the fire. That he was once firmly muscled was clear, but now the muscles were soft, rolling rather than rippling, as he began his dance. His feathered headdress reached to his heels and swayed left and right with each raised footstep, and to Niglíču he looked as though he were dancing in a dream. Ike shook his head in disgust. the man was clearly drunk. The dancer began his song, but Niglíču could not understand the words and was not even sure they *were* words. Repetitive singsong syllables uttered in a deep voice matched the drumbeat, which got progressively faster, reaching a speed that finally surpassed the ability of the dancer to match it. Sweat beaded on the man's face. Soon out of breath, he struggled on.

"I've seen enough," said Bastiat. "This is pitiful." He took Niglíču's hand and led her away. She did not need to see this degradation of Indians.

And then they heard another song, so virile and menacing it sent chills down the priest's spine. The words were clear and Bastiat could make out a few, angry and hateful insults to white men. Perhaps the warrior was dancing a battle, crouched bending and twisting, ducking and jumping and jabbing with a long stick that substituted for a spear.

Loud Bear.

What a dance he was performing! What a magnificent specimen of a man he still looked to be! The crowd loved it and cheered him on and he loved it too as he envisioned stabbing and torturing and even scalping every one of those watching him, every one whom the alcohol had turned into a soldier from the massacre. Tears came to his eyes, but he blinked them aside, dancing until the drumbeat stopped.

"Now, that was dancing!" Texas Charlie said to the other showmen watching. "See if you can get *him* to join up with us!"

Bastiat overheard the conversation and whispered to Ike. "Those people are wretches. Terrible wretches. Go talk to him. Warn him. Don't let him do this!"

"I will try, Padre."

*****

Wašíču wóečhuŋ él wíyopȟeič'iye.

214

He is selling himself into the way of the White Man.

By the time they started back, it was dark. Niglíču was tired. Sitting behind Bastiat on Ned, she rested her cheek against the priest's back and fell asleep, but she woke up as they approached the village they would pass through to get to the bridge.

The night was warm enough for the people to be outside their thípi, but they were not. It was not so late! Surely children should have been playing or at least sitting before an old grandfather hearing stories of the past. Women should have been walking from one campfire to another, talking to relatives. Men should have been gambling and laughing through games of chance, and surely one young couple should have been standing outside a thípi wrapped in a blanket. Surely…but not now. How her world had changed!

The village was too still. She tightened her hug around the priest's waist.

"What's the matter, Niglíču? Are you OK?"

"There is something missing here tonight."

"It looks fine to me. Everything is as it usually is." Bastiat looked around to be sure he was right.

She looked at Ike. "Do you feel it?"

"I feel it after I have been away for a few days. But I know what you mean.

"Maybe Lalá and I should not move here. Maybe we should stay where we have our thípi now."

Bastiat quickly cut in. "You need to be with more people. You should not be out there, just the two of you."

They passed through the village, seemingly unnoticed. No one opened a thípi flap to see who the riders were, and the few who were sitting outside barely lifted a hand in greeting.

Ike, riding his borrowed horse, led the way across the river. That he could always get a horse while she could not have one for herself bothered Niglíču. Ned was content following, but with the extra weight on his back, he stumbled on the rocks as they crossed.

Another reason to have a horse of my own, she thought.

Grasshopper was waiting for them. "You were gone a long time."

Bastiat smiled. That response…and obvious concern…was typical of a grandfather. "She was safe with us."

Niglíču yawned and went into the thípi, leaving the men to talk outside.

Grasshopper turned to Ike. "What happened?"

Sober now, Ike told him about the knife contest and then about Loud Bear.

"This would be wrong. I must go to him before he decides to leave. He is my only grandson..."

"I'm going with you," Ike said.

Reluctant to leave his granddaughter alone, Grasshopper looked at the priest. Bastiat nodded and said, "Yes, I'll stay here with your granddaughter. Take Ned."

The priest sat outside the thípi reflecting on this shift in his relationship with Grasshopper. Somehow he had earned the old warrior's trust.

Tired though she was, Niglíču could not sleep. When she closed her eyes, she'd see Loud Bear dancing. She knew that it was him, but his face was not right. He had a red beard that bounced up and down. He had a scar that slashed half across his face

"Pepére! Pepére!" she called.

"I'm coming!"

It was dark in the thípi with the door flap closed. The embers were burning in a soft, red glow. It was warm, and it smelled earthy. He heard sobbing.

"What's the matter, Petite-Fille?" *Granddaughter. I called her granddaughter!*

"I am afraid. Please stay inside with me."

"Afraid of what? I'm here."

"That man. The one with the beard."

"Sleep. He is not here." He thought for a minute. "Let's say a prayer together. Do you know you have a guardian angel watching over you at all times?"

"What is an angel?"

"A being from God, who watches you and guides you."

"A spirit being? I think I *have* a guide. A wolf."

"No, Little One, not like that. Not like that at all."

She looked confused.

To demonstrate, he prayed out loud to the guardian angels while Niglíču listened. At the conclusion, he said, "There, doesn't that feel better?"

"I still think this angel is my wolf," she said.

216

He couldn't help but smile. He kissed her good night and wondered if Grasshopper also did. He stroked her hair until her eyes closed in peace.

*****

They found Loud Bear where they expected near the medicine show camp, surrounded by a group of boisterous and clearly intoxicated young men, envious of him.

"I am leaving this place! I am going to be free again!" he bragged to the others. "I will roam the plains, see their cities, get drunk on their firewater. And all I have to do is dance!" He laughed uproariously.

"He is a fool." Grasshopper said. Dismounting, and with determined stride, Grasshopper approached the crowd. "Thakóža, come here!"

The young men looked to Loud Bear to see if he was cowed by the commanding voice. Unwilling to lose face, he pretended indifference and swaggered over.

"You have come to say goodbye," he said deceptively. Though displeasing his grandfather whom he so loved rattled him, he pridefully raised his head and set his face dispassionately.

"I have come to tell you to stay."

"I am a warrior. You do not tell me what to do."

At this, Grasshopper narrowed his eyes. "You no longer know what a warrior is, my grandson."

"Maybe you are right, Thuŋkášila. Maybe I am no warrior. But there is no need for warriors here anymore. All the wars are over. All the real warriors are dead."

Those words stabbed Grasshopper. "No, not all dead yet!"

Loud Bear smirked.

At that obvious display of disrespect, Grasshopper knew it was too late to help. Something more than alcohol had poisoned his grandson. His purpose in life had been stolen and a man without a dream does desperate things. Still, Grasshopper tried one more time.

"You are wrong, Thakóža. There is more need for warriors now than ever before. Do you not remember what Sitting Bull said? A real warrior is not someone who fights. He is one who sacrifices himself for the good of others. He is the one who takes care of the elderly, the defenseless, those who cannot take care of themselves and especially the children."

"Women can do this."

"You need to."

A long silence followed. Ike broke it.

"It will not be what you think, Loud Bear. They will use you. You will never be free. I've seen these things happen."

"And if I stay, I can be like you?" he countered.

Ike lowered his head. There wasn't much he could say to refute the implications.

Loud Bear turned his back on his grandfather to rejoin the crowd, tossing his farewell over his shoulder. "Goodbye, Tȟuŋkášila. Maybe someday you will understand."

Months would pass…years…before they would see each other again.

*****

Mniyáta Niglíču iháŋble.
Mniyáta dreamed about Niglíču.

Mniyáta was dying. It was about as natural a death as one could expect from someone who was born before the white man became a serious threat to the Lakȟóta people. He had grown into manhood with the old ways virtually untouched. An occasional rifle could be had in trade but lacking a steady supply of bullets and the gunsmithing required to keep it functioning, the warriors of Mniyáta's youth largely depended on the bow. Looking back, Mniyáta was grateful to have lived during those times. Looking forward, he was worried for the children of the present time who would never know what that freedom was like.

Although he had only known Niglíču for that short time when she was called Brings Fire, she kept appearing in his dreams. Always there would be water. Always she would be standing either in it or over it on a bridge. She would appear with her arms outstretched and her head thrown back. There was nothing more to this fleeting dream, but the thought of it would last for hours. He was tempted to find her. It could not be hard, he thought. He knew which village she had gone to, but his dream had never seemed to be an invitation. But

218

now that he was dying, the dream changed. She was still in the water, but the vision was more like his first one. She was on a horse and it was his horse.

Although his pinto was fast and healthy, the wašíču had never taken his horse. *Perhaps they are afraid of my power,* he would often laugh to himself. Even as an old man, or perhaps because he was an old man and still a formidable figure, the soldiers left him alone. He traveled extensively from village to village, healing both the people and the few horses they still had. His cures were powerful and the same for both horse and man, as he saw a man's horse as an extension of the man rather than a separate being. The health of one affected the health of the other. The luck of one acted in the same way. His healings reflected this bond.

He rested, leaning against the outside of his thípi, and the sun felt warm upon his face. He closed his eyes and the sun shining on his eyelids made him see a warm red background. In the center, he thought he saw a flicker of movement. *Perhaps it is a shadow of a great bird flying overhead,* he thought, but he was too tired to open his eyes to see. He stared, trancelike, at the interior of his eyelids and the movement seemed to take on form. Three shadowy and faceless shapes appeared. Tall figures, one covered in brown and the other in black, flanked each side of the small one. He knew the small one. Niglíču. He felt her smile before the vision disappeared.

*****

All eyes were on Čhaŋkú Wašté *Good Path*; the young man who led the pinto with the short-skirted tail into the village. The magnificent mare caught everyone's attention. *If I had a pony like that,* Bear Teeth said to himself, *I would never walk again!* It was not just the horse that drew the attention though. The stranger's hair was cut raggedly short in the style of mourning. The bandages on his arm had leaked blood, now dried brown. Bear Teeth approached him.

"You are welcome here," he said.

"I have come to find a girl. I do not know her name now, but it used to be Brings Fire. Do you know her?"

"Why do you want to know?" Bear Teeth did indeed know this was Niglíču, but the old man had learned to suspect strangers.

"I have been told to find her. Mniyáta sent me."

219

Bear Teeth squinted. "I have not seen the waphíye here in a long time. You must tell him to come. I am growing older and want to feel less so. His medicine is good!" he laughed.

"The old healer has gone to the spirit world. Before he died, he told me to find this girl."

"Come with me," Bear Teeth said somberly. "She is not far away." Mniyáta had always been a healer to count on. The scar from the bullet wound in his side tingled as he thought of him.

They walked towards Bastiat's cabin. Seeing the church in the clearing surprised Čhaŋkú Wašté.

"She is here?"

"Yes. She learns the white man's talk from the Black Robe."

Čhaŋkú Wašté had lived with Mniyáta for just under two years and had learned enough from the healer to become one himself. The old medicine man had never spoken to him of this girl until the night he died. He had asked Čhaŋkú Wašté to bury him in the fashion of the old ways, on a scaffold, so his spirit could freely find eternity in the other world of the ancestors, but he made one exception. His horse was not to die with him. All he wanted was a long braid from his horse's tail dangling from his scaffold. The mare herself would go to a little girl formerly named Brings Fire. He was insistent about this. And now, a few days after the medicine man's death, Čhaŋkú Wašté was fulfilling the bequest.

Ned nickered a greeting at the sight of another horse. Being corralled alone was unnatural for him. The mare nickered back.

"Seems he likes her," said Bear Teeth.

Mountain bounded towards them, barking, and the mare reared up and whinnied loudly.

"Iníla nážiŋ yo!" Čhaŋkú Wašté tried unsuccessfully to quiet the mare, who danced skittishly before the dog.

Bastiat and Niglíču came to the door to see what the commotion was.

"Oh, it's you, Bear Teeth! What a beautiful horse you have there!" Bastiat said as he walked over and immediately calmed the horse. "Whoa, little lady. Calm down there!" He was proud that he had not lost this gentling touch with horses. As a blacksmith, it had come in quite handy.

"This medicine man has come to see Niglíču," Bear Teeth said.

"Oh? Come in. Come in. Tie the horse there!" Bastiat said,

pointing to a new hitching post on the far side of the cabin.

The medicine man hesitated, but Bear Teeth reassured him. He entered cautiously.

"Sit! Please. Íyotaka yo!" Bastiat said as he pulled a chair out from beneath the table and gestured to it. He was excited to meet a medicine man. If he could make head-roads with him, he might reach more people.

Čhaŋkú Wašté mistook Bastiat's short Lakȟóta command to mean the Black Robe could understand the Lakȟóta language, and so he began speaking rapidly.

Niglíču's eyes opened wide, and she jumped up excitedly.

"What? What?" Bastiat said. "I'm lost here!"

"The horse! She is mine!"

"Wait! What's going on here?" Bastiat was getting nervous. *What kind of custom is this?* And then his mind overreacted. *Horse? For a girl? This young? What? Marriage?*

Niglíču had recently been teaching the priest the past customs of the Lakȟóta. They had been speaking about marriage traditions in both their cultures. Niglíču had told him that horses were often used as marriage proposals. A man would tie horses outside the thípi of a woman he desired as his wife. If she and her family agreed to this marriage, the family would take the horses and add them to their herd. If not, the horses would stay tied there until the unhappy man, embarrassed now before the tribe, took them away. When Bastiat saw the horse and Niglíču's excitement, he panicked.

Children of Niglíču's age surely are not marriageable! thought Bastiat. *Where is Ike when I need him?* The priest relied on Ike for translations in situations like this.

"Niglíču, you can't go with him! I forbid it!" Bastiat blurted out.

The confused look on the face of Čhaŋkú Wašté, who understood not a word, matched that of Niglíču, who understood each one.

"What?" she said.

"What is wrong?" Bear Teeth echoed.

"Marriage!" Bastiat said, exasperated.

"Marriage?" Niglíču and Bear Teeth laughed, tried to calm down, and then looked at each other and started all over again.

Bastiat turned red.

Čhaŋkú Wašté didn't know what to make of the situation and so he sat respectfully with his head down. What he did know was that he was in the presence of another medicine person, albeit a white one. Medicine people could be powerful, and he was not taking any chances by laughing at this.

The door opened and Ike came in. He never knocked, figuring this was just as much his home as any other.

"What's all this laughter in here? And who owns that beautiful horse out there?"

"Thank God you are here, Ike!" Bastiat said at the same time Niglíču called out, "She's mine!"

"Yours? Did some young warrior come and offer the horse so he could take you away with him?"

Niglíču giggled.

"Enough of this! I said enough! She is not going with him or anyone else! That's final!" Bastiat said.

"Padre, what are you talking about?"

"This man comes here, says the horse is hers, they all talk too fast for me to understand, and before you know it, they have arranged a marriage!"

"Padre, that is craziness. Let me talk to him."

Ike spoke to the clearly bewildered Čhaŋkú Wašté. They spoke far too fast for Bastiat to understand them. Finally, the medicine man smiled and then, he too, laughed.

"Padre, Padre." Ike shook his head and tried to control his own smile, which slipped out anyway. "Sit down and let me explain."

*****

Grasshopper crossed the river and headed towards the priest's cabin. He could have used the bridge, which he had used all winter, but now that it was warmer, he preferred stepping from stone to stone to cross over. He frequently did not get his feet wet, but when his foot did slip off a rock and dip into the water, he reassured himself that it wasn't because he was getting old; this had happened before when he was younger.

It had become his habit to accompany Niglíču home on the days she spent with the priest, and he was beginning to enjoy the conversations he had with the man. They were often spirited jousting matches, comparisons of the philosophies of the two cultures that lasted an hour or so. Sometimes they were just about the differences in their everyday lives, and sometimes they even found they stood on common ground.

He rounded a turn and stopped. A horse stood before the priest's cabin and people stood around it. He was too far away to identify all of them. *Niglíču: yes.* And his heart calmed. *The priest? Ike... but who else? Bear Teeth? Who?*

Niglíču saw him and came running. "Lalá! Come see my new horse!"

Čhaŋkú Wašté recognized Grasshopper, a respected warrior admired in his childhood. Remembering that commanding bearing the warrior had displayed riding through his village on his war pony, Čhaŋkú Wašté could still see hints of it now in the old warrior approaching.

"Thuŋkášila." Čhaŋkú Wašté greeted him. "Grandfather, I bring a gift from Mniyáta."

The young medicine man then spoke of the circumstances around the gifting of this horse. During the explanation, Grasshopper could see the excitement dancing in his granddaughter's eyes. He ran his fingers down the legs of this mare, examining her.

"She looks to be in perfect health," Bastiat said, and Grasshopper agreed.

Grasshopper put his hands on Niglíču's shoulders and said, "You cannot keep this horse."

Everyone was shocked.

"Why? Why can't I keep her?"

Ike stepped in to show support. "Why? Where else are you going to get such a magnificent horse?"

He answered slowly, to Niglíču, "You will be noticed."

There was silence.

Finally, Čhaŋkú Wašté addressed Grasshopper again. "Is it wise to not honor the holy man's last request?"

"Is it wise for me to allow my granddaughter to be the focus of wašíču attention? People will wonder how she got such a beautiful mare. They will ask questions. They might say, 'Isn't she the little girl who was with Soft Feather when she died? Isn't she the little girl who threw the knife? Why isn't she in school....or in jail?' Having this horse is dangerous."

"Mniyáta had this horse," Niglíču argued. "No one bothered him!"

"You are not Mniyáta. Listen to me again. Now you are just

223

another girl. You are nothing to the wašíču. They do not see you. But on the horse, they will see you. They will ask questions. You do not want this."

Bastiat broke in. "There is a solution. I will say the horse is mine. A priest can have two horses. I can have ten horses if I want!" He grinned. "I am a wašíču, after all. And the priest who forgives their sins."

Niglíču looked at her grandfather whose face gave no indication of what he was thinking. But he knew he had lost the argument. Mniyáta was a powerful and respected healer. If he saw a reason to give her his horse, should he go against that? And did not the priest offer an alternative that was logical?

"You may someday have the horse, but for now, the mare belongs to the priest until I decide it is safe for you to call her your own. You can ride the other one. In time, things can change."

*****

She whistled and the pinto came to her. The mare was easy to train. She loved her sugar reward for obeying the sound.

"You need to name her," Bastiat said, thinking of all the horses he had tended to. He knew their names better than that of their owners…in fact he listed the horses' name in his ledger before the owners'.

"Does she need a name? Before she was Mniyáta's horse. That was enough. Now she is my horse and that is enough for me."

"God told man to name all the creatures."

"Isn't 'horse' a name?"

Sometimes the priest regretted teaching her how to argue effectively like scholars of old.

"It is, but a special name for this horse might tell about the way the horse is. Is she fast? Pretty? Faithful? Spotted? These questions help you find a word that's right for her."

"That is how you named Ned?"

He rolled his eyes. "No. I suppose I just liked the sound of it."

"Then a name can be a sound? Not a real word?"

"I guess so" he sighed.

"Then I have found a name. It means something and I like the sound of it. It sounds like a bird. Kičhí. That is her name."

224

"But that makes no sense. Kičhí is part of a word. Not the whole idea of a word. Doesn't it mean "with'? Don't you use it to say you work with somebody? Fight with somebody? Respect somebody? Isn't that what you taught me?"

"You can also use kičhí to say you travel with somebody. She travels with me. I travel with her. We travel with each other. I like the sound of Kičhí. This will be her name."

The priest had to admit there was a brightness to the sound, a bright clip in the pronunciation that matched the high spirits of both horse and girl.

Chapter 7

Šinásapa kiŋ Gnugnúška thípi waŋ wašté kíčağiŋ kte.
The Black Robe will make a pleasant house for Grasshopper.

"**L**alá, don't you want to come and see?"

Papers were strewn all over the priest's table. Bastiat, Ike and Niglíču were huddled around it, shuffling papers, drawing, making notations.

"The Black Robe says I cannot have what I want, so why should I look?"

"I told you," Bastiat said, "I do not know how to make a round cabin."

Grasshopper shrugged. It was one of several requests that were denied. He wanted the cabin the size of his thípi which the priest said was 14 feet across. It seemed a simple request but no, the priest said the wood came in 12 foot lengths. He wanted two windows, big ones, one to face east for the sunrise and one west for the sunset to shine through. The priest said this would cost too much money. Grasshopper did not want one room on top of the other, but this too wasn't to be.

"I do not want to sleep in the sky. When I die, then you can put me on a scaffold. Not before."

"Ike, it is Niglíču who will sleep up there. Make him understand this!" Bastiat said.

"I am, Padre. This ain't easy, you know."

After much discussion, it had been decided weeks ago that a cabin would be built near the priest's. Niglíču wanted this. She wanted to be near her horse. Bastiat wanted this to be near Niglíču. Grasshopper was tired of the discussion and so had consented.

"Finally, we have come to a consensus," the priest declared.

Grasshopper stood to look at the drawing they had made. "The door looks too tall. I want a short door. Like thípi."

Ike clamped a hand on Bastiat's shoulder. The priest looked ready to erupt. "You absolutely can NOT have a short door. I refuse to build it. That would be ridiculous!"

Grasshopper glared at him. "I will make the door. I will find a hide."

"Listen," Ike interrupted. "I saw doors cut in half...top and bottom. The top could stay closed if he wanted."

Grasshopper smiled. This time he thought he had won. "And I want the door to face the afternoon sun. It will be good to sit there and be warmed."

Bastiat sat with his lips stretched tight in a line. Barely moving them, he said, "Yeah, we can do that."

"I want the stove there," Grasshopper pointed to the wall opposite the door.

"Sure."

"I want my little windows to slide up and down. I have seen this. It is a good idea."

"He wants them to open and close like the ones they have in town. He says it gets too hot in here."

The priest threw up his hands. "For a man who was living in a house of skins, he has gotten very demanding!"

Grasshopper shrugged again.

"Padre, I can't help it. I only translate here," Ike said.

"I'll bet," countered the priest.

*****

It was easier to dig out rocks from beside the creek than to pry them up from the soil near the cabin. Ned waited patiently while the travois behind him was being filled with the flattest stones they could find. Most of the sedimentary rocks by the creek were unacceptable for what the priest had in mind for a foundation. Yet still they dug, Ike, Bastiat and Grasshopper, passing rocks to each other before their ultimate deposit in the travois. The work was hard, and the day was hot. Only the cool, flowing water made it bearable.

"Back in New York, all we would have to do is to find an old rock wall border made by some farmer long ago and dismantle it. Easy," Bastiat said.

"We are not in New York, Padre. And I am doing most of the

227

heavy work anyway," Ike said.

It was true, Bastiat had to admit. Ike was the only one able to do this heavy wrenching of the rock from the creek bed. It almost seemed wrong to move the rocks that had been there so long. The sucking sound as they were pulled free of the sand and silt seemed a protest. But a tiny cascade of water immediately filled the space and within seconds it was as if the rock had never been there. The priest had to laugh though. The lifting and shifting of so many rocks from the same area had created for him a small tub to bathe in. He stepped into it.

"Look how deep the water is now!" he said standing with the water above his knees. "Ah… that feels so good!"

"Padre, this is never going to get done if you just stand there!"

This would be their fourth trip with the travois and yet the pile of rocks by the intended foundation was nowhere near the amount they would need. Bastiat could see Grasshopper looked tired though he would never admit it. It was becoming more difficult for him to step up the bank slope to deposit the stone on top and he lingered there longer each time before every descent. It was Niglíču's task to roll the stone onto the travois. She worked hard, but the priest could see how often she wiped her hands on her damp clothing. The dirt that clung to the wet rocks had chafed her palms, making them red.

I'm being unreasonable, the priest finally decided. *There is no point to having a full foundation for a cabin that at best would be temporary. The wood would never be painted. Insects would burrow into it. How much longer would Grasshopper…and indeed, myself…live? And Niglíču? She'd be with a husband in hopefully a better cabin than they were making. And Ike? Who knows where he'll settle?*

"I think we have enough stone now. Let's get this back and then we can rest."

"But Pepére, these are not enough to go around even once!"

"I've changed my mind. We only need four corner supports. I think what we have will suffice."

Ike plunked down the rock he had just lifted. Water sprayed up, some splashing the priest.

"You want to play, do you?" Bastiat said. He stretched back his arm and scooped his hand forward, skimming the water and sending it flying at Ike.

228

Retaliating, Ike splashed back, forcefully. Bastiat stepped to the side to avoid being hit but he slipped on a rock and fell backwards into his "tub." They laughed. Niglíču laughed.

Grasshopper watched, happy Ike and Bastiat had found friendship with each other, but each splash tugged more at his heart. He missed his grandsons. He longed for times such as these with them.

*****

Bastiat lay in bed waiting for dawn. Anxious to be putting in the corner supports the cabin, he had neglected proper preparation of the short weekday homily. His mind was so full of measurements, prayer did not come easily either. If he placed the supports incorrectly…too far apart…too short…not at right angles, the cabin would be a disaster. And he knew he would need to get more rocks. A twelve foot span would put tremendous pressure on the floor frame beams. He would need at least another four supports.

He made Mass shorter than usual, but only his most loyal parishioners had come anyway. Then donning what had come to be his work clothes, he squatted where one corner was to be and dug into the soil. The wet clay clung to his fingers. *How can anyone grow vegetables in this?*

But Bastiat knew the people did not depend on farming at all before reservation life, unless the careful management of buffalo herds was considered agriculture. And he knew they had a special, holy place they revered as a mother… a place of dark trees and the bountiful wildlife that sheltered and sustained the people in the winter. The priest had heard Grasshopper and Kills speak wistfully of this place, Ȟesápa, the Black Hills.

It did not come as a surprise that they wanted to somehow obtain a pass from their Indian Agent to go there. What surprised him was that they thought he could get it from the agent.

Grasshopper and Kills came together to see the priest one afternoon, something that had not happened before, something that made Bastiat immediately suspicious of the visit's purpose. Both men looked serious. This was not going to be a time of pleasant exchanges.

"Do you know a man called Penney?" Grasshopper asked.

"Penny? I don't think so. Penny like the coin? That penny? No," he answered, shaking his head.

"This man is the agent here they say. We need to see him. We need a pass."

"Oh? A pass? I'm sure I can't help with that. I have no authority here with those things." Where do you want to go?"

"Ȟesápa," Kills answered.

On rare occasions a pass might be issued to see a child boarding at a school, or to allow a short hunt for game, but the Black Hills was over 100 miles away and the men had no valid reason for going there.

Bastiat shook his head. "Sorry I can't be of more help."

But it bothered him that these men were virtually imprisoned on the reservation. He tossed and turned during the night wondering if it was true that there was nothing he could do to help. By morning he thought he may have found a way.

The priest wrote to his superiors requesting a type of sabbatical vacation. He had not had a day free since he arrived a few years ago, he explained. He wanted to go to their holy place to better understand their faith, he said. They are a misguided people, he explained, although he was not sure he believed this. He wrote that their faiths had similarities he could use for their conversion. The priest did not mention there had been only a few new Catholics so far. He also requested approval for some Lakȟóta guides to accompany him. He wrote stunning reviews of his own work and how he had established a school, leaving out there was but one student.

A few weeks later, an official letter came back with the Jesuit seal upon it. Bastiat was to present it to the reservation authorities, and secure permission. Because he wasn't sure this would be approved by reservation officials, he kept this secret from the two men.

Foolishly he left the letter opened on the table when Ike wandered in. "What's this?" he asked but he was already reading it by the time Bastiat could think up a deceptive answer. Smiling broadly Ike exclaimed, "We're going to the Black Hills?"

The priest hadn't considered Ike. Having no particular affiliation with any band at Pine Ridge and as a mixed breed freighter, Ike was already free to go as he pleased.

"Kills and Grasshopper want to go. But be quiet about it. They know nothing about this."

"And Niglíču? She is going too?"

"I thought maybe she could stay with Pretty Stone and…"

"Wait a minute. Three old men are going alone? Won't you need me? And do you really think Niglíču is gonna like it if you exclude her? Did you think this through?"

*****

Fr. Bastiat did not know where to find the Indian Agent Penney…if indeed he even still was the agent as they seemed to change. He had heard that some who sought the agents wouldn't find them where they were expected to be and had to choose whether to wait or give up the pass quest all together. *But I am not an Indian and so why must I see him at all? Surely a clerk has access to passes. The men would not be traveling alone so the circumstances surely warrant an exception to normal procedure.*

However, the clerk he was to meet with was Mr. Bordeaux. *Bordeaux will be a problem. He hates me… Or maybe he is afraid of me.*

Ever since he refused to baptize Niglíču, the reservation clerk had done his best to avoid the priest. It was an obvious avoidance, too. One day, months before, Bastiat had been standing at the counter of the post office. The street view reflected in the glass of the clerk's window, and the priest saw that Bordeaux was about to enter. Bordeaux had put his hand on the doorknob. He had looked up and had seen the priest. Their eyes met in the reflection, and then Bordeaux had walked away.

Bastiat thought Bordeaux was hiding something, and he was pretty sure it had to do with Soft Feather's death. The government had sent no one to question Niglíču. And it wasn't that she was hiding or difficult to find.

Maybe I will do some detective work. I'll be like Sherlock Holmes when he had disguised himself as a priest in that novel I so enjoyed." He had just finished reading <u>A Scandal in Bohemia</u>, thanks to his generous brother, who thought the priest needed some diversion out on the reservation. Bastiat had to laugh. *This place is never boring!*

But the case of Soft Feather's sudden death, as Bastiat now referred to it, was over a year old.

How did Soft Feather really die? Bastiat wondered. *And how can I find out?*

231

Soon after, he went to town to question the undertaker. Everyone assumed him to be the last person to see Soft Feather. He had, after all, nailed the coffin lid shut. He found the man is his barn hammering six-foot pine planks together.

"Pays to get a head start on these," he grinned as he saw the priest approach. He figured the visit was going to be about a new customer

"No, no one has died," Bastiat told the man, "at least not recently. I want to ask you about someone you took care of before."

"If the coffin is in the ground, Father, I am no longer responsible for anything. Around here it is often best not to remember much."

"You took care of Soft Feather, Mr. Bordeaux's wife."

"I did. She was a good woman. Always cheerful. Trying to make her husband happy. Was a shame she died ... like that."

Bastiat noticed the hesitation. "From falling?"

"She surely did break her neck. Died instantly, I would guess."

"You would say it was an accident?"

"I couldn't tell you that. But I will tell you one thing, Father. If ... well... can you keep a secret?... I like my little business here. I don't want to stir up no trouble, if you know what I mean."

"I keep lots of secrets," the priest replied.

"Well then, I will tell you. That sweet little lady was beat up pretty bad before she fell."

"How can you know that? She would have been hurt falling down those stairs ...."

"She was bleeding before she died, and she died right quick. That neck snapped right through."

"I don't understand."

"She had blood pooling under her skin. Lots of blood. By her bruises. If she died fast, her heart would have stopped pumping that blood right away. No, she was hurtin' pretty bad already before she fell."

"Could a child have hurt her?"

"A child? Beat Soft Feather? That's the funniest thing I ever did hear!" he said, slapping his thighs with his palms, hee-hawing his laugh. "She was a tough woman, that Soft Feather. I saw her outside beating those rugs clean many a time. Some little kid attack her and that kid would go flying. No, she was beat up by a man." The man cupped his chin. "Besides, the woman had lots of wounds on her forearms. You know, like she was trying to defend herself. The kid

232

would've had to stand on a chair to make those bruises." He nodded his head with a satisfied smile on his face, obviously proud of his detective prowess.

"I see."

"Now, you won't go tellin' anyone I said this, you hear? 'Cause I'll deny every word."

"I promise." But to himself he said, *I promise not to tell anyone, but I surely will hint that I know...to Bordeaux.*

Another sleepless night! He thought the evidence was convincing that Soft Feather had been murdered, but it would never be admissible in a court of law. To pursue the case would be fruitless and might even backfire and cast suspicion on Niglíču or her family. And then he tried to convince himself that Soft Feather's death was indeed an accident because, if otherwise, then in a roundabout way, his refusal to baptize the child had led to the woman's death. He tossed and turned, sweated and shivered in bed. He paced the floor. The bottle of wine on the shelf looked very tempting.

"Tomorrow!" he finally decided and said out loud. "I will go to see Bordeaux tomorrow."

Rather than change into his usual work clothes after he celebrated Mass, he instead donned his long black robe for the occasion. Because he was no longer used to it, the robe felt heavy, hot, and confining. And because he was nervous, his hands shook as he tucked the envelope from New York into his pack.

I've never faced a murderer before and asked for a favor. Taking a deep breath, he corrected himself. *Innocent til proven guilty...remember this!*

Bastiat waited in the general store until he saw Bordeaux arrive for work. He was surprised to see the agent escorting a fashionably dressed blonde woman.

"Who's that woman with Mr. Bordeaux?" Bastiat asked the store clerk when he saw Bordeaux bend down to kiss her goodbye quite solidly on her lips.

"Don't know her name, but I hear he is engaged to her. Daughter of an army officer, I think she is," he replied.

Ammunition, Bastiat thought to himself as he walked across the street and into the clerk's office.

"Good morning, Mr. Bordeaux! And how are you this fine and blessed morning?"

"Good morning, Father, what may I do for you today?" Bordeaux replied in a businesslike tone.

"The Jesuits are sending me to the Black Hills on a sabbatical of sorts. I will be taking some of the Indians with me, of course, to show me the way and naturally, I am applying here for permission. Here are my papers."

Bordeaux looked at them critically.

"We have soldiers stationed here who could take you."

"Yes, of course, but I have chosen my guides for spiritual purposes ... for conversion."

"Are you more free with handing out your baptisms now, Father?" Bordeaux asked sarcastically.

"Ah yes. I am forgetting my manners. I am so sorry to hear of your dear wife's passing," the priest said.

"Yes, a horrible accident. Hard to get over."

"Indeed. Terrible the way she was all bruised around the face and all. Swollen. Looked as though she was beaten, I am told." Bastiat looked at him pointedly. "She must have bounced down those steps quite heavily. Oh, I'm sorry. This must be hard for you."

"Who said she looked like she was beaten?"

"Oh, I wouldn't know ... just hearsay, I suppose."

Bordeaux shuffled the papers around. "I have to look them over carefully. Might take a while."

"That's certainly understandable. I will just go outside and walk around as you do this. I believe I saw a young lady I haven't met yet. Blonde. Good looking. You might have noticed her? I want to see if she is Catholic." He winked. "Get to know her better."

"That woman is my fiancée."

"Really? So soon? Well, since she is going to be around here for a while, I certainly should talk to her. Introduce myself. Say how I know you." He changed his tone to have a darker texture. "Tell her how things work around here. Is she Catholic?"

"Yes, she is."

"Wonderful! Maybe she will ride out and celebrate Mass with us. I think I will invite her now." He hesitated. "Oh, maybe not. I might be away for a while ...."

"Just wait here a moment. Let me look at these." A minute passed as he scanned the pages. "It says you need four Indians."

"I do."

"Well, Father, I will tell you what I am going to do. For old time's sake," and then he hesitated and looked at Bastiat with a stern expression, "I am going to send these papers through. When you get approval, just add the names of those you are taking and give them directly to the chief clerk for filing."

"Thank-you, Mr. Bordeaux. I will head back home now. There's a lot of work to be done before I go."

*****

Bastiat watched Grasshopper's face carefully. "You can go, my friend," he said. "You, Kills, Niglíču...you can go to the Black Hills...be gone even a month." Light came into the old warrior's eyes such as the priest had not seen before.

"You have the pass?"

"It only needs me to fill in the names. See...right here."

Grasshopper took the pass and handed it to his granddaughter. "Can you read these signs?"

Niglíču's smile lit up her face. She was going to the Black Hills! A place she had dreamed about but did not remember seeing! "Yes," she answered excitedly.

It was not the usual pass. More like a document than pass, it gave permission for the priest to take four Indians to accompany and guide him on this pilgrimage. She read each word carefully...slowly...and so Grasshopper could not misunderstand the meaning.

He looked at the priest. "You are taking us?"

Bastiat looked down, embarrassed. He knew the man hadn't wanted him to go along. "It was the only way."

*****

"It was the only way," Grasshopper echoed to Kills when he told him. "We would not be allowed to go if not for the priest's lie."

Kills fumed. At first he said nothing, but after a period of silence while the two men smoked, angry words slid from between his clenched teeth. "I do not need the priest's lie. I do not need permission to go to places that our grandfathers fought for. Our people drove the tribes away more than one hundred winters ago.

235

Ȟesápa is our sacred place. It is my sacred place!"

"The priest will not lead us. We decide where we want to go. This is the only way and I feel it is a good one. I will go with Bastiat. My granddaughter will come with me. Ike says he will also go. First we must finish the cabin, the priest says. Then we will go. You decide if you want to come with us."

Grasshopper stood up and left.

*****

Kȟowákataŋhaŋ oíglake.
They moved across the river.

The wagon groaned under the weight of the planks, but the mules plodded on and then rested, a pattern they repeated to Ike's consternation. Flicking the whip over their rumps, Ike urged them forward on that hot spring day.

The frame of the small cabin had been completed and was resting level on the stone supports.

Level. Definitely level. Ike laughed remembering Niglíču's fascination with the wooden bar having the glass vial and sliding bubble within. "Good girl!" the priest had praised her. "Hold it just so while I hammer the nail in!"

Ike could understand why the priest found Grasshopper annoying. The old warrior asked for adaptations to normal cabin building that made Bastiat cringe. For one, Grasshopper did not want the lowest plank of the walls to be hammered securely in.

"Why not?" Bastiat asked, exasperated.

"I will need to take it off in the summer so the breezes can blow in. Like I rolled up the sides of the thípi. And I want a hole in the roof too…like a smoke hole."

Grudgingly, Bastiat hammered the nails on the bottom planks halfway in. He refused to make a hole in the roof.

Within a week, the cabin had sides and a roof, shutters for still glassless windows, and a door cut in half, top and bottom. Their thípi was rolled up and transported to rest against the cabin. Their few belongings were brought inside. As yet they did not have a stove, but it was warm enough at night so one was not needed. Niglíču cooked outside much as her mother had done during the warm months.

Grasshopper found sleeping in the cabin difficult. The squareness of it was too sharp. The walls were too stiff…they did not billow in with the wind, quiver with a strong breeze. Rain did not tap against the sides but rushed off the roof to splash on the ground outside the window. He laid his blankets near that window and angling his body, he could look out and see the stars but within the cabin he no longer felt connected to the sky.

Chapter 8

Akíčita Číkʼa šúŋkawakȟáŋ waŋ ohíye.
Ike won a horse.

The ground swayed when Ike walked. It dipped and tilted. He carried his half empty bottle and sat down on a bench near the Crouch Line railroad tracks. He had just collected his last pay from the freighters he worked for. He told them he needed some time off. They told him that was fine, but don't bother to come back. *Just like that...like I don't count for anything at all.* He took a swig from the bottle, leaned back and fell asleep.

"I got me a Cayuse horse Ah'm willing to bet iffn anyone wants to play some poker!" an old cowboy announced.

Ike woke up to that and the laughter that followed.

"Ah'm serious, I tell ya. Mighty fine piece of horseflesh. Real cow pony."

"Where's he at, old man?" one of the freighters asked.

At least there'll be one taker, the grizzled ex-cowpoke thought. *I gotta get shed of that ole horse before the train comes. Nobody will buy him. Nobody offered to take him for free either.*

"Play me and I'll show you," he said to the other men.

Within a minute, two men, reckless with their money ... and with their guns in case they were swindled and there was no horse to be won ... volunteered to challenge the old cowboy. Within two minutes, there were three.

"Deal me in too," Ike said as he weaved his way over and sat glassy-eyed before them.

The game was tense and difficult for Ike since he could barely focus on the cards, but when it was time to show them, he was shocked to find his two kings beat the two queens the old cowboy had.

"I won! I won a horse!" Ike jumped up, overturning the makeshift

238

barrel table.

"Crazy Injun!" one loser said.

Tucked his winning hand up his sleeve, the old cowboy feigned disappointment. He wanted to lose, after all, and was good enough at cards to make that happen. Adept at cheating to win, this time he had cheated to lose.

"Well, you won fair and square, my friend. Let's go get you that pony. I have a train to catch."

Ike rested his arm on the cowboy's shoulder for support as they walked over to the livery.

"There he is!" he said, pointing to the only horse in the corral. "He's all yours. By the way, he answers well to his name. Dumpling." Not that the cowboy had called the animal's name in the presence of others, but on lonely nights when he skirted the herd, singing softly to the cattle to keep them calm, he had often substituted Dumpling's name for a woman's in the song just to see the horse's reaction. It never failed. The horse would perk up his ears, shake his head and step livelier. "Dumpling, Dumpling, Dumpling," the cowboy would whisper to the horse. "If only Clara was here."

Clara, the only woman with any type of permanency in his life, had named the horse. When the horse was young...indeed when he was young too... he had called the horse dumb in her presence. Clara had corrected him. "He's not dumb. He's just a dumpling," she had giggled, and the name stuck.

But the horse's name meant nothing to Ike, who had no idea what a dumpling was. To him, the syllables were just sounds strung together. "Dumpling," Ike said nuzzling the animal's face. "Dumpling." Ike shook his head and blinked to clear his eyes and the dappled gray swayback horse nibbled his ear.

"You're a beauty, sure enough, old man. I can see it in your eyes."

*****

Ike sobered up after a few hours of sleep in an empty stall. He walked back out to the corral to inspect his prize and hoped his memory of the swayback animal was not the horse's reality. But it was.

It figures, Ike said to himself. *I never was good at poker.*

Not one to brood over losses, being so used to them, Ike decided

239

to look on the bright side. He was out of work and therefore out of a means of transportation back home. The horse might get him there.

"Hmph," he said to the horse, "Home. It's been a long time thinking any place was home."

The horse's eyes were wet and warm, as though he understood.

"Well, Dumpling ..." Ike stopped. He said the name again. "Dumpling? Dumb? Just my luck to get a dumb horse!"

Dumpling stamped his hoof and shook his head. Slowly from left to right and back. Once. Twice. And then he stared Ike in the eye as if to insist he wasn't dumb at all.

"Maybe I ain't so sober," Ike said, disbelieving.

The worn saddle with scarred leather lay over the top rail with the bridle draped across the horn. Ike hoisted it off and prepared to saddle up.

"What do you think you're doin' there, Injun?" the livery owner said.

"I'm taking my horse," Ike replied testily.

"The horse you can take. The bridle and saddle, you leave. The cowboy left those as payment for the boarding of this sad excuse of an animal."

Damn. I was counting on selling those when the horse died. Get something out of the deal at least.

"Do you have a rawhide strip somewhere?" Ike asked.

"I can give you this old piece," the liveryman said, reaching over to a peg on the wall. A strip of leather a bit over an inch wide and eight inches long hung there.

"That'll work," Ike said, and using the leather as a makeshift bit attached to a rope, Ike fashioned an Indian bridle and placed it on the horse. Dumpling did not seem to mind at all.

"You're an Indian pony now and you had better act like one!" Ike said as the horse bobbed his head.

Ike mounted to ride bareback. The day was hot, and his inner thighs became wet with the horse's sweat as they moved along for hours. The horse's gait was smooth, and he seemed to have endurance despite his looks. They stopped along streams and the horse grazed, satisfying his hunger.

But Ike was hungry, the day after a binge he was always excessively hungry, and as they traveled, his eyes scanned the tall grasses for movement. Finally, a rabbit leapt into view.

Ike sat before the fire that night, sucking the meat off the bones of the thin rabbit and thinking. From experience, he estimated it would take four days to get to Pine Ridge at the pace they were traveling if the horse lasted that long. At first he was doubtful the horse had enough strength, but after the first day passed and the horse hadn't seemed to suffer from the exercise, Ike grew more hopeful.

On the second day, Ike estimated they had doubled the distance travelled the first. He had heard these Cayuse ponies could go twice the distance of the Army horses in a day, but he never suspected old Dumpling had that stamina in him. He figured the horse would never repeat the previous day's performance, but on the third day, he did.

Could a horse seem merry to be working so hard? Ike wondered. "Hey, Dumpling, old boy, why do you look so happy?" It was uncanny the way this horse listened to him and responded in ways that seemed like he understood. This time the horse kicked up his heels and Ike, unsuspecting, almost fell off.

By nightfall, they were at the border of the reservation. They spent that night under cottonwood trees near a trickle of a stream. The horse slept standing close to Ike. By now, Ike knew hobbling was unnecessary.

In the morning, a cool dry wind blew up some dust and the slanting sun rays momentarily obscured the image of a young girl riding her horse. Dumpling heard the pounding of hooves and whinnied. Ike sat up and recognized the pinto in the distance. Niglíču was out for an early morning ride. He watched her.

He had been gone almost two weeks and clearly in that time she had bonded with her horse as they now rode together fluidly.

For a moment, he forgot where he was…forgot he was a grown man.

He seemed young once again and there, flying across the grassy plain, was a young woman whose long black hair floated in undulating waves as she raced her pony.

"It cannot be her," he whispered as he came back towards the present, but his pulse had quickened with the fantasy. He shook his head to clear his thoughts. "No, that was then ..."

In 1876 he was but a boy, but that day after Custer's defeat impassioned him beyond his years. The huge encampment along the Little Bighorn River glowed with excitement. They had beaten the wašíču! Now they were free forever, he had thought. And then he

241

saw her, embodying just such freedom and fell in love. He'd never forget her. He'd compare all other women to her.

Niglíču's pony was lathered. She changed directions and headed for the shade and water where he stood. Not wanting to scare her, he called out to her.

Pulling the pony to a halt, she squinted in the sun and then recognized him. "You're back," she yelled. "I missed you."

"My little cousin, you ride your horse so well now!"

"I was hoping you'd be back soon. My grandfather wants to take the priest to Wounded Knee soon. They want me to go...to explain things...like the interpreter.

Ike felt the blood draining from his face. "Why do they want to go there?"

"Pepére wants to bless the graves. He wants to understand."

Her heart pounded as she whispered, "I don't want to go. Will you go ... please?"

When he did not answer, she asked again. "You will go? So I don't have to?"

"They are forcing you to go?"

"No... But they said they need someone to make the words clear."

"I'll go...so you don't have to." He hadn't been back to Wounded Knee Creek since the massacre. He had hoped to never go back again.

They rode back together, and he explained he won the old horse for her grandfather. It wasn't much of a gift, he confessed, but at least he'd have a horse.

*****

Grasshopper smeared axel grease on the brown wrapping paper the priest had provided for him. The grease entered into the spaces between the fibers and turned the paper vaguely translucent. The priest had insisted the cabin wasn't complete unless something covered the windows and so this greased paper would have to do. Grasshopper complied, not expecting such a window covering to last long anyway. Besides they were leaving soon. In the meantime, he could sleep outside under the stars.

Though a little annoyed to see Niglíču on the pinto rather than on Ned like he had wanted, he was distracted by Ike's horse.

242

"You have a horse now?"

"Actually, I brought this horse for you." Ike dismounted and led Dumpling to Grasshopper. "A real Cayuse. Never gets tired. Easy to ride. Responds well. Used to be a cow pony."

Grasshopper ran his hands down and up the steep valley of the horse's back, and the animal shimmied from side to side. He checked Dumpling's teeth, and the horse tried to bite him. He inspected the hooves and almost got kicked. Grasshopper stepped away.

"Easy to handle, you say?" Grasshopper asked sarcastically.

"Try riding him," Ike replied. "Then you will see."

No sooner did Grasshopper get seated and apply pressure to the horse's ribs, than the horse reared up and bucked. Grasshopper slid off quickly, and Dumpling walked over to Ike and laid his head on his shoulder.

"This is your horse," Grasshopper said.

"But ...." Ike stammered.

"Now you can get a horse for me. One that is younger."

Mountain's bark had alerted Bastiat to the new activity at the cabin. Curious as always, he walked over.

"Ike, how was your trip? I'm glad you are back," he said.

"Padre! Good to see you!"

"Where did you find him?" the priest said, nodding to the horse.

"I won him."

"Won? Him?" The priest had to bite his lip to keep from laughing. "That's…quite a horse you have there."

In defense of Dumpling, Ike blurted out, "I'll have you know, this horse, this pure Cayuse horse, can understand every word you say."

"Really?"

"Yes, indeed. He can even do arithmetic." *Damn! Now why did I say that?*

"Numbers, eh? Then let's test him. Would you care to place a bet?"

"A bet?" Ike squirmed. *Please, let me think of something.*

"One dollar says your horse doesn't even know one plus one," challenged the priest.

"Ok…ok." He stalled for time to think of a way out of this. "Let me talk to the horse and see if he agrees."

Think! Think! Finally, the answer came. "You're on!" He looked Dumpling in the eyes and the horse fixed his gaze on Ike.

243

"Dumpling," Ike asked, "what is one plus one?"

The horse nodded twice. Of course he always nodded twice when Ike spoke to him.

"See, I told you so! My dollar please."

"Hmm," Bastiat said, "double or nothing. Does your horse know two plus two?"

"Of course he does," Ike said, praying that this next idea would work.

Sweating now, Ike asked the question. "Dumpling, what is two plus two?" The horse nodded twice as expected. Bastiat started to laugh. But then Ike, with his back to the priest, looked sternly at Dumpling, blinking hard and fast. Because the horse was confused, he nodded twice again. "See! I told you so!"

"Well, Ike, I guess I owe you some money. Except I don't have any to spare right now since I've become involved in the construction business and have some glass panes on order," the priest said, looking pointedly at Grasshopper.

*****

They would leave early in the morning. Though the blanket he lay upon cushioned him from the floor, Ike couldn't sleep. He listened to the priest's soft snores and the dog's dream movements. When the room brightened in the predawn hour, Ike watched the priest prepare. On his knees before the crucifix on the wall, the priest prayed his morning offering. Then he tucked a small bottle into the sack he always carried, already heavy with a Bible. He boiled water for their morning coffee. While the coffee beans seeped, Bastiat folded a purple stole and tucked it smoothly against the Bible. Purple, the color of mourning and repentance: *Maybe I should wear this color,* Ike thought.

Later, the priest opened the door to a flood of sunlight and a bounding Mountain back from his morning explorations. The dog, sensing the impending trip, barked excitedly.

"No. You are not going with me this time. You are to stay with Niglíču, guard her. The dog cocked his head. He understood the word Niglíču and wagged his long, heavy tail.

Ike stretched, stood up and poured himself coffee. "Hard to sleep around here with that noise!"

244

"You weren't sleeping, Ike. I could feel you watching me."

*****

The land was bleak and the noon sun unrelenting as they approached Wounded Knee Creek to water their horses.

We are four men here together, Ike thought, *but we are all in different worlds right now ... all lost in private thoughts.*

Ike crouched on a rock by the water's edge with his head lowered. He swirled his hands in water, round and round in the cold water trickling from the recent rain. They felt dirty, but he did not really think the water could cleanse them...could not erase that type of defilement. Looking at his dripping hands, Ike asked them, *Why did you do nothing? Wasn't there something you could have done? To stop it? To at least try?*

Hands fascinated Ike. Smooth, wrinkled, hard, scarred, they told stories. He watched the other men. Grasshopper, kneeling, bent low to scoop water up to drink with his right hand while clutching his medicine pouch against his chest with his left. *Why the pouch? What medicine did he have in it? Did it give him strength?* Kills In Winter stood tall in the water and looked defiantly towards the hills on which had stood the cannons of a few years ago. His right hand rested on his knife sheath. His left hand held the old rifle, a rifle that he had found under a pile of brush days after the massacre and one he had kept hidden from the soldiers. *I can guess what he is thinking, guess he wants to go back to that time.* And the priest's hands? *Hands that could heal?* Bastiat held up the jar of clouded creek water with its small particles of sand still spiraling to the bottom and he blessed it with his right hand in the Sign of the Cross. *To sprinkle on the graves, he had said.*

The palms of Ike's own hands slid down his thighs to dry them, but the motion continued beyond that. Up. Down. Up. His fingertips raked furrows in the cloth. His thoughts were far away.

The priest had never seen him like this. "Are you OK, Ike?" Bastiat asked in the soft whisper of a voice he used to console a parishioner.

"I'm alright, Padre. It's just hot."

Kills put his hand on Grasshopper's shoulder. "Come, Kȟolá, we should go there now."

245

They mounted their horses and rode towards the hill where the mass grave was. Bastiat murmured prayers. The others rode silently. At the base of the hill, Kills dismounted and, with a match, lit some very dry sweetgrass. Ike thought it strange that the white man's match should light the fire of purification. Kills blew smoke in all directions and over each of the Lakȟóta men. Taking this as a cue, Bastiat lit some of his own incense. Kills set his jaw, struggling not to express his annoyance at what he considered an intrusion. The two scents mingled.

They left their horses at the base of the hill and began their way up. Bastiat knew enough to let the two old warriors lead. Obviously Kills was not happy he was there. And he did feel like an intruder. He stopped halfway up the long slope to pray. He sprinkled holy water on the path right before him, where he had yet to walk. He turned to face the other direction to bless the path behind him but was surprised to see Ike so far back, not walking at all. He went to him.

"What is it, Ike? What's going on? These are your people buried here. You should be up there honoring them."

"I don't belong up there, Padre."

"I don't understand."

"Tell me, Padre. Does your God forgive men who cannot forgive themselves?"

"God can forgive all things if the man is sorry for them, does penance in reparation for them, tries to never commit such sins again. What have you done, Ike, that you cannot forgive yourself?"

"You see these hands, Padre. They're strong. They've hammered men in fights. They've pulled triggers in war. They've released arrows and ended life."

"Yes... go on."

"But on that day...when those people buried up there were slaughtered, I stood on the side of the soldiers. I was scouting for them. When they opened fire, these hands that have killed...they did nothing. I stood there frozen...sickened... and watched. I couldn't have stopped them all, but I could have stopped at least one from firing. And one person up there might still be alive today if I had. How can I go up there? Čhaŋlwáŋmakȟa! Coward! That's what I am. Coward then and coward now."

The priest knew it wasn't cowardice. It wasn't that Ike was afraid

246

to fight. It was that the unexpected horror of the situation overwhelmed him. But still, it wasn't an easy burden to carry.

"When I finally was able to think, the attack had moved from my position. I saw the women running and I started to run after them...to help...and I remember being hit...on my head... I can see myself falling and then I remember nothing at all. When I came to, it was over."

The priest was quiet. Maybe Ike would say more.

"I didn't always drink, Padre."

"You didn't sin, Ike."

"It doesn't matter what you call it, Padre. I know what I am." Ike looked to the hill and his eyes became cold. "How can I face those two? They are warriors."

*****

Mountain carefully guarded Niglíču and the area around the church and the two cabins. This was his territory, and he marked the perimeters generously with his urine. Large and heavily muscled now, when he looked off into the distance with longing in his eyes, Niglíču could easily imagine his wolf ancestry.

But the hair on his back did not rise threateningly when he and Niglíču came back from a hunt, even when they saw flames from her cooking fire and smoke mysteriously rising before her cabin. When she had left the fire hours before, there were but harmless embers.

Niglíču watched the dog as he loped forward calmly sweeping his tail from left to right. She watched the ears of her pony. Did they flick forward in stiff apprehension? No. Were her nostrils flaring? No. Neither animal seemed concerned about the person who obviously was comfortable in her cabin and so she urged the pony into a trot.

Expecting to see one of the cousins, she saw, instead, Oyé Wašté through the open doorway.

"Tukhí! *Oh my!*" Clearly Mountain had surprised the old woman. Laughing, she leaned forward to pet him.

"Uŋčí! *My grandmother!*" Niglíču addressed Oyé Wašté respectfully, although she was surprised to see the old woman had taken down the parfleches and sacks from the wall. "Why are you here?" she asked.

"I came to visit. Am I not welcome?"

"Well, of course you are ... but this is a far walk from the village."

"I was in no hurry. And I am glad I came. You do not have these in the right order. You should not hang food on the wall either."

"Why? We've always hung them this way."

"No. That was when the sides were slanted." She motioned the angle with her hands. "Now, these walls do not let the air behind the sacks. One side will be damp. You must hang them from there!" She pointed to a beam above. "You have nails?"

Apparently, the old woman thought this needed immediate fixing. Once they dragged the table closer and Niglíču climbed on top with hammer and nails, the old woman gave directions for placement.

When the task was completed, Oyé Wašté said she was tired and would nap.

Hours passed. Niglíču had prepared rabbit stew thanks to the hunting prowess of the dog. When the sun was low in the sky, she woke the old woman. "It will be dark soon. You should go back to your daughter-in-law. She will worry about you."

"She will not worry. I told her I will be staying here until your grandfather returns."

"My grandfather knows I can take care of myself."

"Yes, but he said you would be alone. He *did* say you could take care of yourself. You *have* taken good care of yourself. If your grandfather worried for your protection, would he have sent an old woman like me? I came, as he knew I would, because it is the way of our people to stand by each other. Do you understand this?"

Hours later, they both stretched out on top of blankets. Oyé Wašté tossed and turned, uncomfortable in the strange surroundings. Sleepless, she decided to talk instead.

"Once, long ago, I had a girl like you," said the old woman. "She died one winter of the coughing sickness. No one could save her ... although we tried many things." She became quiet before she spoke again.

"Did you know I met your mother? Many years after my daughter died, I saw a young woman that looked and acted like my daughter would have if she had not died. Independent... like you. Your mother loved to ride her pony...just like you. I remember we were at the summer encampment after a great battle. Many people were there, and it was a happy time. I spoke to her...this daughter of a friend. I remember her eyes were warm and wide, and brown with flecks of gold when she was in the sun. A person would not forget those eyes. Yours are like hers...full of sunshine.

"Uŋčí," whispered Niglíču, "sometimes I dream of killing the man who murdered my mother. When I practice shooting with my bow or throwing my knife, I pretend I am aiming for him. I had promised myself I would kill this man, but I do not remember what he looks like. I only see a blurry image and then I start to feel dizzy and my stomach gets sick."

"That was a hard promise to make as a little girl. I would not think too much of what the man looks like now. I think when you are ready, you will know."

Chapter 9

Oíyokiphiyaománipi na ehákela Mnikȟáta kiŋ él ípi.
They were happy as they travelled and arrived at Hot Springs.

T he official permit allowed them to be gone from the beginning of July to the end of August, more time than the priest had expected. However, since he had heard that Bordeaux's marriage would be in July... and that marriage was a social step up for the reservation clerk...he could see why Bordeaux wanted them gone. Bastiat smiled. Yes, he had made Bordeaux uncomfortable as he had hoped. *Let the man wonder what I know about Soft Feather's death!*

But the priest was a bit uncomfortable too. He wasn't proficient with their language yet, but when the warriors conversed there was a hint of expectation that they might not be returning to the reservation at all. Would they dare to risk Niglíču's life as renegades? Could it be true that none of their people roamed free, hiding in the Black Hills? None? Not one?

*****

The priest was locking up the church when two figures approached on horseback. Há Sápa was one of them. He rode beside a coal black man, presumably his father, whom Bastiat had never met.

"Reverend," the older man said as he approached.

Clearly not a Catholic, was Bastiat's immediate thought.

"Reverend, I have a favor to ask you."

"Yes?"

"Take my son with y'all. Please." The man's Southern drawl was evident

"You catch me by surprise," Bastiat stammered. "And I'm not going alone either. Actually, I hardly know where we are going at all.

You would need to ask the others."

"You would have the permit papers. They would not."

"I do. But your son's name is not on them."

"Put it there."

"Why is it so important that you want to send your son off with us?"

"Look at my son. You see there a black boy. He lives with the Lakȟóta and his mother is Lakȟóta but he appears black, and that is the way people will see him. But he is being raised Lakȟóta and I want all people who will know him to have no doubt that Lakȟóta is who he is."

"But he is also his father's son," said Bastiat, pointing to the clearly visible shackle scars on the man's wrists.

"When I was a young boy, I would see the scars on my grandfather's wrists and ankles and the ones that slashed across his back. I would look at them while he talked about a time when his people were free. I want my son to feel some of that freedom. Take him and show how to hunt in the wild. Show him how to be independent! Life on this reservation will not show him that. I can't show him that the same way you can. My wife wants him to go too. She says this might be his last chance to travel with experienced warriors who knew the past ways."

He looked sternly at his son. "He will not be a problem. I have told him the warriors honor him if they let him travel with them. He understands what this means."

Há Sápa nodded his head. Excited for the adventure, the boy was still nervous. This opportunity had come as a surprise to him.

"We are leaving today," Bastiat said. "Can he be ready?"

"He is ready now."

It was then that the priest noticed the satchel slung over the rump of the boy's horse. The horse looked fit. Big. An American horse. Branded.

"Your horse?" the priest asked the father.

The man raised his chin, "Mine now."

The priest's lifted eyebrow was met with a challenging stare.

"Ok then. Go, speak to the men then. If they agree, I will change the papers."

A short time later, Bastiat found himself playing surgeon with his razor. The iron gall ink used on the document could never be erased

251

or smeared but it could be gently scraped off if the paper was thick enough, and it was. The priest painstakingly ran the razor over the number four, obscuring it enough so that his own ink could make it a five. There was already space beyond the last name for the addition of another. Bastiat copied the penmanship style perfectly and was proud of his forgery. He double checked to be sure he packed his long Jesuit robe. His priestly influence might be especially important on this trip.

"Are you ready yet, Padre?" Ike called out impatiently.

"I am. Does Há Sápa have all he needs?" The satchel looked thin and the boy's "saddle" looked to be a blanket that would double as his sleeping mat.

"It's summer, Padre. He has his father's pistol and lots of ammo. That's all he really needs," Ike said.

The first few hours of the trip towards Mnikȟáta *Hot Springs* were pure fun. After saying their goodbyes in the village...Kills to his women...the priest to his parishioners... and receiving gifts of wasná to eat along the way, they left in high spirits. The horses were fresh and the children were not scolded for racing each other. There was no rush to get anywhere and so it did not matter if their horses expended energy off the trail. The yells and laughter... the way the young people taunted and teased each other ... were exhilarating, giving rise to wistful reminiscing by the warriors.

"Do you remember when we did that? My horse was always faster than yours," Kills boasted.

"I held mine back so you would not be embarrassed by the animal you rode," Grasshopper retorted.

Even Dumpling seemed eager to join the racers and Ike gave him free rein to pursue the youngsters.

"I feel young again," Bastiat sighed with head raised to absorb the warm sunshine.

But by late afternoon, the priest felt decidedly older. His leg muscles had stretched to the point of pain. Maintaining leg compression for stability and balance on a bareback pad was exhausting. He longed for a saddle and regretted not getting at least a used one before he left. *Maybe in Hot Springs! Maybe I can get a saddle there cheap.*

He anticipated a long soak in the hot spring water the two warriors were describing that night. Both Grasshopper and Kills had gone there often when they were young men. The warm waters in the moccasin shaped natural bath were soothing, and it had been erotically pleasant hiding on the low cliffs watching the young women bathe. Kills joked with Grasshopper, "Do you think they used to watch us too?"

Grasshopper answered, "My wife said she did."

But Ike warned them again and again that the train from Deadwood was operating there now. Surely it would be different from what they expected to see.

"Even if they build houses there, the waters will still be the same. You cannot change the water that flows up from the earth! We will swim there soon!" Kills said.

The next afternoon, they crested a red rock cliff that overlooked Hot Springs. No longer was it wilderness, and no longer was it even a sleepy town. There were buildings; tall buildings three stories high and a train ran right through town. There were people. Lots of people.

"Wait here," Ike said. With far more experience in these new western towns, he urged Dumpling down a rocky path to get a closer look. He had an uneasy feeling about this place. It was noisy like the mining town of Deadwood he was familiar with, but the sounds coming from here had a different timbre. He could only describe it by saying it was a more civilized sound... voices of people talking rather than yelling, screaming. Music was here, yes, but not the ragged, syncopated beats of saloon music. The music he heard from the distance was smooth. And the gaily colored patterned and striped clothing these people wore differed from the dirt brown of the miners. Comparing the looks of his party wearing cast off reservation clothing to that of the townspeople...men in suits, women in puffed leg-o-mutton sleeved dresses with cinched waists.... Ike was skeptical of their welcome here. If nothing else, they would be very noticeable. Deadwood was so lawless and diversified, an Indian might pass through unnoticed. He wouldn't be served in a saloon... nor could he gamble there... but there were other opportunities for these services in the darker places of town. He doubted the same would hold true here. If his opinion counted, he would say they should bypass this town altogether.

But Bastiat was anxious to go down.

"Padre, look at the people there. They would not welcome us to "dirty" their town."

"But I want to see it! I want to go!" Niglíču implored.

"If you insist, at least do this," said Ike. "Put on your black robe, Padre, and ride double down with Niglíču on Ned. I am sure he is used to the city noises. And no, Niglíču, your horse might not behave well.

"I want to go too," Há Sápa stated emphatically.

"Not this time, little cousin," Ike said with a finality that the boy did not want to question. The priest did not need another racial issue to deal with in this wašíču town. "When it gets dark...after they return...then maybe we'll go."

Ned did not shy away from the crowds. If anything, he bullied his way through them, but no one protested when they saw he was ridden by a priest. Ike was right. The robe made a difference.

Bastiat brought the horse closer to the train station when he heard the whistle of the incoming train. As the engine noise increased, Niglíču tightened her hold around his waist. The steam engine whooshed to a halt right in front of them and the conductor blew the whistle again in response to a little boy jerking his arm up and down. How the boy cheered! The doors opened and a flood of well-dressed people poured out. Gentlemen held out their hands for the ladies to descend the steps daintily, holding up billowing skirts and revealing tall-heeled shoes with buckles and straps.

"So many wašíču, Pepére, so many," Niglíču whispered. "Why do they come here?"

"They come for the same reason your grandfather came. For the water that comes up from the ground. The water that heals."

"Can we go to these waters, Pepére?"

"I'll try to find them."

Soon the whistle blew again, and the train pulled out. A sign on the station wall pointed to Evan's Plunge.

"We'll go this way," Bastiat said pointing right.

They passed the hotels and finally a huge domed structure came into view.

"The waters are in here," he said.

How can this be? Waters inside? Niglíču thought, but as they rode near, she could hear the squeals of joy and laughter of happy people inside.

"Do you want to go in, too?" Bastiat asked.

"Can I?"

"Yes, I think so, but we need the proper clothing," the priest said.

"They wear clothes to bathe?"

"Ssssh. You will see," Bastiat said.

They tied Ned to a hitching post and walked over to the glass. Pressing their noses against its cloudiness, they could see the interior.

"Father, do you and the young lady there need bathing suits? I have some out back. Ten cents for a few hours?" The old entrepreneur gestured to his booth.

"We do, but ... how can I get my ... uh ... grandniece... here into and out of a dressing room by herself?"

"Hmm, Father, I see your point. Your little lady can get dressed back here and for two cents more, I will find some old lady who will walk her through to the pool. You can meet her there?"

"You know someone I can trust?"

"Trust? You don't think I'm trustworthy? Father, I'm Irish. Do you think I'd cheat a priest?"

With a wink, Bastiat said, "Not if you're smart."

It was not hard for the old man to find an aristocratic white woman who said she would gladly take Niglíču through to the pool. She'd wait there by the entrance until Niglíču got changed.

"That was fast!" Bastiat exclaimed.

"Well, Father, to tell the truth I did lie a little. I see your...niece... is Indian. Ever since that little baby Indian girl was found alive at Wounded Knee--what was her name? Lost Bird, I think it was ... yes, it was ... and ever since then, these rich old white women from back East have had a hankering to save another Indian. I told her this little girl was a survivor." Thinking how clever he was, the old man laughed and laughed.

"But, she is," Bastiat said, cutting the man's laughter short.

"Damn...Father, that was a real bad thing the cavalry did. And then they gave out those Medals of Honor? Shameful! But I don't say this out loud around here. Bad for business, you know. I tell you what, though, Father. She can use the bathing suit for free."

Niglíču emerged from the back wearing the too long woolen swimsuit.

"I swim in this? It is so heavy!"

"You'll be fine," Bastiat said, and with a bathing suit draped over his robed arm, they followed the old man to the entrance.

"Mrs. Claiborne, this here is Niglíču," the old man said, "and this

255

is Father ...?"

"Bastiat. It's a pleasure to meet you, Mrs. Claiborne. Thank you for offering to take my grandniece in. It would be most difficult for me," the priest said. He tried to hand her the entrance fee.

"Don't be silly, Father. It's the least I can do," she replied. "Come, my dear, let's go inside and I can pin up your hair."

Mrs. Claiborne walked up to the desk. "Two, please."

The clerk looked at Niglíču. Shaking his head, he planned to protest her entrance.

"Mr. Evans is a good friend of my family. You do work for him, don't you?" She held out the money. He accepted it and the woman took Niglíču by the hand and they walked in.

Niglíču did not say a word as the older woman pinned up her hair, chatting nonstop about how cute she was. The changing room had little stalls and open areas too, and most women were in some process of undressing or dressing. Niglíču had never seen so many white women before in one room, and the white of their near nakedness caused her to avert her eyes.

"Come, child, let's go to the pool."

As they approached the door, the warm sulfuric smell grew stronger. Once inside, Niglíču stood in awe of the huge structure overhead. With head raised and turning this way and that, she did not see Bastiat coming.

"Thank you," Bastiat said to the woman. "C'mon, Niglíču, let's go."

When she turned and saw him, her eyes moved up and down his body, recognizing his face but not his other features. She was tempted to laugh at his tight one-piece suit with no sleeves and short pants that revealed more of the outline of him than she had ever seen before. Putting an end to this close inspection quickly, he grabbed her hand, lifted her into his arms and plunged feet first into the water.

Expecting a chill, she was surprised to feel the warmth of the constant 87-degree water. She squealed with delight and her voice sounded strange in her ears as echoes of her laughter and the other bathers mixed. With his hands under her armpits, Bastiat raised her high and released her. She plunged down into the deep water and, kicking off the bottom, broke the water surface with loosened hair wrapped across her face.

I remember this, but I remember the water freezing cold, she thought. *I remember strong arms that lifted and dropped me and arms that hugged me close when I rose to the surface again. My father, I did this with my father. Somewhere. I must have.*

Bastiat and Niglíču attracted the attention of the white patrons, but the warmth of the waters and the sight of two people with a generation of years in between them, enjoying each other, softened the hearts of the other swimmers watching this unlikely pair.

For those few moments, it did not matter that these curative waters that the white people now claimed as their own, were now shared with a little girl whose people had had them first.

*****

Akíčita Čík'a heyé, "Čhičhíza wačhíŋ šni."
"I don't want to fight you," Ike said.

When hours passed and they still had not returned, the men became uneasy. Ike cautioned them to be patient. He doubted anyone would hurt a priest.

"I will wait no more. I am going to find them," Grasshopper said.

"Find them? How? Will you burst into buildings? Will you take a man by the shoulder and ask where the priest is? This is foolishness," Ike said. "Wait a little more and if they have not returned, I will go down there and get them myself."

"Now you find courage?" Kills threw the question at him. The anger behind it surprised Ike.

"What do you mean by that?"

"Why should we trust you? That day…you were not with us. You were with the soldiers. I heard the people talking."

Grasshopper intervened. "I do not know what this man did then, but I know the man he is now. I trust his words. We will wait until the sun is there." He pointed to the midpoint of the sun's descent. "I will go down then. Any are welcome to follow me." He walked to the edge of the cliff. Ike walked after him.

"The priest will guard her with his life. The name he has asked her to call him… Pepére?…This means grandfather. This is his people's kinship word."

Grasshopper looked straight ahead and swallowed hard. It was hard to accept that a wašíču could feel this for his granddaughter, but

257

he knew it to be true. "It is good that she calls him this," was all he could say.

*****

They sat in silence watching for their return and it was Ike who first saw them, a dot in the distance gradually becoming larger and more distinguishably a horse with two riders.

"They're coming!" Ike shouted. "Over there!"

"I can go to meet them?" Ha Sápa cried.

"Sure," Ike said. "Go!"

Racing his horse down the hillside, he yelled to them, "How was it?"

Niglíču couldn't wait to tell them about the wonders she experienced. "The pool was so big, and it is always the same inside. Never rains and it never gets cold inside there. And the food was so funny! Pink cloud sugar candy that melts in your mouth! On a stick! Popped corn! And a drink that sends bubbles out of your nose!"

"I think we can all go when it is dark tonight," Bastiat said. Carefully avoiding Kills face he continued, "But not in the pool. You would not be allowed there."

"They can still see in the dark. They have special lights," Ike warned.

"Ah...but there will be music. No one will pay attention to anything but The Bower Family Band. Many people will come to listen. With the crowd, it will be safer for all of us. Even so, I assure you, Ike, we will be careful."

"I will not go," Kills said. "I will stay here with the dog and the horses."

"Lalá, you will come?" Seeing his hesitation, she offered, "I will hold your hand, Lalá."

Grasshopper laughed. "I am so old you must lead me now?"

"No. You will protect all of us."

*****

They rode their horses down the dusty switchback path until they were close enough to town to hear the festivities clearly. This was no ordinary day. It was the Fourth of July and now that it was getting

258

dark, the crowd was excited for the anticipated fireworks.

"We will walk from here," Bastiat instructed. Kills took the reins of all the horses. "I will wait for you over the rise there. The moon will be bright tonight. I will see you approach once you pass that curve." Taking a reluctant Mountain with him, Kills led the animals to the more secluded area.

The sudden blast of brass instruments…coronet, baritone horn and trombone…frightened Niglíču whose only experience with any such instrument was the Army bugle, the foreboding sound that preceded an attack. Grasshopper gripped Niglíču's right hand tightly while Bastiat swung her other hand to the rhythm. "Such fun!" he said as the drums beat louder, and the crowd swayed with the music.

Undaunted by the sounds, Há Sápa's face lit with excitement. He wove through the crowd to get closer to the band and Ike, his self-appointed guardian that night, saw the looks of distain these well-dressed people were giving the seemingly black boy who dared push pass them.

Ike grabbed his shoulder, "You can't do that here! C'mon. This way!" he commanded, taking the boy's arm and pulling him aside.

"But look! Look!" Há Sápa protested. "Look at that shine!"

The brass instruments gleamed, but not with the reflection of natural lighting. Hot Springs was now lit by electricity, newly arrived and a marvel to all!

"Wakȟáŋ!" Há Sápa murmured. "Wakȟáŋ! *Holy!*"

Eager to show her grandfather where she had been swimming, Niglíču urged them to go towards Evan's Plunge. As they approached the hotel, the children marveled at the big circle of light before the entranceway.

Niglíču stood in its center and waved her arms, laughing at her shadow dancing below her. Há Sápa cried, "It's a puddle of light!" and he stomped in it as though splashing water. This joyful display caught the attention of the hotel barroom bouncer..

"Hey, you two! Get outta here! We don't want the likes of you around!"

Ike positioned himself between them. "They're kids," he said.

"They're not white," the man growled. "And neither are you."

Ike took a swing at him but was blocked by the priest's arm.

"Enough!" he said. "It's a holiday, after all. The patrons would not want to see a fight," he said to the bouncer. "We're leaving."

Smirking, the bouncer addressed Ike, "Your protector? A priest?"

Ike lunged, but again Bastiat stood in the way while the man closed the door behind himself.

"I fight my own battles!" Ike growled.

Angry at the whole situation, Bastiat answered, "Then go do it...but not when we have children here!"

Grasshopper nodded to Ike. Clearly, he would have supported him and would do so even now should Ike decide to go in after the man. But when he saw his granddaughter, frightened, clinging to Há Sápa, he changed his mind. "There are too many of them," he said to Ike.

Wanting to lift them out of their somber mood, the priest told them about the fireworks and their significance to this holiday. Today was about freedom he said, freedom from a government the people of early America found oppressive. A great war was fought over it and America won! Freedom was won!

"Freedom for everyone, Pepére?"

"No. Sadly not for everyone."

"Then not everyone celebrates this day?"

"I'm not sure. Everyone loves fireworks! Everyone loves a party!"

"That war did not give my people freedom. I do not think I should be happy on this day."

*****

But how could she resist the sparkler the priest got for each of them? Sold in packs of six, these red topped sticklike combustibles were amusement for many in the crowd. Sparks flew in all directions! The faint scent of gunpowder hung in the air. Foolish children yelped in pain for daring to touch the spent hot stick!

"I can have one?" she asked the priest.

"Of course. There's one for each of us...one to bring back for Kills too!

Striking a match against the side of the Diamond box, Bastiat lit his sparkler first. The immediate burst of sparks made the children laugh! "Wičháȟpi! *Stars!*"

"Let's light yours away from the crowd," he suggested and so they moved to a grassy area behind a storage building.

To demonstrate again what could be done with them, Ike would light his next. Sweeping the red phosphorus match head along the outside of the box, he exclaimed, "Instant fire! You try it!" he offered Há Sápa. When the boy was successful after a few stripes, he stared at the flame beaming. "Now light my sparkler," Ike said.

Ike held his sparkler before him, making great figure eights. Há Sápa jabbed and stabbed at imaginary enemies with his magical saber, and Niglíču ran around all of them, encircling them in bobbing waves of light. But it was Grasshopper who brought the priest to happy tears. Ignoring the sting, the old warrior held the sparkler as a child would hold a dandelion seed head and blew hard.

*****

Rather than gather with the crowd vying for a good position to see the fireworks, the men decided it was safer to find a vantage point near the base of the hillside from which they had descended earlier. Settling on the grass there, they had an unobstructed view of the staging area.

"I'm surprised no one is sitting near here," Bastiat said. "I know they would have to walk a ways, but it isn't that far."

"Ladies in their long dresses might trip, Padre," Ike said sarcastically.

A few firecrackers were shot off near the tall fire where the displays were in readiness. Niglíču stiffened with each one.

Bastiat tried to reassure her. "They're just getting ready for the big ones! Getting us all excited in anticipation, that's all. Just wait til the real ones go off!"

The flare of the first rocket brightened the skies with soft red twinkles that made the sudden explosion that preceded it bearable for Niglíču. The second flare sent arching white stars into the sky. The third burst into a V of blue. The fourth was a double explosion that seemed to appear over their heads, showering down green streaks to the earth. Each display became more intense. And each display made Niglíču lean harder into Grasshopper. He put his arm around her and felt her shiver. The next display of multiple rockets made her hide her face in the folds of his loose shirt and Grasshopper saw she was crying.

"We will go now, Tȟakóža. We have heard enough."

She did not want to say it, but he knew for her every boom had become another cannon burst in her ears, every crackle of a

261

firecracker was a gunshot, every scream of delight from the crowd became a cry of terror.

She got up quickly.

"You stay," Grasshopper said to the others. "We are leaving this place."

"I will walk with you, Lekší," Ike said.

Once they rounded the bend, Mountain saw them and bounded down. Niglíču buried her face in the thick fur of his neck and Ike knew they would be safe with the dog. The glow of a small fire on the crest assured Ike that Kills was waiting there. Surely he had heard the barking and knew they were returning. He walked back towards the others.

Sometimes it was easy to see the trail. Other times, when the clouds floated across the moon the path became treacherous, more difficult walking down than it had been ascending. A few times he stumbled, rattling stones that slid away with his footsteps.

But then he heard the crunch of stones behind him. He was not alone. And the other person was getting closer.

"Hey you! You the Injun from town?" Through slurred from inebriation, the voice... but more so the tone... was recognizable. The bouncer.

"I might be. Who's asking?"

"The man you wanted to punch before your priest friend protected you. I don't see no priest here now."

Two more shadows appeared from behind a rock. One was of a woman. And even in the dark he could see she was not of the same class as the men. She stumbled in her elaborate dress. She was not poor. And clearly, she was so drunk she did not seem to mind the company she was with.

"Why not let him join the party?" she offered seductively.

"Why don't you shut up, MRS. Hastings?"

Ike knew he was in trouble. He unsheathed his knife and hoped he would not have to use it. Two against one was not in his favor and the two were big men. Much bigger than he.

"I don't want any trouble." Ike said.

"You did before."

"There was only one of you before."

"Coward!" the burly man taunted as he walked closer.

"I've been called that before. I call it smart," Ike said.

262

Ike turned to walk away, hoping their whiskey bravado would not lead to anything like gunplay. Ike was a gambler after all, and he figured the bouncer would get greater satisfaction from a face-to-face fight before he'd go for the kill. He expected the big man to take his shoulder and spin him around. He was right.

Ike's knife met him but veered a little too much to the right, tearing through his shirt and slashing his belly. Roaring in pain, the burly man attacked with his own knife and sliced Ike's upper left arm across to his chest. The force of the blow and the searing pain sent Ike stumbling backwards. The bouncer was upon him immediately, pinning him to the ground. He raised his arm intent on plunging his knife into Ike's chest.

Dark blood, bluish blood oozed steadily from Ike's arm. A vein was cut and though he was rapidly weakening, his right arm had enough strength to deflect the fatal stab. And then suddenly something slammed into the attacker. Mountain. There was little time for struggle as the great dog bit into the man's neck. The man twitched as his spine was severed, but the dog did not cease shaking his prey until the man became limp.

With fireworks still blazing in the sky, the other man raised his gun to shoot the dog. His first shot missed, but there would not be a second. Kills, racing behind the dog, shot him first.

Terrified, Mrs. Hastings ran to the town. With her hands covering her mouth, her muffled screams were not heard above the din of the grand finale. Shocked into sobriety, she would forever keep secret what she had witnessed on that night of her unfaithfulness in Hot Springs.

The attackers were dead. Kills rushed to Ike struggling to sit up, but the dog, wild now, stood over him with head low and fangs bared, daring anyone to come closer.

Kills raised his rifle.

"Don't!" Niglíču screamed. "Don't shoot! I'll get him!"

"See the blood! If we don't get to him fast, he'll die."

Ignoring Grasshopper's command to step away, Niglíču put herself between the dog and the gun. Fearless, she approached the growling dog. Firmly, she commanded him to move. Miraculously, the dog submitted to her will, stepped over Ike and walked a few feet away.

"Good boy! Good boy!" she whispered. Subdued, the dog let the men approach.

Ike tried to stand, adrenaline fueling his insensitivity to pain, but Kills pushed him down and immediately applied pressure to the wound. Insisting he was ok, Ike struggled against him but soon the periphery of his vision darkened, and he slipped into semi-consciousness.

With heart pounding and struggling for every breath, Grasshopper ran back up to the fire and plunged in his knife. The wound would need cauterization to stop the venous blood flow.

Meanwhile, Kills instructed Niglíču to cut away Ike's shirt to reveal the extent of his injury. In the dim light it appeared the chest wound was superficial. Once sewn it would leave a long straight scar, but the wound was not life threatening. Kills had suffered worse. The arm concerned him more. Such wounds could make the arm useless.

The dog stood up at alert… the long yellowed hairs along the ridge of his spine raised suddenly. "Someone is coming!" Niglíču whispered.

"Give me the gun!" Kills commanded. "You…press down here…as hard as you can!"

When he released the pressure, dark blood commenced flowing. Niglíču pushed against it, but it oozed out between her fingers. Kills aimed the rifle towards the path.

Clouds passed before the moon and so Bastiat could not recognize the figure holding the gun. He pushed Há Sápa behind him. "We mean no harm," the priest called out.

"Pepére, come quickly! Hurry!"

Kills yelled to Há Sápa, "Run! Run up the hill and get the knife! Bring it to me! Hurry!"

The boy did not fully understand the command, but he ran because of the urgency of it. Grasshopper handed him the red-glowing knife. "Take it to him! Before it cools!"

"Hold him down!" Kills ordered the priest, switching positions with Niglíču.

So much blood! And that's Ike! But he immediately straddled Ike, conscious now, panicked, well aware of what was going to happen next. "Padre!" he implored and then the iron pressed into his wound. His yes bulged with the searing pain and yet he was able to bite back his scream. Mercifully he again lost consciousness and so did not smell the burned flesh that gagged the priest.

"The bleeding is stopping. He will live." Kills pulled off his shirt, cut off the sleeves and cut strips of cotton cloth from the rest of it. He wrapped the wound and tied Ike's arm to his body. He stuffed more cloth against the chest wound and bound it. Assuming leadership, he announced. "He will have to travel like this. We cannot stay here."

*****

Líla thečhíȟila.
I love you so.

"He can't travel. You'll kill him!" Bastiat protested.

"If we don't go, we'll all be killed!" Grasshopper agreed with Kills. Staying near two dead white men was in no way wise.

"He will ride with me. We will use his horse. It is short and its back is strong. He will not mind the weight if one rider is Ike."

Grasshopper mounted first and the other men lifted a barely conscious Ike to sit behind him.

"Bind him to Grasshopper with a blanket. You can't use his arms to tie him!" Bastiat was frantic. Transporting someone in Ike's condition was precarious, but he saw the logic of leaving.

They moved slowly but, even so, Ike moaned with every misstep the horse made along the dark rocky trail. He moaned when Dumpling's hoof slipped on river rocks. Any movement caused agony. All he wanted to do was lie down and sleep. They headed northwest towards the Black Hills, riding in water as much as they could to hide their trail, and hours later, but before dawn, they came to a wooded area near a small, warm sulfur spring.

"We will stay here," Kills decided. "The trees will hide us while we take care of the wound. Soon it will be light enough."

But no one slept. Killing a white man could get an Indian hung ... without a trial. They hoped the bodies would not be discovered before morning. They hoped their trail was hidden. They hoped no one would connect these deaths to them. And they really hoped no one would care at all if those scoundrels were missing or dead!

When the sun came up, they examined the wound. Ike was conscious, but in great pain.

"It is a straight cut. Clean," Bastiat said. "The knife used to cauterize was thin so the edges of the wound were not badly burned. It's not too late to try stitching it up. Have any of you done this before?"

None of the men ever did, but it didn't matter because none had a needle or anything they could use as such.

"Lalá, I can do it. I have my mother's needle. In my pouch." Niglíču touched her medicine bag, the one with the crumbled wolf jaw.

Bastiat was quick to respond. "You don't know what you are saying, Petite Fille. This is not an easy thing to do."

She turned to Grasshopper. "Lalá, I can do this thing."

Can she? He believed it possible. There was a mystical quality about her sometimes that made him think she could become a waphíya wíŋyaŋ, *medicine woman.*

Because she had said it, she knew she would have to do it, but tears clouded her eyes when she saw Ike in such pain. Never had she stitched human flesh…any living flesh! But she remembered someone…a grandmother?…saying a hair from a horse's tail could work as thread…a hair from a man's horse would heal him. She wiped away her tears and directed Há Sápa to get a few hairs from Dumpling's tail and wash them well.

Kills addressed Ike, sitting up now, and leaning against a cool rock. "The girl will sew you. It will be hard for her. Do you understand what I am saying?"

Ike nodded. He would hide his pain.

Niglíču did not meet Ike's gaze when she prepared her needle. She estimated how much thread she would need and how she would do this thing she had never imagined doing before. She tried to think this was just sewing. She forced herself away from thinking this was the man she had come to love as her uncle.

Bastiat poured warm sulphuric water over the wounds, cleansing them and softening the skin. Ike closed his eyes and imagined healing. Weak and almost dreaming, he heard her voice from far away.

"I will start now."

He turned his face away while she worked. The piercing was painful, but it was the pulling of the edges together that hurt more. He tried not to imagine the thread sliding through his skin, but he felt

266

it, that, and the knots she made. She worked methodically and when she was done, she turned her back on Ike and walked a few steps away. Crying, she wiped his blood...his blood!.. on the only cloth she had, her dress.

By now he was shivering. The warm water that had soaked his clothing now chilled him. Bastiat was removing this when she turned back to him. "I'm sorry I hurt you," she said. "You need to sleep now." The priest reapplied clean bandaging and covered him with a blanket.

Her knees started to shake, a delayed reaction to the stress. She knelt beside him and took his right hand in hers. "Please get better," she whispered.

Nodding, he closed his oh-so-tired eyes. "I love you, mithúŋžaŋ, *my little niece*," he whispered back.

*****

The meadow near the mineral spring was lush with summer growth the horses enjoyed. Dotted within the tall grasses were bursts of pink/purple, ičáȟpe hú, tall coneflower plants seeking the sun. Niglíču picked off the heads, gathering them in the "basket" she made of her billowy blouse. How beautiful she looked...how remarkably peaceful she appeared to the priest...after the trauma of the past hours. He wondered where she intended to display these vivid flowers with their sunny yellow centers.

He watched as she laid them in a heap upon a flat rock, a bouquet fit for a queen he thought. But then he was shocked to see her press her knife into the pile, shredding petals and green sepals alike, reducing that beauty to a mess of mush.

"What are you doing? They were so beautiful!" he protested.

Surprised, she looked at him, "I am making a paste. For the wounds."

Ike's sleep was ragged. From his moans and garbled sleep speech, she knew nightmares plagued him, but at least his skin was not hot. Her grandfather said they'd have to move again today, further from Hot Springs. And a travois would not be possible for Ike. Not only would it slow them down, but the dragging pole imprints would be an obvious sign to any seeking to find them.

She helped Bastiat wash the wounds with warm mineral water.

267

The skin puckered where she had stitched. He'd bear scars from her work. The slash was red, but did not look angrily so, and a clear and thin oozing liquid streaked with blood emanated from it. She applied the paste directly on top and they wrapped him with mineral washed bandages. He did not awaken during their ministrations, but he did later when they hoisted him on the back of his horse behind Grasshopper.

Semi-conscious and uninhibited, he cried out in pain when he was leaned into Grasshopper's back and blanketed in place.

"You can't make him ride like this all day," Bastiat pleaded.

"We will head east," Kills said. "The woods are deeper, and we can find a place to hide while he heals. A half day's travel...maybe more. He is young...strong. He can do this."

But no one was out looking for the killers. When their buzzard ravaged bodies were discovered late the next day, evidence of the cause of death was destroyed with them. "Frontier justice," the discoverer concluded. Both men were known womanizers, both men hired for their brawn and not their personality. "An angry husband? They deserved it!" was the consensus at the saloon. "Easily forgotten. Easily replaced." And Mr. Hastings had been so drunk that he did not even notice his wife was missing, a blessing she was forever grateful for.

A stand of ponderosa pine, several miles from Wasúŋ Wóniya Wakȟáŋ, the Wind Caves, offered protective shelter. The limestone that had once been shells of the sea, cracked and then eroded into a series of crevices and caves throughout the area, and they found one such small passageway where they could lay Ike. They made him a bed of pine boughs for cushioning and placed a blanket on top. By now he was feverish. Niglíču trickled mineral water into his mouth, sulfur rich water that she had brought from the spring. "You cannot die," she whispered to him. "I will not let you die." That night she pushed meat into his mouth, meat that she had chewed into a tender pulp, and watched him swallow.

"We could stay here, you and I," Kills told Grasshopper as they sat close to the fire when the others were asleep. "They would not find us. Game is plentiful. We could live years here and when we die, our bones will be scattered and become part of this land...a good land...our land."

"My granddaughter...you forgot this? I must care for her until she finds a husband. Where would she find one here?"

"I think there are others like us. Have you not seen signs?"

"The signs I see are the ones the white men leave. Wagon tracks. Roads. This land here? Soon there will be a cabin. Then there will be many cabins."

"Maybe then I will stay here alone."

"You have two women. They would not come."

"They did not have me before."

*****

A thunderstorm had rumbled in the distance that night but brought only a brief drizzle of rain, enough to dampen the ferns and bring out the mosquitoes. Just before dawn, Ike opened his eyes to their buzz around his sweat-salted face. His fever had broken. His left arm, strapped to his side couldn't move much, but a shiver coursed through him when he found how heavy his right arm was. He lifted his head and looked down. Niglíču was there, sleeping on her side against his arm. *My protector*, he thought, smiling for the first time since the fight.

Fully awake now, he saw he was in a small cave, mostly likely at one time home to a cougar or black bear. Not a grizzly. They had all been killed or driven away, extirpated just a few years prior. A tuft of dark fur clinging to jagged stone by the entranceway glistened in the morning sunlight. He remembered pieces of the past days. The fight. The pain. Niglíču. He remembered riding, but all was hazy. He tested his left hand. His fingers flexed fine. The muscles of his upper arm protested but reacted when he pushed out against the wrappings meant to immobilize. *God...I thank-you.*

"Well, I see you're back!" The priest stood blocking the sun. "Think you can sit up?"

Niglíču woke with a start. "How do you feel?" she asked immediately.

"Dizzy," he said and saw her frown. "But thirsty. Hungry...and," he looked at the priest, "I need to get up."

"Go get him some food, Niglíču," Bastiat said. "We must see to some things here."

*****

269

The afternoon was hazy hot, and Ike slept through most of it under the trees. Feisty red squirrels dashed along the branches above, dropping long dry needles in their search for pine seeds. Niglíču, never leaving his side, brushed them out of his hair.

Leaving Mountain behind as protector, the men went hunting. Conserving bullets, Grasshopper brought down a mule deer. Saving the nutrient rich liver for Ike to eat raw, the warriors each took a bite of the dripping heart of the freshly killed deer, hoping the strength and agility of the animal would be imparted into their own being. Bastiat refused the offering, sickened by the blood dripping down the chins of the men and boy.

The stars twinkled in the cloudless sky that night, matching the bioluminescence of the myriad fireflies hovering over the ground. Earth and sky are united by points of light here, the priest observed, imagining what the first man to recognize this must have thought.

Knowing when Ike recovered his strength their next destination would be the Wind Caves, the site of the Lakota creation story, the priest thought he should share his Christian version that night. It was good that they should know this, he thought. Good they should know the real story.

But that night, when Bastiat offered to tell the creation story of Adam and Eve, Grasshopper interrupted him. "They need to know our story. Not yours."

He began at the time when people lived below the earth in a spirit lodge. All was provided for them there. They were tempted by tricksters, one of which was a disguised creature called Iktómi, to seek a food foreign to them…meat. But they had to journey through the cave opening to get it. Thokáhe, the First One, refused to go and many stayed with him. Others went and found life difficult. They pleaded with their Creator to return but were refused and were turned into the first buffalo herd. Time passed and the Creator made the earth ready for the faithful people. The First One led them out. They were instructed to follow the buffalo. These animals would provide all that they needed. "And so they did," Grasshopped ended.

"A beautiful story," Bastiat said, and meant it too. "Such symbolism!"

How wonderful it was that God had revealed the Garden of Eden Creation Story to these people who somehow adapted it to suit their times and culture. It would not be too hard to make the connections to the real story. Ťhokáhe could easily be changed into Adam, this name having multiple meanings, like first man and of the earth. That fit well. Iktómi could be the snake in the Garden of Eden. The priest was confident he could convince them of the truth as he knew it to be.

But the more he thought about what to say, the more he realized his was an equally fantastic story. He tried to see it through their eyes. There was a garden, and a snake convinced the woman to eat the fruit of a certain forbidden tree and after that, they knew they were naked, among other things, and had to leave the garden forever.

The priest became transfixed by the fire, and he let his thoughts roam far away. How could any of these creation stories reconcile with Charles Darwin's discoveries a few decades ago? And hadn't he himself, as a younger man, gone to New Jersey in 1858 to climb down into the marl pit where the almost complete skeleton of the duck billed Hadrosaurus had been found? The realization that a creation story was just that, a story and a teaching, but not historical fact, did not make him as uncomfortable as he would have thought even a year ago.

"Pepére," Niglíču said, tapping him on the shoulder. "The story has ended. We should sleep now."

He smiled at her. "It really is a beautiful story."

Chapter 10

Makȟóčhe waŋ líla wakȟáŋ čha ektá ípi.
They came to a sacred land / place.

There was something he had read about the Wind Caves that hovered on the edge of his memory…there, but elusive…there, and foreboding. Bastiat couldn't sleep and the more he tried to remember what it was, the further away it went. He went through the alphabet. Was it something that began with an A? He thought of negative A words. Assault? No. Aggravation? No. Then B words…Bomb? Brittle? Boast? *Boast. It sounds like boast a little…what is it?* He continued down the alphabet and when he got to H, there it was. *Hoax!*

The Wind Caves had become a tourist attraction because of a hoax. The rumor was that they had found a petrified man, made all of rock, at the entrance. Although the craze of petrified giants starting with the original 10 foot Cardiff man hoax in 1869 was ending, the Wind Cave recent "find" tried to keep it alive. The warriors would not find their sacred place untouched.

"It will not be safe for all of us to go there. It might not be safe for ANY of us to go there. It isn't far from Hot Springs you know. Why don't you all wait until I go in first? Maybe I'm wrong. Maybe the place will be deserted. But, if it's not, at least I can walk around and listen to the talk there. Try to find if anyone is looking for the ones who killed the men."

*****

But the crowd teeming around the cave entrance was not concerned with the prior petrified man hoax. Instead, they wondered if they had been fooled again. Just a few weeks prior, Professor Johnstone, blindfolded, and using his clairvoyant powers, insisted he could find a hat pin hidden in the cave. "Pay me $1,000 and I'll do it," he had proclaimed. His so-called harrowing three-day search, lost in darkness with limited provisions, proved successful. The pin had been found! "Another hoax!" the people gossiped, but their mood was party-light, the hoax a pleasant vacation diversion.

Clearly this sacred place could not be as the warriors had remembered it. The cave had a new and improved blasted out entrance: a log cabin. And guests could stay at the Wind Cave hotel. The priest detected no mystical spirituality about this place given over to commercialism. How disappointed the warriors would be! Such change in so little time!

He did however find the blowhole that sucked air into the cavern, making it appear as though the earth breathed. A small windmill had been placed before it with a handkerchief affixed. The cloth was indeed pulled towards the hole, "proof" that the earth there was alive. Maybe those tourists believed its mystery, but equally likely, a knowledgeable person would know that the phenomenon was the result of the equalization of air pressure between the dense outside air and the sparce inside. Regardless, when no one was looking, the priest removed the handkerchief which seemed to desecrate the sacred spot.

He did not stay long. "We can go when it is dark," he told them upon his return.

Wakȟáŋheža kiŋ tókȟah'aŋpi!
The children are missing!

"I will watch the horses this time while you go. There is a small grove of pine trees near the cave, and I will keep them there with me. We'll be hidden." Bastiat said.

A shadow of wings swept across the ground. Kills looked up at the small flock of prairie pigeons flying overhead. "I remember when there were many."

"And when the skies were darkened by the flocks of the other birds." Grasshopper added shielding his eyes against the sun.

"You must mean the passenger pigeon," Bastiat said.

"The wašíču killed them all too, like the buffalo."

It was true. Billions of these birds. Millions of buffalo. The priest could offer no explanation.

A tail feather fluttered to the ground.

Kills picked it up, reminded of what they should do. "We will smudge before we go."

He reached into his medicine pouch and pulled out a small tight bundle of sage. Their cooking fire had burned to embers but there was enough heat to ignite this offering. Kills fanned the smoke over the others using the feather that would unite the earth and sky and rise taking their bad thoughts with it.

Like my incense, the priest thought. *To purify.* Bastiat held out his hands to Kills. "Here, let me smudge you too."

*****

Though Kills acted as though he had not already scouted the sacred area, he had shadowed the priest earlier in the day. It hadn't been so much that he did not trust the honesty of the priest, it was more he did not trust the priest's powers of observation. In Kill's estimation, the priest was well-meaning but too inexperienced to be a reliable scout. On this day, however, he agreed with the priest's assessment. This place was not safe for them in the daytime.

Even the darkness could not hide the transformation. "This is a wašíču place," Grasshopper said as his heart sank. Disgusted with the changes, they nonetheless found the breath hole and sat respectfully before it, offering tobacco.

Niglíču whispered, "Iná is in there now?"

"Your mother is in the spirit world."

Her grandfather's answer was not adequate. Yes, she knew her mother was in the spirit world but was that world inside this cave? She dared not ask for clarification. Tears rolled down her grandfather's cheeks. He grieved both the loss of the old ways and the people who had passed from this world to the next. She looked at Ike. Maybe he would know, but he sat still with his eyes closed, lips moving in barely audible, prayerful chant.

Sitting for a long period beside a hole in a mountain that bore little significance to him, Há Sápa soon grew bored. He stood up and stretched, but no one seemed to notice. He bent close to Niglíču. "Come with me. Let's look around."

Mountain followed them as they walked through low brush growing near the base of the hill. Because the sky was so clear, the light of the half-moon was enough to cast eerie shadows, enough to enable them to wander further off than they had expected. Niglíču stumbled into a hole and fell.

It appeared to be an entrance to a den but not an active one. The hole was brush covered but the young people, curious, bent and tugged at the vegetation to reveal an opening large enough for a person to crawl into.

"Do you think this is a tunnel that leads to the cave inside?" Niglíču asked.

"Maybe. But we'll never find out."

She poked her head inside and felt around. The walls were damp with dangling roots, the floor littered with what appeared to be small bones. She felt their bony heads. She felt the cracked shaft of some where the marrow had been chewed out. Yes, it had been a den, long ago, but because she could not smell the urine or feces of an animal, she felt safe.

"Come out now! That's far enough," he said when only the lower part of her legs were outside the hole.

She yelled into the hole and her voice seemed to travel well beyond her. "I bet it goes all the way!" *All the way,* she thought. *All the way to my mother inside?* She inched forward another foot.

Há Sápa grabbed her leg. "This is crazy! There could be snakes in there! What's wrong with you?"

At first she didn't hear him. She was listening to another voice…this one inside her head.

"She's not there. You won't find her there." The voice wasn't human. It had the timbre of a low growl, but the enunciation was clear. It frightened her and she arched her back and tried to inch her way out.

But her shirt caught on a gnarled root hanging in the den, trapping her.

*****

The men had noticed them leaving but were not concerned when they saw the dog get up to follow them. However, after a short while without their return, they grew anxious. Calling for them would not be wise and so they split up to search.

Ike heard the dog whining and followed the sound.

275

From what he could see before he approached was the dog digging frantically around a hole and the boy pulling something. He ran to the scene.

"Oyáthake! *She got stuck!*" Há Sápa cried. "Her shirt is stuck. She can't get out!"

Sinking to his knees, Ike heard the panicked sobbing inside the den. "I'm here. Everything will be fine. Can you move forward a little and twist?"

"I can't! I tried!"

"Can you pull out your shirt from being tucked into your skirt?"

"What?"

He repeated the question, calmly, although his heart beat wildly.

"Yes, I just did."

"Good. Now listen to me. Back out of your shirt. That's right. Leave it there and slip out of it. Can you do that?"

The sobbing stopped. "Yes."

"OK. We are going to pull on your legs. Leave your arms straight out until the shirt is off. Will you do that?"

"Yes."

Há Sápa pulled and she wiggled backwards, free within a minute. Free and crying, "I was so scared!" Embarrassed, she covered herself with her arms.

"Go get her shirt!" he commanded Há Sápa. "And don't get stuck."

Ike pulled her close with his right arm and stroked her hair "Mithúŋžaŋ, my little niece, why did you go in there?"

"I wanted to be with her. Iná."

His heart broke with love for her. "Someday, mithúŋžaŋ. Someday, but not now…"

*****

The darkness hid, in part, her disheveled and dusty appearance. "Will you tell my grandfather how foolish I was?"

"Will you do such a thing again?"

"You have my word … never!"

"Then there is nothing to tell, is there?" he smiled.

But he was firmer with Há Sápa. "You should be protecting her. Soon you will be a man. You should have known the danger and stopped her!"

276

"But she…"

"There is no excuse." Ike narrowed his eyes. "None!"

*****

That night Niglíču dreamed an animal presence beside her. Pale yellow eyes staring into her face. Warm panting breath brushing her cheeks.

You did find the right entrance. That tunnel did lead to the home of the Pté Oyáte, the wolf said.

Was I close to it? Niglíču asked in her dream.

Very close.

Why couldn't I get there then?

You were prevented.

Why? Maybe my mother is there—"

She is not there. She is in the past. You cannot go into the past. Your destiny is in your future.

And will I find her there … in the future?

The wolf did not answer.

*****

Days passed. Days of lazy riding and good hunting. Days when they woke up forgetting a month had already gone by. Days when they chose not to remember they would be returning to the desolation of Pine Ridge.

Ike's wound healed well, although his arm lacked the strength it once had. He was confident the stiffness would go away, confident that with exercise it would be as strong as it was before.

They meandered through the Black Hills trying to stay away as much as possible from white men. The initial gold rush was over, but mines still existed and small towns had sprung up throughout the region. But these areas were easy to avoid, and pristine wilderness still existed. Há Sápa hunted every day with the bow and although he was getting skilled, he could not match the ability of Niglíču. They wasted little, feasted on fresh meat, dried some for the winter, and kept the hides that could be prepared using age-old methods.

How hard it will be for these warriors to return to the reservation! the priest thought.

They were but a hard day's ride from the highest peak in South Dakota, Hiŋháŋ Káǧa Pahá, *Making of Owls Hill*. Grasshopper knew of Black Elk's vision there, received when a young boy. And sometimes he believed the wisdom of it. "Sometimes I think it might have been better if we had stayed together and made them kill us all," Black Elk, a powerful holy man now in Pine Ridge, had said. *But is the reservation better than death?* Grasshopper wondered. *It has to be...and I must make it so... for my granddaughter's sake.*

Their plan was to approach the peak from the creek side, watering their horses there before attempting the ascent. How surprised they were to find not a creek but a lake! And not a small lake either. Man-made in 1891, it encompassed 17 acres and had an average depth of 12 feet. Surrounded by dome shaped rocks with vertical striations and towering pines, Niglíču was enchanted.

"Please, can we stay here awhile? Please, can we go swimming?"

"The wašíču must change everything," Kills said with disgust, remembering the creek that had run through the gulch, though even he could not deny how inviting the clear water looked.

"We can stay, but we are not alone." Grasshopper said, pointing to the large building under construction across the lake. Nestled close to the shore, the soon-to-be-open hotel would bring multiple tourists, Bastiat knew. *It's good that we've arrived here before that!*

There were no sounds of construction work on that day, however. No hammers banging against iron nails drowned out the gentle call of birds. No slamming down of heavy wooden planks frightened the family of mallards paddling a v across the lake, nor intimidated the black bear and her twin cubs drinking at the shoreline. *It must be Sunday*, the priest thought, surprised that he had forgotten the days of the week on this trip.

"We can stay the night," Kills announced, seeing how happy the children were splashing in the shallow water by the lake's edge. He watched Ike join them and wade deeper until he stepped off an underwater rocky ledge and tumbled in. Surfacing, he threw back his head in laughter, delighting the children!

"They will remember these wašíču waters," Kills observed with conflicting emotions.

The children scrambled up short rock faces and jumped feet first into the cooling water. It was hot, Kills admitted. The water would feel good against his sweating skin. Surprising everyone, he, too, climbed a rock. He, too, jumped in.

*****

"It's a long, steep walk up to the peak," Kills said. "We should not push our horses to make it to the top. We will take them part way only. And we will go up the southern side. It's a little easier, though not much."

Bastiat looked to the top of the peak. It was indeed high. And the rocks looked treacherous. He had been nervous atop Ned before on switchback trails, not trusting Ned's stability with a weakened hind leg, but so far Ned had not validated his concern. But this? This might be asking too much of the older horse. And maybe too much of himself. He wished he had a true saddle…with a horn to grab onto going uphill and a reassuringly high cantle to lean against going down.

Kills led the way. The priest brought up the rear quite a distance behind the others. But Kills was a wise leader who had concern for the safety of all and so when his horse began to lunge forward, straining to boost himself to the next level, he called a halt. "There is flat land in the clearing there and grass," he said pointing to his left. "We will tie the horses in that place and walk."

With youthful endurance, the children were not fazed, gripping for handholds and pulling themselves up. "Watch for snakes!" Grasshopper warned. Ike followed close behind them, but the priest could see he struggled, sweating, without equal use of both arms. The older warriors were slower still, resting more often, breathing fast, sweating, but they kept pace with each other, probably, Bastiat thought smiling, out of vanity.

But Bastiat had nothing to prove to anyone and so when his legs burned and his lungs heaved, he announced he could go no further. "I'm sorry," he said. "You go ahead. I'll rest here a little and then go back to the horses."

That was not an option for Kills however, determined to bring the priest to the top. "We all will rest a little here," he announced, untying the rope wrapped double around his waist as a belt. "Bring the dog to me."

Knotting the rope around the dog's neck, Kills handed the other end to the priest. "The dog will want to be with the children. He will pull you to the top."

Not used to being restrained, Mountain did indeed pull, wrenching the priest's arm and forcing him forward. Foam fringed the dog's muzzle and flecked the sides of his face as he fought his way upward, panting heavily, gagging, as he almost dragged the priest stumbling along.

At the top, Bastiat fell to his knees. Exhausted...yes...but the view from there was breathtaking. "How great Thou art!" he whispered. "How great Thou art!"

Kills swept his arm across the expanse that would soon be carved into four states. "Look, Black Robe! Look and see all that was ours!"

Bastiat said nothing in reply. *It was theirs, yes...but not always so. Did they not drive away others? Cheyenne? Crow? Kiowa? Pawnee?*

Finally, the priest stood, pointed east and sighed. "My family lived way over there, past the great ocean, in the mountains they call the Pyrenees. Is there a mountain higher than this one from here to there? I wonder. Relatives there, so far away and yet now nothing is in between us but air."

"If your family was there, why did they come here?" Niglíču asked.

"They wanted freedom," the priest responded.

"Couldn't they fight for it over there?"

"I don't know. Maybe so. Maybe so."

Kills next pointed towards the Badlands "Now we just have that where nothing grows, and where few animals choose to live. I should stay here. Live here and die here!"

Bastiat didn't know how to respond. He could not see Kills adapting to reservation life...not after this.

They spent the rest of the day at the top, but when dark approached, they returned to the horses. It had been an exhausting day, but Kills could not sleep. He put a rope around Mountain's neck and started the trek back up to the summit. He wanted to be there with only the moonlight shining over the land. At the top, he perched on a ledge with his legs dangling over the side. He reached for the stick tucked into his belt and struck a match. The sparkler he had saved burst into dazzling stars and, marveling at it, he thought of just one thing: freedom.

*****

They did not hurry as they wound their way up and down the rough terrain of the Black Hills.

Savoring the freedom, they stopped at the hidden and tree protected areas where they had spent their winters as youths. Walking through the area, the old warriors pointed out the cottonwood trees whose inner bark had provided winter nourishment for their horses.

And the children played.

Ike and Bastiat watched them whooping and hollering, racing their ponies across sunny meadows in mock battle with an unseen enemy.

"Joan d'Arc. She's like her," Bastiat smiled, shaking his head at what he perceived to be her similarity to the young warrior saint.

"Who's that, Padre?"

"A freedom fighter from long ago…400 years maybe. A holy woman. She defended France, her nation."

"I was thinking of another woman…a Cheyenne…Buffalo Calf Road Woman. Some say she was the one who knocked Custer off his horse."

"I suppose women can be warriors, but I wouldn't want that life for her," the priest said.

"What war would there be for her to fight, Padre?"

A few moments passed in silence. "We have to start heading back, Ike. It's going to be hard for all of them…freedom vs captivity. But what about you, Ike? You're not stuck like they are. Where will you go? Funny how just having a grandfather who is white keeps you free. A grandfather and a job."

"I can leave the reservation, Padre, but believe me, I am not free." He urged his horse forward, leaving the priest there to wonder.

*****

Niglíču tried to teach the priest how to use the bow. And he did practice, time and time again, but he could not sink an arrow into a tree trunk the width of a man's leg. In the release of an arrow, the priest felt a connection to the target. He imagined the pain of the piercing and concluded that style of hunting was more brutally intimate than a gun and a bullet. It was more a personal contest between predator and prey, a fairer scenario he thought than shooting. Could a bullet hit a target at 1,000 yards? Could so much distance be put between the hunter and the hunted? The new bullets and improved rifles could, they said. Surely an arrow required a distance far less than 100 yards. 30? 40? Close enough to see the animal take its last breath?

*****

Bastiat fumbled through his bag. *I know it's in here! It has to be!* They had been lucky so far. There had been no occasion to show his travel permit, but the cavalry unit they saw in the distance had changed direction and was coming their way. *Finally...here it is!* The writing on the stained and wrinkled paper was still clear...and they had two more weeks until the permit's expiration.

"Should we hide?" Há Sápa asked. "There are trees over there."

"No. They've seen us already. We have the permit. We will ride as we have planned. Meet them when our paths cross," the priest said.

The horses felt their nervousness and grew skittish, wanting to run, but the riders kept them to a slow walk. A few of the cavalry men trotted to them, their rifles across their laps. One raised his hand for the travelers to stop.

"Hello," the captain said, addressing the only white man there. Indistinguishable without clerical garb, Bastiat appeared one of many settlers.

"Hello, Captain. I'm Father Bastiat, a Jesuit priest and these are my companions on my retreat out here in the wide open spaces. I'm evangelizing them… and learning from their sacred places.

"They have rifles."

Kills, Grasshopper and Ike did indeed have their rifles before them, though their hands were not touching them as they rested on their legs.

"My permit says we can hunt."

The officer held out his hand for the permit. Bastiat gave him that, along with the permission from his Jesuit order. Examining the permit, the soldier ran his finger over the scratched surface where the 4 had been changed to 5. He raised an eyebrow.

"The agent was sloppy there, I admit...in a hurry to get to other more important work I suppose. But it was understandable for his little son had tugged on his leg just at that moment and when the agent went to shoo him away with his left hand, his right hand…the one with the pen… became unsteady and the ink…"

The captain looked at the children and decided, because of their presence, the priest might be telling the truth. "Enough. I believe you. Remember your timeline though. Some settlers reported seeing a group like yours in the hills and your presence made them uneasy."

"I surely would not want them to feel that, Captain. We will be leaving the area soon anyway."

"Good, Father. And by the way, my wife is a Catholic. Say a prayer for her. Our baby will be born soon."

"How wonderful! Yes, indeed! I will ask the Blessed Virgin to be with her in her hour of travail."

The captain rode off and Ike brought his horse alongside the priest. "Padre, I never heard you talk so fast!"

"I'm from the Bronx you know. New York City. Everyone talks like that," he said exaggerating his accent.

Ike laughed. "Yeah, and that was some fancy story you made up too. Quick thinking if you ask me. Can everyone do that where you come from?"

"Not all. Just the smart ones." He looked back at the others. "C'mon, let's get outta here. North, right? We're still heading north?"

*****

Šinásapa kiŋ čhaŋlí wapȟáȟta eyá kaǧe.
The priest made some tobacco ties.

It would take days to get to Matȟó Pahá *Bear Butte*, their holy mountain, and Bastiat worried if they would be able to meet the September 1 deadline for returning from such a distance. His map indicated 100 miles. They would need to travel many miles per day. The horses appeared sound still, but this pace would be taxing for the older ones.

Bear Butte…their holy mountain. Bastiat could not help but compare it to the holy mountains in scripture. *Moses on Mount Sinai. Jesus' transfiguration on Mount Tabor.* Around the evening fire, the priest told his stories. He spoke of the Ten Commandments. He

283

spoke of the Beatitudes. He told of the Transfiguration and was encouraged by the warriors' associations between their values and Judeo-Christian ones. He could see from their nods of agreement that they could respect Moses and Jesus.

"They were Shirt Wearers for their people," Kills observed.

"Shirt wearers?"

"Padre, men who were honorable, brave, selfless and caring were given a special shirt to wear as an honor. They could keep the shirt as long as they remained worthy of it. Crazy Horse was given the shirt but it was taken from him when he had relations with another man's wife."

"I see. I would agree that Moses would deserve such a shirt. The saints would, but Jesus? He is so much more. He is God. He is Wakáŋ Tháŋka and a man too."

"I think Kills would have a hard time understanding that, Padre."

Kills had learned to speak English better than before during this trip, but difficult English words and concepts would be hard to express in his native language.

"What is he saying?" Kills asked.

"He says he agrees," Ike lied.

Kills nodded. As their time free was nearing an end, Kills' dreams had taken an ominous turn. *Maybe you are seeing these holy places for the last time,* the dreams said. *Maybe you will not live to see them again.*

For this reason, when he reached the sleeping bear mounds of this mountain, he did not allow the others to make the long ascent to the top. "We will sweat first," he announced. "We will purify ourselves."

Though they did not know the geology of it, the Lakȟóta had tales of the power they felt beneath these mountains. That this underground pressure never erupted into a volcano, did not stop the more spiritual of their people to feel the tension beneath the earth there. Some had felt the ancient echoes of volcanic activity and so it was a mountain all approached with reverence. Atop the mountain, they felt they could get messages from their creator.

Willow grew beside the small lake near the base of the mountain and this was where they decided to stay that night. There was enough light to the day left to prepare a sweat lodge. Sixteen long willow limbs were used to create the frame. When during the construction, one limb broke, Bastiat assured them the fifteen would suffice. "It's only going to be used once," he explained.

"But there must be sixteen," Grasshopper said.

"Why?"

"Four is an important number to us. There are four directions, and there are four stages of a man's life. We can use twelve poles, but I think we need four more. Many will sweat here."

Bastiat offered to go back and cut the last pole. They left the leafy side branches intact to darken the interior. They did not have enough blankets to completely cover the top. Grasshopper explained the Sixteen Great Mysteries, symbolically represented by the positioning of the poles to create the roof. In the sweat lodge, he said, the people would draw power from the water, rocks, fire and air. By nightfall, the lodge was complete.

The morning was already hot, but the first seven stones heated the lodge hotter. The group had fasted for hours, drank plenty of water, and received instructions from Kills, who would lead the experience. After the traditional smudging and prayers, Niglíču, being female, was asked to enter first. She crawled in on her knees, followed by Há Sápa and Grasshopper. Ike motioned for Bastiat to enter next.

Getting on his hands and knees, he crawled into the dark, steamy hot lodge and sat cross-legged like the other men. Kills poured water over the stones creating a plume of steam that filled the lodge. Chanting, he added fragrant sweetgrass and sage to the stones.

The others were quiet. The priest looked at their closed eyes, lost in meditation. The heat induced drenching sweat. The foreign mystery caused the priest's heart to pound with guilt. *What am I doing here? I'm not allowed to engage in pagan religious ceremonies!*

"I'm sorry. I cannot do this," he finally said, crawling from the womb-like lodge. When he stood up, he felt dizzy. Water to be used in the ceremony was near the fire. He drank some, but it was warm and tasted of the bladder container it was stored in. Immediately he became nauseous. *Forgive me, Lord.* Staggering to the lake, he waded in. The cold water refreshed him, but made him incredibly tired. "I'm sorry. I'm so sorry," he whispered as he walked over to the shade of a willow. Leaning against the trunk, he fell asleep.

*****

285

Bastiat, thinking he would be spurned for leaving, avoided the eyes of the two older warriors when they left the sweat lodge, and so he was surprised when Grasshopper walked over to talk.

"We understand," he said to the priest. "You must understand now why we do not feel it is right in your church."

But in mid-afternoon when Niglíču showed him how to make prayer ties, he readily participated. "These are like rosary beads," he said. "These are like the small candles we used to light in the churches back east...symbols of our prayers. Čhaŋlí Wapháhta. Am I saying it correctly?"

"Almost," she replied. "But you are folding the cloth the wrong way. Put the tobacco and your prayers into the center of the cloth. Fold the cloth in thirds and then fold it over."

She watched the priest do it correctly that time and then helped him with the knots; his fingers not nimble enough to string the ties evenly spaced.

"Your hands are clumsy, Pepére."

"I used to watch the nuns make rosary beads. They were so exact. When I see you work, I think of them."

"What you should be doing is concentrating on your prayers for each tie," Niglíču said, and enjoyed saying it too. *I'm teacher now!*

When the ties were finished, they began their walk up to the top of the butte. The incline was gradual in the beginning but got steeper as they ascended. They could see bits of cloth hanging from bushes and trees, remnants of prayers said in past times. They walked by these respectfully in a solemn procession.

Off to the right, a thorny clump of bushes caught Bastiat's eye. The shrub was heavy with fruit. Green, red and almost purple grape-like fruits hung from the thorny canes.

"Are these good to eat?" he asked Niglíču.

"Wičhágnaška ... gooseberry. Yes, you can eat some."

The priest stopped awhile to eat, letting the others go forward. He was tiring easily. They had been traveling for weeks now ... almost two months!... and the physicality of the experience was wearing him down. The view from the top might be magnificent, he thought, but he was content being halfway up. He draped his prayer chain between two thick canes of the shrub, sat on a rock and prayed.

Chapter 11

Hókahé!
Let's do it!

Makȟóšiča, the Badlands. When the priest first saw them in the distance he was awestruck. He was no student of geology and so his initial reaction was spiritual. *The patient hand of God made these layers once. Long ago His gentle hands laid layer upon layer and smoothed them out, patted them down and said it was good.* He smiled, imagining it millions of years ago, flat layers of earth perhaps underneath a sea, with new sediment covering the floor and adding yet another layer.

But then something must have happened. Did the sea recede, carving vast gouges in the layers? Did rivers cut through them, revealing the history of their creation?

How can I describe this to my brother? There was so much to write about, later, when he was home. Home. On a reservation.

But the thought of home gave him inspiration for a description. That, and the desire for something sweet. He was tired of this predominantly meat diet the others so craved and longed for a delicacy… like a cake. And that's when he knew how he could describe this landscape.

Millefeuille …the cake of a thousand leaves. Swallowing the new burst of saliva, Bastiat thought of his grandmother. Layer upon layer of flaky pastry lovingly laid down in a sheet, interspersed with creams, topped with another layer of icing and chocolate. But when she finished, he hadn't been able to see the layers until a knife pushed into it, sectioned it, pulled away a piece. *I'll tell my brother this land looks like this … only it is not sweet at all.*

Kills did not smile when he pointed to the wall of sedimentary rock with its horizontal layers of sandstone, lime and whatever had been washed from the Black Hills giving it the pastel colors light played upon it. No, he did not see the beauty…only the desolation. "This is the land the white man has given us. Grow food here, they say. If the land was good, they would take it for themselves."

"We will go there," Kills continued. "It is the place of my vision quest. My dreams tell me it is where I must go."

One particular dream plagued him. He was at Makȟóšiča, the place of his vision quest. How young he was! How hungry! How thirsty! Looking out from his ledge, the world seemed to quiver with the rising waves of heat. Nearly delirious, he suddenly saw the ram.

"Are you my spirit guide?" he asked.

The ram approached, head down, horns curved upward, lethal appendages waiting to sweep him off the ledge.

See these, the ram seemed to say, *I will fight you for this place!*

But young Kills had not been afraid. He walked up to the ram and surprised him by gripping a horn. They struggled. The horn broke off in Kill's hand. He looked at it in disbelief as the animal backed away.

You have taken my power, the ram said.

The ram's head was lopsided and Kills felt pity for the now disabled animal. He approached the ram again and placed the horn back in its place where it reattached. "You need your power more than I do," he said.

The ledge is yours, the ram said. *It will be your destiny.*

The dream was odd. Kills struggled to make sense of it.

The others did not dispute his decision to travel to that wall dividing the land, although it would considerably alter their course back to Pine Ridge.

*****

They had traveled in a southeasterly direction to get to the place of Kill's vison quest. With otherworldly landscape surrounding him, Bastiat imagined himself on the moon. Like the early daguerreotypes he had seen of the moonscape, here were the mountains and valleys and craters found on the moon, he thought. And like the moon, there was no water to be seen here either.

They would make a quick crossing going directly south. Kills said it wasn't far. The day was scorching hot, and they carried bladders of water to replenish what they sweated.

288

The older horses suffered over this shale-like sliding terrain. Bastiat thought shoes would have helped protect the soft tissue of the hooves, cushioning them against sharp edges, but then again, the iron might slide across the rocks and cause other problems. He looked up and saw a ram. His cloven hooves serve him well, the two toes spreading to grip rock. An impressive animal of over 300 pounds, he bleated an alert.

Kills saw him too, this ram with tilted head whose eyes seem to bore into him. *I am not afraid of you,* the old warrior thought.

Foam coated the flanks of Ned and Dumpling. Bastiat knew his weight was too much for the animal in these conditions and so he dismounted. Ike did the same.

"There are rattlesnakes. Watch where you walk," Kills warned.

Niglíču saw that Bastiat was also tired. "You ride Kičhí, Pepére. I will walk Ned.

"No, you ride. I'm fine," he answered.

They followed Kills, walking across the top of the wall, weaving around the formations, and descending into the dips and gullies. Some formations were higher than others. Kills looked for the ledge he had chosen for his vision quest. There were so many ledges, and many looked the same, all hot, blazing white in the sun.

"How can you know where that one is?" Grasshopper asked, pointing to the miles of Badlands that stretched out before them.

"It was near here. I know it!"

Kills led the way followed closely by Há Sápa. The boy was nearing the time when he could go on his own vision quest and the elusive ledge fascinated him.

Niglíču trailed behind Grasshopper, keeping a steady slow pace for Ike and Bastiat, on foot, to follow. She looked over the vast wasteland and found the intensification of the red, yellow and buff colors bathed in the softer sunlight of late afternoon so mesmerizing that she neglected to be as aware of her surroundings as was her horse. Kičhí suddenly startled, raising on her hind legs.

Ike saw it....the rattlesnake on the ledge to her left, poised to strike. "Siŋtéȟla! *Rattlesnake!*" he warned. The snake rose just as Ike's knife zipped past the horse and pinned the reptile to the dust.

Twisting rapidly to see the snake, Niglíču lost momentary control of her pony. The horse shimmied away from the ledge and slipped on the rocks, almost tumbling. Kičhí jerked herself erect but the unexpected motions unseated Niglíču. She fell, but because the slope on the right was steep, she rolled once and stopped, hovering over the precipice. Clawing the lose shale to pull herself to safety was useless and she slipped over the edge just as Ike's body slammed into the earth reaching for her.

"Niglíču!" the priest yelled, inching his way to the very edge. "Niglíču!"

"I'm here! I'm here!" she yelled back.

Niglíču, clinging onto the edge of a small ledge with feet dangling into space, did not hear the anguished cries of her grandfather from high above her as he was wrestled away from climbing over the ledge to get to her. She heard the frantic barks of Mountain, but she understood them as words, words that came not from him but as soft whispers from her spirit wolf.

You have a choice now, Little Warrior, the voice crooned to her. *You may drop below and join your mother and ancestors, or you may harness my strength and climb onto the ledge. Either way, disaster will happen. Your fingers are slipping now. It will be easier to let go. They say, 'Today is a good day to die.' But if you choose to live, another might die in your stead. You have the choice,* he repeated. *Do you want to live?*

"Yes!" she screamed. "Yes!" Her fingers pushed through the dust and found a solid ridge of rock… and then another. Hand over hand, she pulled herself onto the narrow ledge. Backing up against the wall, she started to cry.

"Are you hurt? Are you hurt?" they screamed at her.

She was scraped, bleeding lightly, but she felt no pain. "I'm ok," she sobbed.

"A rope! A rope!" the men yelled to each other. "Get some rope!"

But a long length of rope was one provision they did not pack.

Knotting what they had from belt and bridle gave them a length of perhaps three yards. That would never be enough. They estimated the ledge to be around fifteen feet below them.

"We'll use our clothes," Kills ordered. Stripping themselves, they twisted their clothing into tubes and knotted them onto the end of the rope.

While the men fashioned the rope, Niglíču started to shiver, reliving the horror. *I fell off Kičhí, I rolled, I fell off the edge, I hit something and rolled and fell again…here. If I crawl to the edge of the ledge I might be able to look up and see my grandfather. It should be so. I did not fall straight down.* But she knew empty space was below the edge of the ledge she was on. Her dangling legs had felt it and so she did not dare move closer. *I'll stay right here. I won't move. I'm safe here.*

A rope of sorts dangled from the precipice above… a temptation to move.

"Grab hold of it and tie it around your waist! We will pull you up!" Ike said as the rope was lowered.

But the rope did not reach her. It was not even close.

"Drop it down more!" she pleaded. "I won't be able to reach it."

Ike crawled to the edge and lowered his arm over with the rope. "Enough now?"

"No!" she cried. "No! No! Help me!"

"How much more?" Bastiat yelled. "Think! Remember the yardstick! Remember the ruler! How many more inches?"

Panicked, she could not remember her lessons. "As big as me!" she called up. "I need more rope as big as me!"

The men looked at each other. "Maybe the saddle blankets? Could we cut them up? Tie them together?"

"My robe!" Bastiat blurted out. "That would give enough length!" They added that extra length and lowered the rope again.

"I can almost touch it," she yelled up, daring now to walk nearer the edge to reach upward.

"She will not have enough to tie around her, even if we can make it longer. I will climb down and get her. I will lift her and see that the rope is secure around her," Kills commanded.

"She is my granddaughter. I will do this!" Grasshopper argued.

"I'm younger…stronger," Ike joined in.

"Your arm is weak. You cannot and no, Black Robe, you are not strong enough. The boy is too young. Kȟolá, I am taller than you. I have always been stronger. You must let me do this."

They wrapped one loop of the rope around a rock that jutted upward by the edge and Grasshopper held the end. Kills took the other end and wrapped it around his hands.

He cried his warrior cry, "Hókahé! *Let's do it!*" Walking backwards he stepped down the incline and jumped to the next ledge. The rope held firm. Relieved, he dropped to the ledge beside Niglíču. The men above cheered. She buried her face against him, and he hugged her tight.

"Little warrior, you must be very brave now. You will climb on my shoulders. I will hold you. Do not be afraid. You are to wrap the rope around your waist and tie a strong knot. Can you do this?"

Her lip quivered, "Yes."

"A warrior does not speak in that little voice. Say it again!" he commanded.

"Yes!" she said firmly now, wanting to please him. She climbed up on his shoulders and tied the knot.

"Good! Now you will use your feet to walk up against the sides while they pull you. You will do that?"

"Yes!" she said with resolve.

"Now you are a warrior! I am proud of you! Yell with me together, "Hókahé!" Their cries rang out over and over, "Hókahé! Hókahé!" and she was hauled up safely.

Again, they lowered the rope. "Does it reach you?" Grasshopper called down.

It was short by a few inches but Kills knew he could leap for it. *Like the ram. Like the ram!* He jumped up and grabbed the end…the priest's robe. He heard the stitches tear, saw a hole by the shoulder seam.

"Are you ok?" they yelled down to him.

"Yes," he lied, doubting the remaining stitches would hold. *It is a good day to die!* "Pull hard! Pull fast!" he yelled back, and they did. Straining every arm muscle, he pulled himself up hand over hand, using his feet when he could to relieve the tension on the tearing seam. He was near the top, close to hands extended down to grab him when the final stitches tore through, arcing him backwards through the air.

"Hókahé!" he yelled. "Hókahé!" he yelled again when he hit the side of the mountain far below. And then there was no sound at all save for the grinding and sliding of rocks carrying his body into the tomblike crevice far below.

*****

She ran her knife across her arms that night while the priest, horrified, looked on. Her grandfather watched her, watched to see the wounds were kept superficial and not like those slashes bleeding from his own arms. Her hair was cut in a ragged line, short to show her grief. Like the hair of her grandfather and Ike. Like Há Sápa. And like the priest himself.

*****

Thiyóšpaye kiŋ hetáŋ hiyú.
From that began the extended family.

They heard the keening even before the village came into sight. News of their return had preceded them. The village knew of the riderless horse and mourned the death of the once great warrior.

Bear Teeth stood at the head of the path into the village. He walked up to Grasshopper and touched the horse he led. "He died a warrior's death?"

"Yes."

"It is good."

Grasshopper dismounted and led Kill's horse to the thípi where Pretty Stone and White Birch stood, Pretty Stone with her chin raised, and her cousin with tears streaming down her cheeks.

"I will not cry for him," Pretty Stone said. "He told us he would not return, and I believed him. His dreams were powerful. He trusted them. I trusted them. He did not want to die here. He wanted to die free. Did he do this?"

"Yes."

"Then when I cry,I will only cry for me. Not for him. He was a great warrior and a good man. I will tell you one more thing he said to me before he left. He said that you, as his kȟolá, would take us in. I told him we did not need this care. He said he knew this. But he said that you need our care. If you want, or when you are ready, we will come to you as sisters. We have talked this over between us. We will help you raise your granddaughter."

He handed the reins to Pretty Stone and, nodding to both women, he turned away.

Two rifles were hidden within his rolled blanket. Only one was his, but the possession of either was forbidden on the reservation. He will return his to its hiding place. The other he will give to the women of his kȟolá. Kills would have wanted this.

The priest expected weeds and prairie grasses to have grown up around the church building. He had abandoned it to nature for the summer months after all and so assumed nature would have begun to reclaim the area. How surprised he was to see this was not so! Not only had his someone kept the weeds away, but there was also a bouquet of wild flowers standing freshly erect in a jar in front of the locked church door.

He dismounted and led Ned to the corral. Fresh water was in the bucket. Dry hay was piled beside it. Who was it that had cared for this place while he was away?

And then he saw the small thípi behind his cabin. And the small fire before it. And the old woman stirring the pot. Oyé Wašté.

*****

The man before the mirror was a stranger...so bronze skinned that his blue eyes seemed beacons of light, the whites blaring from wrinkled lids. A greying beard inches long flared in wavy disarray framing his cheeks. The uneven wispy edges of a shorn forelock above his face laid in stark contrast to twisted curls of dust encrusted hair that reached well below his ears.

The priest looked at himself, rubbed his beard and pushed back his hair. *Have I ever looked more of a man?*

Warm water filled the basin before him. He lathered his hands and teased the suds through his thick beard. His razor was sharp. Each stroke of the blade revealed the pale white skin beneath it. *For two months I was one of them.*

*****

Though it was hardly necessary, Ike escorted Há Sápa to his cabin. Seeing how happy the parents were to see their son was painful for Ike who had no one waiting for him to come home. This wouldn't have bothered him before the trip, but now? Now he longed for the companionship he knew he would be missing.

He spent the night with the family, welcomed and feasted with them. So many stories were told...and each tugged a little harder at

Ike's heart.

When he left the next day, he headed for a small way station called Black. Maybe he would find freighting work there along the Chamberlain Road. He supposed…and hoped… the railroads had not eaten up all the freight work between Chamberlain and the Black Hills, a two hundred fifty mile stretch. Luckily, George Johnson had a job for him. He couldn't guarantee steady work, but at least this was an opportunity to get some money because he had none.

*****

Oyé Wašté returned to her daughter-in-laws' thípi when the travelers returned. She had enjoyed her summer by the church. Working at her slow pace, she still felt useful and in the quiet of night she would sit under the stars and pretend she was young again, waiting for her warrior husband to return home. In the morning, the singing birds were her family, and she did not have to avert her eyes from her daughter-in-law's new man who, though polite, resented her presence.

Balancing herself with her walking stick, she made her way to the church one morning a few days after Niglíču returned. She carried a gift tucked under her arm. The leather pouch was narrow and old, dried and cracking. The fringes had long ago disintegrated and only a few beads remained. The quillwork was faded. The gift was valuable to the old woman, and she wanted to give it to Niglíču. Inside the pouch was one eagle feather.

The old woman had missed Niglíču while she was away. She had dreamed of her as she sat in the cool shade near her thípi, and through the dreams, she had come to think of the girl as granddaughter. It was pleasant to think this way. She had no daughter of her own and her son's wife had given her a grandson, but she missed having a little girl. She had hoped to give this gift to her as she had been given it by her own grandmother. Now, she decided, was the time she would pass this on to Niglíču.

She found Niglíču untangling the long tail of her horse. Burrs had knotted it into bunches, and Niglíču stood beside Kičhí as she gently raked her spread fingers through the tangles. Niglíču had been at this task for a while, and she found it soothing rather than frustrating.

"You like to do this, I see," Oyé Wašté said in greeting.

295

"Oh, hello," Niglíču replied, surprised. "I do."

"Why?"

As Oye Waste had grown older, she had become less subtle. Niglíču was troubled and Grasshopper had asked the old woman to talk to her. Niglíču would not speak to him about it, nor even to the priest, but he was certain his granddaughter felt guilt over Kill's death.

Niglíču pulled hard on a burr causing Kičhí to twist away, but it came free. "Because this I can fix," she replied as she held the burr with long horse hairs streaming off it.

The old woman patted the horse's rump to calm her. "Steady, Wótheȟila *Treasured One*, you sweet one whom this little girl loves. Be still now while we make you beautiful again."

To Niglíču she said, "May I help?"

They sat with the horse, young subtle fingers working with the gnarled, work hardened hands of the old woman, pulling the hairs apart, separating them from the burrs that held them together.

"Do you think when you love someone, you should only expect happy things to happen?" the old woman asked Niglíču, fully expecting that the girl would say no. Her whole life, after all, was proof that bad things happen.

Niglíču shook her head.

"Sometimes when I do things like this," and the old woman held up a hand tangled in the hair, "I think about how one thing teaches me about another. Do you ever do this?"

Niglíču shook her head, not really understanding what the old woman meant.

"Look at these hairs. They run side by side. Could they be paths that we follow? Could one be yours and another be mine? Sometimes they meet, right? Sometimes they get twisted together? We make braids, do we not, and can't we say paths cross and make something pretty? But look here! A burr! Sometimes something else happens and things get all tangled up. We try to fix it, but then, look again!" The old woman held up a hair that had come loose. "Sometimes the paths break away even though we do not choose this." She held up her hand that held the loose hair and a breeze took the strand away. "This hair has not changed, but it is free and on its own path again. We do not know where it will go. It will go where the wind takes it.

"A burr came into your life and tangled lives together in a way you did not like. The time seemed to stop when you tried to untangle the burr. Then it started again. Time stopped for Kills in Winter when he tried to save you. It was not your fault. It was not anyone's fault. But remember, now he is free, just like the hair."

They continued with the tail in silence and when finished, Oyé Wašté spoke again.

"I brought you a gift. My grandmother earned it. I wanted to hand it on to a daughter or granddaughter. I now give it to you."

Niglíču took the pouch reverently, realizing this was something precious. With the old woman nodding that she should do so, Niglíču reached inside and pinched the thick shaft of a tail feather. Withdrawing it, she saw the bronze coloring splashed with irregular white striping of waŋblí, the golden eagle.

"My grandmother was a warrior woman. She fought beside her husband. Few women earned a feather. My grandmother earned several. This is one that I have been able to save."

"Uŋčí, I have done nothing to earn this. This is for a warrior."

"Your grandfather told me one of the last things Kills In Winter said. He heard his kȟolá say you are a little warrior woman now. I gift this to you in his name. He has judged you worthy."

Niglíču protested. The old woman hushed her. "I judge you worthy for another reason. A warrior woman does not have to show bravery in battle, as a man must. There are other ways too. Tell me, who saved the life of Ike? Did you not stitch the wound and allow it to heal properly so he did not end up with a useless arm? Or none at all? Had you ever done such a thing before? Is that not the same bravery as pulling a man onto your horse if he fell in battle? I see it as the same. The gift is yours. It is deserved."

*****

Ike missed the trees. Reservation land had some, here and there, but not enough to break up the endless sky, not enough to hide an impending storm. And a storm was coming. Angry grey-black clouds darkened the horizon. If he hurried Dumpling along, he might make it to shelter before the rain.

He jingled the coins in his pocket, a paltry sum, surprised they were still all there a day after he was paid. A bottle at the way station had tempted him, but he didn't have a desire to be numbed by its effects. A woman behind the way station had invited him, but that wasn't the need he wanted to satisfy. What he wanted was companionship, and the feeling that he belonged somewhere. He headed towards the village.

The rain outraced him, drenched him shivering cold. He dismounted at Bastiat's corral and Dumpling pushed his way into a spot of the shelter already occupied by Ned and Kičhí, his head thus protected, though not his rump.

Pale light suffused through a cloudy windowpane. The priest was awake. The dog knew he was there. He could hear him snuffling at the edge of the door.

"What's the matter, Mountain?"

Ike knocked. Chair legs ground across the uneven floor. "I'm coming…"

Wide eyes matched the priest's bright smile as he welcomed Ike in. Like a father, Bastiat embraced him.

Like a mother, he took Ike's dripping clothes and hung them over the line stretched behind the stove and handed him the blanket from his bed.

Like friends, they talked deep into the night until they both yawned deeply and laughed because of it.

The priest stood up first and walked to the wall where a newly made ladder lay horizontally before it. "It's heavy. Help me with this?"

Together they leaned the ladder against a cross beam. Planks had been laid the prior week to make a loft floor. "I have blankets up there…for you."

*****

Day after day Oyé Wašté walked the quarter mile to the church compound. Nine hundred steps. She counted them, one to one hundred, as far as she could count, nine times, closing one finger at a time into her fist. The counting helped with the pain of arthritic walking and once the fingers of one hand were all closed, she stopped and rested, confident that after the pain subsided, she could make it the rest of the way.

Though she could not do much, she helped the others who were

298

making the new cabin for the cousins. She brought them fresh water from the barrel next to the priest's cabin. She picked up scraps of wood to use later as kindling. And although it was hard to bend and grasp them, she collected the bent nails...these men were not carpenters and many a nail bent before being fully slammed into the planks......and even tried to hammer them straight again. *How interesting to nail wood together rather than lash pieces together with strips of rawhide! The nail was a good thing to have!*

"I will carry this," Grasshopper told her one day when she struggled with a basket of wood scraps. "The work is too hard for you, Old Woman."

She smiled at him. "The work is hard, but it is good to be useful."

"Each day you come to help and then you leave when the sun goes down...a long walk when you are already tired. You could stay here. My cabin needs a woman to tend to it. My granddaughter is still young. She does not know how to cook good food yet. She needs someone to teach her. I grow thin," he laughed, pulling in his stomach.

"Too thin," she teased, although the two months of feasting rounded his belly and made him look quite robust. "I will think about this."

*****

Although there were no baptisms, no official memberships, the Church community grew as summer waned into the crispness of fall. Mass was celebrated every Sunday, and sporadically on other days, and the attendees kept the church building full. The people felt comfortable with the "new" Bastiat. He was more relaxed about the details of Catholicism, though he still demanded baptism and education before receiving the Eucharist.

They were therefore not too surprised when one day they saw Čhaŋkú Wašté directing the priest in the proper construction of a sweat lodge. This particular sweat lodge did not look to be a temporary structure; it stood solidly behind the church. The arched saplings were substantial and well anchored, and the wood was lashed together tightly. With the cattle hides Ike procured, somehow, Pretty Stone and White Birch sewed a thick covering that could be stored until necessary. A pile of wood was stacked nearby in readiness. Stones were piled near the entrance.

The two cousins' cabin was near both the priest's and Grasshopper's. Its positioning somewhat across from the priest's cabin and church, and Grasshopper's cabin created a central and welcoming circular space that all doors faced.

"This is getting to be like a thiyóšpaye *extended family,*" Ike said with hands on hips surveying what was becoming known as the "other village."

There in front of the as yet unfinished cousin's cabin was a hide stretched on a rack...*a hide from the Black Hills!* A slow fire breathed insect inhibiting smoke beneath it.

There outside Grasshopper's cabin, the old woman added harvested thíŋpsiŋla *prairie turnip* to an iron pot filled with stew, thickening it. Niglíču was there stirring the meal that all would share that night.

There between the priest's cabin...*my cabin too,* Ike thought, stood the tall wooden cross the priest erected that Good Friday, a day which seemed so long ago.

Part Three
1900

Chapter 1

Niglíču heyé, "Wičhóoyake waŋží oblákiŋ kte."
Niglíču said, "I will tell a story."

"I do everything. All I need is some cash up front. I've done this before, Bordeaux. I know how it works." The red-headed man was dead serious.

"Selling whiskey on a reservation is strictly forbidden. Times have changed. This isn't like when these Indians were brought here almost ten years ago! I worked hard to get where I am today! I'd lose my position. Heck, they'd send me to jail."

Bordeaux was not making this easy for Dawes. He was going to give the man the money, but he was hedging to make the pot sweeter when it came to his "commission."

"I set this up in the store and you give me only ten percent of the take? That's not worth the risk," Bordeaux said dismissively.

"Fifteen," Dawes countered.

"Twenty-five or there is no use talking any further," Bordeaux said, standing up, preparing to usher Dawes out the office door.

"OK. Deal. Twenty-five percent."

That was too easy, Bordeaux thought to himself. *He's planning to skim, I know, but I can skim too.*

"Fine, but why should I believe you know anything about handling money? To be honest, you smell like you drink a good portion of the alcohol yourself."

"Me? Well, you are right about that, Bordeaux. I was never good with cash, and I do like my whiskey. But I got me a secret."

"A secret?"

"I got me a counting machine of a woman. A Chinee girl. She knows her numbers, she does."

"Why would I trust her?"

Dawes placed his palms on the desk, leaned forward a little too

302

close to Bordeaux's face and said, "Because she likes to live, if you get what I mean."

Bordeaux pulled back. There was evil in Dawes' countenance. That strange gleam in his eye. The sweat that speckled his forehead? He could almost smell it, sickeningly sweet. "You can't sell directly from the store. You'll get caught right away."

"Now," Dawes spoke in a conspiratorial manner, "I know that. I also got me someone who will sell directly to the injuns. He's one himself.

"Who? Do I know him?"

"He's been gone from here a while. Been traveling with a medicine show. A dancer. A drunken dancer!" Dawes guffawed. "Don't worry. He's perfect. He's been around the seedier section of our great society, let's say. He knows the ropes. And if he gets caught and squeals, ain't nobody gonna believe him, anyway."

"Sounds like you got it all planned, Dawes," Bordeaux said.

"I do indeed."

*****

She did not want a big ceremony that involved the whole village. Niglíču wanted only her thiyóšpaye to honor her passage into womanhood. She emerged from the išnáthi thípi bearing beaded gifts for the people and then prepared them a meal. She was now a woman in the eyes of all.

After she had made her thípi of thirteen poles, one for each moon, she was cared for by Oyé Wašté, Pretty Stone and White Birch. During her four days of seclusion, she did not feed herself or even touch herself. Niglíču was treated like a baby for the last time, while she was also instructed in all the ways of a Lakȟóta woman. Niglíču submitted to this treatment, and was even honored by it, but she did feel uncomfortable. This woman she was taught to be was not the person she knew she was. Her first menses had come later than others of similar age, concerning the other women of the thiyóšpaye, but Niglíču erroneously thought it was because she had willed it so. Becoming a woman in the traditional sense would be restrictive. *Why would I want that?*

And yet now it felt strangely wonderful to be looked upon as desirable to men. Their eyes, sweeping her body, at first had made her feel uneasy, but now they told her she was beautiful. Há Sápa's dark eyes veiled under long curled lashes told her so. Ike's quickly averted eyes attested to her beauty. And when she looked into the mirror in the priest's cabin, she saw her beautiful mother. Tall now, and lean, her hips had rounded, and her breasts pushed against clothing that had once hung loosely on her, revealing nipples hardened by her own observation of the bodies of men. *Am I so unlike the other young women of the camp?* A few had even taken husbands. One already had a child.

But she was different. How could she possibly be the same as her peers when each day over the past several years she had listened to Pepére teach her the ways of the world beyond the bounds of the reservation? She could quote Pepére's relative, the real "Bastiat," of France. How often was she admonished with the words of Kant, "Dare to know! Have courage to use your own reason!" To Niglíču, the world was one big "Why?" and she was hungry to understand it. She took Jefferson's "All men are created equal," to include her Lakȟóta people and herself as female. She read voraciously and learned the thoughts of mankind's great philosophers. She learned to express herself in writing.

Yet she did not turn wašíču in her heart. The priest had not aimed to "kill the Indian" as many boarding schools attempted to do. His desire was for her to understand the world she was in, for the newly begun twentieth century offered opportunities to go forward … to ultimately leave the barren reservation.

Pine Ridge was a place of both economic poverty and poverty of spirit. Lakȟóta traditions were discouraged or outright forbidden. Every effort was made to discourage the use of the Lakȟóta language. The wašíču demeaned it. Schools forbade it. And so the English language snaked into their vernacular. Wašíču customs and inventions had no Lakȟóta counterparts. How could they describe Edison's phonograph, a machine displayed in the white man's store that scratched out indecipherable noise? What word best describes electricity without speaking of spirit power?

Grasshopper helped her to maintain her heritage by resisting change. He continued singing his morning song. He offered his pipe to the six energies: the four directions and the earth and sky. He maintained his connection to his creator in traditional ways. While he appreciated Bastiat's education efforts, he refused to learn to read or write himself. He'd often say he could see, hear and speak. What need did he have for the written word? Why was this presumed to be more important because it rested on dried leaves?

And yet Niglíču did see the written word as important. She could no longer remember all of the stories of valor she was told as a child. She could hardly remember the funny stories of Iktómi, the trickster, that she had loved so much before. If *she* couldn't remember them, how could she pass them on to her own children?

My children? she thought. Now she was a woman! That she would have children became very real.

If these stories were written down, then she would not have to trust her memory at all. The stories would live on without a living storyteller. She had decided she would first write down what she could remember, and then ask the older people for help. She would write these stories in English, but more importantly to her, she would try to write them in Lakȟóta also, although she soon found English orthography did not adequately convey her pronunciation.

*****

The Spring evening was cool, and Ike sat outside Bastiat's cabin on one of the rotting log benches that had been used as seating for the first—and outdoor—Masses. He saw Niglíču sitting at her table through the open door. Rarely did they shut that door.

"Come, sit by me and read me one of your stories," he called to her.

Niglíču loved reading to him. Her fluency allowed her to read with emotion, mesmerizing Ike.

"You should be the camp storyteller," he said to her as she came out with her notebook. "I can picture you in a warm thípi with the winter winds howling. Gathered around you would be the camp children, each trying to sit as close to you as possible."

"I just finished this one. Want to hear it?"

"Yes," came a deep voice from behind them, "What story will you tell the little boy today?"

Ike stood up immediately and turned, angered at the insult. Loud Bear again, he saw. *Why doesn't he just stay away?*

Niglíču stiffened. It wouldn't take much for these two men to fight, she knew. She suspected her cousin was jealous of the elevated

305

position Ike seemed to have in her family. That Grasshopper had compared the two men was evident in his demeanor towards them, and clearly Loud Bear was judged the lesser of the two. Loud Bear was selling whiskey, after all, an action Grasshopper found despicable.

"How's business?" Ike asked, his sarcasm evident in his dismissive tone.

Loud Bear pointed to the supple buffalo robe that was hanging outside the door to air out.

"I see my grandfather did not mind my gift to him. It will keep him warm in winter."

Ike shot back, "It would chill him to know how you got it."

With the buffalo population nearing extinction, the chance of getting a buffalo hide to make into a robe was near zero. Loud Bear could not have gotten it through legal means, though he told his grandfather it was a gift from the traveling medicine show.

Ike walked to his cabin and closed the door behind him, darkening the room. Bastiat looked up from his book, annoyed at the door closure which made reading difficult. He was about to complain when he saw Ike's furrowed brow and clenched fists.

"He's back again," was all Ike needed to say.

*****

Wičhása waŋ yúza čhíŋ
A man wants to marry her.

"Why do the Black Robes never take a woman?"

The question came as a surprise to the priest. He and Čhaŋkú Wašté had been having more conversations now that the intelligent young holy man was becoming more fluent in English, but the question of Christian marriage had not yet been broached.

"I was married before," Bastiat said, "My wife died. But when I became a priest, I married the Church. The ring I wear suggests this."

"To marry a church is an odd thing," Čhaŋkú Wašté said.

"What it means is that since Jesus did not marry and I am supposed to take his place, I should not marry either. In this way, I am not divided between a wife and the people I serve."

"Why wouldn't the right wife make it easier for you to serve? You

306

could serve together.

Bastiat knew celibacy was hard for any man, but he thought it was particularly difficult for a man who had been previously married…like himself. Nights were the most difficult. How could he control his dreams? And was it sin if he dreamed it?

It now seemed insufficient, this notion he was taught, that since one does not marry in Heaven, a priest is better prepared for that state than the rest of humanity who marries. Still, he gave this reason to the shaman, but he could see that Čhaŋkú Wašté was not convinced.

"If I went to your Heaven, I would learn to adapt," the young man said.

"Ah," Bastiat laughed. "You are still young! And your people allow you to marry, even if you are a holy man."

"My people do not make rules about who can and cannot marry."

Just then, Niglíču walked her pony into the clearing. Not aware that she was being watched, she slid off her horse, her skirt rising with the slide exposing much of her legs. The young shaman's gaze locked on her, and the priest heard his sudden intake of breath when she turned towards them, face, flushed from the ride, hair, breeze-lifted off her shoulders.

"She is very young yet," Bastiat said.

"She is a woman now," Čhaŋkú Wašté replied, still looking at her.

*****

It was on the way to pick up their allotment that Niglíču saw the second Mrs. Bordeaux ride past on her bicycle. An attached wheeled wicker cart for children rolled along behind her and the Bordeaux's twin sons waved gaily at the wagon full of Lakȟóta women. The Bordeaux family, it was said, did not lack material things, and some gossipers wondered how the agency clerk could have that much money. The kinder people said Mrs. Bordeaux had an inheritance they were drawing from. Niglíču just felt sorry for this woman who had married a murderer.

What attracted Niglíču were the clothes Mrs. Bordeaux was wearing. Her skirt was split up the middle and sewn into two balloon like legs allowing the woman to pump the pedals unhindered by a long skirt. "I need this," Niglíču said to herself.

307

She imagined it would not be difficult to change her long skirt into one like that. Lay the skirt out flat. Cut it up the middle most of the way and then sew the pieces into billowing legs. With some trepidation, she presented the idea to Oyé Wašté.

How the old woman laughed! "Yes! Yes!" she exclaimed gleefully. "Cut mine too! I do not like these wašíču clothes!"

The next morning Grasshopper thought something was different about the old woman as she served him breakfast, but it was not until she squatted down to pick up a dropped ladle that he saw the skirt. *And now did she just bend over on purpose to show me the split?* He tightened his lips to hide a smile, deciding to wait until later to say something. This attire was suspiciously familiar… *Did I see it in town?*…but he was not willing to give the old woman any satisfaction as she looked to be flaunting this new apparel before him. But when he saw Niglíču dressed in similar fashion, he laughed. He was not about to fight two women and the new style skirt suited his granddaughter well.

Having Oyé Wašté live with them had been an excellent solution. She was the ideal feminine presence for his granddaughter.

*****

Oyé Wašté did not like Loud Bear. Niglíču, out of childhood loyalty, tried to defend him. But it was difficult when he came staggering in, drunk, boisterous and full of stories of his adventures traveling around the west, stories in which he most frequently ended up a hero in some form or another. He had thwarted a robbery, rescued an abducted child, stopped the stampeding horses who almost pulled the medicine show wagon off a cliff. "And how the wašíču were afraid of me when I danced! You should have seen them cower! I swung my club and they stepped back! I laughed, stabbing my spear in the ground and they cringed!" The list went on and on, and Oyé Wašté looked at the man and knew he was more capable of evoking their scorn than their admiration.

"Maybe he once was such a man, maybe once he was brave, but that was long ago," she told Niglíču.

That Grasshopper was so lenient with him surprised Niglíču, but what she did not know was that his plan was to win back Loud Bear's trust by not being critical. Hopefully, and gradually,

308

Grasshopper was sure he could turn his grandson's life around if he was gentle with him. If he could get him to spend more time with the thiyóšpaye, maybe a change could be effected. He thought too, that he might enlist the aid of the shaman, Čhaŋkú Wašté.

Despite his bravado, Loud Bear was having a difficult time back on the reservation. When he travelled with the medicine show he wasn't exactly free, performing when he was told to, but at least he had garnered some attention, even some applause and money.

Money. Money bought a fringed jacket, machine stitched. Tooled cowboy boots that blistered his wide feet. A belt of rattlesnake skin. A wide-rimmed hat, a Stetson of the creased top Carlsbad model. He bought Levi jeans which proudly sported a pocket patch that read "The only kind made by white labor." Of course he didn't wear any of these when he danced. Beads and a breechclout were his uniform, with trailing undeserved eagle feathers in his hair.

Money. Enough to dress him like a wašíču. Enough to buy him whiskey to forget who he had become.

But the wašíču obsession with dancing Indians had faded. The medicine show no longer wanted him.

And so to satisfy his alcohol addiction, he had to continue to make money and Dawes offered him the easiest way. Sell whiskey. The demand for it was surely there.

*****

Há Sápa pteáwaŋyakiŋ kta čhíŋ.
Há Sápa wants to be a cowboy.

Her given name was Venus. Venus. Even at young age playing with the master's daughter she learned Venus was some kind of goddess…goddess of love, Lucretia had said. Lucretia meant wealth. Her master's family surely had that. But it seemed to Venus that her name really meant sex. By the time she was sixteen she already had a child with Massah, though the light skinned baby died mysteriously after he was born.

But now that she was old, bent over and wrinkled from field work she had somehow survived, she preferred the name Granny. She was proud of her name, wore it like a title, a testament to having a son who bore a son. Her only grandson, Há Sápa.

309

His paternal grandmother had just recently entered his life. Venus had lost track of her emancipated son who joined the army but when a letter from him, with money in it, found its way into her hands, she couldn't believe what it said. "Read it to me again!" she said over and over to the postmaster in Georgia. "My boy sent for me? He wants me to come to him where? To a reservation? What? I have a grandson?"

She stuffed her clothes into an old carpetbag, bought a ticket to wherever far the money would take her, sent her son a wire she hoped he'd get and got on a train. When she somehow, by the grace of God she had said, reached Rapid City he wasn't there to meet her...right away...but he did come.

This sun-wizened, feisty woman delighted in Há Sápa. "You're like your father. You're not an Indian!" she said. "Just look at yourself! Black like me. Black like your father. I asked your father, 'Why you give your boy that Indian name? Black Skin?' Do you know what he said? He said, 'That name don't mean just no skin color. It says where his people are from! Africa!' See, your father knows who your people are! You don't have to stay here! This place will hold you close, and suck you so dry, you won't ever know what freedom is!"

But this wasn't true. Há Sápa knew what freedom was. That trip had changed Há Sápa's life.

What his grandmother did not recognize, though, was that he was also the child of his Indian mother. She so had taught him to respect the customs of her people that he was more Lakhóta than the full-blooded young men, his peers, who had lost hope.

"Be a cowboy!" she urged. "Lots of black men become cowboys and you can ride! I see you out there on your horse, racing that girl. You know what you're doin'. Listen to me! Get out of here and be a cowboy!"

Ike had told him about Belle Fourche. Not much further north than where they had been in the Black Hills, the city was all about cattle. He told the boy that he would never even be able to imagine the number of those animals loaded onto trains.

And so Há Sápa decided he would leave. He was a man now, after all. "My grandmother says that because I ride so well and because my skin is so dark, like my father's, I can become a cowboy," he told Niglíču.

"A cowboy?" she said incredulously. What little she knew about cowboy life came from chance encounters with dime novels and there was nothing particularly hopeful about the way people with dark skin were treated in those. "A cowboy?" she repeated. "You're leaving?" She wanted to add "me"...You're leaving me?" but pride prevented her.

Before he could say more, she turned her back to him, and mounted her horse.

"I'm coming back. I promise I'll be back!"

With tears in her eyes that he couldn't see, she rode away.

*****

Ič'íčhağe.
He transformed himself.

Dawes' store was not a place where people lingered. Customers did not go there to gossip, nor did they peruse merchandise positioned to tempt. Flour. Sugar. Coffee. Beans. Bolts of fabric. A few tools, guns. There was nothing fancy. Just the basics. It was as though Dawes was doing his customers a favor by providing anything at all. *He might as well put up a sign that says 'Just Buy It and get the hell outta here!* Bastiat thought. *He should improve his inventory. There are people around here with money to spend...like the Bordeauxs.*

A young Chinese woman worked the counter there, Dawes' woman it was said, although their interactions did not suggest they were even fond of each other. His words to her were sharp. Her responses, in broken but understandable English, were clipped. She smiled shyly at customers but did not engage them in conversation nor even meet their eyes with her own. Diligently she worked adding account information to her long ledger. Her notations were of characters looking far more artistic than their dry meanings would require. Date. Name. Item Purchased. Cost. Her thick brush tapered to a point, fresh from the ink block, rested each character on the page. And she wielded the rubber stamp with such fluidity and grace, the word PAID over the entry was barely perceptible. A so meticulous woman in her appearance and actions, she didn't seem real and Bastiat suspected her calm façade hid secrets, secrets which bound her to Dawes.

311

The talk around town was that Dawes had met this woman in Deadwood, although the veil Dawes used as he introduced her to male customers was 'rescued'. The priest had overheard a conversation once and caught words like "talented" and "popular" used to refer to her sexual attraction and skills. Not wanting to hear more, Bastiat walked away.

"I wonder what's her story?" the priest asked Ike one evening.

Ike shrugged. "But you know what's going on with the store, right?"

"Know? What?"

"It's a cover for the whiskey Dawes is selling with Loud Bear's help," Ike said.

"What?" the priest yelled. "I'll report him!"

"Who will you report him to? Bordeaux?" Ike laughed sarcastically.

"I'll go above him!"

"And Loud Bear will go to prison. Let me tell you, prison ain't a pretty place for an Indian."

"You've been there, haven't you?"

"I've been in jail a few times. Bad, but not quite the same as a prison."

*****

Grasshopper couldn't decide which was worse…those many years he did not know where his grandson was at all, or these times when he did know…or at least suspected he did. Alcohol was consuming his grandson and that was horrible, but the suspicion that Loud Bear's nightly activities were destroying the lives of others sickened him. What could he have traded for the ornate silver ring that he flaunted on his left hand? How did he get that knife with the carved ivory handle that peeked out above its sheath on his grandson's belt? Whose treasure was the turquoise stone that hung from his pierced ear? He did not have these things when he returned from the medicine show circuit.

Long after the store closed for the night, Dawes left whiskey bottles in crates under the back steps. Loud Bear would wrap each bottle before putting it into his sack and so, without the clink of glass, he would sneak off deeper into the reservation to meet with his usual

312

customers. How the men got the cash for their purchases he didn't care to know. And if a little coercion initiated a gift as well as the cost, Bordeaux was none the wiser.

The white whiskey, or moonshine as it was called, was procured from a connection Dawes had. An unsuccessful gold miner turned entrepreneur bypassed the government taxes and operated his still, distilling the corn, barley and rye into a rather horrible tasting but still potent, unaged clear liquid that burned on the way down, and enabled a fast oblivion. It was purchased by the gallon with Bordeaux's money. Dawes would bottle it, cut it with water by ten percent and hide that profit from Bordeaux.

One night, Loud Bear met with a new customer, a former warrior once respected in the village. They could not agree on the price and the middle-aged man ripped the bottle from Loud Bear's grip. A fight ensued and Loud Bear wrestled him to the ground, wrapped his hands around the man's throat and squeezed. The man's eyes bulged as he tried to force out a scream. "Like a woman!" Loud Bear yelled and then released him, disgusted at the man's degradation. Loud Bear watched the man stagger away and suddenly had a vision that he, too, must look like that when he was drunk.

Disgusted with himself now, he uncorked a bottle and took a long burning swallow. And another. But this time the alcohol effects only intensified his self-loathing.

He lay in the darkness against a tree and his customers filtered through the woods to make their purchases. The new customer returned, but this time he was not alone. The man dragged along a frightened young woman, young enough to be his daughter. Shoving the girl at Loud Bear, he growled, "You can have her for the night… in trade," he said. The girl was attractive. Loud Bear grabbed her leg before she could pull away.

Another man intervened, taking the former warrior's arm. "That's your daughter!" he protested. "Your daughter!"

Shamed, the father pulled his daughter's away. Shocked, Loud Bear released her. Appalled by his own behavior, Loud Bear threw his bottle against a tree. It didn't break and the other men around rushed to get it.

Loud Bear's eyes were opened that night. He smashed the few bottles he had left to sell and hurried back into town. Dawes awoke to the banging on the back door of the store and the yelling. He opened it and saw Loud Bear ranting.

"I'm done with this!" Loud Bear hollered as he threw down the empty sack and pelted Dawes with the coins he had earned that day. "Take it! All of it! This is wrong!" he shouted.

Merely amused, Dawes responded, "Go sleep it off, you worthless dog! I'll see you back here tomorrow night ... or else!"

*****

Loud Bear managed four days without drinking. On day five he woke up feeling great. No more headache. No more shaking. And his heart stopped pounding, slowly disappearing until not being felt at all. *I don't need whiskey anymore!* He walked into an open field of grasses, spread wide his arms and embraced the day. He gave thanks to his Creator, sat and soaked up healing warmth until the sun rose high in the sky, and then he asked himself, "What will I do today?"

And there it was. The beginning of the real test of his sobriety...the simple question that begat a suggestion. *Since I'm cured, I can certainly have a drink...just a little one...later. How could just a little bit hurt?*

But the day stretched long before the 'later' he promised he'd wait until...the later when he would reward himself for his self-control.

He could not think how to fill this long day when his body felt so alive, so alive that he could almost taste the sweet tang of a good life...so alive that he wanted to experience it...enhanced... with the colors even brighter and the touching more sensuous. Surely one drink would bring him this...surely one drink would make everything even better.

No. No, it wouldn't! He pulled back from the temptation and sank into misery. *There's no good in this world! I'm not a man. I'm worthless like Dawes said. Why should I expect anything more?*

The goodness of the world disappeared for him. Whiskey wouldn't make the world better, but it might just make it all go away.

*****

Sitting outside his grandfather's cabin brooding, Loud Bear soured the thiyóšpaye.

"Bad apple," Bastiat muttered, thinking of sermons he had heard

314

about the corrupting influence of sinners. *Have I ever spoken this way to my congregations? Would Jesus? No, he decided, Jesus would have sat down and ate with them.*

"Loud Bear, come share some coffee with me!" he invited cheerily with his lips, but not quite so with his heart.

They sat in silence while the priest poured the coffee. Loud Bear poured in sugar from the jar and stirred it into his cup, swirling it left, then right, then left again, never looking at the priest. Finally, he raised his eyes as he raised the cup. "What do you want of me? Are you offering me coffee... or salvation?" He took a long swallow. "I will drink your coffee. I do not want your god." With no further word, he stood up and walked out the door.

*****

"Bastard!" Dawes slammed the door shut rattling the dainty lidded Chinese teacup Ah-Duo had set on the shelf next to the chipped plates stacked neatly there. She didn't ask who the day's bastard was. Dawes was always cursing somebody. "He never showed up! The bottles are still there!"

Now she knew the offender. And it was unlike him to miss a day either. "Maybe he is sick," she offered as a lame excuse.

"He's sick alright and when I get my hands on him, he's gonna be worse than that!"

She set the coffee pot on the table next to his cup. The bottom was scorching hot, but she didn't care whether it marked the wood of the table. There were several burnt rings there already, and she could have covered one with the pot. Instead she made another ring knowing full well it would aggravate him more. Some things he was meticulous about.

"What are you doing?" he yelled.

Feigning innocence, she apologized, "I'm sorry." Only the word did not come out as sorry but as solly, annoying him even more. "Damn Chinee" he muttered. But the coffee was good he had to admit and that mellowed him some. "Come over here."

She went nearer to him, and he grabbed her waist and sat her on his lap. "Feel that?"

Disgusted, she tried to pull away, but he held her firm.

Suddenly a bell tinkled. The shop door had opened. "Dawes,

315

wherever the hell you are, get out here!"

Shoving Ah Duo away, he grabbed the sack stuffed with coins and bills and entered the storefront.

Bordeaux emptied the money on the counter and totaled it. "You're short," he declared. "A day."

"My distributor didn't show up last night."

"Distributor?" Bordeaux spat on the floor, still wet from Ah Duo's mop. "You mean that drunken Indian you've been paying off. I told you not to trust him!"

"He'll be back."

"He better be. He knows too much!" Bordeaux growled, slamming his fist on the counter, jiggling the hard candy in the lidded jars there.

"He won't talk," Dawes said.

"Make sure of it!"

*****

It is good that he rides the taller horse, Čhaŋkú Wašté thought looking to his right seeing Loud Bear astride the tall bay. *He looks confident up there. It is good too that I lied to him.* The holy man did not need company, or the protection of another man, when he traveled to other villages in the vast reservation. But Loud Bear didn't need to know this and now the former warrior turned dancer turned…turned… Čhaŋkú Wašté did not want to put words onto what had become of Loud Bear because now the man was changing as his addiction to alcohol waned. Loud Bear had a purpose. Protect the holy man.

And doing this for Loud Bear had more than one purpose for Čhaŋkú Wašté. It gave him an excuse to spend time with Grasshopper and, in turn, Niglíču.

She was lonely without her friend, Há Sápa, his competition. The boy had become a man and Čhaŋkú Wašté knew he would be coming back to take her for his wife. He'd be a fool not to.

And I'd be a fool not to, also, he thought.

*****

Wówapi waŋ Há Sápa etáŋ ičú.

316

She received a letter from Há Sápa.

The cast iron boot scraper was screwed into the porch floorboards right next to the stairs. Dawes gift to her ("Don't you like it? I had it made special for you!") was effective for those who bothered to use it. Most didn't. Most could not even imagine why that bent iron bar with flat top was there. Ah-Duo swept the dirt around it back into the dusty street. Dawes tacked up a poster beside the door.

Niglíču always attracted attention when she rode into town with her lively pinto, one reason Bastiat preferred her to ride Ned there. Now the pony kicked up dust, her steady trot screening her long white legs. Dawes watched her approach. He always watched attractive women.

He watched her swing her leg over the horse's back and dismount. While the new skirt hid the outline of her legs, it accentuated her buttocks. He smiled. Ah-Duo rolled her eyes, disgusted with him.

Dawes opened the door for her and placed his hand too far down her back to usher her in. Niglíču glared at him. "Do not touch me!"

He laughed and threw his hands in the air in mock surrender.

If she didn't need to, she never would have gone into his store knowing how he used Loud Bear to his advantage. But her last notebook was filled with stories she had collected from the elders of the village. Her penmanship precise, she was proud of the way the letters looked in her book, proud of the way they told the stories.

"I want to buy a notebook," she said.

"Now why would a pretty gal like you want a notebook? Do you want to draw pictures on the paper? I have some paper in the back. Do you want to see if you would like it?"

"I want to buy a notebook," she repeated.

"You want to draw pictures, do you? How nice."

She swallowed her anger. He was playing with her, but she could play the game too. She nodded solemnly. She just wanted to buy the book and leave.

Interested in their interactions, Ah-Duo came into the store and walked behind the counter. She admired this young Lakȟóta woman. She opened the ledger and took her brush, ready to record the transaction.

"Would you want a brush to paint with?" he asked. He took hold of the top of Ah-Duo's brush, her favorite, and pulled.

317

Before Niglíču could answer no, Ah-Duo grabbed her brush from Dawes' hand. Retaliating, he backhanded her across the face.

"Don't you ever!" he growled.

Niglíču's initial reaction was to intervene, but she sized up the situation quickly. If she interfered, the woman would be beaten more. Now it had stopped. She locked eyes with Ah-Duo who held her hand over a reddening cheek. *I'm with you!* Niglíču's stare told her.

The tiny bells above the door jingled as Mrs. Bordeaux entered the store. She stopped dead still, aware of the tension, but then Dawes turned on the charm.

"Mrs. Bordeaux," he said cheerfully. "Where are your two sons? The candy they like just came in yesterday. I was hoping to give them some."

"Good morning," she replied coldly. "Yes, I will buy the candy, but she was being served first. Please complete that transaction." Her formal language always seemed to put him in his place. She despised him. Something about him seemed evil.

He quickly handed Niglíču the notebook and accepted her few coins. With her head down, Ah-Duo recorded the sale.

"Your cheek looks red this morning, Ah-Duo," the clerk's wife observed. "Did you bump into something?" Without waiting for an answer, she then looked at Dawes. "You should get her some ice to put on that."

As the door closed behind her, Niglíču glanced at the newly hung poster. In bold words it said, "Archery Contest." Next to it was given the location near Fort Robinson, Nebraska.

Reading further, Niglíču learned the contest was being offered to celebrate the first Olympic archery events held in Paris that year. Women who had competed against the US National Archery Women's Champion, Lida Scott Howell, were expected to participate in the event. It also said the contest was open to anyone. *Maybe I can go...*

*****

"What does the Olympics mean?" Niglíču asked Bastiat.

"The Olympics? Why, that's a competition between athletes from all over the world. Why do you ask?"

"It says there was the first archery contest in the Olympics this

318

year," she replied.

The priest got excited. "Yes, in Paris. Men's archery though, They are talking about maybe having women compete in the next Olympics. 1904.

"Why, Pepére, if the wašíču have so many guns, why would they want to use bows and arrows?"

"A good question indeed! Some do it for fun. Others because after the Civil War, the confederate soldiers were forbidden to have firearms, but they still wanted to hunt. Later, and because they liked it, it became a sport. And then there were contests."

"There is going to be a contest here, too. The poster says anyone can enter."

"And?"

"I want to enter it."

*****

Fort Robinson was but a two-day ride from Pine Ridge if they traveled cross country and did not stick to winding roads. Bastiat could make it happen. They would take a chance going without an official pass, assuming, as before, that his priesthood would protect them from intense questioning.

Though they decided they would keep her upcoming participation a secret, one of the cousins let the news slip and the village became excited for her. Young boys were encouraged to watch her practice. Young girls spied on her in defiance of their elders, leaving their quills and beadwork to see this unusual young woman practice with her weapon.

It did not take long for the news to reach Čhaŋkú Wašté. He followed her one early morning when she walked off to practice away from the eyes of the village. With the rising sun as his background, he strode confidently across the open area to where she stood with her back to him.

"I bring you a gift," he said, surprising her as he announced his presence. How magnificent he looked in traditional buckskin garb! Admiring the long fringes that waved from his arms and the intricate beadwork on his shirt, she felt a stab of jealousy. *What woman had made this for him?*

"It is wakáŋ. Wear this that day when you compete."

319

She marveled at the traditional breastplate he handed to her. Two columns of forty white hair pipes were separated by rows of five brass beads. Long leather fringes lined each side. One perfect cowrie shell and a purple silk ribbon hung from the left.

"I will be honored to wear it," she said.

*****

Niglíču had outgrown her original bow, but she still kept it, protected from moisture, hanging from a ceiling beam in the corner. Together she and Grasshopper had made her new bow to fit her height. The green ash had been measured from the tip of her left center finger, when her arm was outstretched, to her right hip at the joint. The wood had been properly aged over a fire and sinew was used for cordage. The double curved short bow measured about 40 inches. It was designed for quick and reflexive arrow release that had once given it the advantage over single shot rifles. The arrows she would use were made based on the length of her arm and were fletched with turkey feathers. Grasshopper had judged it to be an excellent bow. An adequate bow could embed an arrow in buffalo hide. An arrow shot from a superior bow would pass through the animal. This bow fell somewhere in between. It would sink the arrow in up to its fletching.

Niglíču did not know exactly what the contest would entail, but she prepared for both stationary and moving targets. She practiced daily.

They set out a few days before the event: Bastiat, Grasshopper, Ike, and herself.

*****

White military tents dotted the area of the flat plains where the contest was to take place. Horses grazed nearby, freed from the sometimes ornate carriages they had pulled to the site. The people wore impractical clothing. Velveteen jackets on the men.

"They look like people who were at Hot Springs," Niglíču confided to Bastiat.

Men wore summer straw boater hats with colorful hatbands. Their necks sweated under their detachable starched collars and stiff bibs and their fake cuffs stuck out from their jacket sleeves. How Niglíču giggled when she saw a man semi-stripped, preparing to cool himself by a water trough behind a tent. "He isn't wearing a shirt at all, just those pieces." she whispered to Ike.

The sun blazed on that hot day. The sky was clear and heat shimmered over the wilted grasses. With trepidation, Niglíču walked to the registration table with Bastiat in his new black robe at her side. The official looked over the rim of his glasses at this young Indian woman in a long, beaded buckskin dress covered by an ornate breastplate that jangled as she moved.

"Yes?" he asked.

"I want to register for the competition." When he hesitated, she added, "The rules say it is open to all women."

He pursed his lips and pinched them in consternation. The rules did say that. He handed her the pen.

"Write your name here," he pointed.

When she returned the form, he handed it back to her. "Your last name too," he ordered smugly. With this technicality he hoped to disqualify her for noncompliance.

"I am Lakȟóta," she began. "We don't...."

Bastiat cut her short. "Stop being silly," he said to her. "You know how to write my name. Bastiat. B...a..."

The registrar was startled. Bastiat was, after all, dressed in full Jesuit attire.

"My daughter wants to enter the contest. Is there a problem?"

This feels so devilishly good! Bastiat thought.

Niglíču had a hard time controlling her smile. *Daughter?* But she added Bastiat to her name on the entrance form.

Away from the table, Grasshopper asked, "Was something wrong?"

The priest replied, "Nothing we couldn't solve."

She entered the lineup, assigned last in the long row of elaborately dressed women holding their English longbows, bows as tall as they were. Quivers hung from their waists.

And they weren't alone out there on the line. Men presumed to be husbands stood behind them.

Ike stepped up behind her, his hair wet slicked back in the attempt to look good for her.

She smiled, took a deep breath, and joined the line facing the large

321

bullseye targets. The distances would be at 60, 50 and then 40 meters. There would be 6 arrows shot in a four-minute period per distance. She would need to shoot many arrows that day.

The crowd cheered as the competition was about to start, but one jeer was heard from the bystanders nearest Niglíču. Niglíču thought she recognized it and turned. Dawes leered at her.

"Ignore him!" Ike commanded.

She did not begin shooting when the others did. She knew she had plenty of time to release six arrows in four minutes. She could easily do that in less than one.

With arrow nocked, but with string slack, she offered her bow to the four directions, the sky and the earth, and then pointed the arrow directly towards Dawes and held that position for a long second. The crowd gasped as she pulled the arrow into position. Dawes stepped behind the stranger who stood next to him, while Niglíču whipped around and rapidly fired her six arrows effortlessly towards the center of the bull's eye. She turned again, met Dawes' eyes, and smiled. The threat was not lost on him.

The crowd was stunned at both her speed and accuracy. Not all arrows hit their mark, but enough did to impress. Ike let out a warrior whoop matched only by Grasshopper. Tears welled in the priest's eyes.

Dawes slunk to the back of the crowd as it was announced that she had won that particular part of the contest.

*****

They received a warrior's welcome when they returned to the village. "Lelelelele!" the women cheered. Children ran along beside them. They dismounted before Grasshopper's old lodge. Čhaŋkú Wašté and Loud Bear were there to greet them. Niglíču unwrapped the breastplate from her blanket and handed it back to the shaman.

"Thank-you. It helped me," she said shyly.

When they arrived back at their cabins, Bastiat remembered the letter he had picked up at the post office. He handed it to Niglíču. "It's from Há Sápa," he said.

She went inside her cabin and climbed up into the loft. With nervous fingers she opened the first letter she had ever received. It was short and said simply,

"Wait for me."

*****

Napé líla makȟáte.
My hand is very hot.

Wait for me...but for when? And for what? Há Sápa had been gone for months and then there was just this three-word letter. She wondered what it would be like to be loved by him in a man/woman, and not just friend, way.

Čhaŋkú Wašté had approached Grasshopper about the benefits she would have in marrying a man older than she. He was settled. He was respected. And he respected her. He suggested she could be a helpmate. Already she had the propensity for being a healer and surely the interest. She gathered herbs and mixed potions under the tutelage of the old woman, but he could teach her more.

Grasshopper spoke to her about this because he was skeptical. The shaman would want a traditional wife and his granddaughter was not that.

She had been walking along the creek, a walk that took her miles from the cabin without her realizing it. Mountain was with her, and he splashed through the streaming water. A mature dog now, he was past his prime but still vigorous and eager to accompany her.

Stopping to scoop up some water to drink, the milky, translucent whiteness of a wet stone in the shallow river caught her eye. She bent to pick it up and was immediately struck by its smoothness. River stones were smooth, but not like this, she thought. She held it against her cheek and slid it over her lips, a cold kiss.

The stone warmed in her palm, and she absentmindedly caressed it as she walked home.

"Look what I found!" she said to Bastiat, outside spreading hay for Ned.

He laughed. "A heart! How nice is that!"

"A heart?" She was unfamiliar with the symbol. "No, look, Pepére! See how smooth this is. There are none like this here."

He took it and rubbed it with his thumb and was immediately brought back in time.

"You are right! This stone is from the ocean."

323

"The ocean? That's so far away! Oh, Pepére, I wish I could see the ocean."

How can I describe the ocean? How can I make her envision tall dark waves breaking into a cascade of white? How can I make her feel the foamy bubbles that tickled my feet and swept away the sand beneath them? How can I explain sinking deeper into the soft sand with each retreating wave? Can I make her see the elusive clam shell floating back into the sea, or feel the shiver of stepping on a beached jellyfish? How can I make her hear the seagulls or smell the briny perfume of salt air?

He held the stone in his hand and examined it, rolling it over in his palm. He told her the shape, although far from perfect, resembled a heart which, among the white people, was a symbol for love.

"I bet one day a miner lost this. Maybe he died? I bet his girlfriend, or his wife gave this stone to him and said to keep it to remember her," the priest said imbuing the stone with a romantic background.

Maybe that's what I felt when I picked it up. Niglíču thought.

"When I was a little boy…," Bastiat began dreamily.

"Pepére, wait! Let me get my notebook," Niglíču ordered.

"Why?"

"I write down everyone else's story. Shouldn't I write down yours?"

The priest laughed but waited. He thought that no one would be interested in his story when he was gone. His family would never even miss him. He had been away a long time.

With pencil in hand, Niglíču prepared to take notes.

"I didn't know what salt water was, and I never saw the ocean. I lived in a part of New York City called the Bronx and there is salt water there, but my family had no desire to take me to see it. My mother's brother came to visit one summer, and he was wealthy. He decided to take my mother, my younger brother and me to see the ocean."

"How big is the ocean, Pepére?" Niglíču asked.

"Do you remember when we were standing on that high mountaintop and we thought we could see forever? An ocean is many times bigger than what we saw then. If you look, you cannot see the other side. If you traveled across it for many days, you still could not see the other side of it."

He continued with his eyes half closed. With her pencil ready, she

324

was prepared to capture his experience.

"We took a carriage into Manhattan, and then I got on my first boat. It was magnificent! A steamer with a side wheel! My mother gasped when she saw how expensive it was to board. Fifty cents a person! When we landed two hours later, we went directly to the Coney Island House hotel and changed into bathing suits. I remember how windy it was! And how hot the sand was on my bare feet! Burning! I ran straight ahead and splashed into the water. How cold it felt! I jumped up and down, slapping my hands against the water, and it bounced up all around me and showered over my face. The salt stung my eyes, but I squeezed them shut and didn't care! Paradise!"

"And then, with no warning, I was spinning in the water and couldn't find my way up, even though the water was only a few feet deep. I panicked. My mouth was full of sand, and I spat that out, sputtering, as I tried to stand up in the soft sand that I kept sinking into. After what seemed like forever, I stood up with my bathing suit hanging low with the sand it had collected and looked towards the shore. I'll never forget this next thing. My mother was laughing at me! There I was, utterly humiliated that the ocean bested me, and she laughed!"

"Did you hate the ocean after that?" Niglíču asked.

"No, I loved it! It challenged me and I fought back! I learned how to dive through waves or jump over them, and my brother and I had a glorious time that weekend!"

Will I ever see the ocean? she wondered. *Will I ever be able to see the world he has lived in?* The reservation suddenly seemed so small. Deep in reflection, she walked to her cabin and placed the notebook and stone on the table.

"What's that, Ťhakóža?" Grasshopper asked.

"I found this stone, Lalá. It's from the ocean." She held it out to him."Pepére says it is probably from a wašíču who died around here. Maybe he was killed. See? It's heart shaped. We think maybe it was a gift from the man's woman to remember her by."

"You see a story in everything!"

Drawn to it, he picked up the stone later when he was alone and smoothed his thumb over it. *It feels hot,* he thought. *Hotter than it should.*

Dismissing it as part of his imagination, he nonetheless laid his hand against his shirt, assuring himself his medicine bag with the photo inside was still there.

Chapter 2

Ečháŋni t'iŋ kte.
He will die soon.

Wanting to become a cowboy and actually becoming one were two different things, Há Sápa soon found out after he reached Belle Fourche. As the open range was being divided up by homesteaders and turned to agriculture, cattle ranching was forced to adapt. Cattle ranches moved closer to the cities from which the cattle were shipped and distributed to the nation via the railroad. Belle Fourche had a glut of cowhands and there was little need for a young inexperienced man to take a job a seasoned professional could perform for the same pay.

"What you want to do, young man," a black cowboy smiling his leatherlike face into deep creases said, "is to go east to Evarts. The Chicago, Milwaukee and St. Paul railroad just reached there, and it's turning into a cow town. It's a bit of a journey, but they need men to work cattle near that Missouri River. It's a tricky one, for sure."

Há Sápa soon began the two-hundred-mile journey there, leaving hungry and arriving thinner than before. As he rode his exhausted horse into town, he was greeted on the outskirts by women in varying forms of undergarments fanning themselves on their porch.

"We're closed now, Sweetie, but if you come back in a few hours, we can teach you things," one said, suggestively running her hands over the curves of her body.

"Daisy," another said, "that boy ain't got enough money to pay for a peck on his cheek."

"But he sure looks mighty fine," Daisy teased.

"You don't get paid for lookin!" an older whore said, and the other women laughed.

The stench of cattle filled the air and Há Sápa thought every fly in South Dakota had come over to taste him. Stockyards were filled with bellowing beasts, Four hundred frightened beasts were routinely prodded into cramped stockcars and every three hours a loaded train would pull away with them.

Há Sápa was amazed when he saw the pontoon bridge. It spanned the Missouri River! Groups of 20 cattle were herded over it, each controlled by only one cowhand.

"Maybe I can do that!" Há Sápa thought.

He was quickly hired, but not as a cowboy. He had to prove his worth, they said, and so he was directed to dig out what would become another chemical pond, a dipping facility they called it. There, a lime, sulfur and antiparasitic bath was prepared for the cattle who were forced to swim through it so their scabies and Texas fever would be eliminated.

The hours were long, and the pay was barely enough to buy the exorbitantly priced food. He developed a taste for coffee, the only drink other than alcohol that the cowboys consumed. Drinking-water was polluted, and a cowboy learned to enjoy the hot coffee that killed the bacteria swimming in it. But within two weeks, Há Sápa earned the respect of his boss and was offered a cowboy job on the Strip, an eighty mile long and six mile wide lane that fed the cattle into Evarts.

Though they sang "Home on the Range" by the campfire, these men were not on the range nor exactly home either. Deer and antelope did not play where they were. There were just cattle, scared, thirsty, hungry beasts. And flies.

One in four men working these cattle were black men. During working hours, men were judged by the ability to perform their job and not by their skin color. But equality was hardly perfected. CowBOY was applied to black men while cowHAND referred to white men. And men who on the trail or working the pens were comrades, segregated when in town especially in the presence of white women.

Besides their forays into town, there were other times of amusement, but they were at the expense of the driven cattle. The animals were expected to travel 12 miles a day and it was so planned that at the end of the day they spent the night at a watering hole. Texas cattle were used to being watered out of steel tanks or shallow ponds so when they met a true South Dakota watering hole with deep water, they innocently waded in and sank. The cattle drivers laughed watching the animals disappear and then rise up, startled, and confused. Há Sápa found the scene painful to watch.

Often at night, Há Sápa would think of the stories he had been told of buffalo hunts. Man against beast…a contest either could lose. He imagined himself on a pony hugging close to the herd, drawing back the arrow…the aim… the release…the thud of arrow into tough hide. He tried to think that being a cowboy was like that, but he could not convince himself. This was just cruelty, he thought. Total slaughter of all with no regard for the dignity of the animal. Being a cowboy was not what he had expected, and every morning he had to convince himself not to leave. *I'll stay… for the money.*

One morning a bred heifer that had escaped last year's round-up, but not this one, gave birth to her calf on the final leg of the Strip. Há Sápa waited with the cow during the birthing and saw the afterbirth still hanging from the cow while the calf had its first drink of the colostrum it needed to survive. The trail boss yelled for him to drive the cow forward.

Because the calf was yet too weak to be traveling, not even yet dry from the birthing, it stumbled along a few yards, falling and rising before it collapsed, exhausted. The cow tried to hang back to protect it, but the herd propelled her forward, mooing piteously. The calf was destined to be trampled.

But the calf's cries unnerved Há Sápa. Risking injury by dismounting in the middle of the herd, he shoved the cattle aside, swept up the bull calf and slung it, squirming, over his horse's neck.

"Put that thing down," his foreman yelled as he approached the herd. "Leave it. We have work to do."

"It will die," Há Sápa pleaded.

"Does it matter? They are all going to die in a day or two," came the response.

"It matters to this one," Há Sápa replied, refusing to put it down.

The foreman rode off laughing. "That cowboy has developed a conscience!" he called to the others.

The calf flailed its spindly front legs, kicking him as he mounted behind it.

By the time they reached the dipping facility, the mother cow was lost in the anonymity of the herd struggling to escape the burning waters. Há Sápa's boss rode up to him. "Drop the damned thing!" he said.

Há Sápa blurted out, "I want to buy this calf."

"You want to do what?"

"Buy him."

"Ten dollars."

"Ten? You are only getting six dollars for a hundred pounds for these," Há Sápa said, pointing to the masses of cattle in the holding pens.

"Seven. A week's wages, and if you argue, I'll shoot you for being a cattle thief." He drew his pistol and pointed to Há Sápa. This boss would not tolerate belligerence. Stick with the routine! Be orderly! Not complying would cost him money, and it could cost his men their lives.

However impulsive was Há Sápa's decision, he stuck with it.

"Ok, seven. You can take it out of my wages."

"Hah! You'd don't even make that much! Think about it, boy. The calf will be dead by morning."

"Seven," Há Sápa said, though imagining his disappointed father. *You left because of a goddamn calf?*

"Fine! And good riddance to you!" the boss hollered, jerking his horse's head around to join the rest of the men. "We sure as hell don't need any sentimental cowboys around here!"

Há Sápa left the herd with taunting jeers stinging his ears. "Gonna turn that thing into tatanka are you?" the cowhands laughed. He rode over to the shack, collected his wages and added more to pay for the bull calf, now barely able to raise its head to wheeze out a call for his mother. Paid, the bill of sale said. The animal was his, but this calf needed milk. Something he foolishly did not consider… a problem he would need to rapidly solve. He knew nothing about raising a calf. He was not aware that a calf needs to suckle milk equivalent to ten percent of its body weight a day…quarts and quarts of milk.

And the cattle heading to slaughter were not accessible to him, even if they had milk.

At first he naively thought it would not be difficult to find a dairy cow in or around town. Surely he could buy some milk although the money wad in his pocket was not nearly as thick as it had been before. But he soon learned this town did not attract families. Dairy cows did not graze on meadow grass around homesteads to provide families with milk, butter and cheese. But he remembered seeing one such cow, although he could not recall where.

330

And then he remembered.

A cow grazed behind a house ... the house on the outskirts of town with the women on the porch.

He rode up to the white picket gate, dismounted, and laid the calf on the grass beside his horse. There was little risk of the calf wandering off. It seemed barely alive.

No one was outside that day. He walked up to the door, hat in hand, and knocked. Business must have been slow that Monday, however, as Daisy opened the door immediately.

"Well, hello," she said. "I remember you. Come on inside."

"I need a favor," he said. "I will be willing to pay for it."

"Of course, sweetie, I'm sure we have just what you need. You have money now?"

He blushed, felt it rise in his cheeks, although with his dark skin he knew she could hardly see it.

"Not that kind of favor," he said, and speaking rapidly, continued. "I need milk for my calf over there and I see you have a cow out back and her bag looks to be full, and I wonder if you would allow my calf to nurse from her for a few days until he gets stronger to travel. I'll work for you to repay your kindness. That fence over there looks like it could use a little fixing."

She called over her shoulder, giggling, "Girls, come on over here if you are not ... busy ... and listen to this cowboy!"

Há Sápa's plight charmed the women, and their maternal instincts were directed towards the calf. The calf was introduced to the cow who did not happily accept him, but eventually submitted to the nursing.

But the calf would need more than days to nurse and so began Há Sápa's several weeks as a repairman and handy man at the brothel, while his calf grew old enough to eat grass and travel.

Business in that cowtown was steady and the women entertained often. The brothel madame made a healthy profit and she was generous with Há Sápa's fees. A hard worker, he hired himself out doing heavy work, chopping wood, painting, whatever needed done. His money roll grew thicker along with his confidence that when he returned home, his parents could be proud of him. And because the calf thrived, he figured he should be home by the first snow.

Over the course of those weeks Há Sápa realized he had not made a mistake with his young bull calf at all. Imagining his future, he

331

figured the calf could someday be herd sire on his ranch

Someday. Someday I will own land. Someday have a wife...children...

Soon the nights grew cold and the unheated shed of a barn he shared with the cow, calf and chickens chilled him. The women offered him, again, nights in a warm bed and he was sorely tempted, but he knew the time had come to leave.

*****

The porch faced the sunset, and no tree blocked it. There was just the long shadowy road that disappeared into nothing when the sky darkened. Molly, the proprietress of the whorehouse, sat on the swing next to her long ago customer, but now friend, Horace. The evening was chilly, and he held her close while the chains creaked bearing their weight. Molly preferred being outside. The grunts and groans of the men and the false-passioned responses of her women bored her. She had been in the business too long.

"You say that boy workin' for you is leavin'? Going south to the reservation? Hell, that's 300 miles if he sticks to the roads and God help him if he doesn't. He'll get lost for sure. And he's takin' the calf? Thing'll be dead in a week. Damn shame. The calf's put on some good weight with all the fussin' your ladies is givin' him. I seen them feeding him bouquets of pink flowered clover like he's some god or something to be worshipped. Glory be but that meat's gonna be right tender. Tell him to leave the calf here. I'll help with the butcherin' when it's time."

She swatted him with the tasseled end of her shawl. "You'll do no such thing!"

"But the calf will die without milk. That's a powerful long walk he'll be takin' with no milk to boost him up. Might last a week or two but he'll die for sure. Goddamn shame."

"He says he'll stop in towns...get milk there... or from homesteaders."

"Molly, I'm tellin' you there ain't nobody or nuthin' between here and there. He don't know that? Damn. Maybe he's gonna die too."

They rocked in silence. A customer inside yelped and hollered his release. Molly rolled her eyes. Horace chuckled. "We was like that once." He kissed the top of her head, his gray beard thick against her gray strands.

"I'll tell you what, Mol. Why don't you send him with the cow too? You don't need her anymore now that kid and his whorin' mother are gone."

"Send Daisy?"

"Now, I been meanin' to tell you, Daisy ain't no name for that cow. She ain't no farm critter. Half Holstein yeah…Holstein from those creamery fever Danish people up north makin' all that butter. But she's Hereford too, and should have a fittin' name. Name like Queenie maybe bein' those Herefords come from England and all. Queen Victoria! That's what she should be called!"

"Do you know what he calls his calf? Tȟatȟáŋka. Likes he's a buffalo," Molly laughed.

"Give him the cow, Molly. You ain't got no use for her. If he travels slow, they'll make it. The boy's got grit. Mebbe he'll make somethin' of hisself."

"I'll think on it."

They swung back and forth, back and forth, and then he burst out laughing.

"What? What's so funny?"

"I was picturing them injuns sitting around the fire at night, fartin' up a storm."

"What?"

"Injuns' bodies cain't handle no milk. I'd like to be there after they sample some of Queen Victoria's. Give him the cow, Molly. Let them fart away!"

*****

The cow was tethered to his horse. The calf would follow obediently. The women waved to Há Sápa from the porch that early morning when he said good-bye. He hoped he would remember them that way…looking like ordinary women without makeup, wearing modest shifts that only hinted of what they hid. Women with flyaway hair and gentle hearts. Women who hoped someday for a better life.

333

Chapter 3

Oȟágye.
He poisoned him.

B ear Teeth did not want a cabin. He couldn't remember how many winters he had spent warm in his thípi and saw no need to spend the rest of them surrounded by wood. Even small cabins built around the village were too spacious to heat. He watched the people every evening gravitate to the church where the iron stove radiated warmth that penetrated to their bones.

But his thípi was not in a protected area surrounded by towering pines to buffer the wind. His thípi was not ringed with heavy brush that dared the winter winds to pass through, nor was the army canvas insulated with grasses. Despite his best efforts to guard against the cold, his thípi did not stay warm. There was never enough branches to be found and no buffalo chips for the fire at all.

And so as fall waned, he too went to the church building for the comfort of the stove and the company of the people. The church building had evolved into a meeting place where stories were told and children played tag around the church benches. At first the priest was appalled to see this behavior all under the light of the sanctuary lamp that said Jesus was present there in the Eucharist. But then he remembered the scripture which said God delighted in His people. Wouldn't Jesus in the Real Presence rejoice in this community?

And if a couple had a naming ceremony for their newborn there in the church, would Jesus be offended if Čhaŋkú Wašté conducted it? And would not Jesus rejoice to see Loud Bear, seemingly transformed, assisting with the fanning and smudging?

Loud Bear transformed. The speed of it both pleased and worried him. He had seen this before in his years as pastor; a sinner repents, becomes overzealous, and then falls harder than before.

Loud Bear thrived during the day following the shaman and assisting when he could, but it was the long nights that brought him haunting dreams, dreams always of laughter. High pitched laughter. And directed at him. People pointing to him, laughing at him. He would wake up sweating, his heart beating wildly. One little girl's face would float in. A wašíču girl, blonde, ice-blue eyes and stunningly beautiful. Maybe three years old. He remembered her. How could he forget? It was at a show. He was dancing, and he saw her watching, and he had smiled at her. *Such rare beauty,* he had thought. *Innocence.* The next thing he remembered was seeing her face contort, bursting into laughter. She tugged at her mother's arm. "Funny man!" she said. "Look, Mommy, at the funny man!"

Some nights were worse than others and one night, the laughter would not leave.

Just one drink. Not the whole bottle. Just enough to make her go away!

He walked into town as the first snowflakes fell. Despite the dark, the well-worn ruts made the road easy to travel and yet he walked slowly, hesitant to get there, knowing it was the wrong thing to do but doing it anyway.

No lights were on in the house. Dawes was probably asleep. Thinking that there were bottles under the porch steps waiting to be picked up, Loud Bear approached cautiously, intent on stealing one. His hands shook as he leaned under the stairs and felt around in the dark. The familiar sack was not there.

Nor anywhere else. He searched likely hiding places, even lifted the lid of the feed bin by the barn and reached in, but the noise set the hens to clucking and a light to be lit in the window.

Loud Bear hid in the shadows until the light went out. Frustration and the wait intensified his need. He wanted a whole bottle now, remembering the burning and the glow.

Maybe the bottles are in the barn?

He slid along the side, turned the corner and pushed against the edge of the door. It slid to the left allowing him space to squeeze in. The horse whinnied and he froze.

A window rattled open. "Who's out there?"

Fear deflated his desire. Dawes would not blink an eye killing an

335

intruder. "Loud Bear," he called back.

"Step out of the barn…real slow."

"I want a bottle. I'll pay you double."

Dawes laughed, "That's why you were in the barn, eh? To pay me double?"

Loud Bear could feel the rifle pointed at him. He said nothing. Dawes said nothing. A minute passed.

"Go to the back door. I'll give you a bottle. For old times' sake." Dawes closed the window and went downstairs. A lantern was lit in the kitchen.

Desperate enough to want to believe Dawes, Loud Bear went to the base of the stairs. From there he could not see Dawes stretch to the top of the cabinet and take down a dainty blue bottle. He could not see the white powder poured from it into the whiskey.

Ah-Duo heard the noises downstairs as Dawes fumbled around in the kitchen and pantry. She watched, terrified into silence, as Dawes brushed the excess strychnine powder onto the floor. Shaking the bottle vigorously, he walked to the back door and handed Loud Bear the bottle.

"For old times' sake," Dawes repeated.

Finally, relief! Loud Bear thought, uncorking the bottle, gulping the milky liquid.

Finally, relief! thought Dawes, knowing his whiskey-selling business would remain, for now, a secret.

Loud Bear carried the bottle with him to the street and, disgusted with himself, he slammed the cork into the top. He raised the bottle high and was going to toss it away but then the ever present temptation of addiction cautioned him to save it…just in case. He ran his tongue over the inside of his lips and across his teeth. His mouth had a bitter taste. Spitting didn't relieve it. He started to walk back but within minutes he felt agitated. An owl screeched exceedingly loud and he covered his ears. The cold felt colder. As the poison worked its way into his spinal cord, his back muscles spasmed. He felt sick and tried to walk faster to reach his grandfather's cabin, but his legs tightened up. And hurt. He stumbled and fell.

*****

Damn! It's cold! Ike breathed condensing fog onto his hands and shuddered. It had barely dawned as he smoothed the saddle padding on Dumpling's back. "Yeah. I know. You'd rather not go but it's my last chance to get some money before it really snows." The promised freighting job would have him away for weeks. "Get through this and you can rest all winter," he assured his horse.

Bastiat came out of the cabin carrying a bundle. "Biscuits. You might get hungry."

The new dusting of snow was slippery in spots and Dumpling stepped gingerly, a slow walk that made Ike impatient. They had miles to travel that day, but he did not push the horse harder. This was at least better than walking, the only other alternative.

But when Dumpling stopped and refused to walk further, Ike got angry. He prodded him, but the horse shied, snorting. *Damn horse!*

He dismounted. "It's just a little snow! It's not that icy! Thought you were a cow pony!" Ike slid his feet over the fresh snow to prove his point, but then he laughed. *I'm talking to my horse like he's a person!* "Dumpling. Dumpling. C'mon. Let's go."

Back on the horse, he urged him forward but still he wouldn't move. And that is when Ike saw the snow covered mound on the path ahead.

Dismounting again he recognized the mound as a body, feet in the road, head on the uneven and rocky side, arms flung outwards. Brushing the snow off the corpse's face, Ike identified the body. His heart pounded. Loud Bear!

There was no need to put his head to the Loud Bear's chest. He was dead. Face gray. Body stiff. One hand locked onto the whiskey bottle.

Disgusted, he became angry. "Couldn't stay away from it, could you! Do you know…do you know what this is gonna do to the old man!" *And Niglíču.*

He began to cry. Crouching, Ike slipping his arm behind Loud Bear's head and under his thighs trying to lift him, but Loud Bear was a big man and heavy. He was able to raise the body a foot, two, and then Ike fell back on his heels. He'd have to pull the stiff body up and pray he could get him over the back of his already nervous horse.

While he thought about how to do this, he noticed his jacket sleeve was darkened. He brushed his hand over what appeared a stain. *Blood?* Bending close to the body now, he gently raised Loud Bear's head enough to get his hand beneath. *Yes. Blood. Yes. A sharp-edged rock underneath.* Ike looked at the bottle he had angrily pulled from Loud Bear's grip. It was nearly full.

You weren't drunk, were you. You fell. You slipped on the goddamn ice and hit your head and died.

Ike rocked on his heels, tears flowing freely. He slammed the corked bottle on the rocks, shattering it and sat watching the amber liquid color the snow orange.

*****

There was quiet in this other village of the thiyóšpaye. No one stirred. Lazy smoke rose from the clay chimneys and all doors were closed. He tied Dumpling behind Bastiat's cabin, hiding the horse and the body in case anyone awoke. He knew the priest would be saying his morning prayers by now, lips moving in whispered thanksgiving. Ike could hardly bear disturbing this peace.

Mountain was aware of his presence, already sniffing at the door before Ike opened it.

"You are back," Bastiat said. "What's wrong?"

"Come outside."

When Bastiat saw the body stiffly hanging over the saddle, he made the Sign of the Cross.

"Oh, God!" he moaned. "Who?"

"Loud Bear."

Together they carried the body in and laid him on the priest's bed. Bastiat knelt beside him and prayed. "Eternal rest grant unto him, O Lord, and let perpetual light shine upon him…"

Rising, he said, "We must go to them."

A gentle knock roused Grasshopper, but not Niglíču still sleeping peacefully next to Oyé Wašté. Filled with foreboding, the old warrior pulled the blanket around himself tighter and went to the door. Opening it, he saw Ike and then the priest in the background. In answer to Grasshopper's questioning eyes, Bastiat only said, "Loud Bear."

It was enough to make the old man's knees buckle. Ike grabbed hold of him before he could fall. With his arm around him, Ike led Grasshopper to Bastiat's cabin.

He is just sleeping, Grasshopper thought, desperately denying the obvious truth. *He is ill, I will care for my grandson, and he will get better.*

But then Bastiat took his hand. "He is with God now."

Images of Loud Bear as an infant, young boy, man, swam in the tears that clouded Grasshopper's eyes. He sat on the bed, touched Loud Bear's face, and then stretched out beside his grandson and pulled him into his arms. Burying his face in Loud Bear's hair, he cried.

They did not see Niglíču and Oyé Wašté standing in the open doorway. The old woman began a low wail. Niglíču stood silently and then walked away. Bastiat followed her.

"No," said Ike. "Stay with Grasshopper. I will go."

After a short pursuit, Ike called softly to her. "Wait for me!"

She turned to face him. "How?" she said coldly. "How did this happen?" she demanded.

He told her the story and did not spare her the details. She would only appreciate the truth.

"Tell me again," she said.

He did.

"Again," she insisted.

"Why? I told you all I know. I left nothing out."

But she knew there was something missing. She was sure of it. Something was not right, and she was determined to find what that was.

*****

Čhaŋkú Wašté solemnly cut a lock of hair from Loud Bear's purified body and held it above burning sweetgrass. Then he wrapped it in buckskin and handed it to Grasshopper. The Naǧí Gluhápi *Keeping the Soul Ceremony* had concluded, and the package would be kept safe in the cabin and visited for a year before it was released ceremonially.

Bastiat said his prayers and blessings silently. It was not the time to evangelize. He sat beside Grasshopper in watchful waiting beside the burial scaffold, a practice that transcended cultures. Sitting shiva, Christian wakes and now this ceremony the priest knew aided the grieving process and allowed for the letting go, the acceptance that

339

the deceased had passed into another life.

After one week, Grasshopper determined it was enough. He would visit with the spirit of his grandson in the cabin and leave his body to return to the earth from which it had been born.

*****

Her mourning was not usual. Though both Grasshopper and Bastiat knew anger was often part of grieving, her anger was more obsessive…driven.

Niglíču confided her concerns about the circumstances of Loud Bear's death to Čhaŋkú Wašté but they were dismissed. "It was an accident. People fall. People die."

The shaman had become quite attentive to her, showing her rituals and customs, potions and medicines, but in this other way he failed her. And not only did he dismiss her intuition, he told her the anger she felt was selfish.

But Bastiat had taught her to think. He taught her the importance of questioning, of clarification. Čhaŋkú Wašté discouraged it. Knowing the old ways was good enough.

"It is a custom among our people," he teased, "that when a man desires a woman as wife, he asks her to stand with him, outside her father's thípi, with a robe covering both of them. Have you seen this?"

"I have."

"Have you done this?"

He never expected her response. She wanted to hurt him for not acknowledging her suspicions.

"I have," she replied, remembering the day she and Há Sápa had played at this.

Čhaŋkú Wašté's face hardened. Though he was handsome and would be a good provider, it was his dominating demeanor that dampened her ardor.

"But I was just a child," she added to soften her statement.

His face relaxed and he smiled at her. She smiled back and lowered her eyes like he expected her to do, but then she remembered another day when she had smiled, and he had not.

Under Čhaŋkú Wašté's watchful tutelage, she had been grinding a prescribed mixture of roots and leaves, a potion to cure the many illnesses he was describing to her, when Ike walked over to them. Later she would wonder why he had picked that specific time to show off what he had learned from her.

Ike unfolded a piece of the priest's crisp white paper. "Look at this!" he said proudly. In the chunky, all capital letter printing of a young student, he had written:

HELLO NIGLÍČU. MY NAME IS IKE.

*****

Há Sápa glí.
Há Sápa has come home.

The road through the town had been well traveled since the last snow, and because the day was warm, the horse's plodding hooves splashed muddied slush on the cow and calf walking behind it. The long trail had taken a toll on the animals. They were lean and weary, the cow barely producing enough milk for the bull calf. Há Sápa was almost home, with money in his pocket and the start of a herd behind him. He sat straight and proud on his horse, riding past the store with the spindly pine on the porch waiting to be brought inside and become a Christmas tree.

"Hey, you! Boy! Look here! Where'd you get those animals?" Dawes called from the open doorway.

"Bought 'em," Há Sápa answered assertively, ready to withdraw the paperwork from his pocket to prove it.

"I'll buy that calf from you. Folks around here are looking for some veal for Christmas dinner."

"Sorry, Sir. He's not for sale."

Dawes persisted, "Maybe you did not get my meaning, Boy. I want that calf and will offer money for it."

Há Sápa stiffened. His months as a cowboy had changed him. He was not going to be pushed around. "Not for sale," he said and walked on.

The horse picked up his pace when he realized he was heading home. The cow protested, mooing. Há Sápa knew she had small stones embedded in her left front hoof, but he did not have tools to remove them without damaging softer tissue beyond the sole. He could see evidence from when she had probably stepped down hard

341

onto a rock, pushing pebbles into white line fissures. Only luck had saved her from going lame.

With thoughts of Niglíču occupying his mind, he almost missed the snow covered burial scaffold. Affecting cowboy mannerisms, he respectfully tipped his hat to it, wondering who had died.

Oyé Wašté squinted and shaded her eyes against the reflected sun glare when she saw them approach. Finally, she recognized him.

"He is back!" she called excitedly. "Há Sápa is back, and he has brought fresh meat!"

*****

Later, when they were alone, Há Sápa held her. "Did you get my letter?" he asked Niglíču.

"Yes."

"Have you waited for me?"

"Yes." She raised her face to his and he kissed her.

*****

Ah-Duo was not Christian, nor did she see any reason to become one. The Christians who had owned her mother in Deadwood, using her for their own pleasure and plying her with opium, were not admirable. The drug had dulled her mother until she became emotionless. She dressed herself to attract men but found no pleasure in their attention. She sold her body for drugs. She later sold her only daughter too…for $400.

Ah-Duo was told her father was one of her mother's many customers. Growing up, she wondered which one. She guessed he was a customer who came often, and she hoped it was the elderly Tanka man, a boat person from Southern China, who always treated her kindly and never asked for her body.

Her mother, too, was a Tanka, but she had had the misfortune of being conceived on a boat nursery with a specific breeding plan aimed at producing girls to be sold into the sex trade. Ah-Duo knew she was at least luckier than that, although her fate up to this time, had been the same. Still, she was in America, and there was hope for her future.

This man she took to be her father knew how to read and write

Chinese, though how that had come to be was always a mystery. Tanka men were barred from such education. Maybe that was why he valued it more.

And maybe that was why he taught Ah-Duo what he knew, although he did not live to teach her to read and write English too. His persistent cough killed him slowly. He visited her less and less until he finally stopped coming. Days after he perished, his pungent decomposition prompted the discovery of his body in the hotel room. A book rested on the table beside the bed. A note peeked out of it: "Give this to Ah-Duo."

*****

Ah-Duo lugged the drying pine tree inside, tipping it over to clear the entrance, scattering needles that would need to be swept. Dawes had cut the tree weeks ago but had never watered it. She hadn't wanted to either. Christmas meant nothing to her. "It brings business!" Dawes said of the tree. She would decorate the tree with a paper chain and hang the red paper Chinese lanterns she made by herself that Dawes hated on the branches.

"Such an unusual tree!" the customers would exclaim, and she would smile dutifully as she snipped squares of white paper... unlucky white!.. and drew the character for the number 4...unlucky 4!...death!... on them to hang beside the lanterns.

"The red lanterns are for me, and the white squares are for Mr. Dawes," she would exclaim, smiling. She made many more white squares than lanterns for the tree.

"How sweet!" they would say.

Dawes was getting supplies that day...probably some kind of alcohol for the upcoming celebrations...and she was alone at the store. Business was slow and she leaned on the counter when she should been dusting shelves and read her only book, Tao Te Ching by Laozi, the book her Tanka father had bequeathed her.

The bells on the door startled her smile away.

"What are you reading that makes you smile like that?" Ike asked casually. His job was over, and he wanted to return home with candy for everyone, a new custom he delighted in.

"Oh, nothing," she replied. "How can I help you?"

"No, tell me. I am interested in books. My niece writes them."

343

"She does? Well, this book tells the way life is. It tells The Way."

"That sounds like the Bible. Bastiat would say Jesus is the Way."

"The words are different here, I think."

"Tell me."

"I was reading from Chapter 76. 'The big and strong will take an inferior position. The soft and gentle will take a superior position.'

"Well," Ike flirted. "Soft and gentle...like you."

She frowned. "How can I help you?" she repeated a little less friendly than the first time.

He ignored that. "I like those inferior superior sentences. There's truth in them."

Surprised this Indian man even knew the words superior and inferior, she looked directly at him. "Laozi wrote many true things."

"Like Jesus in the Bible," he offered. "He was gentle ,but He was powerful. A good example to follow. Too bad most people don't."

Ah-Duo nodded her head.

He asked her to read more, and they talked about what the sentences might mean. Several minutes passed and a customer came in. Ike stepped aside while that business was conducted.

After the customer departed, Ike offered, "On Sunday the store is closed. Why don't you come to the church and listen to the stories we tell there."

Seeing a flash of panic cross her face, he said, "Dawes won't allow that, will he?"

She nodded, but then brightened. "He drinks a lot on Saturday night and sleeps late in the morning after. Maybe I can go."

*****

"Do you know that little Chinese woman that Dawes keeps?" Ike asked.

"I don't know her, but she seems pleasant enough," the priest responded.

"Do you think they are married?" Ike asked.

"Married? Like officially? I doubt it. Why?"

"Just wondering. She said she might come to church one Sunday."

Bastiat burst out laughing, choking on the juices from his mouthful of stew. "You are a missionary now?"

Neither man knew Ah-Duo's actual circumstances, but the priest suspected the woman was Dawes' indentured servant. She would not be free to walk away without repercussions. Many of the Chinese prostitutes were indentured and after the agreed upon time, they expected to be released from their servitude. While seeming a reasonable trade-off, once time was taken off for sick days, menstruation, pregnancy and childbirth, the reality became that freedom was never attainable. When Dawes bought Ah-Duo, he wanted her for himself, more a slave than a servant. And only when he tired of her, would he let her go.

*****

Há Sápa listened attentively while Niglíču explained the circumstances surrounding Loud Bear's death. He agreed something was suspicious. True, the man could have just fallen and hit his head. True, it was dark and there was some snow. But there was that nearly full bottle he was holding. Corked.

"He did not drink enough alcohol to have been drunk!" she insisted. "He was not clumsy."

Há Sápa thought her suspicions had some worth but they were hardly conclusive. Still, because she was so adamant, he allowed himself to think of other scenarios.

"Where did he get his alcohol?" Há Sápa asked.

"Probably from Dawes."

"Did Dawes make it himself? Did he bottle it?" Há Sápa knew about the homemade brews and how they were cut with water. Cowboys always complained about that. "Maybe something was wrong with the whiskey," he said.

Niglíču thought for a moment. "A woman lives with Dawes. She is Chinese. I wonder if she knows something."

*****

Ah-Duo dreaded Saturday nights. That was when Dawes was most abusive. Whatever limited self- control he had during the week, he lost then. He wasn't an alcoholic in the true sense of the word. He was able to keep fairly sober during the week but on Saturday after he emerged from his "temple,"…his own word for the padlocked shed behind the barn…he was more evil than the most drunken

345

patrons her mother had serviced. And more energized.

Alcohol did that to him in the early stages of its consumption. He'd come out of the shed exhilarated, waving the half empty bottle around, singing bawdy ballads. He'd grab her and force him to dance with him, his now clumsy feet stepping on hers as he'd swing her around and pull her close. She'd tolerate it and even pretend to enjoy it, encouraging him to drink more and more. If she was lucky, he'd drink enough to dull his passion, drink enough to go upstairs and collapse on the bed unconscious til late Sunday morning. If she was unlucky, he'd stop before the alcohol rendered him impotent and drag her to bed with him.

She was lucky that December night. He left the shed staggering, grabbed a second bottle and headed upstairs alone. It was easy for her to slip away unnoticed early in the morning.

She had not been to the village before and once on the path she began to have misgivings. *Why would I think I would be safe going there alone?* The doubt distorted the surroundings. She shrank from the rustle of dry grasses. Shadows became unfamiliar shapes. But still she walked.

She stopped on the outskirts of the village. Mostly it was quiet save for the barking of dogs who did not recognize her. A line of people were slowly walking away, engaged in hushed conversations. A bell jingled and they immediately picked up their pace. She followed behind them.

Hesitantly she stood in the doorway of the church while the villagers took their seats on the long benches and faced the altar. Fr. Bastiat appeared behind her, prepared to process in, Bible upraised before him. A small Indian boy stood next to him carrying a crucifix. A young girl held a bowl of flatbread and a cruet of wine. Ah-Duo backed out and stood to the side. The priest smiled and beckoned her to go in. She sat on the bench closest to the door and wrapped her shawl tightly around her.

*****

"Ah-Duo is a beautiful name," Niglíču said after Mass. She had convinced Ah-Duo to stay for the breakfast they all shared after the Celebration. "What does it mean?"

"One too many, I guess."

346

"One too many of what?"

"Daughters."

"How can a person have too many daughters?"

"I heard in my country there are four hundred million people now. With so many, you can have too many daughters."

"Can your people have too many sons?"

Ah-Duo laughed. "No, I don't think there will ever be too many sons!"

In her society, a woman joined her husband's family, but the son would stay to support his parents in their old age. It was no wonder sons were more valued by their parents.

Million was a concept Niglíču could not imagine. What could or would she count that had so many members? Surely not her people. Surely not the buffalo. She asked Ah-Duo to explain.

"Can you imagine all the people, *all of the people*, in America all together? Do that a little more than five times and that is four hundred million," Ah-Duo answered.

But Niglíču could not imagine all the people in America. All she knew was that there seemed to be no end to the number of white men.

"So many!" Niglíču exclaimed.

"Yes, maybe too many," Ah-Duo laughed again.

"The Lakȟóta never had too many people. And now we have too few."

They were both quiet as Niglíču thought of how to frame the question she wanted to ask.

"Did you know my cousin Loud Bear?" she asked. "I think he sold whiskey for Dawes."

In truth, Ah-Duo did not know Loud Bear, or at least not by name. She had been told to never go to the back door at night, never to ask questions about anyone she might see out there in the dark. This was his business, he had told her. "Stay out of it!" he had warned.

Niglíču pressed harder. "Did a Lakȟóta man come weeks ago when something seemed different?"

Ah-Duo tried to remember and then she recalled the commotion outside that night that had prompted her to walk down the stairs.

"There was one night. A man came. Dawes filled him a bottle, but he put a powder in it too."

"A powder? What powder?"

"That I do not know," she said.

347

Niglíču could not wait until she saw Há Sápa again.

*****

Wóšpipi!
Christmas!

"Didn't you think I'd notice you were gone?"

Dawes was sitting in the parlor when she returned. She immediately became compliant.

"I didn't want to wake you. I just wanted fresh air. I thought I'd go for a walk. You were sleeping. I tried to be quiet. I wanted you to sleep."

"I'll bet you wanted me to sleep!" Her short, clipped sentences betrayed her. She was lying and he knew it. "Whore!"

"I went for a walk! I did nothing!"

"Bitch! Who was he?" He grabbed her. "Lyin' whore!" She tried to twist away but he pinned her to the couch.

"You're a whore alright but you're supposed to be a *faithful* whore!" He held her there with one hand pushing against her throat.

"I did nothing!" she tried to scream.

"Oh yeah? Where'd you go then?"

She said nothing. How could she tell him? Even if he believed her, it wouldn't make a difference. And if he did believe her, would he hurt them?

"Right. Don't tell on your lover. Well, we'll see what your lover thinks of you after this!" He reached to the sheath at his belt and withdrew his knife.

"Do you know what the Indians do to cheating wives? They cut off the tips of their noses."

She screamed, and he shoved his hand over her mouth. "Quiet, bitch! I ain't gonna hurt your pretty face 'cause I like looking at it." His large left hand covered the side of her face as he pushed her head deep into the cushion. He slapped the knife point against the very tip of her ear, cutting it away, nicking the side of her jaw. He released her. "There! Remember that next time you wanna to go for a walk!"

*****

On the Friday before Christmas, Ike volunteered, as the priest knew he would, to go into town. Bastiat hoped the gift from his brother would have arrived, the one gift he would get for Christmas! The excitement always made him feel like a little boy again! But the priest had not heard from his brother in many months, and he was concerned about his brother's wellbeing.

But it wasn't for the post office that Ike wanted to go. Ah-Duo was the attraction.

"And can you pick up a sack of sugar at the store. I've never seen people pour so much sugar into their coffee as my parishioners!"

"You, too, Padre. I've been watching you."

He would take old Dumpling for the short ride into town. The horse walked slower now, but taking him was better than listening to his incessant whinnying if he was left behind.

Ike was disappointed to see both Dawes and Ah-Duo working the counter. He waited his turn and watched Ah-Duo make her transactions. She looked different, softer, with her hair lowered. One side draped down over her ear before being swept into a low braid in the back. Tendrils had pulled loose. He wanted to touch them, touch her.

"No credit here! Cash only," Dawes said, stepping in front of Ah-Duo when it was Ike's turn.

"I'm buying this for the priest. Sugar. He said you should add it to his account. He'll pay you next time he comes to town."

"So, you're the one livin' with the old guy. Keeps you as his slave, I suppose."

Ike caught Ah-Duo's warning glance, and he winked at her when Dawes reached back for the sack of sugar on the shelf behind him.

Affecting a Southern drawl, Ike replied, "Yassuh, Massuh suh. I's does all he says, and he lets me sleep by da fire at night and stay cozy warm. I's shore beholdin' to dat der priest."

"Smart ass Injun!" Dawes rolled his eyes at the next customer, a white man. "I try to be patient with the injuns," Dawes said.

*****

On Christmas morning, two gifts lay under the tree. One, from Ike, was secretly tucked behind the tree and obscured by the hanging branches. The other, a big box from Bastiat's brother, was in clear view and had been a temptation to the priest since Ike brought it back.

A third gift was hidden behind a pot on the shelf above the stove. It was small and wrapped in ink decorated paper, the priest's handiwork: Bastiat's gift to Ike.

Ike, who was rarely up first, had the coffee ready before the priest finished his prayers. He sat at the table waiting, excited to give Bastiat his gift.

Rising from his knees, Bastiat reached behind the pot and held a small box out to Ike. "For you," he said, "in gratitude." A gift was not expected, and Ike fumbled with the wrappings.

A tiny circular brass case was revealed. "A clock?" Ike guessed.

"Not a clock, not a pocket watch. Open it."

Once unlatched, the cap could be removed, but Ike did not know what the gift was with its strange markings, NSEW lettering and shimmering magnetic needle. "What?"

"It's a compass. It will show you the way home."

Ike's eyes clouded. He stretched behind the tree retrieving his secret gift. The brown box had neither wrappings nor label. "For you," Ike said. "To keep you safe."

Bastiat was moved to tears when he opened the box. Inside was an almost new, but oiled and shining, 1858 New Army Revolver.

"How?"

"Padre, I have ways."

The priest cocked his head and squinted his eyes, suspicious.

"Don't worry. I didn't steal it."

*****

Later, when all were gathered, Bastiat made a big show of opening the gift from his brother. He tore the paper covering slowly, drawing out the suspense, and revealed a box with Sears stamped on it. It was tightly sealed, but Ike offered him his knife and the contents were revealed. "A fiddle?!" Bastiat exclaimed.

He drew it out and without adjusting the four strings, he took the bow and swept it across them.

"That screech is horrible!" cried Oyé Wašté. "Let me try!"

All the women were equally bad, and Mountain, whining, stood by the door eager to be let out.

"Padre, that gift will not make you a lot of friends," Ike laughed.

*****

When the two of them were alone later, Bastiat showed Ike how to use the compass.

"I think I understand it now," Ike said closing the compass in its case. "And it's something I can use." He was quiet then, rubbing his fingers over the brass casing. "Padre, I can't stay here. You've shown me that I have to make my way in the world. I can't be living off your generosity. And I don't want to be relying on the government for what I need. Being a freighter is over. The railroad is taking all the business. I don't know how to do much, but I can drive a wagon, work mules and all, and there's still a need for that... but...at the mines. They got a mine up in Deadwood that's hiring for the winter. The Homestake Mine. I don't like them digging in the Black Hills, Padre, but you can't stop progress. I can't just stay here all winter doing nothing. I know myself. I know what I'll turn into and I don't want that."

"I understand." And he did, but the anticipation of an empty cabin again saddened him.

"I'll be back though. The job's just temporary. Hard to find men to work in the winter and it's damn cold there."

"When will you be leaving?"

"Soon...a week... maybe less."

351

Chapter 4

Mázawakȟáŋ kiŋ okšú.
He loaded the gun.

Ah-Duo was the only woman Niglíču had ever befriended who was not in some way connected to her people. Conversations were different with her. They did not speak of reservation life or old customs, traditions, family or neighbors. The world beyond the confines of the reservation was opened to Niglíču. She had known there was a place called Africa thanks to Há Sápa's grandmother. But that there were other places like China, India, and South America astonished her. "How do you know these things?" she asked her new friend.

Though they looked to be of similar age, Ah-Duo was several years older than Niglíču and she did not want to explain the circumstances of her knowing. Deadwood was only one place where she had worked. Other towns closer to the coast had a more diverse population and drunken men talk, bragging about the places they had been to. Ah-Duo received a dubious but colorful geography education that she gladly shared.

"There are people in India called Hindus. They won't eat cows because they are considered holy."

Niglíču could relate to that.

"But in a place called South America the people used to sacrifice their children to make their gods happy."

Impossible! Niglíču thought. *Kill a baby? A child? How could any person do that? And why would their gods want the children back? Weren't they gifts?"*

It was only because Dawes adhered to a rigid daily schedule that the two young women could meet at all. He was there at the store's opening but, on alternating days he disappeared in the early afternoon when business was slow, hitching his horse to a wagon and rattling empty bottles in the bed of it as he drove out of town.

Ike took advantage of those afternoons too, cultivating a friendship that was becoming more intimate. One afternoon he followed her into the back room where the supplies were stored, stack upon stack of dusty flour with mice chewed corners spilling a white cascade from one bag to another, bumpy sacks of beans piled and looking to tip, bags of sugar solidified into bricks towering to the low ceiling. He leaned her back against the bolts of bright cotton and tentatively kissed her. She didn't pull away.

Encouraged, he ran his fingers through the shine of her hair and held her head firmly while he parted her lips and explored. Feeling her hesitation, he ended the kiss, sliding his fingers forward, his thumbs brushing her ear lobes. He felt it then, the scabbed over wound her hair had disguised.

He turned her head and lifted her hair. "What happened? Who did this?"

She blushed and lied. "Oh, that? What a silly accident! A scissor! I should have used a mirror. My hair had gotten all tangled..." She thought fast. "The honey had spilled. I bent down to clean it up and my hair..."

"He hurt you?"

"No. No! An accident." She quickly pulled her hair to cover the scab. She couldn't let him know the truth. Dawes was deadly...a killer. Was Ike?

"You should go now. People will be suspicious. Here!" She handed him a small bag of coffee beans. "Take this. Let the people know you bought something."

That night Ike spoke to Niglíču. "You think Dawes killed Loud Bear, don't you."

"I'm almost sure he did. Why?"

"Do you think he'd kill Ah-Duo? I mean, if he caught her with another man?"

"He needs her. I don't think he'd kill her. But he could make her life miserable."

"More than it is now?"

*****

"I have business to take care of tonight. I won't be home," Dawes

353

said the night of Dec.28. "Don't go anywhere. And NObody comes here either. Do you understand? Nobody!"

A night to myself! Ah-Duo hoped he'd freeze to death wherever he was going. She watched him go into the shed and come out with a sack.

She burned so much wood that night that even the drafty house was warm. How free she felt to meditate in peace! How free to walk from room to room without his vigilance! How free to steep a cup of tea and read a book by candlelight!

How free to climb up on the counter and see what was in that jar on the very top shelf.

Poison. That's what it was.

She remembered she had seen him use that before, sprinkled on bread crumbs on a plate and placed in the corners of the kitchen for the mice to consume.

And this is what Dawes poured into the whiskey bottle too.

What would a little do to a man? A little each day.

She went to bed thinking about it.

He came back before noon the next day, disheveled and hungry. Cold.

"Another anniversary well celebrated!" he announced, although what anniversary it was and why it was celebrated she did not know. "That felt gooood!" he bragged.

She showed no interest.

"Did you miss me last night?" he asked, undressing, leaving his soiled and whiskey splashed clothing on the floor at his feet. "Look at me!" he demanded.

"Of course," she said, averting her eyes away from his arousal.

"Let's go upstairs after I eat."

"The store is open."

"Close it."

She thought he wasn't looking and so she slid the white powder on the cloth closer to his dish. *One pinch. One pinch today,* she thought. She raised her fingers with the powder between the tips.

"What's that?" he growled, grabbing her hand. The powder sprinkled onto the counter.

"Nothing. A spice," she said as nonchalantly as she could with shaking knees.

"You taste it then. See if its good." He licked his finger and swiped it across the powder and pushed it against her lips. She jerked away.

"You were going to poison me, you bitch!" He shoved her to the floor and kicked her. Hard. Once. Twice. "If I didn't need you for the books, I'd ...." She rolled into a ball with her hands clasped over her head. He kicked her again. "Don't touch my food! You hear me?" He grabbed her hair and dragged her upstairs.

*****

The next morning Bastiat found her curled on the floor under the lit sanctuary lamp, shivering.

"Ah-Duo! Ah-Duo! Sit up! What happened? What happened to you?"

"I can't go back," she said sobbing. "He'll kill me. Can I stay here? Please! Until I find a place..."

"Oh my God!" he exclaimed when he saw her face. "Are you hurt anywhere else?"

"He kicked me. My ribs." She looked around. "Ike?"

"He's not here. Found some work up north. Not sure when he'll be back. He didn't tell you?"

"No, but I don't want him to know. He might do something. They'll hang him."

He brought her into his cabin, laid her on his bed. "Wait here. I'll get the women."

While the women tended to her, Father Bastiat got his new pistol, tucked it into his belt, saddled Ned, and headed to town.

*****

"I'm afraid I know nothing about this pistol," Bastiat said innocently as he laid the gun on the counter. "Do you have the ammunition for it?"

"I surely do, Father. I have the powder, balls, caps and some beeswax. All you need," Dawes said amiably.

"That's wonderful! And could I impose on you to show me how to load this thing?"

"Why, of course!"

Bastiat saw there was a pleasant side to this man, after all. Strange how people can be so two- sided, he thought.

Dawes began his lesson. "First, you pour about 30 grains of this black powder into each chamber." Dawes did that, revolving the chambers around until all six were charged with the powder. "Next, use the lever to ram the ball down. It's tight. You might shave off the outer ring of lead, but that's fine. You try it."

Bastiat did this to each of the six chambers and brushed the excess lead off to the side.

"Now you rub a big gob of beeswax over the opening." Dawes demonstrated with one and had Bastiat do the rest. "And finally, the caps," Dawes said. Again, there was a demonstration and again Bastiat finished them off.

"You are all set, Father. Ready to shoot," Dawes said with a genuine smile on his face.

"Good," the priest said, and he held up the gun, cocked the trigger, and pointed it at Dawes' face.

"Whoa there, Father! What the hell do you think you're doing with that thing?" Dawes' skin above his beard blanched white, but not as white as the jagged scar that hid beneath it.

"Listen to me really good now, Dawes," Bastiat began. "Ah-Duo is a member of my church and as such, I intend to keep her safe. Do you get my meaning?" He shook the gun a little and raised it higher, in line with Dawes' nose. "I don't take kindly to my parishioners showing up for Mass all beat up, and with the Lord behind me, I will surely slay the evildoers."

"Father, she was trying to kill me!"

"You can't prove that, Dawes. And right now, but maybe not for long, I can't prove some other things. About you, Dawes. But I'm thinking seriously about it."

He hesitated and raised the gun higher, level now with Dawes' sweating forehead. "You're from down South. I hear it in your voice. I bet you are a Bible Christian ... or were. Do you remember this? Isaiah 3:11, 'Woe to the wicked. It will go badly for them. For what he deserves will be done to him.' Keep that in mind, Dawes."

He lowered the pistol and changed his demeanor, completely throwing Dawes off guard. "Now how much do I owe you for the ammunition ... and the lesson?"

Bastiat paid what he owed, eased the gun behind his belt, walked out the door and mounted Ned. With knees shaking so strongly that

Ned was confused about what pace his rider wanted him to travel, Bastiat rode home.

*****

Dawes did not find sleep easily in the days that followed. He kept thinking about the past.

On that sweat dripping, sweltering Southern summer afternoon in 1865, Atticus Dawes had returned home with his gray, tattered uniform hanging off his undernourished and thoroughly exhausted body. His wife greeted him.

She was standing outside, barefoot, with their five-year-old son Hugh clinging to her apron. He barely recognized the boy. He had been away a long time.

"Well, Ah see y'all have all yer parts with ya. Welcome home, Atticus," she had said.

Despite the heavy fighting he had been involved in, Atticus had sustained only a few cuts and scrapes. But, in fact, he had not returned home with all his parts because he had lost his humanity. A man given to depression before the war, after he sank into despair. He took to drinking whiskey to lift his spirits, but inebriation, rather than soothe him, ignited a violent streak he previously had under control.

He tried to find peace by working hard on their little farm, but the crops failed in the overworked and depleted soil. He tried to find it in their bedroom where each night he sought the erasing of the war's horror by pouring himself into his wife's tired body. He thought maybe he had succeeded when a year later his second son, Murdoch, was born, but the robust baby drained what little strength his wife had left until she became a shadow of the woman Atticus had married. How he resented the baby for that! The child should be strong while his wife was withering away?

When whiskey wasn't enough, he hoped a fundamentalist approach to religion was the answer. The combination made him abominable. He became adept at quoting Bible verses, tossing them like curses upon his children for normal childhood indiscretions. Isaiah 3:11 was a favorite. "Woe to the wicked..."

Hugh was ten years old the day Atticus finally had enough of his son's "transgression." And it was a minor offense, insolence, the

357

rolling of the eyes, that set Atticus off and steamrolled into tragedy. It was a sweep of the arm that held the ladle, a sweep propelled by a powerful arm that caught the side of Hugh's head and knocked him off his chair, a fall that twisted his neck, a crack before Hugh lay motionless on the floor.

Lorna dropped to her knees and cradled her son. He was dead. He was no longer there behind sightless open eyes.

Murdoch remembered little else besides his father screaming how it was an accident. An accident! Murdoch had witnessed the murder of his brother and because he was a little boy and dependent on his parents, he kept his feelings inside and never said a word about the "accident" to anyone.

He remembered the graveside service…how they all said God had called Hugh home. He couldn't help but think that it wasn't God who had called his brother. It was his father who had sent him to heaven. How afraid of Atticus he became! The boy buried his hurt and hid his fear until it moldered inside, until he was old enough to release it with the accuracy of his rifle. Bam.

And now Murdoch Dawes felt that tension again and "woe to the wicked" played over and over in his dreams.

*****

Wóopȟe ogná héčhetu.
It is legal.

"How the hell do I know what you should do?" Bordeaux fumed. Dawes had just come to him with yet another of his problems. This time his whore…bookkeeper…whatever he wanted to call her…left him. He knew she was with the priest at his "little village" but he wanted assistance to get her back. "Is she yours, legally? You have paperwork that she's indentured to you? She signed it?"

"I do. Right here! See, that's her name in that Chinee writing. She's mine. Four more years. It says it right there!"

"So just get her."

"What if she won't come? I have your permission to hurt some Indians to get her?"

"Goddamn you, Dawes! No, you do NOT have my permission even if it was mine to give…which it is not. You got her from

358

Deadwood? A whore? Well, whoring's illegal even if you'll never find a lawyer to attest to that around here. Why don't you just tell them she's broken two laws. Servitude escaping and whoring. Tell her you'll get the law after her. Threaten jail time. Tell the priest he has permission to have his church here...but that can be revoked."

Dawes nodded his head eagerly. Now he had leverage. He'd ride out there that day.

*****

The people wondered about Dawes' purpose as he rode boldly through the main village, his rifle prominently displayed across his lap. They wondered why he veered off the main road to take the path to the church. Later, they wondered what had happened that the little Chinese lady, crying, sat before him on the horse heading back into town.

*****

"Why did you let him take the woman?" Grasshopper asked angrily. "You are a white man. Couldn't you have stopped him?"

"The law was on his side. I had no choice."

"You have a law that gives a man the right to steal a woman against her wishes?"

"He had the legal papers. If she did not go, worse things could happen to her. She had signed the paper. She had agreed to the contract."

"This contract...it is like a treaty?"

"Yes...a little like that."

"Then the writing on it means nothing...nothing to the woman...only to the white man. The words only mean what he wants them to mean."

"I warned Dawes. I told him he had better not abuse her."

"And you think your words are greater than the writing on paper? Even I know the white man's writing is stronger than the words he speaks when he wants it to be. You cannot trust the white man's word and you cannot trust the white man's paper."

Bastiat's face fell. Was he also not to be trusted?

Grasshopper responded to his hurt expression. "You are no longer

359

just a white man."

*****

Dawes had poisoned Loud Bear? That was no longer a question to Niglíču. But could Ah-Duo's evidence be used against Dawes? Who would believe her? Who would care that the side-show Indian was dead now?

White man's justice would keep Dawes free. But how his face haunted Niglíču at night! She knew that face from another time. She knew the red hair when it was not streaked with gray. But from when? From where? It seemed so important to remember...mandatory that she remember!

*****

The sweat lodge behind the church was no flimsy structure that allowed light in. It was not like the lodge they had hastily built near Bear Butte. When the shaman closed off the entrance behind him, the interior of the dome was blackened. Niglíču could not see him. The heat was suffocating and the steam hissing off the stones hung unseen in the air.

There were just the two of them there. Her monthly menses had just ended and so he was safe with her. While menstruating, her power could have overcome his. He offered his prayers and incantations to the beat of a small drum and slowly she dissolved her identity and melded with the spirit world...hoping for a vision to purify her dreams, hoping to put an end to the mystery behind Dawes' face and hair. By the fourth round of steaming, her vision was painfully succinct. There was her mother. There, pointing to Dawes floating towards her. There in the distance, the padlocked shed behind the store. There, out in the open… there, Wind Woman stood with her knife raised.

Niglíču cried out and the vision was gone. Čhaŋkú Wašté pulled aside the entrance flap and cold air rushed in. He held her in his arms while she sobbed.

The shaman was hesitant to explain the vision. He knew what it pointed to, but he was equally aware the vision could have been fed from her imagination and not be true.

360

Dawes...the man with red hair who had killed her mother. Dawes...the man who had promised to kill.

*****

Dawes enjoyed the challenge. Living with a woman who had tried to kill him and maybe was plotting to again was invigorating. Especially when the woman thought she was under the protection of the priest... and that young Indian woman with her bow. Flaunting it. He had to admit that Indian both scared and excited him. Subduing her would be a powerful thrill!

Life had become a game and he reveled in it. He watched Ah-Duo's every move...shadowed her...surprised her with alternating threats and gifts. Such fun knowing she could not predict his behavior! It made her nervous. He could see it in her shaking hands, startled exclamations. He thought maybe he'd pick her a bouquet of flowers that day. Maybe he'll smile and compliment her. Make her tea. Buy a sweet cake from the widow woman in town and give it to her. Yes, he'd be so nice to her today. Oh, he'd make sweet love to her tonight...soft kisses, gentle caresses. Yes.

And tomorrow morning he'd find an excuse to beat her.

*****

An arrow was imbedded in the door frame of the store. Dawes bumped his nose against it when he opened the door. Another was deep in the beam above his horse's stall. Someone had been in the barn. The arrow snapped when he reached up and broke off the shaft. Nervous, he looked around, but no one was there.

*****

Weevils in the flour he sold. Pale beetle larvae in sacks of beans. His customers were furious thinking he was selling them Indian rations and they complained mightily. Dawes' anger flamed against Ah-Duo but she insisted on her innocence. There could be only one other explanation.

*****

Ȟugnáȟye.
He burned it down.

Dawes wasn't drunk the night he slipped into the unlocked church. What a fool the priest was to be so trusting! And how nice to leave the light on.

Light from the sanctuary lamp effused the area around the tabernacle and Dawes set the kerosene can on the altar so to be free to jiggle the tabernacle's tiny wooden door.

"Knock. Knock. Jesus. Anybody home?" *Stupid Catholics believing God was in there in a piece of bread.* "Hey, Jesus," Dawes whispered, "Come on out and let's have us a little talk."

The dark church had a vaguely familiar feeling he likened to the interior of his shed. Maybe it was the candle. He had one there…a candelabra of sorts he put on his altar… but instead of the brass holder he had a human skull…an Indian skull… and two candles peeked out from the eyes. He too had an altar cloth but his wasn't pristine white and lace trimmed, although his blood stained one made from a shirt did have a few holes here and there. Dawes took a deep breath. A heavy fragrance of incense permeated the building the way his tobacco smoke had soaked into the splintery pine of his shed.

He was eerily comfortable in the church, leaning his elbows on the altar and addressing the tabernacle behind it. "So tell me, Jesus, why did you let my brother die?" It felt good to ask the question that had burned his mind the many times his father brought him to the meeting hall and cried "Alleluia" as though he was innocent. "Why did you let my father get away with it?"

Dawes cringed thinking about the fingers his parents shook in his face. "Don't you tell!" they threatened. "Don't you ever tell what happened to your brother! It's our secret…our family secret!"

"I'm gonna tell you another secret, Jesus. I'm gonna burn this place down and you in it. Why? Because that little bitch thinks she can scare me with her bugs and her arrows. I don't know what she knows about me…me and that drunk Indian…but she needs a lesson. Don't mess with me 'cause I ALWAYS win!"

He walked up to the tabernacle and tilted the candle there. Wax dripped onto the cloth beneath the holy box. He tilted the candle more until the flame touched the cloth and browned a ring.

"Look, Jesus," he said as he fanned the little flame, "Just like the injun smudging!" Drops of his spit landed on the tip of the flame, almost extinguishing it, but then, fueled by the cloth, it burst into a fiery column. "Your priest thought he could make a fool of me, Jesus. What kind of man is that, I ask? And then ... and then," he hissed, "and then he had the nerve to change my woman! HIS parishioner he says. No. Not his. MY woman!"

Dawes lifted the altar cloth, and the flame tracked towards the tabernacle and blackened a corner.

"Gonna be getting a bit warm in there, Jesus. You might want to come out now."

He took a stem of dried flowers from the vase on the altar and fed it to the flames. He carried the Lectionary over closer to it, ripped out a page and ignited it.

"Gotta go now, Jesus!"

Dawes took the kerosene can he didn't have to use and rode back to town.

*****

Nothing they could do could save the church. Though their screams and the towering flames brought the villagers with their buckets, the fire ripped through the building and licked out onto the roofs of the nearest cabins. Soon the tarpaper ignited into black smoke while the people looked on, horrified at the inferno.

And then it snowed. A squalling storm smothered the fire before the roofless cabins were completely destroyed. A blanket of snow buried the charred remains. A blanket of snow buried any tracks Dawes' horse made on the way back to town.

*****

"We are all safe," Oyé Wašté said, wrapping bandages around the singed hands of the priest. They had gathered in the cabin of the cousins, the only one that had escaped the flames. "We are all safe," she repeated looking into the tearful eyes of the priest.

At first light they picked through the ruins and evaluated the damage to the cabins. They had enough wood to repair one cabin but not the other. The priest's cabin was bigger and so the decision was made to salvage the wood from Grasshopper's cabin for the repair.

The horses hadn't gone far. There was enough charred wood to make them a shelter and build an enclosure. Grasshopper delegated tasks and all were put to work.

Father Bastiat was too devastated to help. He sat with his head in his hands. "I'm too old to start over," he cried. "This is too much! Who would do this?"

White Birch tapped his shoulder and handed him the ivory corpus fallen from the crucifix consumed in the flames. "Jesus lives," she said to him. "He is no longer on the cross."

*****

Bastiat stood before the ruins of his church. "I should have locked the door. I know the candle was OK. It should have burned out soon, anyway. I knew it needed replacing. I checked. I checked."

If she had more courage, Niglíču would have admitted that she was in the church after he had checked it for the night. Sometimes when she couldn't sleep, she'd go there. She didn't think she prayed there ...or at least not the way the priest did with memorized words and specific gestures... but she did feel close to God...the Great Spirit...the nameless spiritual entity who had created the world and sustains it. Sometimes she became lost in the closeness, as she had that past night. Reality seemed to change then, and she had uttered meaningless sounds as chants and so seemed to communicate in a timeless sense. Sometimes she dreamed she was a little girl. She did that night, a very clear vision of the little girl she had been before. Before. Before when she was Brings Fire. She didn't remember leaving the church that night. She must have still been in that other dream reality. *Did I touch the candle?* She couldn't remember. *Did I bring the fire?*

*****

The only person she felt comfortable with sharing her suspicion was Oyé Wašté. She told the old woman about her dream of being a little girl. She told her she went into the church that night.

"But you are a responsible young woman. You would never have

364

been so careless. You were honored with your childhood name because you did something good. It is not right to change the meaning to something bad. You did not make the fire, but I think you might know who did. Dawes is a dangerous man. I know what you have been doing to taunt him. You will not win this way. He has nothing to lose. You have many people he can hurt."

"I think he killed Loud Bear. I think he killed my mother."

"I told you once you would know the man someday. Now you must make sure."

*****

Ah-Duo learned of the fire in the morning. "The Lord works in mysterious ways," one customer snickered to Dawes as he paid his bill. Dawes laughed. "Yes, he does!"

She hardly expected Dawes to be sympathetic, but he was downright gleeful all morning. *Could the fire have explained the acrid smokey smell on his hair when he heaved his cold body under the covers in the middle of the night?*

Chapter 5

Makȟóčhe igláȟniǧe.
He chose a piece of land for himself.

T he Dawes Act of 1887 only coincidentally bore the same
name as the storekeeper, although he claimed relationship
with the senator from Massachusetts who had authored it.
"See how fair we are to the Indians? 160 acres free to each family!"
Murdock Dawes boasted of the splitting up of reservation land into
allotments. He did not mention that there was quite a bit of gray area
in the execution of this. Somehow white settlers got choice pieces of
land by marrying an Indian or showing other proof of such
relationship. Sometimes settlers purchased land rights the Indians
didn't even know they had. Official allotment took place in 1904 but
in prior years it was difficult to see the "fairness" Dawes boasted of.

*****

Julia Bordeaux was the only child of her military officer father.
Together with her mother, she followed the man from one end of the
country to the other, earning her the unofficial designation of an
attached traveler, the abbreviated and Americanized form of the
British Regiment Attached Traveler or BRAT. Julia, strong and
resilient, faltered only once in her decision making and that was after
her mother died unexpectantly. In her vulnerability at that time, she
fell in love with a man who displayed all the strengths of her father,
but actually had none of them. A dashing man who told heroic lies of
living with the dispossessed Indians he was guiding into the
twentieth century, Bordeaux won her heart. Going against her
father's advice, she married him and now, with two children, she
was trying to make the best of a miserable situation.

Her horsemanship was superb and her horse superior to any she had seen on the reservation save for the pinto ridden by the Indian girl her husband had wanted to adopt. Bordeaux never told her the whole story of the painful death of his first wife but had vaguely linked it to the little girl who had lived with them that short time long ago.

"I don't want to talk about it," her husband always insisted but Julia was always curious about this young woman now living as a sort of protégé of the priest. The Indian woman owed her education to Fr. Bastiat and Julia often considered visiting the young woman, but her husband forbade this.

Julia, wiser now as his wife of several years, rarely submitted to Bordeaux's wishes unless they corresponded with hers, but in this one thing she was compliant. She believed some battles weren't worth fighting.

The twins were at school this late winter morning, the house was in order and she was free to do as she wished. The ground had softened from an early thaw but wasn't yet muddied. The sun was shining and the sky clear of clouds: a perfect day to give her mare the exercise winter had denied her!

The dark bay danced in her eagerness, her black legs lifting up and down while she tossed her black mane and flagged her tail in the corral at Julia's approach with the saddle. The horse's excitement ignited her own. They would gallop today!

The ride exhilarated both and when they finally slowed to a walk near a copse of cottonwood, Julia saw a black man emerge from the shadows of the trees. She pulled up short and her hand went to her pistol.

"Mrs. Bordeaux! Mrs. Bordeaux!" he called to her. "May I speak to you for a minute?"

"Do I know you?"

"No, Ma'am, I don't think so, but I remember when you was a child. I rode alongside your father a few times and saw you at the fort." He let that sink in and watched her face. There was no recognition, but he was determined to push forward. "I come askin' for some help, Ma'am."

"In what way?" she asked, suspicious now.

"My Momma and I each want to file papers for intent to homestead. My boy and I found two nice pieces of land on the reservation. My wife is Lakȟóta. I'm not sure if someone else claimed those pieces before me, although ain't no sign of that on the land itself, no marker I mean, and when I asked over at the land office, they wouldn't talk to me. Southern boys workin' there, if you know what I mean, Ma'am. My Momma and me are both United States citizens and we surely are over 21 years old. I fought for the Union army too. I figure since my wife is an Indian, maybe we could get the land. And since my son is half Indian, surely he is entitled to land too which he will own with my momma until he comes of age.

I wonder, could you help us? Maybe use your husband's influence? I know I have no call to be expecting you to, but everyone around here knows how you try to help the Indians through your church work."

His plight touched her heart. Here he had been a soldier! And with her father! Surely he was eligible because of his wife. Didn't her husband get land that same way because of the Indian he had married? Now this man can't get land? Preposterous!

"Could you ride with me over there now, Mr. ?"

"Call me Amos, Ma'am.

"Ok, Amos, can you ride with me now? Let's set things right."

They rode together to the government offices, and she strode confidently in with Amos behind her. She had a commanding presence and men stood up in respect as she passed by.

"I need to see a map of the homestead claims on this reservation. I know you have it and I know good land has been given out to people who are not Indian, too."

The clerk cringed under her scrutiny. He fumbled through some papers, but ultimately produced the map.

"Amos," she said, "Can you show me on this map the land you were thinking of?"

The office workers watched the two intently. This was a highly unusual distraction from their boring jobs.

"I can, Ma'am." The land he chose was not prime farmland. He was too realistic to choose that, because he knew somehow he would not be allowed to keep it. His chosen pieces had potential though. With careful irrigation, some of it could be turned into farmland. The rest looked like cattle could graze there. He pointed to the area.

"It seems like no one has claimed these," she said to the clerk. "This man does so now. He understands the rules. Within six months he must relocate there and build a 12 by 14 structure. He will make improvements on the land, and after the allotted time, he can file for the land to be his. His time will be shortened, of course. He has served our nation in the military. The claim for his mother, in trust for her grandson, though, is for the 5 years."

"His mother?" the clerk asked.

"Yes, another eligible citizen. I'd like to see their names written down now and when the paperwork is completed, please have it sent directly to me. Two days will be enough time for this, I'm sure?"

"Yes, Mrs. Bordeaux."

"Oh, and if you see Mr. Bordeaux, tell him I'm making him his favorite dinner and not to be late. He'll understand."

As they walked away, Amos overheard one clerk say snidely to another, "I wonder if Bordeaux knew what he was getting when he married HER?"

*****

Bastiat found Amos' land acquisition intriguing. He had never considered homesteading and couldn't imagine himself as a farmer now, but what about Ike? He would be eligible. Maybe together they could get their own 160 acres.

160 acres! In New York that would seem huge, but strangely on this dry open land that acreage might not even be enough to support a small herd. However combined? His. Amos'. Há Sápa's? Now that would be a mighty holding!

He had asked Grasshopper about applying, but the old warrior had no interest in owning a piece of land cut out of the prairie. "What about for your granddaughter?" the priest persisted.

The priest presented his idea. "There would be 4 pieces of land and one corner of each would be at the center. We would build four cabins in these corners, close to each other. It would almost be like what we had here...only better. When we die, the next generation will live there. They will have each other. We should plan for this before the land is cut up and we are told what land will be ours."

*****

Dawes iyé he?
Is he Dawes?

369

Every Saturday morning, Ah-Duo would drink a cup of juniper berry tea. She'd have another on Sunday, Monday, and Tuesday, just to be sure. The "recipe" only called for three days, but she would do four. The Chinese were hesitant about the number four. The sound of the word for the number four was close to the sound of the word for to die. *But isn't that I want?* she thought to herself. *To want something to die?*

Dawes followed a set pattern. On Saturday nights, regardless of the season or the weather, he would walk out to what was once a smokehouse with a full bottle of whiskey in hand, open the padlocked door, and lock himself in the windowless shed. There he would stay for hours. Afterwards he would enter the house, drunk and wild-eyed, and rape her. Each week Ah-Duo hoped the tea would prevent a conceived baby from holding on to her, drawing life from her. She did not want Dawes' child. Any child of his would be better off dead!

But her menstruation was late this month, and she was nervous. The snows were gone, and the world was springing with new life. It was too early to note any visible changes in her body, but she felt she was pregnant. The teas had not worked. She knew what she had to do, although she had never had to do it before. Where was she supposed to get cotton root bark now?

She knew she could get the decoction in a city. It was often purchased in Deadwood as the whores used it to bring on uterine contractions and abort their children. She did not think she could get it in Pine Ridge. She would need to find someone who could travel to get it for her.

*****

Ike returned with the good weather, a healthier man than when he left. His thick hair was pulled tightly back into a low tail that had a wavy end, testimony to his Spanish heritage. His clothing bore little trace of the Lakȟóta. His one pair of Levi jeans with their copper rivets and snapped fly were worn through at the knees and cuffed at his ankles. His heavy leather boots were scuffed and blackened. A color-rich Pendleton wool blanket shawl with zigzagging geometric patterns was draped over his shoulders and descended to cover the rump of his weary horse.

His first stop was the general store. Many lonely nights had been spent dreaming about   Ah-Duo. He hoped she was still there. He hoped he would see sparkle in her eyes when he surprised her.

He wasn't disappointed. Clearly she was happy to see him although she could not voice it with Dawes there beside her. Ike thought she looked sickly. She was too pale.

When Dawes went in the back to get his order, Ike pretended to look at the items in the counter's glass display while he whispered. "I want to see you. Speak to you. When?"

"I feed the animals in the morning. At dawn. Dawes isn't up yet. The barn?" she whispered.

*****

How shocked Ike was to see the ruins! How guilty he felt for not being there! But the little village was bustling with people rebuilding Bastiat's cabin with the charred wood from Grasshopper's. What was left of the old warrior's cabin now looked more like a lean to, but it was serving as shelter for the horses who stood beside the toppled chimney chewing hay strewn on the floorboards.

The church was gone and so despite the activity... despite the construction...the little village seemed empty. Its heart was gone.

Ike dismounted outside the work area and found Bastiat supervising the raising of a roof beam.

"Padre."

The priest turned at the recognition of his voice. "Ike! You're back!" His smile brought youth to features that had aged in the past months.

"They told me in the village. I would've come back if I had known."

"You're here now," he said and opened his arms to hug him.

*****

Ah-Duo didn't tell Ike at first. He'd ride to town a few mornings a week to meet secretly in the barn for the short time it took her to care for the animals. At first he didn't touch her...they only talked, casting nervous glances at the door the whole time. After a few meetings she invited him to kiss her. She allowed his eager hands to explore her body beneath her clothing and then she abruptly stopped him, pushing him away.

"I need a favor," she asked, choosing his vulnerable moment to work up to the indelicate question. She felt guilty teasing him this way, but she was desperate. "Didn't you say you were going to Rapid City soon?"

"Yes, I leave tomorrow. 'Will be gone less than a week, though. What do you want?"

"I have some money saved. Can you buy something for me?"

He nodded yes, and said he would, of course, buy her anything if he could find it.

"I need cotton root bark," she said. "A medicine."

"You are sick?" His eyes looked frightened. She was being very serious.

"No, not sick." She knew she had to say it. Risk it. "Pregnant."

She did not expect his response. His eyes softened and he touched her belly. But then he realized who the father must be and withdrew his hand.

"Medicine for the baby?"

She didn't answer.

"You will have his baby?"

Because she hung her head and again made no response, he suddenly realized what she was asking for.

"No! You can't do this!"

"You won't get it for me?"

"To kill your baby? No, I will not!"

And more out of frustration than in anger, she slapped him, turned around and left him standing alone in the barn.

*****

Ike sat on the bank of the creek tossing pebbles into the water. Oyé Wašté noted for the past few days that the man was brooding over something, and most probably over the woman who worked with Dawes. No longer did he go into town early in the morning. No longer did he volunteer to check to see if the letter Bastiat hoped for had come. She watched him from behind and then walked up to him, surprising him with her hand on his shoulder. "She put your moccasins outside the thípi." She set the water bucket down and sat beside him saying nothing more. He kept looking straight ahead and blinked to clear his vision of tears.

"She likes Dawes better?" She knew this was not true, but she hoped her words would get him to respond.

"She's carrying his baby ... or was anyway."

"This is hard for you," she said softly.

"I know she does not love him, but she wants to kill the baby. How can she want that? The child is part of her!"

"A long time ago I could not understand why a spirit child so often chose two other people as parents and did not choose my husband and me. We waited a long time for my son to be born. I wonder why this child chose them."

"Yeah." She saw his jaw muscles twitch as he tightened down on the next word. "Right!" A minute passed before he continued. "A bad decision! He's gonna have a short life."

She put her hand over his. "Maybe the spirit child knows something none of us do."

"Like what?" Ike stood up. "Like Dawes is gonna turn into a good man?"

*****

She tried to hide it, but Dawes could hear the retching and smell the vomit of her morning sickness while he lay in bed trying to think how long it had been since her last menstruation. *Six weeks now? Seven?* Her belly was still flat, he knew that, but he was pretty sure she was pregnant. One part of him was proud of his virility as though this was a great accomplishment. But the child wouldn't be white. *At least the kid won't be a nigga, or an injun!* He wasn't sure part Chinese was that much better though. He liked slanty eyes, found them attractive in a woman, but whether he could accept this in his own child, he didn't know. He thought about it. Sometimes he figured a son might be nice. The child might not look so Chinese. Other times, when he pictured himself walking through town with a mixed-blood son, he cringed from the stares he knew he would receive. He never considered he might have a daughter.

Some nights he would awaken drenched in sweat. Maybe he wasn't the father at all! What a laughing stock he would be if the

373

baby had thick kinky hair and full lips. Dark brown skin. Or what if the straight black hair was not Chinese at all…but Indian!

He couldn't decide if he should take the chance. Maybe it would just be easier if the baby died. Not all babies survive childbirth after all.

*****

Trying to be as inconspicuous as possible, Niglíču walked to the store one early morning.

Ah-Duo sat on the step. "No need for the deception. He's not here. Come. Sit with me."

"Ike sent you?"

"No."

"Tell him I didn't do it," Ah-Duo said. "Tell him I could not bear having him think of me that way."

"You've made a hard decision, miťhámaške." Seeing her raised eyebrows, Niglíču translated, "My friend."

"I'm afraid," Ah-Duo confessed.

"Tell me, why did you change your mind?"

"Because of my father," Ah-Duo explained. "Or the man I think was my father."

"Tell me about him."

"He was a lonely old man. His name was Yang Ya-tang. He was born to a wealthy family in Cheng Du. That is somewhere in China. His father was a man who fought against his corrupt government. When the father, my grandfather died in the rebellion, Yang Ya-tang went to live with his uncle. This man liked the Ching Dynasty, so my father did not fit in. He was, after all, the son of a rebel. The uncle used my father, who was an outstanding student, to take the Imperial Examination for his own lazy son. After that, my father was no longer needed and was told to leave the family. Yang Ya-tang decided he would only be safe if he left the country and so he traveled the ocean to come to the Old Gold Mountain in America. He worked on the railroad starting there in San Francisco and ended up in Deadwood somehow. He met my mother there. She did not love him, but he gave her money to support her opium habit. When I was born, he was like a mother and father to me. I was all he had. I will be all my baby will have too."

"I think you are wrong about that," Niglíču said. "I think, if you want, your baby can have a father too…and not Dawes."

*****

The day was so hot. She had just returned from an unsuccessful hunt and needed to cool off. Kičhí stepped into the cool stream to drink while Niglíču slid from her back into water up to her knees. Laughter coming from a winding area downstream drew her attention. Leaning on her horse's neck to balance herself on the slippery rocks, together they splashed to the bend.

Three adolescent girls were drenching themselves with buckets of water. Their thin cotton clothing clung to their bodies. They were innocently unaware the white material of their blouses had become translucent and attracted the attention of a man Niglíču could see emerging from the bushes that lined the creek.

Still mostly hidden by the bend, Niglíču watched.

"Hey! Can I play too?" The man was Dawes. Pretending to stumble on the rocks, Dawes teetered and laughed, fell into the waist deep water, much to the amusement of the girls who laughed with him. He skimmed his hand over the water sending breaking waves to the girls who giggled and hid their faces. He inched towards them until he reached such an uncomfortable closeness, the girls stepped back. He reached for one, grabbing her arm, but she screamed her fear.

"Stop!"

He looked up to see Niglíču on her horse, bow in hand. She withdrew an arrow from the quiver and readied for the shot. "Stop!" she yelled again.

Dawes released the girl. "We were just playing. Playing. That's all." He turned towards the girl scrambling up the bank. His head was soaked. His beard askew. "Weren't we?"

Something is wrong with his face! There's a scar! A long scar! The beard hid it… but not now!

The image jolted her memory, shook her to the core, and she tightened her hand on the bow shaft. *I could be wrong,* she hesitated. *It was so long ago.*

"Go home!" she yelled to the girls. "Don't come here alone again!"

"And I'll be watching you!" she hissed at Dawes before following

375

the girls.

Mnič'ápi waŋ k'ápi.
They dug a well.

"This is impossible," Bastiat sighed, watching bucket after bucket of dry earth being pulled up.

"Impossible for you when you just sit there," Ike said, dusting off a layer of dirt before he raised the ladle of warm water Oyć Wašté handed him. It was hot in the hole, but at least the sun wasn't beating down on him as it was now. Water trickled down his chin onto his chest, wavy rivulets streaking the dirt there. "Why don't you do something useful. You're a priest. Ask God for water."

"What do you think I have been doing here, anyway? He's not listening to me."

"Maybe we need a Baptist minister," Amos said. "Maybe God ain't too fond of Catholics."

"Maybe we should get a water dowser. One of those forked sticks?" Bastiat said.

"Sure," Grasshopper added sarcastically. "You can just see how this forest has found all the water here!" he said, motioning to the long stretches of empty grassland. "Maybe we should dig by a tree," he suggested.

"There are no trees where these four pieces of land meet," Há Sápa protested, "And I'm not digging more than one well either ... at least for now."

Pine Ridge Reservation sits on a sedimentary rock aquifer. Thirty feet under layers of sandstone, silt, gravel and clay, usable water could be found. The digging was difficult. Propping up the sides of the hole was even more so given the lack of materials the men were working with.

The junction of the four land allotments was chosen for the well site so accessibility to each cabin would be at a similar distance. They had not yet begun construction on the cabins. Money from the sale of Bastiat's inherited land had not yet come to him. He had kept the land as a safety net, having not relinquished it to his Jesuit Order. They knew nothing of it. And he hadn't expected to claim his inheritance thinking his share would, upon his death, go to his brother's children, but now he had need of the money. To keep the land in the family, his brother had purchased it, but the legal transfer of land and money was taking more time than the priest had anticipated.

As the days wore on, their comments became a bit more jagged and the sarcasm more painful. The women stayed as far away as they could in the beginning. Regardless of their luck in creating a well, food had to be gathered for winter. Thíŋpsiŋla, prairie turnip, grew abundantly on this as yet undeveloped land. Harvested in June, for which the Lakȟóta month was named, the women wove the roots together and made braids of them to dry. Eaten in many ways, it was a staple food.

It soon became apparent that the men needed assistance. The first well began to cave in at a depth of 30 feet and was abandoned when no water was found. The intense digging work fell to Ike, Há Sápa, and Amos. Grasshopper and Bastiat strained under the weight of heavy buckets of dirt needing to be hauled away.

Pretty Stone, White Birch and Niglíču intervened. "We will carry the buckets you pull up. The work will go faster."

One day, when the second attempted well neared a depth of 20 feet with no moisture found, Čhaŋkú Wašté surprised them with a visit. This break from monotony and discouragement was welcome.

"We will be digging down to China," Bastiat said to Čhaŋkú, "before we reach anything."

Ike yelled from down the hole, "China?"

"It's a figure of speech, Ike. You will never get to China."

"I think you are wrong, Padre. I'm digging pretty fast down here."

"Maybe you are digging in the wrong place," Čhaŋkú offered as a possibility.

"You know how to find the right place?" Bastiat asked.

"I have never looked for underground water, but I have used branches to help me find things that are lost. Maybe we can say the water is lost? I can try if you want."

"We'd like that!" the two cousins said. "We are tired of hearing them complain."

Čhaŋkú took the sack that hung from his horse's saddle and pulled out a small medicine wheel. He prepared grasses for smudging and then aligned the wheel to the north. Holding the sticks before him, he paced a few steps forward. The sticks crossed. He stopped and faced another direction. They again crossed. He turned, and the sticks

377

stayed apart and so he walked further in that same direction. He continued left, right, forward with the sticks crossing and staying apart until he reached a spot a hundred feet to the west of their last attempt where the sticks spread wide.

"If there is water to be found, it is here," he said. He asked for a shovel and, while singing various incantations, he dug. The ground appeared soft and the digging was relatively easy for him. He dug down to excavate an area two feet deep with an approximate diameter of four feet. Then he left it to the others to finish. Days and days of hard labor passed, and the sides of the hole would often cave in and need to be supported by branches that were difficult to get. Finally, Ike picked into the earth and a shovelful of shale glistened in the shaft of high noon sunlight. Not believing it, he dug further and finally, a small puddle formed. "Water!" he yelled, his voice hollowing its way up out of the hole. "We have water!"

*****

Ike only went to town when it was necessary to do so. The distance from their well to town was considerably longer than from the little village and so a trip would demand hours away from the labor of cabin building.

He missed Ah-Duo. It hurt to think of her with Dawes. He hammered his frustration away. Obsessing with building the cabin, he was sloppy with his carpentry, using far too many nails and too little use of the level. The walls of the minimally required 12 by14 structure bowed in on one side and out on the other giving the cabin the appearance of yielding to the incessant wind. Bastiat was too tired to object. "Just let it stand," he told Ike. I don't care what it looks like."

They had finished Grasshopper's cabin first. It exceeded the required dimensions by four feet but the 16 by 20 structure was divided down the middle. On one side would live Grasshopper, Oyé Wašté and Niglíču. On the other: the two cousins. "Why not share a wall?" the cousins argued. "Less wood." While they would be entitled to homestead acreage of their own, neither wanted the responsibility.

It had been Pretty Bird's idea. Both cousins were growing old and were not as independent as they had been before when their bodies

378

were stronger. And they did not want to return to the original village. They considered themselves part of the extended family of Bastiat's church and did not want to leave the security of it. And even after the many years since Kill's death, Pretty Bird still thought she would one day be accepted as Grasshopper's woman. "He is too old now to want a woman," White Birch chided. "I will make him feel young if he will let me," Pretty Bird retorted, imagining a doorway that could someday be cut into the shared wall.

Grasshopper thought about the arrangement and came to the conclusion that four women in what would seem like one big cabin would be more than he could handle. One day when the priest stood appraising the near completed work, Grasshopper walked over to him.

"The cabins look wonderful, don't they? Standing near each other like that...like a camp circle, right?" Bastiat observed.

"My side of the cabin is not big enough. I snore. The old woman snores. My granddaughter has no space in half the loft. We need more room."

Exasperated, Bastiat protested, "You agreed to the space. We can't make it bigger now. Maybe in the spring?"

Grasshopper shook his head. "We need more room now."

"How is that supposed to happen? You tell me!"

"I will take your cabin. You will take mine. You have two people. I have three. This is more..." He struggled with the word. "Logical."

The priest had to agree with the logic. Two women on one side. Two men on the other.

*****

Oyé Wašté reached into the old nail keg and pulled out a handful of the rusted nails they had been able to buy cheap. Having assigned herself to be Ike's helper, she handed him two at a time. One he clasped between his teeth. The other he slammed into the wood.

"We will not have enough nails for tomorrow," she observed. This was not true though. She had taken handfuls of nails from the bucket and hid them that morning. The deception would force Ike to go to town. "You will need to get more."

"Someone else can go. I have work to do here."

"Not without nails."

Their relationship had grown stronger. He called her Uŋčí *Grandmother* and she called him Thákóža *Grandson*. One evening when they sat alone, talking by the fire, she lamented the loss of her usefulness. Looking at her knobby arthritic hands, she confessed her fears. "There are few things I can do with these anymore." Ike saw beyond the words. "I will take care of you. I promise you this."

The old woman nodded, grateful. "Niglíču says she asks about you."

"Who? Who asks?"

Oyé Wašté didn't answer directly. "I think you need to go to the store."

*****

Dawes pačégčeg iyéye.
Dawes shoved her, making her stagger.

The dew of a fall morning dotted the tall and dry buffalo grass, wetting Dumpling's legs and Ike's dangling feet as he sat bareback astride his aged horse. They travelled slowly. Ike was in no hurry to get to the store. It had been many months since he had spoken to Ah-Duo and he was hesitant about the reception he would receive. Still, the plan was to arrive near the store before it opened and wait for her somewhat hidden by the bushes several yards away.

Focusing his binoculars on the door, he was taken aback when he saw her. Her round belly billowed out her skirt and her blouse strained at the buttons. Her hair was caught up in a knot and held in place with a smooth stick. She was so beautiful ... so beautiful and so pregnant!

But then she was not alone. Dawes came out and sat on the step. Ike waited. Maybe the man would leave.

*****

Two young cavalry soldiers rode into town. Dawes immediately perked up. He enjoyed interactions with his "fellows."

"Hurry up with your sweeping. We got customers comin'."

The men dismounted in front of the store. "You sell chewin' tobacco?"

For an answer, Dawes spit a stream of brown saliva to the dirt. "'Course Ah do."

"Tiger?"

"The only kind I sell."

"Have you heard any more news about McKinley?" the young soldier asked. "Last I heard, the President seemed to be recovering."

"Nah, nothing," Dawes said, and quickly changed the subject. To Dawes, the President was a good man, but nothing more. That someone had tried to assassinate him days before was a tragedy that did not, however, supersede the need for Dawes to talk about himself.

"I was a sharpshooter for the calvary," he said to the young soldier, who, meticulous about his uniform, was brushing the horsehair from his pant legs.

"With all due respect, Sir, the word is cavalry, not calvary," the young man said.

"Right, that's what I said. I worked in the calvary. I was there at that Wounded Knee fight. Bullets and arrows buzzin' by my ear, but we fought them savages off real good, we did. Ended all Indian wars, we did, once and for all. I'm mighty proud of that day."

The young man seemed more impressed with the improper use of the word than with the heroics of the day. "Cavalry, Sir. Not Calvary."

"What?"

"Jesus died on Calvary. You rode in the cavalry. Jesus: c a l, you: c a v a l."

Ah-Duo was sweeping the area next to where Dawes sat. She made a mistake and dared to snicker.

"Calvary, cavalry, It's all the same to me!" Dawes blurted out as he stood up, indignant. With a swift arm motion, he shoved Ah-Duo out of the way. She stumbled backwards, twisted and tried to right herself, but her belly slammed into the arm of the bench. She gasped and fell to her knees. One soldier came to her aid, helping her onto a chair. The other slammed Dawes against the wall.

"What the hell do you think you're doin'? Can't you see she's with child?"

Although Ike could not hear the proceedings, he saw what happened and ran over to intervene, infuriating Dawes even more.

"Ain't my kid she's carryin'," he yelled, struggling to get loose. "She's mah woman but that's the man who fucked her...raped

381

her…I saw them… would've killed him but he ran so fast buck nekkid outta there."

Ike lunged at Dawes but was restrained by the other soldier. The commotion attracted a small crowd.

"Arrest him! Let me go!" Dawes yelled. "Bitch! No good whore!"

Just then, a shout echoed through the crowd. "He's dead! The president has died!"

All attention swung to the announcer. "What happened? He was getting better!"

"Oh, dear God!"

"Gangrene!" the announcer shouted. "Gangrene got him!"

Even Dawes, released now, got caught up in the excitement.

"Hurry! Come with me!" Ike commanded Ah-Duo. "Hurry!" He pulled her to her feet, and they ran to his horse. She was breathing heavily from the exertion while Ike boosted her onto Dumpling's back. "You can ride, can't you?" Without waiting for an answer, Ike took the reins and began running with the horse.

"Hey! He's stealin' my woman!" Dawes cried and started after them. Again, the soldiers grabbed him.

"You're not goin' anywhere, mister!"

Out of sight of the town, Ike slowed the horse to a walk.

"Is he coming?" Ah-Duo cried. "Do you see him?"

"No. No," Ike gasped, trying to catch his breath. "But we'd better keep moving fast."

Ah-Duo clutched her belly. "Ahhhh. Something's wrong…."

"He'll catch up with us! We can't stop!" Ike demanded.

"Oooh…it's too early…," Ah-Duo moaned.

"Hang on…a little bit more," he lied. "We're almost there."

But Ike did not head for the village, guessing Dawes would search there first. He turned towards the new homestead, turned towards her new home.

*****

"She is bleeding. She may lose the baby," White Birch said to Ike after examining Ah-Duo.

"There must be medicine?"

Niglíču offered, "The shaman has something he traded for that comes from the Cherokee. It doesn't grow around here though.

382

'Asgina' something. I can't remember. Had to do with a devil biting some part of the root? I didn't understand the story. It stops the bleeding and cramping though."

"Then, I'll find him," Ike said, worried he might be guilty of pushing Ah-Duo too hard on the ride.

"No. Go first to the village and see if the hokšíyuza *midwife*, is there. She might have gotten this from him."

The older woman, the hokšíyuza, was not there, but her daughter knew where her mother left some medicinal herbal supplies in case she was gone long. She found the required root soaking in alcohol, ironically purchased from Dawes. She gave Ike some of the tincture, along with instructions her mother had told her for its administration. When he returned, he found Ah-Duo less stressful and resting more comfortably. Because of this peace of mind, and the medicine, the bleeding and cramping had stopped by morning. The baby was still alive and moved within her.

Niglíču Dawes theȟíya khuwá.
Niglíču harasses Dawes.

Julia looked across the table at her husband after the children were excused from the dining room. "Isn't this a horrible day! Our President killed! Impossible to believe!"

Bordeaux agreed, but kept sipping his postprandial glass of port.

"I wish you would not drink in this house. It unsettles me, and it is not good for the children to see this at home. Here I am looking for a higher position in the Women's Christian Temperance Union and my own husband flaunts his drinking before the children!"

Bordeaux ignored her as he usually did when she started talking temperance. The 1890 Prohibition was over, and for several years now, drinking was fine. He expected her to next speak about suffrage, another of her causes. He smiled to himself when he predicted correctly.

"Poor Ida McKinley! I have great respect for that woman who, despite her illnesses, continues to promote women's rights. I did not like that she was not for prohibition, but at least she made up for it by speaking for equality!

Bordeaux didn't think women should be allowed to vote. He agreed with the breweries. If they vote, prohibition will return.

"I hope Mr. Roosevelt will champion women's rights! Alice, his wife that died, surely was for it!"

Bordeaux sipped again, disinterested.

"Oh, by the way, did you hear about the fight that happened between Dawes, some soldiers and that Indian today?" Julia asked.

He had, but he pretended he hadn't. Dawes had come crying to him that afternoon about the injustice of it all. His woman was gone, he said. Rode off with the Indian. Dawes was humiliated and all because of that strange family out there with the priest. "Thinks he's Friar Tuck, he does," Bordeaux muttered to himself.

"What did you say?" Julia asked.

"Oh, nothing. I just sighed. So many issues with those Indians!"

"Personally," Julia added, "I think Dawes is an issue. Why you allow him to operate here, I do not know," Julia retorted.

Bordeaux wished he could say what he was thinking out loud. He would say, sarcastically, *Julia, my darling, do you really think I had a rich uncle who left me a lot of money so you can have these pretty things you like to give the children? Do you think my salary here on the reservation would afford this house and all the modern conveniences it has? No, Julia, my love, it is because of Dawes and that alcohol you are so against that you live like you do.*

What he did say was, "Julia, this is a free country. Dawes can operate his business as he wishes. The way he treats his whore is not your affair or mine, either."

"That girl is barely a woman and the way I hear it, she was born in this country, and so she is American! She has rights too! I'm glad she's out of there!"

"No one has tied her there, Julia. She had signed the papers after all. And the age of consent around here is ten, you know."

"That is horrendous, Mr. Bordeaux, and you know it! Think of the children! We need to change this country. Our watchwords are ...."

"Oh my GOD, Julia! How many times do I have to hear it! 'Agitate, Educate, Legislate.' Do I have it right? Your WCTU is all you think about ... all you talk about lately. What happened to the woman I married?"

"She grew up, MR. Bordeaux. Get used to it."

It was pointless arguing with her. Maybe he would have been better off with Soft Feather, he thought. This issue with Dawes, though, was troubling. The man had spilled all his concerns out to him, whining about his woman's friendship with that Indian girl, Niglíču, and how the friendship had changed her. Niglíču! How Bordeaux hated that name! He avoided mentioning her at all...best to keep all that in the past... He had listened to Dawes whine about the so-called harassment by Niglíču; how she would appear in the oddest places and just watch him, scrutinizing him with piercing eyes, holding her bow with an arrow ready to be nocked.

Maybe my wife is right, Bordeaux said to himself. *Maybe I should get rid of that hothead Dawes before he stirs the pot too much and causes problems for me. I can find someone else to sell whiskey here. It's not like Dawes owns the still.*

*****

Khukhúše núŋpa wičháyuha.
She had two pigs.

Ah-Duo had told Niglíču of Dawes' middle of the night forays. "He must be getting the whiskey, but I don't know from where." It was not unusual for Niglíču to have sleepless nights where walking would calm her and so she knew her absence would not cause concern if she was missing a few hours. One night, Niglíču decided to follow him.

Although Prohibition was over, alcohol was still prohibited on the reservation. That, however, did not diminish the need for it.

Dawes headed towards a homestead on land not too far from town where pigs were raised. With the breeze in her face, Niglíču could smell the pigs long before she reached the barn Dawes stopped his wagon in front of. She tied her pony to a clump of bushes to hide her. A man left the shack and met Dawes at the pigsty. Soon after they both went inside, the pigs squealed. "Move! Get outta the way," the homesteader commanded, shoving and kicking the animals aside.

The ill-fitting boards of the sty afforded Niglíču a good view. She watched the men clear the fetid pig litter from the top of a door in the flooring. When the trapdoor was raised, the pungent fumes of fermentation rose from the pit. *Clever,* she thought, *how one smell hides the other.*

The homesteader climbed down into the pit and began handing gallon jugs up and then, tired, told Dawes to load them onto the

385

wagon himself. It took a while before the jugs were all in place. The whiskey jugs were set in the rear of the wagon and Dawes latched the flap so that the bottles would not slip out as he ascended the rocky hill on the way back to town.

Niglíču smiled. The bottles in the back gave her an idea. When Dawes urged the horse forward, Niglíču crept up and unlatched the hook. Then, running parallel to the wagon under cover of the trees, she raced several yards ahead. There she waited in the hollow between two rocks. When the horse, struggling with a heavy wagon and uphill climb, reached Niglíču, the young woman let loose a powerful growl. At the sound, the horse reared, and the wagon backed down, only to be jerked up as the horse took off again. The jugs shifted and slid off the wagon, breaking on the rocks. Stifling a laugh, Niglíču did not wait to see Dawes' reaction. There was more she had to do.

She ran back to the barn. The shack was dark, and assuming the homesteader had gone to sleep, Niglíču quietly entered the pigsty. She made soft sounds as she touched the animals so as not to frighten them. They milled around her, looking for food, as she worked. She found the kerosene lamp and the box of matches for it lying on the cobwebbed sill. Still speaking in soothing whispers to the pigs, she prepared to light the lantern. She had to work fast to escape detection. A quick survey showed about ten pigs. One sow had very young nursing piglets. After thanking the protesting sow, Niglíču tucked two squirming and squealing piglets into her blouse, a painful decision. The four tiny digits of the piglets' hooves scraped her belly. Wielding a broom, she chased the rest of the panicking pigs from the sty. Quickly, she dropped the kerosene lamp into the pit containing the still and raced away. The pigsty burst into flames.

*****

She was flushed with excitement when she reached the cabin and returned her pony to the corral. Her belly hurt, scratched and raw from the still squealing piglets' struggles. Mountain barked. Bastiat, preparing to celebrate Mass, threw on a blanket and went outside to check.

"What are you doing out here?" he whispered to her. "And what do you have there?" he said, pointing to the moving bulge in her

386

tucked in shirt.

"Baby pigs."

"Piglets? Where did you get those?"

"They needed a new home. Their pigsty burned. I'm giving them to Há Sápa. Don't worry. They won't be staying here."

But she didn't count on Ah-Duo's enthusiasm for them! "No! No! Let them stay here!" she said in the morning when she heard their cries. "I will care for them!"

Pork was not a favored meat for the rest of the thiyóšpaye. Mostly they associated it with the rancid bacon the agency distributed. But Ah-Duo saw the pigs as future meat for a variety of culinary uses.

"Little piggies!" she exclaimed. "How cute they are!!" Ike shook his head and smiled.

"You like pigs?" Ike asked.

"I like sausage." She told him her father had told her of the pigs kept by Chinese families and the importance of pork to the Chinese diet. The word for pig and meat were the same in Mandarin. Although hard to bend her ever growing pregnant body, she traced the character for "family" in the dirt. She explained the character was a pig under a roof. Ike found this particularly funny.

"So, if I was to think about a character for 'Lakȟóta family', I would draw a buffalo in a thípi?"

She rolled her eyes.

"We have a boar and a sow. You did well, Niglíču. In a few years we can have many, many pigs. Think of all the sausage I can make! We can sell it everywhere," Ah-Duo said.

Ike shook his head. The industriousness of this little Chinese woman astounded him. She had such big plans!

Chapter 6

Mázawakȟaŋ čík'ala waŋ yuhá.
She has a small gun.

*W*hy *is Dawes here in the middle of the night?* Julia wondered. *It's bad enough that we have to deal with him in the store with his overly pleasant, phony ways! Yes, Ma'am, No Ma'am, Beautiful day, Ma'am.* She mimicked him, angry that all the while he was bullying that Chinese girl! *What is my husband up to with him?* She stood on the stairs and listened. She had heard the pebbles hit the window before and saw her husband jerk awake. He had been signaled.

"I was afraid to come to tell you, but last week the still blew up and the supply of whiskey was dumped, and so I have no money to bring you tonight." Dawes' words were mumbled. Julia was sure he stood with his head lowered, his mouth buried in his shirt collar muffling his words.

"What do you mean, no money? I was expecting a bundle. Two weeks ago, you said tonight you would have it all!" Bordeaux hissed the words. Julia knew if it were daylight, the neighbors would have heard them.

"It might have been an accident," Dawes said.

"Might have?"

"Just seems peculiar, that's all," Dawes had thought this out beforehand. He had no idea how the still burned, but he was going to somehow implicate the Indians and he said so.

"Indians or Indian?"

"Don't know. But maybe it was that squaw that's been stalking me. Niglíču," Dawes said, hoping that name would ease the pressure off him.

Julia had heard enough. *Good for Niglíču!* went through her mind. She hurried upstairs. She had some thinking to do.

388

Feigning sleep that night, Julia thought of her options. She looked around her room, looked at the opulence of the draperies; silk taffeta, ...and the furnishings; ornate Eastlake style... and knew now that her husband's salary could never have afforded all this. *Why hadn't I thought of that before?*

In the morning, she arose, seemingly cheerful, kissed her husband on the cheek as she poured his coffee, sat across from him with her cup and questioned him.

"At our meeting the other day, the women were talking about their lack of knowledge of family expenditures and savings. Some ladies said their husbands would never allow them to see the finances. I told them that was silly. You certainly would, wouldn't you?"

"Yes, of course, dear," he said absentmindedly.

"Some said their husbands hide their accounting ledgers from them. I know where yours is, right?"

"Yes, dear."

"I would like to look at it after breakfast. Is that OK with you?" Julia continued.

That caught Bordeaux's attention. "Why would you want to do that, dear? Are you not satisfied with what I have provided for our family?"

He assured her that his books were in order and that he had, in fact, left the ledger in the office. He would bring it home tonight, he said.

Mr. Bordeaux was a cautious man. Never would he leave records of family finances in his cubbyhole of an office. The books had to be in this house, she thought.

"Thank-you, dear. Maybe you can teach me how to read them later?"

"Of course. Of course," he said. Julia, relieved, knew by his tone that he suspected nothing.

After he left, Julia decided to do some housekeeping, or so it looked to the children, but what she was actually doing was searching for the books. She found them easily enough. She opened the ledger flat on his long desk.

How stupid he is! she said to herself. *He writes the entries in French, so, he thinks, no one will be able to understand, but doesn't he see that the words are so similar to English?*

She copied the words down. She would find someone who would confirm their meaning. It didn't take her long to find a name. Bastiat.

A French name. Maybe he would know, and she could speak to him in confidence. As a priest, he was bound by that, she thought. Perhaps, once the children were in school, she could ride out to see him.

Luckily, he was still in the village late in the morning as one of his parishioners had taken ill and he wanted to bring her the Eucharist. She found him saddling Ned to leave.

"Father, may I speak to you for a moment, please?"

Bastiat was very surprised to see Mrs. Bordeaux in the village. He did not remember her visiting the people before. "Why certainly," he said. He was suddenly very aware of his clothing. Not one article spoke of his priesthood.

"Do you know French?" she asked.

He explained that his knowledge was very limited, but that he would help if he could. She showed him the neatly printed words and asked for their translation.

"Why, these words appear to come from some sort of financial recording, I would guess," he said. "They are misspelled, or at least some are, and they are not all the most common usage but see, this word here, '*payson*'. That means peasant. This word, 'sauvage,' means savage and I suppose refers to the Indians. *Recettes* is income, *dette* means debt, *dois* is to owe, *perte* means loss, *emprunt* has to do with loans, *boissons* is booze, *cruche* is jug. Mrs. Bordeaux, what are you really asking me?"

"May I speak to you in confidence, Father?"

"Of course."

"I believe my husband is involved with the alcohol on this reservation."

"That is a serious charge, Mrs. Bordeaux."

She couldn't help it but blurted out the question that had nagged her for years. "How did Soft Feather die?"

He grew quiet and then said, "Niglíču did not do it. I know that for sure."

"Was she a suicidal person? Was she likely to accidentally fall down the stairs? I need to know this!"

"I have no proof of anything. I'm sorry." He hesitated, then asked, "Are you in danger?"

A sly smile crossed her face, and her eyes narrowed as she reached into her dress and pulled the pearl handled derringer out from between her breasts.

"That is one beautiful gun!" Bastiat exclaimed. "May I hold it?"

With the metal still warm from her skin, Bastiat caressed the ornate sculpturing on the barrel. The gun possessed a sensuous power to it, and he handed it back to her, blushing.

"I always keep this with me and he knows it. I am no fool, Father Bastiat. I'm the daughter of an officer and proud of it. Mine is not a happy marriage. I made a mistake, but I can fix that too," she said. "Thank you for your help. I should leave now."

*****

Julia went home and considered her options. She decided to place the ledger back where she found it and say nothing about it right away. She made a lovely dinner and awaited the return of her husband.

"Julia, dear," Bordeaux said to his wife upon completion of that dinner, "Dinner was excellent! I brought home our financial records and think we should go over them as you suggested. You should know what we have, you know, just in case."

"Thank you! I'm not sure how much I will understand but seeing it all written down will surely help." She even went so far as to bat her long eyelashes at him. He was beginning to feel the night would be very pleasant.

When the table was cleared, Bordeaux produced the books. They were neatly done, Julia noted, and in perfect English too. There was the inheritance recorded. Quite a decent sum of money, she saw. His salary was listed next and then in the expense column, all the outflow of their money was recorded and subtracted accurately. Despite what she said, Julia was very good with numbers. His deception was impressive, and he carefully explained each entry so that even an idiot would understand.

"I feel so much better now," she sighed, enjoying this role as an actress. Now she knew what action to take.

Two days later, as Mr Bordeaux was riding home, he saw a neighbor, whom he really did not know very well, with a wagonload of expensive looking furniture. "He must be doing well!" Bordeaux thought, "That appears to be quality." He put his horse in the barn and entered his home. The evening passed uneventfully, and he soon

391

felt ready for bed, but not ready for sleep.

"Come here, Julia."

She went to him, and he sat her on his lap. "Why don't we go to bed?" he said as he kissed her neck and felt under her dress.

"Good idea," she said dreamily. "Why don't you go upstairs first? I'll be right up."

He wasted no time going up, and she stood on the bottom of the stairs, pistol in hand, *just in case,* she thought laughingly, knowing he'd be down very soon.

"Julia!" she heard him yell as he slammed the bedroom door behind him. "Where is our furniture?"

"I know," was all she said as she watched his face contort. She held out her revolver. "I wouldn't try anything either. I'm not the only one who knows about your business dealings."

He was fuming.

"I gave the money from the furniture sale to the church to be used for the Indians. It is their money, after all. Not ours. And now I give you a choice, which is more than generous. For the sake of the children, I will agree to allow you to stay here…yes, in this house, although maybe jail would be a better place for you. Yes, you heard correctly, allow you. You may sleep on the couch tonight. Tomorrow it will be gone along with the dining room set.

"We can start over, I suppose, again as I said, for the sake of the children, but there will be conditions. We will live on your salary alone, or, I will take the children and leave. I will expect your decision in the morning. Good night, Mr. Bordeaux."

*****

Dawes waŋná líla šičáwekta.
Dawes now had many nightmares.

The military career of Murdock Dawes began at the end of the Civil War. Sixteen year old Murdock, in an act of spiteful hatred, joined the Union Army early in 1865 against his southern parents' wishes. He wanted to go to war, but on the winning side, and clearly the South was losing. Initially stationed at Fort Scott, Kansas, he started as a promising soldier noted for his marksmanship skills, but he soon discovered following rules was a requirement. He despised authority.

He despised the black soldiers of the First Kansas (Colored) Infantry stationed there with him,

But mostly it was punishments for his transgressions that he despised most.

"You want to be in the cavalry?" his superior sneered after pulling Dawes from a drunken brawl. "We'll let you ride the mule first! Teach you a few things!"

The mule was a wooden torture device: a log hewn to a point on the top side supported by four spread legs. Given a head and tail to enhance the mockery, the offender was straddled upon the mule's back, weights were attached to his feet and an exaggeratedly heavy wooden sword was placed over his shoulder. There he was made to sit for hours. What first started as uncomfortable, soon became unbearably painful. After several encounters with the mule, Dawes learned to respect the officers and the rules and just took out his hatred on the enemy.

When the war ended too soon for Dawes' liking, he directed his energies towards annihilating Indians. And he was good at it. Each kill bolstered his pride. He started taking souvenirs. Strings of beads at first that he wore around his neck. Scalps that he fastened to his saddle. Fingers that he hung to shrink and dry. Pubic mounds from the Indian women he raped, turned into purses. Those sold for a good price on the black market and the money kept him well supplied in alcohol.

He was forced to leave the military on a Bad Conduct Discharge shortly after the Wounded Knee massacre. His behavior had become too erratic... "dangerous" was the word his commander used.

Dawes traveled around for a while with his souvenirs, selling some, before ending up at Pine Ridge, close to his greatest military achievement. Wounded Knee hill became his temple. His shed became his shrine.

*****

He missed Ah-Duo. Their relationship, twisted though it had been, lasted the longest of any of his short-lived affairs with women. When he was young, he had been quite handsome and could be very charming. Women were attracted to him, but none stayed longer than it took to realize how abusive he could be. He may have fathered

393

other children, but no one ever said he did, no one wanted that attachment that acknowledging his paternity would give.

And now he was going to be a father. Though he ranted about Ah-Duo's supposed affair with the Indian, he didn't...he couldn't...believe the child was not his. His demented pride would not allow that another man planted the seed he had not.

Though he would never admit it, he was afraid of the night. Not of the dark. The dark was comforting, a blanket. But night itself...especially right before dawn, when he thought the world slept and he alone was awake, the demons would come to haunt him. Having Ah-Duo in the house made him feel safer, as though her presence would keep the evilest of the demons away.

But now that she was gone, the dark spirits romped through his mind, laughing and sneering, screaming and crying, and sometimes they had tortured faces, bronzed faces, male and female. Sometimes he would swear he could smell them...smokey...musky...and sometimes he could feel their blood, sticky on his hands. They called him and he went to them, behind the house in the shed.

*****

Niglíču wanted to see what was inside, to see what Dawes guarded so protectively that he had beat Ah-Duo one day for fumbling with the lock.

Grasshopper respected her independence, but he worried about her night walks. They weren't walks. He knew she was lying when she said they were to help her sleep. How could she think she could go past him, open the door and leave without him watching where she went? She would take her pony and disappear, and his grandfather heart would follow her.

But she had been uncustomarily agitated that evening. Her movements were jerky. Her words were clipped. Grasshopper knew that if she went out that night, he would tail her.

He lay still and then he heard the soft creak of the loft ladder. She stopped on the bottom rung, listening. The old woman's snores assured her she was asleep, but her grandfather's quiet breathing told her he was awake.

"Lalá, I cannot sleep. I'm going outside for a while."

"Where are you going?"

It was not easy to lie to him directly. But it was harder to contain the thoughts that had been plaguing her. "I need to ride to the town. There's something I must see." Even as she spoke, she saw how foolish her idea was. Go to town. Try to get into Dawes' shed. Alone? At night? She was lucky she didn't get caught the first time with the pigs. Would she be as successful again? "Will you come with me?"

*****

Have I ever ridden beside my grown granddaughter? The way she sits with such confidence astride her pony reminds me of her mother. The gentle way she pats her pony's neck when the animal shies makes me think of my wife. The horses always loved her more. It seemed she knew what they were thinking. In my granddaughter I ride beside both of those women. Truly the child beloved has grown to be an honor to our people. He took some credit for that, but he knew he shared this with the priest. *Would she have become what she is now without Bastiat's influence?* He remembered the traumatized little girl after the massacre...he remembered her crushed spirit and how he had thought he had lost her too.

It was only when they neared town that she told him her purpose. "The shed holds secrets. I must know what they are."

They tied the horses to a tree outside of town and walked to within sight of the store. A lantern was lit in a downstairs window. Dawes was awake. Pale light flickered through the cracks in the shed wall. Dawes was inside.

"Good. The light would let me see inside," she told Grasshopper. He protested. "I should go. You stay here," but she put her hand on his arm. "No. This is something I must do. But have your rifle ready in case something goes wrong."

The heavy rifle felt light in his arms as a surge of adrenaline coursed through his body. "I will follow behind you," he insisted.

She glided unnoticed from shadow to shadow and stopped a few feet away from the shed. She heard talking. *Are there two inside?* She motioned for her grandfather to stop while she crept closer to the widest crack.

"How are my lovelies today?" Dawes whispered. His speech was slurred. Already he was drunk. She peered through the crack and saw him fondling long dark braids before the candlelit skull. Next, he pushed tobacco into the bowl of a pipe and lit it. He puffed to start the burning and then placed the stem between the skull's teeth.

"We had some good times, didn't we, Chief? Some mighty fine battles. Y'all didn't stand a chance against me and my rifle, but you tried pretty hard. Gotta give you credit for that." Dawes lit his own pipe. "Feels good to sit and smoke with you, doesn't it? Talkin' about the old days is mighty comforting."

The light inside the shed was so dim it was difficult to see anything, but the candle glow illuminated the wall behind the "altar." There she saw weapons...a bow...feathered arrows of different styles... old muskets...a spear head...knives of all sorts...rusted silver, shiny black...

"Dawes! You in there?"

Niglíču's heart raced. She squatted to the ground and eased her way around the corner.

"Dawes?"

"Goddamn you! I'm busy! I told you never to bother me!"

"The whiskey....it's not under the steps..."

Now Dawes cursed himself for forgetting to put out the bottles for his distributors. "I'm comin', I'm comin'," he yelled from the shed.

He slammed the door behind him but neglected to lock it.

Should I? Should I go inside?

The decision was made for her. Grasshopper tugged on her sleeve. "Hurry. They won't see us if we leave now."

*****

Waníyetu na ičámna.
It was now winter, and it snowed.

Life for Ah-Duo was easier in the warmer weather. She was outside all day. Now that it had turned cold and the first snow had already fallen, she longed to sit by the stove. Her hands were so cold! Her feet felt frozen, but still she made excuses to stay outside much of the day. Three women in the tiny half cabin were one too many. And like her name suggested, she was the one.

The cousins hadn't considered adding another person to their home. They certainly did not expect a pregnant Chinese woman who knew little of their customs and even less of their language. And when they took her in and settled the baby within her, they didn't expect she would be staying.

But where else could she go?

*****

With the cabins completed, Ike went back to freighting...small jobs here and there that did not keep him from the group for long. It was hard being away from Ah-Duo. He had grown to love her and knew, given the chance, he would marry her and accept her child as his own.

But he wasn't sure that the love was reciprocated. Ah-Duo seemed distant, their relationship reduced to greetings and insignificant conversation. In his insecurity, he justified her behavior. What kind of man was he? He still drank, though not as much. As Indian, he was no skilled hunter nor warrior. As a white man, he had neither money nor good prospects of attaining it.

*****

Ah-Duo struggled to walk. Her ankles were swollen. Her belly off-balanced her. Yet she wrapped a shawl around her shoulders and walked away from the cabin to be alone, worrying. *What will happen to me? I am a Chinese prostitute living in a Lakȟóta thiyóšpaye carrying the child of a crazed high-nose white man. How long will they let me stay?* And then she thought the unthinkable. *What if I die and my baby lives?*

It was a reasonable fear. At the time, one in a thousand women died either in the birthing process or from infections and complications later.

Oyé Wašté watched her leave from the open doorway of her cabin. There she sat by the table quietly struggling to push the needle through the leather as she beaded the lizard shaped čhekpá ognáke, umbilical cord pouch, for Ah-Duo's son. And Ah-Duo insisted this was a son and for this reason the old woman chose the lizard. Because it regrows its tail, this animal represents adaptability and the ability to care for oneself, qualities valued in a boy. But just in case this was a girl child, she designed the pouch so that simple

397

adaptations could turn the lizard into a turtle, signifying longevity.

Feeling sympathy for Ah-Duo, Oyé Wašté got up, threw a blanket across her shoulders and followed her. "You are upset," she said when she found the young woman sobbing. "Why?"

"I'm afraid."

"All new mothers are afraid."

"But I cannot stay here without a man. Where will I go? I am so different from them. They won't let me stay."

"I think you are wrong. They will not turn you away, but I see you are wrong too about other things. You do not try to learn from the women. You do not try to learn their language. We speak…you and I…in the white man's tongue. They have learned this for the priest. Why don't you learn the ways and the words of our people? Everyone will see that you want to belong here."

What the old woman said was true. Ah-Duo admitted she had not made the effort. She was too busy feeling sorry for herself.

"Năinai," Ah-Duo said, addressing the old woman with the Mandarin word for granny, "I cannot stay here without a man. Ike stays away from me. He has not asked me to marry him. He has not asked me to be his woman."

"So, this is the real problem?" the old woman laughed. "You need not worry about his love. Are you blind to the yearning in his eyes? You will see. After the baby is born, he will ask you. And you need not worry about belonging here. Your baby will be good for all of us. Can you picture the old priest bouncing the baby on his bony old knees?" She lowered her voice and spoke her advice with compassion. "But remember what I told you about learning our ways. Then you will feel better. Come back with me now. I will show you what I am making for you. And you should ask the others to show you how to make clothes for your little one."

*****

Hokšíčhaŋtkiyapi héčha.
She is a Child Beloved.

"Pȟéta Akú! Pȟéta Akú!" In her dream, shadowy figures cried out to Niglíču using her childhood name, Brings Fire. "Avenge us! Avenge us!" they sobbed, tears streaming from eyeless sockets in skeletal faces.

Niglíču woke with a pounding heart. She was afraid to go back to sleep. Like other nights, she feared this dream might precede another...another of a knife slashing through a cheek, carving the flesh into a curved grin...giving a man with red hair two mouths...one a smile...the other a tortured O.

Čhaŋkú Wašté visited them the next day. He did not come as often as when he had considered Niglíču for a wife. His initial attraction had turned to admiration. She was a powerful woman. Her spirit might best his, overpower it, weaken it, and his vanity could not accept that in a wife. Her masculine mannerisms did not intimidate him. In fact, her superior horsemanship, her skill in weaponry, excited him. He fantasized the challenge of coaxing her into submission to his virility. Such a union would be powerful medicine. Such a union would create exceptional children.

It was her mind that dissuaded him, and for that he blamed the priest. Čhaŋkú Wašté could not abide a woman who could out-think him, could not tolerate a woman who already knew more of the world than he ever would in his lifetime. Books. Because of books he lost the woman he had hoped for.

And so they remained friends, an unusual relationship between adults of different sexes who lacked kinship. Because he was a shaman, people accepted this cultural irregularity. Someday he might teach her how to become a medicine woman.

"My friend," she said to Čhaŋkú Wašté. "I need your advice. Will you walk with me?"

When they were far enough away so that no one else could hear, she told him of her dreams and about her suspicions concerning Dawes. After thinking about it and asking for clarification of details, he spoke.

"This man has been woven into your life path. What that means for you now is to be seen. But what is most interesting is that in your dreams, you were called by your other name. I think now is finally the time for you to decide what that name means for you. What fire do you bring? What is its nature?"

"I'm not sure."

"You were once honored with the Child Beloved ceremony. You were given special responsibility to care for the people. Have you done that? Have you lived up to that responsibility? It is in that direction that your thoughts should travel. There is where you will understand the meaning of your dream."

*****

That night, once again she dreamed....the faces, the man, and this time the knife became clear. It was black...shiny...her mother's knife... but this time the red-headed man was holding it.

*****

"Pepére, in your Holy Book, what does fire mean?" Fire was a word frequently used in his Bible readings. Now the word took on particular significance.

Unaware of her conversations with Grasshopper or the shaman, the answer he gave, partial though it was, exactly fit her thinking.

"In the Bible, the fire of God often meant vengeance. St. Paul speaks of Jesus coming from Heaven in a blazing fire with his mighty angels, presumably to judge the wicked. The Bible often paints a picture of God's glory as a fire."

Niglíču imagined it. Angelic white spirits like those she had seen in Bastiat's books, now bringing fire to the evil ones. Gentle Jesus, now with eye's burning with anger. Clearly Bastiat's God understood revenge.

And now this challenge fell on her. Her responsibility! A reason to be warrior-like. Finally.

*****

Wičháša kiŋ lé ikíphi šni.
This man is unworthy of it.

Yes, the counterfeit Medal of Honor looked genuine. "Conspicuous bravery in action against Indians concealed in a ravine on 29 December 1890." That's what the award stated. The back of the medal was engraved accurately too, except for the name. The authentic medal had the Irish born Pvt. Thomas Sullivan there. Dawes had the counterfeiter engrave his own name instead.

Dawes sat in his shed and rubbed a soft cloth over the metal,

400

shining it. He held it close to the candlelight and smiled. "The Congress to Cpl. Murdoch Dawes, Troop E, 7th Cavalry, for bravery at Wounded Knee Creek, S.D., December 29, 1890."

He deserved the medal even more than the twenty soldiers who had received it!

Reverently he traced his finger along the eagle's wings and around the five stars. He kissed the fabric of the flag and hung the medal next to an authentic Wounded Knee souvenir, the obsidian knife he had taken from Wind Woman.

*****

Why didn't I think of it before? Ah-Duo asked herself. She had overheard Niglíču and Ike talk about the black knife in Dawes' shed. They were going to break into the shed and steal it one night. *Dangerous business. But I could get that knife...easily too I think. All I need is a ride to town. Dawes always found an excuse to be gone on Distribution Day. He couldn't stand looking at the savages, he would say.*

A few days later, she climbed onto Amos' wagon, joining the others he was transporting to the center. "Why do you want to go?" they asked her. It was easy to lie. Easy to say that because Dawes would be away, she could enter the house and get her belongings. They were rightly hers, she told them. She knew where he hid the key too.

She didn't exactly know where the key to the shed was, but she was confident she could find it. Many times she had heard the hens squawk when he went out there. The key must be somewhere in the coop! And she would have time to search. The lines were long to get the food. She would not be sneaky either. She would act as though she had returned, greeting neighbors as she saw them.

The coop wasn't large and there were only a few dozen hens. Maybe she'd even help herself to a few. Dawes would never know the difference. She searched all the corners. Inside the nest boxes. On top of the frame. No key and she was tired from bending. Supported by one hand to rest leaning against the barn wall to which the coop was attached, she felt a plank give. She jiggled it loose. There, hung on a nail, was the key. Hurriedly she went to the shed.

Once inside she did not linger to be sickened by the grotesque souvenirs. She found the knife in question and tucked it into her waistband. She did not recognize the significance of the medal next to it, but since it was prominently displayed she figured he attached importance to it and so snatched it off the wall too. Carefully she relocked the shed, shoved two panicked hens into a sack and waited on the porch. She had no desire for her clothing....no desire to re-enter that house and give him more reason to go after her.

"Did you get what you needed?" they asked her when she was helped up onto the wagon. "No," she replied. "He threw everything away."

*****

That night Ah-Duo showed Niglíču the knife. "Is this the one? Did this belong to your mother?"

"How..?"

"Never mind that...is this it?"

Niglíču's fingers trembled as she reached to touch it. Tears filled her eyes. It was the knife. She was sure of it...the bone handle with dark stains in pocked imperfections...the chip at the end of the handle her mother had sanded smooth...the blade still sharp with the large nick, a mistake of the chiseler, near the inserted base.

"Hold it," Ah-Duo offered. "Be sure."

"I can't." The knife was too precious...too wakáŋ. She thought if she held it, she wouldn't be able to stand.

"Here...Take my hand...We will hold it together."

*****

Niglíču secreted the knife away. She would not tell her grandfather. His reaction would be to kill Dawes, not caring if he lost his life in the process. He'd be proud to die such a warrior's death, but Niglíču would deny him that honor. She would kill him.

*****

Because they had planned to get the knife together, Ike had to be told about Ah-Duo's adventure, but he was not told the truth. They told him the knife was not in the shed and to say nothing about its

402

supposed existence. They showed him the medal.

*****

"Why did you do it?" Ike asked angrily. "That was dangerous! You should have asked me!" He fired questions at Ah-Duo. "What about the baby? What if he had found you?"

The chastisement brought her to tears. He softened his tone. "Don't you know how much I care about you? I wouldn't want anything to happen to you…or the baby."

His admission, the first declaration of his feelings, both warmed and emboldened her. "It was something I could do. Something to show I want to belong here."

*****

"How do soldiers get this thing called the Medal of Honor?" Niglíču asked the men. It had become routine for many of them to gather in one cabin when the sun set. On this day they drank their coffee in Amos' cabin with Granny serving them.

"That's an odd question. Why do you want to know?" Amos asked.

Niglíču set the medal on the table. Há Sápa picked it up and turned it over. "Dawes? Dawes got a medal for Wounded Knee?"

"Ah-Duo got it from his shed."

"For shooting women and children? Unarmed old men?" Amos was incredulous. "Used to be for risking your life above and beyond the call of duty. That was just slaughter! Where's the honor in that?"

The familiar knot tightened in Grasshopper's chest. He rubbed it and brushed aside the medicine bag hanging there to do so. *Honor.* He had always thought of himself as a warrior of honor … except for that one day when he was so angry, so furious, at the flow of people into the Black Hills. It was almost thirty years before, he figured, when at the beginning of the gold rush, the new town of Deadwood was created to service the miners. A steady stream of would-be prospectors headed northwest from Sioux City to desecrate the Lakȟóta holy place with their picks and shovels slamming into the earth. *And then he had to come,* Grasshopper thought, *with his wagonload of tools clanking down the road. How stupid he was to*

403

think he could just pass through!

Grasshopper stood up. His heart was racing. "I leave now," he said abruptly. The sky was clear, and the moon lit the well trampled grasses on the path to his cabin. He stopped just outside and removed the photo from his medicine pouch, angling it so it shone in the moon rays.

The stone-faced people in the photograph look deprived of life, devoid of spirit dressed in their elaborate white man's clothing. The emotionless expressions on the man, woman and younger boy did not disturb him, but life was captured in the face of the older son. His face was slightly turned to the right and his upturned eyes were glued on the father whose hand rested firmly on his shoulder. Clearly, the boy loved this man; adored him. *The boy there was like I was long ago. How I had loved my father! How I still carry hatred for the man who killed him! This boy, now a grown man, would hate his father's killer, especially if he knew the cowardly way the man's life had been ended.*

Pretty Stone had not gone to Amos' cabin that evening. She rarely did. The conversations were only infrequently about things that interested her. She worried about a lonely winter. The homestead was quite a distance from the village. It wouldn't be an easy walk in the biting cold and wind driven snows. What news would there be to talk about here? What friendly woman's gossip? Who would be the storyteller to make them forget the long dark and confining winter moons? What children would they hold under their blanket shawls while the storyteller kept them spellbound with stories from the past?

She stepped outside to look at the moon and they saw each other. Immediately he shoved the photograph into his bundle.

"What do you hide there?" she teased. He mumbled an incoherent response and she saw how troubled he was. Boldly, she reached out and took his hand. "Come inside with me and keep warm."

*****

White Birch saw how the relationship between Grasshopper and Pretty Bird had changed. But Grasshopper was not a man like Kills. He would not want two women. White Birch knew he would not cast her out, but she also knew she would not be an equal wife. Frightened by the future, she turned to Bastiat.

404

"I do not hear your morning prayers anymore," she said to him one morning while they sipped coffee together. The new wood planks of the wall that separated the two cabins had shrunk with the stove heat, leaving spaces which limited their privacy.

"I'm quiet. I don't want to wake you." Her bed rested on the opposite side of the wall as was his. Though he celebrated his private Mass on his knees before the bed turned altar, she had heard his words clearly enough to follow along every morning, her whispers unheard by him.

"But how do you know I pray?"

"I can hear you." She paused. "I can see you too, through the cracks."

He blushed red.

"Can I pray with you?" she asked. "Through the wall?"

The priest only went to the village a few times a week to celebrate Mass. Always on Sundays. Sporadically on other days. It was harder for him to travel in the cold weather. His arthritis had stiffened him. Riding was painful in the morning.

"I know the words now," she continued.

Chapter 7

Wéčikte kte!
I will kill him for her!

Dawes opened the store from the inside. A white sheet of paper tacked to the door fluttered in his face. He ripped it free and read it. Five words. Five words that chilled him. "That was my mother's knife!"

*****

"Dammit, Dawes! Why are you coming to me with this stupidity?" Bordeaux said, quickly ushering the man outside of his office to talk privately. "Stay away from me!"

"She knows what I have in my shed out back," Dawes countered. "You might care about that."

"What are you talking about?"

"Look, Ah-Duo took the knife. People saw her go to the shed when I wasn't there. The knife is missing. She brought it back to those Indians she's with."

"What's that to me?"

"You have a short memory, Bordeaux. I believe I got me a few receipts for some souvenirs you purchased from me. I document my sales, you know."

"What do you want me to do? Send the police out there to arrest her for a damned knife she took?"

"We have to get rid of her. Before she talks too much…about what's in the shed. Her and that Indian girl you had here. Get rid of both of them! It won't be hurtin' me so much as you if they talk. I can always leave here. No one would care. But can you?"

He let that sink in. "And about that girl, Niglíču. And your first wife…Soft Feather was it? Wasn't there something peculiar about how she died? The girl didn't push her. Funny how your wife just fell like that…"

"Are you trying to blackmail me?"

"Just concerned about your reputation, is all."

"So, you are telling me you want them arrested or else you're going to blackmail me? You are treading on soft ground, Dawes."

"I said nothing about arrested, Bordeaux… maybe an accident…you know…like your wife had."

"Goddamn you! You have nothing on me, and you know it!"

"Them two have mouths and I have a mouth. Which do you think you should shut up most?"

Dawes was no fool. Hurting either Niglíču or Ah-Duo would bring down the weight of the law. The priest would see to that. But let that fall on Bordeaux! The Indians might also retaliate. The priest had built up a quite a following. *Yes, let Bordeaux take care of it!*

*****

Whose mouth should I shut up? Your mouth, Dawes! That would solve the whole problem, wouldn't it? Bordeaux thought.

*****

A letter came, addressed to him in his sister-in-law's handwriting. The priest's hands shook as he opened it. Tears blurred his vision…he read the letter twice to be sure but yes, his brother was dying. "Come soon if you want to see him alive."

He could not go. How could he? Almost all his inheritance money had gone into building the cabins, and the reserve he had secreted away was for a time that they might need food. He had no income from the church anymore having lost contact months ago. His superiors probably thought he was dead. Strangely this didn't bother him. He would always be a priest but now he was an independent one. And the thiyóšpaye had no income save for what Ike got for his freighting and odd jobs. Bastiat did not know for sure what the train fare back East actually was, but he guessed it might even be fifty dollars! It did not matter, he told himself, for he had nothing to spare.

The letter to his sister-in-law was difficult to write.

Bear Teeth would not move to the homestead. He would not move
into a cabin. He knew he would die soon and wanted to spend his
last days in the old way. The women of the village buffered his small
thípi with brush they had gathered and lined the interior with
colorful government issued blankets, laid firewood inside the
entrance and brought him food. It was warm inside and he was not
hungry.

"Come. Sit by me!" he said to Niglíču. "My ears are weak, and
my eyes are dull, but I am still grateful for the presence of a
beautiful woman." He wriggled to straighten his posture to look
healthier. Niglíču moved closer and adjusted his sagging blanket
which had slipped to only half cover his shoulders.

"You are well?" she asked, giving him the dignity to say he was,
although his pain-sunken eyes would betray his response.

"Yes. The people take care of me. Here, eat!" He reached to his
side and picked up his empty bowl and handed it to her. "Take some,"
he said pointing to the pot handing over the fire. "The women made
a good stew."

He spoke again while she ladled stew into the bowl. "I hear
someone has been in town bothering Dawes. Stole a knife. That was
you, wasn't it?"

"The Chinese woman stole it."

"But you have it?"

"Yes." She took it from her belt and handed it to him. Reverently,
he turned it over and gently ran his fingers across the edges where it
had been flaked. "A good knife. It is still sharp. But why is it
important to you?"

Niglíču's breathing was tight. Speaking in short, strained
sentences, she struggled not to cry.

"Dawes killed my mother. He tried to kill me. He had my
mother's knife. He probably killed Loud Bear, too."

"And you want to avenge their deaths? Those and all the others?
And for this you have come to me?"

"Yes. I knew you would understand."

"You could not speak to the others? Your grandfather? This was
his daughter. His grandson."

"I had promised I would kill him. That day I had said it."

He laughed. "You have a warrior's heart." It was difficult for him to talk, hard for him to find the breath to push out the words he so deeply felt.

"I would ride with you. I would give anything to ride with you to grind this man into the dust. I was once a strong warrior, you know. Many danced in my honor." At this, he closed his eyes, smiling still and remembering. When his eyes fluttered open, he continued, "But you would not want me with you. I can see that. You want to do this alone. It is good."

Niglíču did not know what to say. He reached out his clawed hand out and brushed away a tear that had drifted down her cheek.

"There are few warriors left now. I do not know any more worthy than you are. Come closer. Let me give you this gift."

His hands went to his neck, and he pulled his bear teeth necklace over his head. "I want you to have this," he said, as he adorned her with it. "This is for the warrior you have become."

Her hands fondled the old teeth, stained brown, but still hard.

Then his fingers played with the top buttons of his plaid shirt. He could not undo them and his eyes asked Niglíču for help. She opened one, then two, and finally three, before he told her to stop. He pulled apart the shirt, revealing the bear claw necklace he had always worn unseen.

"I always wore this for courage. And protection. I was afraid to fight. Without this, I would have been a coward. That is why I wore it under my shirt. I did not want anyone to know I needed it. I still don't want anyone to know."

This necklace hung over a scarred chest where, over the years, the points of the claws had raked across his flesh. Tiny arcs of scars laced the skin over his heart.

"But I do not need this anymore. I am not afraid of death. Wear it for me when you get Dawes. I can think I am there with you."

He removed this necklace and placed it in her open palms, cupping his hand over it one last time. "Wear this on that day. Not before." He closed his eyes then and drifted into sleep. She waited there a while with him feeding sticks into the fire, but when after a time he did not reawaken, she pulled his robe to cover his chest and walked out.

The bear claw necklace she hid in the loft, but Niglíču would not take off the bear teeth necklace. She had been lax in recording the stories of her people but now she returned with fervor to this task. "The old ones are dying…I cannot let their stories die too!" she explained to Bastiat while sitting at his table to work. The necklace was long. Teeth jangled against the paper as she leaned over her work in the dim lighting, annoying the priest.

She shouldn't be wearing this! It makes her look too… Indian! The thought surprised him, and he realized that he no longer saw her as Lakȟóta. She was the granddaughter of his heart, better educated than most white women of the time!

"That necklace is too heavy for you," he said. "Maybe I should shorten it and then you can tuck it inside your blouse."

"I like it this way," she responded, never looking up. Her left hand fingered it as she wrote, rubbing the teeth as though they were beads of a rosary.

Ike noticed the necklace right away. "Bear Teeth's? How'd you get it?"

She explained it was a gift and left out the details. The priest shook his head.

"Well," he said. "I like it. It makes you look different."

Not only did it make her look different, but it emboldened her stride, and gave her an air of masculine confidence that Ike found attractive. He thought of the woman he had fallen in boyish love with so long ago. *It must have been her mother…they are so alike in looks and mannerisms.*

*****

That night she thought about killing Dawes. *What would it feel like to take a person's life?* The priest would forbid such thoughts. These come from Satan he would say. The Prince of Darkness! Fallen angel! And yet she kept thinking of it. Her language had many words for killing, very specific words for how the killing was done. *Will I kill by choking, stomping, punching, kicking, or knocking somebody down? Will I kill for myself or for someone else?"* She stopped there. *"Wéčikte kte,"* she said to herself. *"I will kill him for her!"*

The priest swept the crumbs off the table. Usually Mountain was there to lick them up but now the dog was perplexed. The four chicks had gotten there first, pecking and peeping. "Leave them alone," Bastiat warned, smiling. He remembered the first egg the stolen hens had laid. How happy he was to fry it! How appalled Ah-Duo was when she banged on his door and demanded to know why he took the egg! "We need chicks!" she said. "You cannot eat the eggs! We have no rooster!"

The priest saw no logic to that. No rooster meant no chicks, but Ah-Duo disagreed. "We have two weeks after she has been with the rooster!" And she was right. One of the hens went broody on several eggs despite the season and four did indeed hatch. It was too cold for them outside and the cousins would not tolerate the hens in their cabin, so the chicks found a new home near Bastiat's stove. It was fine when they were soft and fuzzy. Now that they had feathers and their dropping squished on the floor, it was time for them to be relocated.

The housing for the animals had become a problem. Two fast growing piglets, six chickens …hopefully one was a rooster!...and the horses needed shelter. And what about the bull? And the milk cow? Would they tolerate the winter in the lean to Amos had for his horse?

The issue…and always it was the issue…was the lack of wood to build such a structure. What they had now was a frame of sorts covered with old canvas tent material. It would collapse under the weight of heavy snow. They had no funds for new wood, and they had already scavenged the still usable wood from the fire.

Once again it was the ever resourceful Ike who brought the solution. Back from a job, he told them of his discovery.

"Do you remember Chápa Wakpá Othúŋwahe *Beaver River City,*" Ike asked Grasshopper when the men were all together. "Two days ride from here in Nebraska? Now it's called Chadron. They had made their village in one place and then when the train did not come through at that spot, they took all the buildings and moved them six miles away. Except they were sloppy. They left lots of wood pieces too small for their houses in the first place they were. The prairie

411

covered it. I rode through there coming home. Lots of wood! Some boards rotten but most were good enough to build a shed or maybe even a small barn."

Há Sápa was immediately interested. "We have a wagon! Let's go get it!"

Ike volunteered to guide them to the site, but he said he wouldn't stay. He had promised Ah-Duo he wouldn't leave again until after the baby was born.

Amos and Há Sápa left soon after with hammers, ax, and saws, not knowing what they would find. They did not expect the work to be easy, but it would have to be completed before snow covered the ground.

The trail was overgrown and rutted, making for slow travel. Nights were frigid with unrelenting wind, but father and son spooned together to draw heat from each other. They threw an old blanket over the horse, feeling sorry for its lack of protection.

Two-foot, three-foot splintering planks were strewn all over but hiding under wind bent dry grasses. Nails were pulled from worm holed beams and, if usable, both were salvaged. In a few days, the wagon bed was full and would tax the strength of the lone horse who would pull it.

But they found treasure there! The more affluent townspeople had left behind once valued possessions that had fallen none too gracefully into old age. A rust-lidded jar of buttons! How Niglíču would love them! A dented and chipped mass produced enamel bucket with a wooden grip on the handle! A metal ladle! A white porcelain flower edged plate with only hairline cracks! A ring of safety pins! A blue speckled basin mineral stained brown! These and more, all now river washed clean and piled in a sack the men would hide until Christmas morning!

*****

Bastiat was not concentrating on the Mass he was celebrating through the wall with White Birch and that made her angry. Clearly he was distracted. She narrowed her eyes and scrunched up her nose when he ended Mass abruptly before the closing prayer.

Niglíču had gone outside. He saw her through the window, took his jacket off the hook and went to her.

412

"Can I speak with you while you work?" Bastiat asked. She was grooming her horse, apparently preparing to go for a ride.

"Of course, Pepére."

While Ned nuzzled the priest, Bastiat began his questioning.

"You like that necklace, don't you?"

"Yes, I do," she said as her fingers separated the tangles in Kičhí's mane.

"It is unusual for a woman, is it not? Bear teeth?"

"I think so," she said, as she turned to untangling the mare's burr infested tail. Addressing the horse, she then said, "How did you manage to get your tail into so much trouble?"

Using that word to get to his point, as it seemed she was not going to volunteer information, the priest, "Are you in trouble?"

"No. Why?"

"There was talk in town. About you."

"There is always talk in town. About somebody."

He took the plunge. "Are you going after Dawes?"

When she did not answer, he pushed on. "Things are different now, Petite-fille."

Her heart clenched at that name. It had been a long time since he had called her granddaughter in French.

"You cannot act this way. There are laws. Courts. A justice system. We will find proof that will stand in a court of law."

"What proof will say my mother was murdered at Wounded Knee? What proof…what law will punish the soldiers they gave medals to?"

He ignored her questions because they were valid. "But he is white, and you are not. You cannot trust a jury to treat you fairly if you are caught."

"I did not say I was doing anything."

"You did not say you were not either. Remember, 'Vengeance is mine,' says the Lord. I don't know what you are planning, but please think about what our Lord would want you to do."

"I act as a warrior now. I will do what all my grandfathers before me did."

All? His exclusion stung.

"That may be true, Niglíču. But you will always be my little girl. From the time I carried you into the village, sitting before me, shivering and wrapped in my robe, I knew you had my heart."

"I carry you in my heart too, Pepére. I always will. Mičhaŋté él

413

čhiyúze."

"Then you will think of what I said?"

"I will."

*****

The common well had its advantages and Oyé Wašté admitted it was a shorter walk than going to the river to get water every day. But pulling up the bucket that had to go so deep into the well was hard work. She struggled with it, leaning her weight against the rope that passed through the pulley, but when the bucket reached the top and she had to pull it onto the ledge, the rope would so often slip and down the bucket would go. Such frustration! But she refused help from the others although they offered and even insisted on it.

"No!" she said firmly. "This is something I can do!" Her eyes pleaded that this simple usefulness not be taken from her.

Amos' mother, Granny, watched her. They had their own well by now right next to the cabin and she thought it shameful that the others let the old woman work so hard. *Her son would never have permitted this!*

One morning she saw Oyé Wašté fall. The long skirt she wore was an impediment and she had tripped over it. *I can hem that,* Granny thought. *And I can help her since no one else is doing it!*

"That's it!" she said indignantly to no one but Amos' wife who rarely responded. "If nobody there has the common decency to help an old woman, I'm gonna do it myself!" She wrapped a fringed shawl around her shoulders and went outside.

"Wait!" she called when she was a reasonable distance away so that she could be heard above the incessant wind. "I'm coming to help."

The two women knew each other, but they had never really talked much. The English Oyé Wašté spoke was difficult to understand. Her words were out of order. *Maybe they put these words another way in Lakȟóta?*

"Help I want no," Oyé Wašté responded.

"I didn't ask if you needed help. I said I was helping, and I am! We'll do this together."

Accepting help from another old woman did not hurt Oyé Wašté's pride. They finished the task together, both out of breath but happy

414

in each other's company. Oyé Wašté asked for Granny's real name. She knew it had to be more than just the kinship name the Lakhóta use.

"My name? Lordy, it's been ages since anyone asked my given name. I've been Granny for almost as long as I can remember. My name is Coffee."

"Coffee?"

"Massah thought my skin was the color of his morning cup of coffee. My momma worked in the big house kitchen and Massah liked his coffee with cream. She made it for him every mornin'. Momma had given me another name, I was told, but Massah would have none of it. 'Said, "That's child's name is Coffee.' and what he said was law."

"Your father? He mad?"

"I ... I'm not sure who my pappy is."

Oyé Wašté was appalled.

"In a way, I was lucky though. Momma married a fine black man later, the only pappy I ever knew." She paused. "I talk too much, I know, but it's a pleasure to find anyone who listens. When I do find a listener ... like you," she said affectionately, "then I run on and on! My goodness, I surely do!"

Chapter 8

Waníkiya Tȟúŋpi Aŋpétu wašté yuhá po!
Happy Christmas to all of you!

G ranny decided that Christmas Day celebrations would be
held in her cabin which, as the largest one, would be most
accommodating for the festivities she planned. She
remembered Christmas as her favorite day! Oh, the planning for it
then! The baking and decorating! Happiness seemed to permeate the
walls of the Big House and grace the entire plantation! Though the
"house niggas" were never treated as equals, on those days before
Christmas they were treated most kindly, as though the Baby Jesus
would look on Massah and Missus with loving eyes and forget all
the evil things they did the rest of the year.

She knew the others thought it odd that she had harvested so many
orange-red rose hips in the fall…thought it odd that she threaded
string through them and the dried white beans from the
distribution…hip, bean, hip, bean until she had long garland to wrap
around the braided grass wreaths she made for every door.

Tears came to the priest's eyes when she presented him a cradle
made from the scrap wood she had lashed together with wild grape
vines. Atop a bed of dried grass, she had laid a cornhusk Jesus and
gave Him shiny button eyes pulled from her own blouse whose
sparkle seemed to give the doll life. "Sprinkle him with some of that
water you priests use so he'll be holy!"

And yes, there'd be music too! Amos could play Bastiat's fiddle.
His timing was sloppy, but he was capable of screeching out some
semblance of a rhythm to dance to. Indians were supposed to be
good with drums, she had thought, but she could not get them to say
they'd bang a beat on her old pot. She'd do it herself! On this day,
they'd be merry!

On Christmas Eve, Ah-Duo experienced pre-labor pains as her

416

body prepared for birthing. She was afraid and hoped they'd go away. Walking was difficult. The baby was in a head down position now and the pressure on her pelvis made movement cumbersome. Still, she helped Granny with the decorating, tying colorful strips of scrap cloth into bright bows to be hung on the inside of the windows.

On Christmas Eve, Niglíču gave no thought to celebrating or decorating or the Christ Child soon to come. Her mind tortured her with plans of how she would kill Dawes in a few days. It would be on the 29th, the day of the massacre. It would take place on Wounded Knee hill, the place to which he went each year to relive that day.

Twisted thoughts had entered her dreams of the past few days. The wolf, her spirit guide, slept in a manger, awakening to make the Sign of the Cross with his paws and howling, "Kill him! Kill him!" The dreams were short and mostly incoherent. They evaporated on her waking, leaving her only feelings of unrest. The priest. The wolf. The Bible. The necklace. Her mind embraced one and then the other. Her mood was foul. Because the others had been so involved with barn building and decorating, she was able to hide her ill temper from everyone except the dog.

So attuned to her moods, Mountain followed her everywhere, in silent support. Niglíču noticed, although the others did not, how the hairs on the back of his neck lifted ever so slightly when someone approached her. "It's ok," she reassured the dog. "I'm fine," she said rubbing his neck behind his ears.

"He likes you more than me!" Bastiat teased, but Niglíču didn't smile. He called Mountain to come to him but the dog uncharacteristically refused. The priest, still worried about what plans she had, sent up a prayer. "Lord, let the dog protect her if she travels in harm's way."

*****

A sprig of jade plant decorated with a red bow hung upside on the top of the door frame in the Bordeaux home. There was no mistletoe, so Julia took a cutting from the precious old jade plant she had inherited from her now deceased mother. But Mr. Bordeaux did not kiss her as they squeezed past each other to carry the appetizers into the dining room. He would, later, when the guests arrived. Then there'd be an audience of the most affluent townspeople. And she'd kiss him back too with sparkle in her eyes because her father, The Captain as he was affectionally called by those who knew and loved him, would also be there and she did not want him to know how much she despised her husband.

Because Dawes was also a prominent person of the town as a store owner, he, too, was invited that Christmas Eve night. His impeccable dress did not, however, match his uncouth behavior. As self-appointed bartender, he was generous in pouring the alcohol for the other guests but was free-handedly more liberal in pouring whiskey for himself. Soon he became boisterous.

The Captain took Julia aside. "Why is he here? Isn't there something shady about his business dealings with the Indians?

"I know, Papa, but Mr. Bordeaux wanted all the town's business people invited, showing no favoritism, and so Dawes could not be excluded. Let me go speak to him and see if I can quiet him down."

Dawes watched her approach, his lecherous stare fixed on the lacey low cut bodice of her dress.

"Julia," he said, and the use of her first name insinuated an intimacy they never shared, "May I pour you a drink?"

"Actually, MISTER Dawes, I came over to ask that you refrain from drinking any more. Frankly, you are becoming quite loud."

"Am I? Hmm. Then why don't you and I go into that little room over there and you can show me how to be really quiet?"

She swallowed hard. How she wanted to slap him! But was it worth ruining the party? Red-faced, she walked away with his clipped snicker echoing in her ears.

But Mr. Bordeaux saw her flaming face from across the room. He strode over to her. "What did he say to you?"

"Nothing, really. He's drunk. The party is almost over. He'll be gone soon. Let it be."

"I will NOT just let it be!" he said loud enough for heads to turn in his direction. He smiled to reassure the guests and walked over to Dawes. "Let's go outside…to talk."

"I'd like that a lot, Bordeaux. Sure you're man enough?"

They walked into the privacy behind the house. Bordeaux did not plan to talk, nor did Dawes anticipate conversation. But Dawes did not expect Bordeaux to whip out a pistol and aim it at his face.

"Hear me and hear me good," he said. "Get out of here and stay out of here. Leave town. It's not safe for you here, if you get what I mean."

"Go ahead and pull the trigger, big man. See If you can explain my brains splattered all over the Christmas snow in your neat little yard. You would not dare. Face it, Bordeaux. I know who you are and what you did with Soft Feather. I know, and I wrote it down too. Gave it to someone for safekeeping, I did. If I show up dead one day, the authorities will know where to look."

Boldly, Dawes slapped away the gun and spat on the ground. "Watch yourself, Bordeaux. Watch yourself!"

He staggered back to the store through the dusting of snow and never noticed the other footprints in the back of Bordeaux's house. Two guests, married to other people, had separated from the party for their own merrymaking in the barn. They had seen and heard it all.

*****

Silent night. Holy night. All is calm. All is… "Not all calm. Not here," Bastiat mumbled, interrupting his own rendition of the hymn that he imagined himself singing with a choir. He had argued with White Birch an hour before. She insisted that it was going to snow and snow hard in the morning. "Don't go to the village! You can say Mass for them another day!"

Reasoning wasn't working. Christmas Day Mass must be celebrated on Christmas Day, he explained. Maybe the night before, he conceded, but never the day after!

"Does it matter?" she argued. "Are you sure it was on THAT day that Jesus was born? I don't know on what day I was born. What is important is that I was born!" Seeing his hard face, she switched tactics.

"Aren't you happy I was born? Even if you don't know what day?"

"Of course!" he admitted.

"Then the people will still be happy Jesus was born on the day after Christmas?"

"I surely hope so."

"Then you will celebrate that they are happy…when it isn't snowing. When you won't get lost in a storm or freeze to death."

He sighed. This felt like being married.

419

But she was right. It did snow on Christmas morning…big heavy flakes that quickly accumulated into a few inches. He was up before dawn, said Mass quietly so as not to wake anyone, and went out to the horses. He had a special treat for them! The peppermint sticks Dawes sold had an artistic flair to them now… a red stripe was added, twisting around the white J for Jesus, or shepherd's staff depending on how the candy was held. The priest did not think about the supposed symbolic message of the candy…white for purity, red for Christ's blood. He did not think of folkloric origin as a way to keep children quiet during the long Christmas Mass. As he crunched one between his teeth, he only thought of the flavor! He broke off a piece and gave it to Ned.

"Merry Christmas, my friend." Another he gave to Dumpling. "And to you too, old man. Now don't go breaking your teeth on these!" The other animals demanded theirs and he gave them pieces such as they could handle.

He took down a hammer from the wall and laid the remaining sticks between two layers of the cloth. Then he smashed them! He would put some crumbs in the hotcakes, some in the coffee and make a treat for everyone!

Shortly after, Ike heard him bustling around the stove and soon a uniquely springtime scent filled the air. Mint? Coffee? Hotcakes? He peered over the edge of the loft. "What are you making down there?"

"Come and see! Get dressed and go call everyone to come for breakfast!"

The cow had produced enough cream for butter and the priest slathered it over the large stacks of brown cakes. As a gift to all of them, he had purchased a large bottle of maple syrup from New York. He placed it on the table as though a centerpiece.

When all had gathered, eager for the meal, Grasshopper stopped them. "This is the priest's special day. On this morning, we will ask the priest to make his special ceremony, his Mass. We all will listen to his words. We all will thank the Creator, the Great Spirit, for what we have. Then we will eat!"

"You honor me," Bastiat said, with tears welling over his eyelids. After a brief preparation, he began the readings with Isaiah:

"For a child has been born for us, a son has been given us …."

*****

420

Tȟašíyagmuŋka *Meadowlark,* Amos' wife, was not comfortable with the idea that everyone should be in her cabin. She didn't like visitors or anything that broke her routine. Though she was not physically injured at the massacre, her gentle nature could not find a way to integrate the past horror with present circumstances.

She had not been part of the caravan on the way to Wounded Knee. With Amos and her son, they had already established a home on the reservation, but she had been happy knowing more relatives were coming. "I will go meet them!" she had said excitedly, her face beaming with anticipation. "You stay here!" she told Amos. "Do not go near the cavalry!"

He needed no coaxing. His military career had started more to the south and their targets were the Comanche and Apache. The senseless killing on both sides had sickened him. The slaughter of a people's food source, the buffalo, was incomprehensible. And he couldn't believe the ex-slaves' pretention that white men would think everyone was equal. He was tired of watching these same black men treat Indians with the same lack of respect, the same inhumanity, they were shown by whites.

One day he was so disgusted, he just rode away. As a deserter, he could not have risked going to Wounded Knee with his wife that day. He could have been recognized.

When their first guests arrived, Meadowlark retreated to her chair in the far corner by the window and sat looking out at the falling snow.

Ike and Bastiat were greeted with the heavy smell of roasting turkey. How that propelled the priest back in time and place to his childhood home! "How did you ever get turkey?" the priest exclaimed with his nose up in the air, drawing in the grease-gamey smell with a smile on his face.

"I sent my grandson. He was not to come home until he found a turkey. He found two!" she bragged.

*****

After dinner, Amos dragged the heavy sacks in, laden with the treasure they found at the deserted town site. One by one, he took out the pieces and only Bastiat and Granny recognized them as the cast-offs that they were. The small pot Oyé Wašté was so excited to see, Granny recognized as a chamber pot. The old pliers Ike opened and closed Bastiat knew would soon break apart at the rusted bolt The speckled enamel coffee pot the cousins admired would be found to leak. The hairline crack across the china plate would split the dish in two after several scrubbings. The zinc that coated the galvanized washboard was already flaking off. The rust would stain the clothes more than whiten them. But how appreciative the people were! Even if the treasures were short-lived in their usefulness, all would remember the novelty of them!

Amos played the fiddle though no one danced to the music. Instead, they swayed back and forth to the unfamiliar beat. Há Sápa put his arm around Niglíču. "Are you happy today?" She nodded yes. Today she was. Today she did not let herself think of what she was going to do. She leaned into him and he kissed her hair.

*****

Hokšíyuha kte.
She is going to have a baby.

Ah-Duo looked at all her gifts. There was the parfleche stuffed filled with cattail down from Oyé Wašté. "For the ačhésli *diaper*. It keeps the baby dry." Ah-Duo pictured the old woman by the riverbank, bending the long stalks to get to the dried flower spikes.

Niglíču had given her soft doeskin squares which when folded would hold the diaper fluff in place. Pretty Bird and White Birch had sewn long gowns from blanket material. "A winter baby needs warm clothes." Granny knitted thick-stitched booties.

She lifted Ike's soft gift, a cup shaped pouch of rabbit skin, and held it to her face. The fur tickled her nose and she sneezed. Ah-Duo had not wanted a cradleboard. She wanted a mei dai, a traditional Chinese baby sling. Wanting to please her, Ike had found a Chinese seamstress in Deadwood who cut and measured the wide scarf…longer than his height…that Ah-Duo would someday wrap around herself and the baby and knot in the back. Ike designed the pouch to keep the baby warm in the sling. "For… uŋkíčhiŋčapi," he had said when he shyly handed her his gift and walked away. Not understanding, Ah-Duo had looked at Niglíču for translation, "Our child" she had whispered back.

*****

In roundabout ways, Niglíču confirmed Dawes' habits. Without arousing suspicion, she now knew that Dawes went to Wounded Knee hill the afternoon of Dec. 28 and did not return until the next night. Ah-Duo described how he dressed himself in his old uniform, went to the shed and left carrying a bulky satchel.

On the 27th, Niglíču went to town and tacked another note on a door: the shed door this time. It simply said, "I'll meet you there."

*****

Ah-Duo's back hurt. She arched her spine and bent back her head, but it didn't help.

"The baby sits lower today," Pretty Stone observed. "He is getting ready."

"But do not worry. We are here with you. We have seen many babies born and we know what to do," White Birch added confidently.

*****

Bastiat kept a handwritten calendar, crossing out each day as evening approached. No mark was yet on the 28th. The sun was yet high in the sky. Niglíču knew Há Sápa was taking his mother to visit relatives for a few days, so she was sure he would not come to see her. She would lie and say she was going hunting with him in the morning. She would lie again and say she should be there the night before too, so they could get an early start together. It would not be unheard of. Grasshopper would think she was safe, and he would not know that she was already on her way to Wounded Knee. Niglíču felt uncomfortable with the deception, but knew it was a necessary one. They would have never let her go alone.

Her grandfather was napping when she left in the late afternoon.

*****

Dawes stood before his hand-hewn, rectangular, floor-length mirror, wearing only his faded, red union suit. Sucking in his still well-muscled abdomen, he smoothed the material over it and twisted from frontal view to side, admiring himself. The room was chilly. He had let the fire go out. His cavalry uniform was neatly draped over a chair. His shiny black boots rested on the floor beside it.

He took a scissor and trimmed his beard precisely, being careful not to uncover his scar, and the tiny red hairs fell in miniature piles at his feet. He combed back his hair and cut off the errant curl that had rolled over his earlobe.

After he was finished dressing, he again admired himself, adjusting the tilt of the mirror to his full advantage. "Those eleven years never even touched me," he said out loud. "I look as good as I did before and maybe better," he continued, notching his belt one hole tighter only to prove that he could.

He disapproved of the faint blood stains on the knees of his light blue pants. He wouldn't have minded them anywhere else. *A soldier should have blood stains after all,* he told himself. It wasn't, however, doing a soldier's deed that gave him those blood-stained knees. He wasn't being a soldier when he raped Wind Woman.

"Dammit!" he cursed. He hated it when his mind did that to him. Hated it when his conscience told him he had been... and was... a coward to go after women. He picked up the bottle on the windowsill and guzzled enough to numb those thoughts.

*****

Is this supposed to be happening? Shouldn't the cramps be in the front? She could have asked the women, but they weren't there. *Where? Why aren't you here?* They would have assured her it was normal, but because she was uncertain, she endured the pain alone until liquid dripped down her legs and puddled on the floor next to her bed. *Where are they?* She bent to wipe it up, not sure because of the color if it was urine, but then a deep, intense pain squeezed her abdomen. Bending forward, panicking, she moaned.

Ike heard her through the wall. "What's wrong? Are you ok?"

Another wave of pain ripped through her. "Help me! Please help me!"

He rushed into her cabin, saw her pale face, her tears, her arms gripping her bulging belly.

"I'll get the women!"

Pretty Stone took the leadership role while the others assisted. She examined her and declared she would give birth to the child soon. They made Ah-duo squat. One woman balanced her arms in front while another other rubbed and supported her back.

"You are open," Pretty Stone said. "Push."

*****

The three men sat in Bastiat's cabin, but the sounds pierced the walls. Moans turned into cries, cries turned into screams. Hours passed. Screams became exhausted moans. Ike couldn't stand it any longer and went outside in the cold, leaving Grasshopper and Bastiat alone.

"Should it take this long?" Bastiat asked. His hands shaking from nervousness jiggled the coffee in his cup.

"Sometimes it does. Sometimes it can be days."

"Days?"

The old warrior nodded. He did not add that if it took that long there was not usually a good outcome for either mother or child.

"Shouldn't they get a midwife?"

"She went away. She never came back."

Ike passed by the window. "He acts like a father," Bastiat said. Grasshopper nodded.

The priest continued, "If my wife hadn't died, I would have had a child. Maybe more than one."

Both men became quiet. Only muffled sounds came through the wall. Maybe Ah-Duo had fallen asleep.

Grasshopper opened his medicine pouch and took out the tintype he had been carrying there for so many years. He handed it to the priest. "Look at this. The man was a father."

"Who are these people?"

"I don't know their names."

"But you knew them?"

"Only one. The father. For just a little while." The old warrior became quiet again and then asked a seemingly unrelated question.

"Catholics tell you things they have done wrong. Things you call sins. And you forgive them. This is true? How can this be that you

425

can forgive another person who has done nothing wrong to you?"

Bastiat gave the Church-appropriate answer. "The Lord works through me. I am just his instrument. Only God forgives sins."

"Does your God forgive every sin?"

"It is not that simple. The person has to be sorry for it. The person has to try never to do the sin again. And the person must do penance."

"Penance?"

"Make up for that sin."

"This penance is hard to do?"

"Sometimes."

"I think I have done this thing you call sin," Grasshopper confessed.

"Tell me." Bastiat lowered his eyes and made The Sign of the Cross.

*****

"The day was hot, and I was sitting on a small hill overlooking the banks of Wounded Knee Creek. I can even now see the slow water flowing. Peaceful. Flies buzzed around. I swatted at them. My horse grazed in the thick grass in the small dip of the land behind me. I could hear the swish of his tail. It was a day for dreaming.

"I was almost asleep, nodding I think, when I heard the splashing. There, coming around the bend, was the wašíču kicking over rocks in the stream making the water flow ugly brown. What was he looking for? Gold? Was there ever gold here? Stupid wašíču! Two pack animals... mules...followed along on the banks, pulling up the grasses as they grazed. They carried tools. I could see the handles. Who would he sell them to? More wašíču to rip up the land?

"My rifle was beside me, and I picked it up and aimed for his head. I did not intend to shoot him, but I enjoyed keeping his head in my sights as he splashed along. Then he stopped. Opened his pants. Urinated in the water. I thought, my people will drink this water with the wašíču urine in it. It angered me. I fired a shot high over his head as a warning.

"I think if he had become afraid and rushed to his animals and tried to get away, I would have let him go. Even if he approached me boldly, I might have spared him for his courage. But no. He was terrified of me. His body showed me this, but he waved his arms in

426

greeting and shouted 'Kola!" over and over, pointing to himself.

'Kola!' As though he was my friend! But he could not even say the word correctly. My khóla! I became more angry! He was still yelling 'Kola! Kola!' when he reached his mules. My 'kola' pulled his rifle to shoot me, but the fool did not have it loaded.

"I did not want to waste more bullets on this man. I took an arrow and sent it into the ground by his feet. He jumped out of the way still fumbling with the gun, putting bullets in it. I sent another arrow to block this move, and so I made him dance to the left and right as I spent my arrows. Finally, he got his gun loaded and he aimed it at me. I yelled to him, "Khóla" and I sent an arrow into his heart."

They sat in a long silence.

"What did you do next?" Bastiat said evenly and, without emotion, as years of practice allowed him to do.

"I walked down to his body and made sure he was dead. Then I took his mules and left him there. Later, when I opened the bags, I found the picture. It meant nothing to me at first, but then I kept seeing the boy looking up to his father. He would not see this man again and would never know what had happened to him. This made me sad. I have kept the picture with me ever since and it's always hung heavy around my neck."

"Are you sorry for what you did?"

Grasshopper knew what the priest expected him to say; that he was sorry for killing an innocent man. He was not sorry for that, though. *Not really,* he thought to himself. *I would do that again. He was the enemy of my people.* But he was sorry for how his actions would have affected the boy. He knew that feeling well. He tried to explain this to Bastiat.

"You ask for forgiveness for what you did to that boy?" Bastiat asked softly.

"Yes."

"If God forgives you, you must do penance. You must do something to counteract your sin."

"What?"

"I don't know. I cannot see how anything would fit the offense."

"Then I am not forgiven?"

Bastiat thought about this carefully. This warrior was not Catholic. He had never lived by the rules the Church had put forth. Could a priest possibly absolve him of a killing that in his warrior's eyes was not a sin? Could he forgive a man for what was done indirectly to another person if the original offense was not a sin?

"I think," the priest said slowly, "that only you can absolve yourself of this sin. I think you must find a way in your own heart to make this right."

Chapter 9

Wičhóȟ'aŋ kiŋ lé ečhúŋ.
She has done this deed.

T he last thing Dawes did before he went to the shed to get his ritual supplies was to reverently take down his Whitworth rifle from its hooks above the fireplace. The barrel gleamed. While dust covered the mantle and cobwebs looped in ceiling corners, the rifle was kept pristine. He caressed the rifle, running his fingers sensuously down the nearly yard long barrel.

"Ah, do you remember Spotsylvania Courthouse how Sedgwick chided his men for ducking in ditches when they heard your bullet fly? Like a whistle it was! Said not to fear. 'They couldn't hit an elephant at that range!' That's what he told them. He didn't know your power! He didn't know the skill our snipers had! Yeah, well, he learned! One lovely bullet hit old Sedg's head!"

He laughed and then wrapped a woolen blanket around his rifle, locked the door behind him and went to the shed.

*****

Partway there, Niglíču rested and prepared her horse for battle. Burrs had knotted up the horse's long tail, but she didn't have time to untangle it. Instead, she poked feathers in it, a crude version of a war bonnet train.

She then opened a small buckskin bag that contained red paint. Rubbing some onto her wet hands, she made a paste that covered her palms. She put two upside down handprints on either side of the horse's neck like the old warriors had said they did. Applying this 'do-or-die' mission symbol was supposed to give her courage, but instead it frightened her. *I could die today. Is it ever a good day to*

429

die?

To her own face, she painted an angle resembling an open snout. With the vertex by her ear, one leg of the angle stretched to the corner of her eye and the other halfway to her chin. When she added upper and lower fangs, she hoped she had created the illusion of a wolf's bloody jaw. On impulse, she took her reddened finger and painted a cross on her forehead.

The bear claw necklace was in her medicine pouch. She took it out, held it to her nose and breathed in the spirit of it. Its faint musky scent soothed her, but when she put it on and the cold claws touched her breast, she shivered.

Stay calm! She mounted Kičhí and headed for Wounded Knee.

*****

Unknown to Niglíču, Mountain lagged behind. The pony's familiar scent was easy to follow, and the old dog was compelled to be with her.

*****

Dawes urged his horse into a trot. The rise of the burial ground was in sight. *Has it been a whole year since I was last here?* Before the ascent, he paused to savor the feeling of arrival. He closed his eyes and raised his head to the sun and prayed.

I tried to be true, Father, to the mission you called me to do. They are almost all gone now. The ones left I have subdued. The old ones are dying away. I heard another one wandered out into the snow somehow. Had some crazy injun name about teeth. Haha! Yessir! Almost all the warriors, gone! Whoever is left is wasting his life as a drunk, thanks to me!"

He bowed his head. *I am your servant, Lord. Clearing the Promised land for the Chosen People.*

But then a voice whispered to him. *Not all. Not all. Not all gone.* He looked for its source. It had seemed so real!

"YET!" he yelled aloud. "Not all dead YET!"

One more bitch to go. One more! he thought to himself.

He set up his small tent by the soft, sloping side of the mound, and imagined with perverse pleasure what had happened here eleven years before. He started his fire with the wood he had brought. The flames snapped in the whipping bitterly cold wind and he stood to the side watching them and thinking of the note. "I'll meet you there."

I'm ready for you, bitch. I know you wrote that and I'm surely ready!

The sky was clear, and the night would be bright. There had been a full moon on Christmas Day.

When the flames died down, he crouched warming his hands over the coals. *Damn! Were my fingers this cold that day?*

Then he figured the rifle barrel would have given off so much heat from round after round of shooting that he wouldn't have noticed the cold at all! The thought made him laugh. *What a day that was!*

But he wasn't using his Whitworth that day. No, that was hardly a sniper attack where one bullet counted for everything. He needed to fire lots of bullets, and fast! There was so much pleasure to be had watching Indian after Indian fall. Pop! Pop! Pop! and down they crumbled! Beautiful in his eyes! That Springfield unloaded 8 to 10 rounds per minute. 8 to 10 deaths he had hoped!

His Whitworth leaned against the tent, loaded. Once she was in his sights, one bullet was all he'd need.

*****

Both White Birch and Pretty Stone were panicking, although they hid this from Ah-Duo. "You're fine," they encouraged. "Just a little more time," they said. And yet, though the contractions were strong and the birth canal wide, no baby head was crowning. *How could this be? The baby's head was surely down. Why didn't it descend?*

Ah-Duo's tortured cries had reduced Ike to tears. Finally, the door opened and Pretty Stone walked in.

"The child cannot be born."

Not comprehending at first, the men looked at her, dazed. Finally, Grasshopper spoke.

"The baby is dead?"

"No, not yet."

"The mother?"

"No." There was a pause, and a barely audible whisper, "Not yet."

Ike jumped up. "NO!" he cried, but Grasshopper's still strong arm restrained him from immediately going to Ah-Duo.

431

"Tell us. What has happened?" Bastiat asked.

"The arm is being born first," she whispered.

The words hammered Ike back to his childhood. It was another long winter night in a succession of hungry ones. Winter had been hard. Their thiyóšpaye had been looking forward to the arrival of this baby. Ike had longed for a little cousin to bring smiles to their faces again, but this was not to be. While his uncle went to get a woman from another village known for her midwifery skills, his aunt hemorrhaged. Both baby and mother died.

"No! No!" Ike pulled away from Grasshopper and left the cabin.

"Isn't there anything you can do?" Bastiat moaned.

"We are not wíŋyaŋ hokšíyuzapi. We don't know what to do ... and the midwife is too far away."

Ike burst into the other cabin and Oyé Wašté immediately drew up the blanket to cover Ah-Duo's nakedness. "Quiet!" she commanded. "She is resting."

But Ah-Duo's eyes were open and yet vacant. Exhaustion and pain had driven her into semiconsciousness. He could see her body grip with the next contraction but no reaction to pain appeared on her features.

"Hold her," Oyé Wašté said. "She has not much longer to live."

That's impossible! Impossible! She cannot die! If the arm is in the way, move the arm! Get it out of the way! Do it! his mind screamed. *"Oh God! Help us! Help me think!"*

And with those words, his mind cleared the clutter away. He only saw himself with horses and one mare in particular. She had struggled to give birth and his father had reached into her and moved the baby somehow, pulled the forelegs forward and the filly slipped out alive. He must reach into Ah-Duo! But even as he thought it, he looked at his large hands. Never could he do it. He turned his head away from her.

Oyé Wašté laid her hand upon his to comfort him. How skeletal her bony hand appeared! Weakened tendons and joints had folded her hand over lengthwise, slimming it. So narrow it was now, almost useless, with thick blue veins popping out over the dry papery skin.

So tiny, he thought. *So tiny.*

He looked at the old woman. "Will you help me?"

"How?" she asked hopelessly, but then when she saw the seriousness of his expression, she added, "If I can."

432

"Maybe we can move the baby around." He pulled the blanket back, shocked at the blood.

I will not think. I just will do. Forcing back nausea, he divorced himself from the reality of the scene. *There is a task to do. I will do it.*

Too weak to squat, she lay on her back with legs spread and knees apart. Methodically, his hand went to her vagina. With the next contraction, a little hand appeared. He touched it. The fingers bent. Astonished, he tried to clasp it but when the contraction ceased, it retracted.

Love surged through him.

"I can't do it! My hands are too big," he said to the old woman. Taking her hand, he pleaded. "Your hand…it's so small and narrow…push the arm back…push the shoulder back so the head can move into place!"

"No, no! I will break the arm! Do not ask me to do this thing!"

"Stop this!" Pretty Stone commanded, pushing Oyé Wašté aside. "What are you doing!" White Birch exclaimed. "You will kill her!"

"Go! Both of you, go! Go, or I will make you go!" The cousins stepped back.

He turned to Oyé Wašté. "You have to do this," he said.

"My hands! I can't."

"No. This hand is perfect. All you need to do is slide the arm backwards. I will do the rest."

After the next futile contraction, the old woman pinched the tiny hand between her two fingers and pushed it higher up the birth canal. Another contraction forced it forward again.

"You have to take a chance!" Ike urged. "If the arm breaks, we will heal it. Push it back until the hand points backwards." She paled but did as he said. Finally, the pressure released.

"I think it has turned," she said. "I think it did not break."

No hand appeared with the next contraction. Ike massaged Ah-Duo's belly hoping to manipulate the body so the head would shift into position.

Ah-Duo's body convulsed with another contraction, her eyelids fluttered open and she moaned with the pain. Through a haze, she saw Ike and Oyé Wašté, but they seemed miles away.

"Push now!" they yelled to her. "Push!"

She screamed with the next contraction, but the baby's head

crowned. After another, the head was born and with the next, the baby boy slid out into Ike's hands. He held him, wet and bloody, dumbfounded with the joy of it.

*****

Niglíču saw him on the hill next to the white plume of rising smoke. Saw his uniform: dark blue jacket, light blue pants against the grey sky. Saw his little tent. Saw his hobbled chestnut horse, like Ned save for the white blaze, facing away from the wind. She was close. Close enough to see he was holding a bottle. Close enough to see the rifle against the tent.

I could shoot him right now and end this. But he wouldn't know who did it. He'd be dead before he could even turn around, but even if still alive, the sun behind me would blind him. No, I won't kill him yet. It's too early. Tomorrow is the day. Tomorrow morning he will die. She slid back down the hill and hurried to her horse hidden in a copse of trees.

*****

Ah-Duo moaned and her hand went to her belly. Deflated. The baby had been born. Now she remembered. She remembered Ike holding her baby. "Hokšílala, a little boy," Ike had said as he laid the newborn near her breast. The child's lips moved. He seemed to be searching, so Ike lifted him closer. The infant soon found her nipple and sucked sporadically. Content, but exhausted from the long birth and significant blood loss, Ah-Duo, shivering, fell into a twilight sleep. He covered her. He wrapped a blanket around the baby.

"Hokšílala, mičhíŋkši, my son," he whispered, "will you let me be your father?" He fondled the infant's pink fingers. "You reached out your hand to me. If you were my true son, I would name you Napé Yuǧáte, He Raises His Hand."

Napé, Hand, a good name, Oyé Wašté thought. "Let me hold him," she said.

*****

I want him to know I'm here. She felt perverse deliciousness thinking

434

about him wondering when she'd attack. *Would he sleep? Would he spend the night in watchful waiting?*

She hugged her horse. "Will you do this with me? Will you take me through this?" Kičhí snorted. "Sssssssh…he'll hear you."

She broke a branch from the willow and prepared it as a coup stick, tying feathers she took from the horse's battle ornaments to the top. Swishing the branch around frightened the horse. "No. Be calm." she whispered. "I won't hit you."

Her decision to count coup on him in the dark was frightening, and yet she felt exhilarated. The trick was to surprise him. But the wind whooshed across the grasses noisily. The sound would deaden the thud of the horse's hooves against the hillside.

Dawes sat by his fire, facing the disappearing sunset. She'd approach from his back…taking the horse on a slow walk until she reached the crest. Then she'd charge…touch him… and race off. Before he could use his gun. She'd have to be fast!

They ascended the hill. Kičhí, sensing her rider's nervousness was difficult to keep to a walk. At the crest, Niglíču propelled her forward, charging towards Dawes, charging towards the fire. Dawes heard her coming. Shocked, he twisted around…went to draw his pistol.

But Kičhí was no warhorse. She had never charged a man. Never charged to a fire. Dawes was standing when she swerved at the last minute. Her hindquarters slammed into his chest, and he fell backwards. Landing on his right shoulder, his arm dipped into the fire. He screamed his rage.

With the opportunity to count coup gone, Niglíču disappeared into the darkness. She may not have touched him as planned, but now he definitely knew she was there!

*****

His hand blistered immediately. He rolled over onto his arm to smother the heavy but now scorching material covering his forearm and saved the skin there. But his shoulder was damaged. He couldn't raise his arm above his waist. Now he was scared. *How can I use the rifle?*

The unbearable pain came later. He added more wood to the fire to enlighten the area around him, laid on his belly with his cocked multi shot Springfield beneath him resting on his left arm, burned right index finger curled over the trigger, and waited for her return.

*****

Niglíču did not know how badly he was injured. That he was injured at all made him both more vulnerable and more desperately dangerous. Gone was the innocent bravado of before. This was no game and she was thoroughly frightened. She touched the bear claw necklace under her blanket shawl and thought of Bear Teeth. *I know what you mean now.*

Breathing heavily, she crouched beside her horse and scanned the hill, wondering if he was still there. Suddenly the bushes behind her rustled. She whipped around, knife in readiness, when she heard a familiar bark. Mountain! The exhausted dog padded over to her and sank to the ground. She cradled his head. "Oh, Mountain," she said tearfully. "You've walked so far!" He closed his eyes, content to be with her now, while she rubbed behind his ears.

"Hey Bitch! You out there still?"

She didn't answer… did not want to reveal her location. His voice seemed from far away on the hill, so she was safe.

"Come mornin', let's you and me talk. I got no hankerin' to be killin' you. You'd only get in trouble for killing me. They'd come after that little homestead ya'll have out there. Might get ugly."

She stayed quiet.

"You ain't answering, but I'm bettin' you're out there. Lemme see if I can find you."

He aimed for a random shot and pulled the trigger. The bullet sped into the darkness, far from where she was. He aimed again and fired. This time he was even farther away. A few seconds later he changed directions. She heard the bullet whiz. Kičhí whinnied.

Dawes laughed. "I know where you're hidin' now." He fired again to where the sound had originated, but by then she was gone.

She retreated out of range and sat down, shaking. *How am I going to do this?* Grateful for the dog's watchfulness, she closed her eyes.

*****

"Come. Sit here on my lap. Let's look at this book together." She

436

was a little girl and the strange man in a black robe called her to him. The book fascinated her. It was heavy. It had many pages and colored ribbons separated them. Pictures of bearded white men in long robes and a soft faced woman with a blue head shawl were hiding in the book. She had once searched for them. There were a few sad pictures too.

"Look here," he said. "These are numbers. See? One, two, three. Let's count them." He pointed to the strange shapes, and they said the words together. Numbers.

"Each number has a rule. Number 1 says to love God. You do love God, don't you?" She nodded yes to please him. He went down the list. "Number 5 says to never kill. Never kill another person. You must remember that. Never!"

*****

She startled awake. The dog had nudged her. There was motion on the hill. It was almost morning.

"Ready to talk?" he yelled. His voice split the frigid air.

"Why should I trust you won't shoot?" she yelled back.

"I won't have a rifle. I'll lay down my pistol." *She was talking. Good. Weakness. She's wavering.*

"Walk down the hill a little. Leave the weapons behind where I can see them."

When she steps from her cover, I can get her then, he thought. *But that would be too easy. Wanna play with her a little.*

He stepped into the open. Laid down the weapons. Walked a few steps down the hill. *Damn! My arm hurts! Ha! But my fingers are too cold to feel anything!*

"Put your hands up!" she yelled.

"I can try. But my arm...it's hurt...it won't raise up." He lifted one. The other was a half salute.

"Stay here!" she commanded the dog. She stepped into the open with her bow drawn.

"Now, that ain't friendly. I don't have weapons. Why should you?" She lowered the bow. "Let's talk here. Like this."

"What do you have against me, anyway?" he asked, affecting sincerity. "Yeah, I was at Wounded Knee. So were a lot of others. Why pick me?"

437

"You had my mother's knife."

"So what? I found it there. Nice knife. But you have it back. Ain't that enough?"

"You killed her!"

"How could you know that? You ain't barely past being a girl now. That was long ago."

"You have a scar. My mother cut you. I saw it."

"Listen now. I know you're upset. Losing someone ain't easy. I lost my brother. I know." He stepped forward. *If she was going to kill me outright, she'd have shot already. Let me lure her.* He stumbled. Fell. Careful he didn't hurt that arm. Cried out in pain. Lay there moaning.

With bow drawn again, she approached him cautiously. When she got close, he twisted his body, threw out his leg and tripped her. Immediately he was on her. Almost immediately Mountain was there, baring his fangs.

"Let me go or I'll tell him to kill you. He's killed before."

Dawes didn't doubt it. The dog was wolflike with lips drawn up and eyes slitted. He got off her slowly.

"Hold him!" she commanded as she had when the dog worked with the bull and cow. With hair raised along his back and head lowered and snarling, Dawes didn't dare move.

"I should kill you right now," Niglíču said.

Dawes didn't doubt that either, but he tried one last persuasion. "Tell me, before I die, did I have a...*say daughter*, he thought. *Daughter like I wanted one...* daughter?"

He saw a flicker of guilt. *She has a conscience. The priest got to her.*

She thought of her dream of long ago. The buck. She had the power of life over death for him. The knife was ready at his throat....

"I'll let you go if you promise to never come near here again. If you do, I'll kill you."

"That's an easy promise. Sure. Let me go and I'm outta this godforsaken place. For good. You have my word."

She walked behind him to his horse. He put his left hand on the horse's mane. Lifted his leg to the stirrup. His right hand did not go to the saddle but instead slid to his boot. She hadn't seen the derringer peeking over the top. Ignoring the pain, he whipped it out.

But Mountain saw the fast move and leapt at him. The gun

discharged. The dog fell. The arrow was released.

*****

Dawes lay gasping, blood spurting from his chest. Niglíču rushed to Mountain, but seeing there was no longer life in him, in fury, she turned to Dawes. His eyes locked onto hers, pleading for help. Straddling him, she snarled, "Feel my arrow!" Crying, she twisted it out of him. His eyes started to glaze. She pulled the obsidian knife from its sheath and lifted his beard. There was the scar. She jerked his head to the side and, thinking of her mother, sliced the other side of his face, linking the two. His eyes rolled back. "Go to Hell smiling!" she said standing up.

*****

I killed a man. She looked around at the bloody scene. There, his body, eyes open, hands on his chest as though to hold the blood in. *I did that.* There, on his side with gaping mouth, Mountain. She started to shake. *I need to leave here.*

Dawes' body, jellylike soft, wasn't easy to move but she wanted him off the grave. She dragged him to the edge of the hill and flipped him over, hoping he would roll. He did not. She flipped him once again and left him there, arms and legs unnaturally askew, staring at the sky.

She tore down the small tent and used the canvas to shroud Mountain. She tucked his legs into a natural pose of sleep. She would take him home. Only because she had trained her pony to kneel, a trick to impress Há Sápa, was she able to drape the heavy dog over the horses' shoulders. Kičhí danced nervously. "Stop! You've carried game before," she said thinking of the few times she had brought home a deer.

Dawes' horse, still hobbled from the night, had not wandered far. She freed his legs and slapped him on the rump. He'd go back to town riderless. She wondered if anyone would care.

The rifles, the pistol, even the derringer she took. Shivering, she mounted the pony and headed home.

Chapter 10

Uŋkíthawapi kiŋ iyéčhel ičháȟ'uŋyaŋpi kte.
We will raise him as if he were ours.

T he door to the priest's cabin opened and Bastiat passed wood back to a person inside. Niglíču heard a cry. Ah-Duo's child had been born. Dawes' child. Dawes…the man she had just killed that morning.

The door opened again, and Ike came out. He walked to the barn and did not see her watching him. Kičhí, hungry, whinnied and stamped her feet. He turned.

What will I say to him? She rode forward.

At first, he thought she had a successful hunt; the deer slung over the horse would be most welcome. But when he saw her face, the blood on her clothing, the shrouded kill, he made no sound when he went to greet her. She dismounted, looked him in the eyes and suddenly her knees felt weak. She reached for the horse to steady herself but grabbed onto the canvas shroud.

The enormity of her emotions overwhelmed her, and she started to fall. Immediately he caught her and held her against him. "What happened. Tell me!"

Feeling so safe in his embrace, she started to cry, pouring out her story between sobs. He caressed her hair, laid his unmoving lips against the top of her head and told her he loved her.

But then he held her off from him, inches that felt like miles, inches that felt like years away when he dreamed of holding her mother in just that way. A love that hadn't been realized. A love that could never be.

"I love you, mithúŋžaŋ, *my little niece*."

When have I said that before? Years ago. At Hot Springs. Years ago, when I realized the daughter could never be her mother.

"You did what needed to be done. You did what a warrior would do."

He pulled her close again and told her how proud he was of her. "I have a son," he finally said.

*****

"I will take care of the horse...the dog. If you want, I will tell the priest and the others." She nodded gratefully. "Go to your grandfather. You must tell him."

"Thakóža." That was all he said when he saw her take off her blanket, revealing the bloodied blouse and the two necklaces, teeth and claws, against it. She was different now. He could see it in her bearing. Fire. He called her by her child beloved name. "Phéta Akú".

"No. I keep my name. I will always be Niglíču. It is a name I have earned."

"He is dead?" Oyé Wašté said. "In a dream I saw you."

"Yes."

They had worried about her. Amos and his family had returned that morning without her. There had been no mention of a hunt.

She again told her story and could see the pride in their faces.

"You left him there? On the hill?"

"Yes."

"The child has been born."

"Yes. I saw Ike. When I am clean, I will go to see the baby."

She climbed the ladder into the loft, changed her clothes, removed the bear claw necklace, hung it on a nail and, nervous, left.

"The body cannot stay there," Grasshopper said. "It must be hidden."

Oyé Wašté knew what he was saying. He would ride there. "Take her pony. Even tired, she is fastest."

*****

Bastiat watched for her. When he saw her head for his cabin he went outside. With arms flung wide, he looked to her like Jesus.

"Granddaughter! Granddaughter!" he called to her, and she ran to him...into his embrace.

Never had he held her so tightly...never except once...when she

441

sat before him as a little girl on his horse that first time. "It was self-defense…self-defense," he said over and over, convincing himself while absolving her

The cousins moved aside shyly when she walked in. She had gained status in their eyes. Ike stood next to Ah-Duo, his arm on her shoulder. "Come and see our child," she said, pulling aside the blanket to show the baby's face.

A face of innocence. Creamy white skin. Black slanted eyes that looked, as yet unseeing, at her. Bristly dark hair with a glint of red.

*****

Cold. Like that day, Grasshopper thought riding through the open plains dusted with snow. It was better in the summer with the heat waving off the parched earth. Better brushing through the dried grass. Better when he was a boy and had not known what was to come.

He forced himself to think of good times. He thought of a day when he was but eight winters old, the day he got his name. He thought of the little girl there running with him through the arched grasses tickling their bare legs. They had hopped like the grasshoppers exposed by their paths. Hopped and laughed! Jumped and fell, rolling over each other in their innocence. When they walked back to the encampment he surprised her with his captured treasure. "Look what I hunted!" he had laughed showing her the grasshoppers he had tucked into the folded hem of his long shirt. "Food for all!" she had laughed back at him. "But you eat them first!"

Suddenly he no longer felt just a boy. Suddenly it was important that he impress her. He put the insect in his mouth and the tiny claws on its feet dug into the inside of his cheeks. He swished it around with his tongue and bit into its crunchiness. Swallowing hard, he looked at her triumphant. "Eat another," she dared him, calling him his new name, "Grasshopper, eat them all!"

It was easier to think of these things than the alternative nagging thought. *I should have killed him.*

The ride was hard on his stiff muscles although the pony's gait was smooth. This horse was worthy of a warrior. She responded to his every subtle coaxing…the slightest pressure from his knees, the reins across her neck…He was thankful that his granddaughter had such a horse in these times.

From a distance he squinted, seeing the black silhouettes of birds flying above the pure white of the snow dusted mound. Buzzards? Crows? Clearly they had found the body, their treasure in this land of scarcity. He slowed the pony to walk and approached the sacred place reverently.

He thought of that night of waiting eleven years before. The door to the church building would open and all eyes turned in hope of seeing a relative. Only some had been satisfied. Whose bodies were within that mound? Whose skeletal bones were embracing there? My grandson? He is there?

The supplies Dawes had brought with him were there near the neat firepit he had made of stone. Stones in a circle, carefully placed against each other to contain a fire. What kind of man took such care and yet caused so much destruction?

A flurry of wings greeted him when he crested the hill and looked down the side. The body had been ravaged. Red specks dotted the footprinted snow. He dismounted and walked closer, his body heating to a sweat.

A glow of satisfaction warmed him even more when he saw his granddaughter's handiwork, the face sliced into a smile, one side a fresh wound, the other an ugly scar. He crouched beside the body and pulled aside his jacket. The arrow had gone straight to his heart. He would have died quickly.

"Penance... Only you can absolve yourself of this sin."

He spoke to the body that he would later hide. "My revenge is this. I will love your son. I will raise him in our ways. I will teach him to be all that you were not. I will protect him with my life."

He walked to the top of the mound, lifted his face to the sky. He raised his arms, open to the power of the Wakáŋ.

"Grandfather of all beings! Spirit of all directions, I call to you. Hear me!

This I will do!"

About the Author
Paul Oscar Wybrant

Educated at Stanford, Yale and National Taiwan University, Oscar Wybrant is now retired from a colorful career as Air Force linguist, government liaison and world traveling engineering consultant. Residing in California with his wife, he finds peace in his garden with his birds and squirrels but continues his education with a passion for history and the preservation of our great American heritage.

Raised in dust bowl Colorado, his early life drove his obsession with the culture of indigenous peoples. Later he used his linguistic skills to become an early member of the Lakota Language Consortium, with the goal of learning and then passing on the language to the people with whom the language originated.

Inspired at the graveside of Ziŋtkála Núni on Wounded Knee hill, Wybrant's story of a fictionalized survivor, Niglíču, was born and later developed into this novel of struggle, adaptation and triumph set in the years following the massacre.

About the Author
Florence D'Angelo

In a world marked by division, it is my privilege to present a story of people of different cultures who, once divided by tragedy, are now united by first, understanding, then, forgiveness and finally by love. And who is better to illustrate how that can be achieved than a child, vulnerable and yet so powerful?

As a former elementary school teacher, I know how uniting behind the best interests of children transforms lives. In my novel, Niglíču, you will see this. Though the setting is well over a hundred years ago, the message is timeless. We are more alike than different, and we are called by God to love each other.

Raised on a small island in the Bronx, I am an unlikely person to tell a story of the Lakȟóta people but, strangely, I was drawn to study the language of a people whose words had been taken away. What a tragedy to lose words! What a tragedy to lose stories that could have...should have...been told!

You will see many Lakȟóta words in this novel and that is thanks to my co-author, a man dedicated to preserving the language of the indigenous people. <u>Niglíču</u> is a fictionalized story rooted in history that he wanted to tell. I helped to put it into words.

In my so called retirement, I strive to be a storyteller. Stories can tell truths in a way people can relate to.

You will see this for tweens in my novel, <u>The Balance of Wings</u>. You will see this in my historical fiction novel, <u>O'Toole.</u> And hopefully for many stories to come.

Printed in the USA
CPSIA information can be obtained
at www.ICGtesting.com
LVHW050537190823
755600LV00001B/25